WILDCAT

A THOMAS IRONCUTTER NOVEL

DAVID ACHORD

SEVERED PRESS
HOBART TASMANIA

WILDCAT

WWW.SEVEREDPRESS.COM

ISBN: 978-1-925493-22-1

Chapter 1

I'd thought this through. Really, no joke. The plan was brilliant. I retrieved a folding metal chair out of my trunk, walked across the parking lot, and planted my butt in a parking space which had the word "reserved" carelessly scrawled on the asphalt with red paint.

Getting comfortable, which meant I took a sip out of my flask and lit a cigar, I looked around and fixed on the faux neon sign mounted over the entrance. The only thing I could think of was, gentlemen's club my ass. This was a titty bar, a place where men frittered away their money watching naked girls dance provocatively. Not that I'd ever been so foolish. You believe me, right?

The business had changed names a few times over the years. Currently, it was called the Red Lynx. Back when I investigated my first murder, it was called Cutie Cats. In fact, it'd happened right here in this parking lot, a few feet from where I was currently sitting. I scoffed at the memory and absently noted my cigar was almost down to the nub.

I looked at my watch and then looked at the marquee again. It said the club opened at four, fifteen minutes from now. One would think at least a few of the employees would be here by now. You know, to turn the lights on, things like that, but apparently, astute business practices didn't apply in this venue. I forced myself to be patient. After all, a good character trait for a PI is patience.

I checked my watch again.

Looking around, I couldn't help but notice the parking lot was clean, not even one single cigarette butt. Management must have used one of those annoyingly loud vacuum trucks that woke you up at four in the morning. I flicked my cigar stub in a high arc and watched it land, right in the middle of the pristine lot. There, now it looked better.

Finally, a bright blue compact car shaped like a cube entered the lot and parked three spaces down. The thin aluminum of the automobile was literally vibrating from the vehicle's oversized sound system, reminding me of how much I hated how most modern cars looked nowadays.

I watched the driver curiously. She continued to sit in her car a few minutes, eyes closed, swaying to the rhythm of a mindless rap song for a minute before getting out. She was a woman in her early twenties, slightly taller than the average female, light brown hair which didn't quite touch her shoulders, and long slender legs trailing out of a pair of old cutoffs. A pink midriff shirt revealed a flat, toned stomach. No bra. Very cute. And young.

She acted as if I was invisible as she walked by me carrying an oversized canvas shoulder bag, but then I heard her footsteps stop. I turned my head and saw her staring at me quizzically. It might've been because I was sitting in a chair in the parking lot, or maybe because I was wearing a business casual sports coat outside on a hot June afternoon, or, better yet, she was staring at me because I was so devilishly handsome.

"Good afternoon," I said courteously.

"Hey big guy, I've no idea what you're up to, but you're sitting in Bull's parking space."

"Bull?" I asked innocently.

"Yeah, he's one of the bouncers, and he's nobody to mess with," she replied.

"Would you happen to know his full name?" I asked.

She now eyed me warily. "Who the hell are you?" she countered.

I set the plain manila file folder I was holding aside, reached into my pocket, pulled out a couple of twenties, and held them up for her to see. She stared at me while I acted like I didn't notice her nipples were now poking out through the sheer material of her shirt. I guess it was one of those natural reactions for strippers when they see a man holding money. After a moment of indecisiveness, temptation won out over caution. She looked around, walked back to me and reached for the money. I tightened my grip.

"Name please," I asked pleasantly.

Her hand lingered on mine. "His real name is Robert Turnbull. He'll be here any minute now."

Bingo. I had confirmation. I relaxed my grip and she slowly removed the money from my hand.

"Are you a cop or something?" she asked as she looked at me with a combination of curiosity and caution.

I shook my head. "I'm not a cop." Not anymore, I thought silently.

She appraised me. "You look like a cop."

"What's your name, your real name?" All strippers had at least one alias.

She gave a small, coy smile before responding. "It's Anna, what's yours?"

"Thomas." I started to say more, but was stymied by the deep-throated exhaust pipes of multiple motorcycles approaching from down the street.

She looked toward the noise. "Listen, I'm not sure I want to be seen talking to you." There was a sudden tone of concern in her voice as she looked down the street. "You be careful. Bull is big and mean, and he's got friends."

I understood. I quickly retrieved a business card from my jacket pocket and handed it to her. "Thanks," I said. "Maybe I can do you a favor one day."

She hesitated for a second before grabbing it and hurrying inside. The door was unlocked. So, maybe there was somebody inside after all. If I didn't have other pressing matters, I would have told them to turn the damn sign on.

I turned away as three bikers, riding customized versions of Harleys, roared into the parking lot. And, all three were wearing outlaw biker cuts, dirty denim vests displaying their club name and other patches of cryptic insignia. These types proudly referred to themselves as one-percenters. They scorned mainstream society and had a loathing disdain for law enforcement.

I knew the type.

The three of them stopped their bikes within inches of me and revved their throttles a few times. I guess the loudness was supposed to intimidate me. I sat quietly and waited. After a few seconds of their nonsense, the oldest of the three killed his engine and motioned for the other two to do the same.

One of them was thin, wiry, with a long greasy goatee, and dark little weasel eyes. The other two were quite a bit larger. The older one was about an inch taller than me and close to my age, but weighed several pounds more. Some of it was muscle, some of it was fat. He had the standard beer gut of most of your older bikers. Spider web tattoos adorned both elbows that connected to big beefy arms, one of which had a long scar along the bicep. He had a long walrus style moustache, like the guy in that reality show who always yelled at his sons. His crooked nose belied the fact he'd been in a few brawls in his time. At least, that's why mine was crooked. He appeared to be the one in charge, but he wasn't the reason I was there. At least, not the main reason.

The one I was looking for, Bull, was the biggest one. He was over six and a half feet, easily weighed over three fifty, and built like a football lineman. However, I suspected his personality prevented him from playing any kind of organized sports. His arms were covered in tattoos, which given the size of the appendages, the amount of ink required had to be at least a gallon. His legs were the size of tree trunks and his biker boots appeared to be triple-wide size sixteens. I briefly glanced across the parking lot where my car was parked, making sure my backup was paying attention.

Bull edged his front wheel right up against my foot, scuffing the spit-shine on my black wingtips. "What the hell are you doing in my parking space?" he growled.

I clasped the file folder, and putting on my best apologetic expression, stood in feigned nervousness. "Oh dear, please accept my apologies, but it's my understanding this particular parking space is reserved for Robert Turnbull." The older one of the three narrowed his eyes in sudden suspicion. Perhaps my use of Bull's legal name alerted him, but before he could say anything, Bull piped up.

"That's me, motherfucker," he snarled. "So move your ass out of the way."

I nodded, as if duly chastened. "Right away, sir," I replied and moved to grab the chair, but made a display of the manila folder causing my hands to operate ineffectively. Acting exasperated, as if embarrassed how clumsy I appeared, I thrust the folder toward him.

"Here, hold this please, sir." He grabbed the file folder without thinking. I folded the chair, picked it up, and began walking away.

"Yo, dumbass, here's your folder." He flung it at me, and the papers inside it went flying. The weasel started laughing. I glanced at the older one. He was staring at me hard. He knew I was up to something. I looked back at Turnbull.

"Oh, I won't need it, Bull. Those are for you. You've been duly served." I looked at the other two. Specifically, I was looking at their body language and to make sure nobody was reaching for any concealed weapon.

"What?" Bull bellowed as he climbed off of his bike and began walking toward me. I held up a finger, then I opened my jacket, revealing my baby. She's a Springfield Armory model XD forty-five semiautomatic handgun, highly modified, and she was currently tucked into a holster on my belt.

"Bull!" the older one shouted. Bull stopped short and looked back.

"Listen to the man, Bull," I said.

Bull glared at me. "You think I'm scared of your ass?"

"Maybe not me, but you should definitely be scared of the old man over there." I hooked a thumb over my shoulder where my Uncle Mike, a retired police captain, was sitting in my car, a 1961 Eldorado convertible. It was a lustrous jet black Cadillac with lots of chrome, gangster whitewalls, and a white top. It took me almost a year to fully restore it, but worth every minute. He had a shotgun stuck out of the opened window, and it was pointed in our general direction. A cigarette dangled from his mouth and he looked on with armor-piercing dark brown eyes.

"Bull, get inside!" the older one yelled. Bull glared at me for a long moment, as if to tacitly tell me this wasn't over, before walking inside. The older one got off of his bike and picked up a couple of the papers. He scanned them briefly and looked over at me.

"What's this shit?" he demanded.

I started to tell him if he wanted to know, he should read the damn papers, but I stopped myself. He did me a favor by diffusing what could have been a bad situation, and besides, he probably couldn't read.

"Apparently, your buddy beat the crap out of a man back a few months ago. He's suing Bull and the business."

He glanced at the papers a moment and then looked at me with no small amount of unfriendliness. "I remember this idiot. He went too far with one of the girls. When he was being escorted out, he sucker punched Bull. He got what he deserved."

I shrugged and walked to my car. He was probably exactly right, the idiot deserved it, but I wasn't the person to judge the matter. My job ended when the papers were served. My uncle slid over to the passenger side as I put the folding chair in the trunk.

"You sure know how to make friends," he said as I got in. I lit a fresh cigar and he lit another cigarette. It was our way of dealing with the tension. He kept the shotgun sitting across his lap, just in case. Putting his lighter away, he held out a hand in silent expectation. I pulled the flask out of my jacket, took a long pull, and handed it to him.

"We have one more stop to make. It's on the way home," I said as I maneuvered the Cadillac onto Division Street, waited for the light, and merged onto the I-40.

"I seem to recall you working a murder at that place," he remarked. I glanced over at him. Old age was taking a toll on him but his memory was still intact. The afternoon sunlight highlighted the wrinkles on his face.

"Yeah, it was my first as primary. The boyfriend was jealous of his stripper girlfriend. He tolerated the stripping, but she was also doing a little business on the side. He must've disagreed with her extracurricular activity. One night, he waited on her to get off work and shot her in the parking lot."

"What kind of side business?" he asked.

"Prostitution."

He scoffed and took a drag off of his cigarette. "So the whore deserved it," he said. I didn't reply. I had no idea if she deserved it or not. I was about to say it was a pretty harsh punishment, but decided it wasn't worth debating.

"What happened to the boyfriend?"

"He went home and ate his gun," I responded.

My uncle nodded slightly, as if tacitly saying it was the right thing to do. He took a long pull and flicked his cigarette butt onto the Interstate. "Do we need the shotgun on this one?"

"Nope. This one is a client," I said as I changed lanes and quickly accelerated up to eighty. He nodded in satisfaction and took another long pull off of the flask before finally handing it back to me. Fifteen minutes later, I parked the car in front of a Starbucks, located in a strip mall on the south side of the city.

"Who's this one?" he asked.

"A man who has more money than common sense," I replied.

Uncle Mike snorted. "There's a lot of that going around."

Almose Larkins, who preferred to be called Al, was a nondescript, pudgy man with short dark hair, a quick smile and easygoing manner. He was a successful wholesale liquor sales rep who, by virtue of his homely looks, found his women only through the Internet and dark bars. He was currently engaged to one of those women. She was the cause for him to hire me. He was sitting at an outdoor table and smiled as I walked up.

"Hi, Thomas," he said cheerfully as I sat down. I sighed to myself. He wasn't going to be smiling in a few minutes.

"Hi, Al." We shook hands. "Okay, I've got the information for you, along with the invoice. The rest of the bill is thirteen hundred and three dollars. Let's make it an even thirteen." I'd given him a substantial discount because I considered him a friend. Even so, I had bills to pay.

Al nodded, pulled out a checkbook, and hurriedly filled one out. I waited patiently. When he handed it to me, I quickly eyed it to ensure everything was proper, folded it, and put it in my pocket.

"Alright, let's recap your case." I reached into the folder and retrieved an 8x10 head shot of a stunningly beautiful Arabian woman with long flowing raven hair and almond-colored eyes.

"That's my baby," Al said proudly. I nodded in agreement and continued.

"Starting about a month ago, the two of you began receiving several obscene and threatening text messages. All of them were directed toward her."

Al sighed. “Yeah, and the cops didn’t do anything,” he griped. I paused for a moment, mentally searching for the right words to explain why the police did nothing.

“Here’re your copies of the reports contained in the detective’s case file.” I pulled them out of the folder and slid them over. “As you can see, the detective who investigated the case filed a judicial subpoena for the cell phone records.”

I sorted through the folder and retrieved the appropriate paperwork. “The report from the cell phone provider shows all of the phone records. You can read them at your convenience, but right now I want to discuss the detective’s final report.” I slid it over and let him read it. Especially the sentences I’d highlighted in fluorescent yellow. “In her summarization, she concluded all of the texts were sent by a spoofed phone number,” I said.

“What’s a spoofed number?” he asked.

“It’s one of those cell phone apps a person can download to make the caller I.D. of the person you’re calling show a number different from the number you’re actually calling from. It’s illegal, but it’s seldom prosecuted. I’d like to point out one particular sentence the detective wrote. It referred to the past history of your fiancé.”

I pointed at the highlighted sentence. “This is the reason she closed the case.” Al read it slowly, reread it, and finally looked up at me. Confusion was etched on his face.

“I found the sentence interesting, and so I did a little research.” I reached into the folder and retrieved approximately a dozen reports which I had held together with a binder clip.

“What are those?” he asked.

“These are police reports your fiancé has filed over the previous three years. If you’ll read them over, you’ll see they’re various reports of stalking, harassment, threats, etcetera. The detectives who investigated closed all of the cases because of the victim’s apparent lack of cooperation.”

I paused and let him look the reports over for a minute before continuing. “I went a little bit further with the phone texts,” I said and pulled out one final report. “The spoofed numbers and her cell phone number are hitting the same cell phone tower at the same time." I set the report in front of him. "She's the one who has been sending the text messages," I said quietly.

Al stared at me incredulously. "She has? But, why?" he asked. His tone was one of disbelief, childlike.

"It's hard to explain people's behavior sometimes, Al. Persecution delusion is a phrase some doctors might use. You mentioned to me once she had a traumatic childhood. It might've caused some issues to manifest themselves later in life. I'm not a psychiatrist, so I'm only speculating. All I can say is, if you love this woman, you're going to be going through more issues like this. You should try to talk her into seeing a therapist."

Al had nothing to say, and instead kept rereading the reports. The ensuing silence was becoming awkward, so I stood up and quietly left. My uncle handed me my flask as I got in. It was almost empty.

"You got anywhere you need to go before I drop you off?" I asked. He shook his head and lit a cigarette. I tapped an icon on my phone and spoke into it. "The subpoena on Turnbull has been served."

"Who're you speaking to?"

"I'm texting William," I answered. William was William Goldman, a fresh attorney who seemed to be determined to sue everyone in the city of Nashville. Not that I'm complaining, I got paid a decent fee for every subpoena I served.

"Texting?" My Uncle Mike was a typical sixty-something; he hadn't bothered keeping up with technology. He grunted in disgust. "Most normal people talk on the phone to another live human," he muttered.

I smiled. "Yeah, well, if it was Sherman, I'd talk to him, but it's his grandson, who I'd rather communicate with by texting." Sherman was William's grandfather. I admired and respected Sherman. I tolerated William.

I dropped Uncle Mike at his house on Vine Ridge Road before heading home.

Chapter 2

My morning began with a pot of coffee and then forcing myself into a grueling workout. I'd been lazy lately, but the encounter with those bikers caused me to rethink my laziness.

My fists were aching when I stopped pounding on the canvas bag and I was wheezing like an old vacuum cleaner. I pulled the mitts off and made a face as I flexed my hands. The stiffness seemed more pronounced than I remembered in my younger days.

After my breathing returned to normal, I sat down and lit a cigar, rationalizing it was a reward for a good workout. I enjoyed the flavor as I looked around the prefab metal building. It served as both my gym, garage, and repository of various kinds of, what most people would consider, junk. There were currently two cars in various states of disrepair parked alongside my pride and joy, the black convertible.

My only other working vehicle was a 2010 Ford F150 pickup truck. I'd bought it used, but with the exception of a new set of tires, brakes, and a battery replacement, it'd never had any problems. The other two vehicles were a couple of sixties-era muscle cars, a 1968 Dodge Challenger and a 1971 Chevy Camaro SS. I got them both at a reasonable price and fully intended to refurbish and flip them, but a lack of money was preventing that endeavor. Coming to a decision, I made a mental note to put both of them on Craigslist. I hated to do it, but money was tight lately. If something didn't change soon, I was going to have to quit smoking expensive cigars.

I saw my dog looking at me. He was an ugly, seventy-something pound multicolored cur with an intemperate disposition during most of his waking hours. "What do you think, Henry?" I asked. He apparently had no opinion on the matter and walked off without comment.

I piddled around in my garage until I finished my cigar, then went inside and filled Henry's bowl with some overpriced food my veterinarian insisted I use and took a long hot shower before getting down to business. After getting dressed, I picked up my phone and stared at it for ten seconds or so. It was a nice iPhone. The latest version.

I hated it.

Humans had grown too dependent on them, me included. Many times I wanted to smash it with a hammer or throw it out of the window as I was driving down the interstate. But, without it, I may as well shut down my business.

"I guess it's time to go to work," I muttered and turned it back on again. There were four voice mails and one text message.

The voicemails were from people who wanted to hire me to prove their spouses were having an affair. Even though I needed the money, I deleted them. Chasing around unfaithful spouses was a tremendous pain in the ass and it was always difficult getting the client to pay.

The text message was from William, the attorney who had hired me to serve the papers on Turnbull. I read it with a frown. He'd responded to the text I'd sent him yesterday evening stating he had four more subpoenas to serve and wondered if I could take care of them ASAP.

"You little shit, you didn't think to warn me he was an outlaw biker." Yeah, I talk to myself a lot. I guess it's common for anyone over the age of forty who live by themselves. As I stood in my kitchen, I thought about it, tapped the appropriate icon and spoke loudly.

"You still owe me money for the last four. Pay me or go fuck yourself – exclamation point." To my annoyance, the app typed out the words "exclamation point" instead of inserting the symbol.

"Fucking electronic contraptions," I muttered and hit send anyway. My phone rang less than thirty seconds later. Looking at the caller I.D., I saw it was from the Goldman law firm.

"Well, that didn't take long," I muttered before answering.

"Hello, Thomas, this is Sherman. How are you?"

He didn't have to identify himself, I recognized the voice immediately. It was an old friend of mine, Sherman Goldman. He was the senior partner of one of the more prestigious law firms in the city. We'd met several years ago, back when I was a rookie officer. He introduced himself one day after court and complimented my demeanor on the stand.

"Hello, Sherman," I replied. "I've been doing well. I'd be doing better if your grandson ever pays me for my services. How've you been?" His grandson was a self-perceived hotshot lawyer. In less than three months after passing the bar, he probably had seven or eight lawsuits pending, a testament to his nature. As a favor to his grandfather, I'd been helping him, but the little fucker had yet to write me a single check.

"Oh? How much would that be?"

"About two thousand, give or take," I replied. I knew the amount was chump change to Sherman, but like I said, my cash flow wasn't the best these days. Sherman must have sensed my, shall we say, cash flow issue.

"Well, let's see if we can remedy that. Why don't you come down to the office, I'll see to it you get a check and we'll discuss another job."

"That'd be good."

"Let's say an hour then. I look forward to seeing you." He hung up before I could respond with a different time. That was Sherman for you. My phone chimed again. The caller I.D. showed a number I didn't recognize, which wasn't unusual. I answered with my standard salutation. "Ironcutter Investigations."

"Hello, is this uh, a private investigator?" It sounded like an older woman. The kind who eats prunes for breakfast.

"Yes it is. This is Thomas Ironcutter. What can I do for you?"

"Well good. I need to hire you for an investigation," she said.

"Very good, ma'am. Are you aware of my rates? I charge one thousand a week, one week minimum plus expenses. The first week's pay is required in advance."

"One thousand dollars a week? Why, that's outrageous!" she exclaimed indignantly.

I sighed. I got this type of reaction frequently. I'm not sure why people felt they needed to complain. If they didn't like my fees, all they had to do was hang up. But no, it never worked that way. I imagined they thought if they pissed and griped and moaned and bellowed long enough, the outcome would be something like:

"Oh, my, I'm terribly sorry, ma'am. Please, oh, please allow me to atone for my heinous transgression, I'll work your case for free! Oh wait, even better, let me pay you!"

Or something like that. In the past, I'd try to be professional and explain the rationale behind my fee, but it never worked. So, I developed an ingenious, foolproof solution when I encountered a person like this; I'd hang up. It usually worked. Usually.

This time it didn't.

She called back immediately. "Mister Ironcutter, did you hang up on me?" she demanded with an air of righteous indignation.

"Why yes, I did. Why on earth did you call back?" I asked. There was a long silence. I guess my question confused her. I was about to hang up again.

"I don't know who you think you are, but you do not hang up on a potential customer. Any competent business person would know this," she replied.

"Lady, when I advised you of my fee, your response told me all I needed to know about you. You can't afford me, and now you're merely wanting to argue with me." There was another moment of stunned silence. I waited for some kind of imaginative response while I poured myself a glass of water.

"Young man, you know nothing about me," she responded icily. Not very imaginative. Boring. I had better things to do.

"You're correct, I don't know you at all. Shall we leave it at that?" It wasn't the first response I had in mind, but I was trying to be civil.

"Most certainly not. We are now going to discuss my case," she demanded.

"I hope it doesn't have anything to do with your spouse fooling around on you. I specifically do not investigate adultery cases," I proclaimed. I had a sneaking suspicion this is exactly what she wanted.

"And why not?" she demanded.

I took my phone away from my ear and actually stared at it a moment. My God, this woman was looking for anything to argue about. I had to take a deep breath in order not to say things I might or might not regret.

"Madam, I do not owe you an explanation for anything. If I wanted to have someone around whom I was required to answer to, I'd get married or move in with my mother." I hung up without waiting for a response.

"Fuck me, it's going to be one of those days." I took care of a few things around the house, like ensuring my flask was full of scotch, and headed into town.

Twenty minutes later, I was sitting in the reception area of the Goldman law firm. It was a modern office that occupied the entire twentieth floor of a skyscraper in downtown Nashville.

I'd not yet got my butt attuned to the expensive-looking leather sofa when a very attractive woman walked in from one of the back doors. She appraised me through a pair of nerdy glasses with hazel green eyes for a moment as I did the same to her, but with brown eyes and no glasses. I guessed her to be in her late-thirties, slender, and long dark hair she currently had up in a messy bun and held in place with what looked like Chinese chopsticks. A perky nose held that set of nerdy glasses, which I thought was damned cute.

"Mister Ironcutter?" she asked in a pleasant voice which held a wisp of a southern accent. I quickly stood. She smiled pleasantly. "I'm Simone Carson, Sherman's personal assistant." She offered a hand and I probably shook it a little too much. She waited patiently for me to finish, like she was used to men acting goofy in her presence.

"Follow me, please."

She needn't have asked. She cut a fine figure in what women called a professional business outfit. It clung to her curves in all the right places. I would have gladly followed her all over the building. She led me into a corner office with a beautiful view overlooking the Titan's stadium. Sherman was sitting behind a large, ornately carved walnut desk talking to a man the same age as him. He looked up and smiled as I walked into the office.

"Thomas," he said warmly. He was an older man, approaching the back side of his seventies, with a cherubic face and bald head with tufts of white hair on the sides. When he smiled, his eyes squinted in a pleasant expression. "It's so good to see you." I shook his hand and he gestured at his guest.

"This is Judge Barrett Conway." Judge Conway appeared to be close to the same age as Sherman, that is, in his seventies. Clean shaven, his short gray hair was thinning on top and he gazed at me with clear blue eyes through a pair of wire-framed bifocals. He shook my hand as Sherman explained. "The two of us go way back, we went to law school together."

I nodded. Sherman Goldman had been practicing law for a little over fifty years now, so their friendship indeed went way back. After the pleasantries, Sherman motioned toward a chair. Simone, who'd left the room, walked back in a moment later carrying a coffee cup and a carafe.

"Coffee, Thomas?" she asked. I nodded gratefully and found myself liking her more and more as I watched her pour with a graceful hand. When she finished, she took a seat near Sherman.

"Thomas, Barrett is a judge for the middle Tennessee district of the Federal Bankruptcy Court." Judge Conway nodded and then stood. It was then I noticed he was using a cane. It wasn't a gentleman's cane either. I'd seen canes like this before. It was made of hardwood ash and I suspected a quick twist of the handle would produce an edged instrument. One can never be too careful, I suppose.

"I'll be moving along now." He gave me a stern expression. "I was never here, Thomas." I gave him a slow nod of semi-understanding. He shook hands with Sherman before leaving.

"I assured him you'd be discrete," Sherman said after Judge Conway left.

"What's going on, Sherman?" I asked.

"Barrett has asked me for a personal favor and appointed me as a trustee for a Chapter Eleven case."

Simone reached over and handed me a thick file. The tab on it identified the business in question as Robard Trucking. I scanned the first page, which was merely a summary.

I spoke as I made a superficial scan of the file. "If I remember correctly, Chapter Eleven is merely a means to enable a business to reorganize their debts while at the same time blocking creditors from suing."

Sherman smiled. "Very good, Thomas."

"But, I'm sensing a problem."

"Barrett says he smells a rat, and after reviewing the file, I must agree. We've discussed it at length and I suggested bringing you in."

"I can serve a few subpoenas, if that's what you want," I said.

Sherman leaned forward in his chair. "Perhaps I should explain. When a business files a petition of relief under Chapter Eleven, certain things happen. One of those things is the debtor in possession must file a proposed plan of confirmation within one hundred and twenty days. Which is to say, they must write out a legitimate plan specifying how they are going to get themselves out of debt. The president of Robard Trucking has not done so. Furthermore, we believe the company's officers have made several preferential payments prior to filing the petition."

"And, that's why the judge decided to appoint a trustee," I said. Sherman nodded. "But, why you?"

"Like I said before, we go way back. There's a lot of history between us." He said it in a manner indicating he was not going to explain further and I left it at that. I mean, Sherman could have easily passed this off to one of his junior associates, but for whatever reason, he chose not to, and it was obvious the reason, or reasons why, were none of my business.

Sherman changed the subject and gestured at his lovely assistant. "Miss Carson has the necessary paperwork for you."

I glanced over at Simone, noting how Sherman called her Miss instead of Missus. I tried my best to be subtle when I glanced down at her left ring finger. It was bare. A good sign. At least, it was a good sign for me.

"I'm still not sure how I can help," I said.

"I believe your unconventional methodologies may be apt for this case." I glanced over at Simone. She was looking at me with a pair of beautiful hazel eyes, but no outward emotion. I had no idea how much she knew about me and what she was thinking.

"You want me to find the money."

Sherman nodded slightly. "And any hard assets."

"I suppose you already have a contract drawn up." It was a needless question. Sherman lived and died by the law, contracts were a way of life to him. Simone reached over, picked the file folder up off of my lap and opened it. There was a contract on the front page.

"Yeah, figures," I muttered. It was a standard contract, along with a lengthy non-disclosure agreement clause. She handed me a pen and I signed it.

"I'll make you a copy," she said and left the office. I found myself staring at her backside, again and quickly looked away before Sherman caught me.

"Inside the file, you'll find information about William and Leona Spieth, the president and vice president, who also happen to be husband and wife," he said. I looked in the file and found them. I made a quick scan before looking up at Sherman.

"You think they're hiding assets?" I asked.

"It appears so. This is where I believe your unconventional methods may come into play."

I looked at him and he grinned. He was referring to my friend, Ronald, an introverted young man who always looked like he was in the beginning stages of anorexia, and who also happened to be a computer genius. Sherman was tacitly telling me he expected results, but, and oh, if any of said activity was discovered and led to legal prosecution, he was innocent and blissfully unaware of said nefarious acts. Typical lawyer. At least he was going to pay me.

"Okay," I said. "You've given me a lot to work on. Now, let's talk about your grandson."

Sherman held up a finger and picked up his telephone. "Get in here," he said tersely.

A minute later, William Goldman sauntered into the office. A handsome man of twenty-five, he walked with a swagger in his step as if he personally made the law firm the bastion it currently was. He pulled up short when he saw me before quickly smiling and held out his hand.

"Hey, Thomas, boy am I glad to see you! I hope you're here for work. I've got a few more subpoenas that need to be served," he said. I imagine William was a version of who Sherman was, back in the day. A Vanderbilt law school graduate, the young man was wearing an expensive tailored suit and had a diamond Rolex peeking out of his left cuff. He used ample amounts of mousse in his brown hair and was a regular at the trendy nightclubs in the Gulch and music row area.

Sherman held up a finger, indicating William should shut his mouth and listen. "He's here to collect on a past due bill, William. Is there an issue with paying Thomas that I need to be aware of?" Sherman's tone was pleasant, but there was no missing the underlying tone.

William absently adjusted his tie. "No, sir, not at all." He looked over at me. "I'm terribly sorry, Thomas, there was some kind of mix up with the billing. I'll personally see to it that a check is drawn up for you."

"See to it immediately, William. I expect Thomas to be paid in full before he leaves this office."

"But, accounting doesn't issue checks for another two weeks," he replied.

"Is it Thomas's fault you did not turn in the invoice on time?" Sherman rejoined. William didn't answer. "If you have to pay him out of your own wallet, you will do so."

William's cheeks turned red. "Yes, sir," he muttered and hurried out.

Sherman's smile returned. "Now then, I believe the only thing we've not yet discussed is when we're going to get out and hit some golf balls."

I was curious about William and Leona Spieth, so I found their home address in the file and spoke into my iPhone. The Spieth residence was a single-story ranch style located in a well-established neighborhood of west Nashville known as West Meade. The houses were moderate in size, most having large yards, and very well maintained. I circled the block once or twice, noted an in-ground pool in the backyard surrounded by an ornate wrought iron fence, but nothing else of consequence. No cars were in the driveway.

"Robard Trucking Company," I said into the phone and started in the direction the disembodied female voice told me to go. I stopped five times during the trek in order to write down the names and addresses of banks along the route.

"Might be something," I mumbled.

An hour later, I was at my favorite spot, a cigar store located on the southern edge of town near I-65. My phone vibrated as I parked. It was a text message, with the same prefix as the number from the crazy woman. I'd already forgotten the last four numbers, but had no doubt it was her. I shut off my car and read the text.

We need to talk.

I groaned as I fished out my flask and took a swig. This woman was going to drive me crazy. But, maybe she actually did have the money, and after all, I had bills to pay. I responded to the text. This time by typing.

If you really desire to speak with me, I'll speak to you in person and we'll discuss your situation. I'll be at a business called Mick's Place for the next hour or so.

I typed the address, hit send, and went inside.

Mick O'Hara, the proprietor of the shop, was sitting on an overstuffed leather couch, a much more comfortable version than the one in Sherman's reception area, reading a newspaper. He didn't bother looking up. "You going in the humidor?" he asked.

"I am."

"Well then, be a good dago and bring me out a Padron. You know which one," he said as he turned the page of his newspaper. This is how it usually went, and he'd usually wait until I got seated before telling me I should have refreshed his coffee as well. Today, I took preemptive action and filled both of our cups before sitting down on the couch adjacent to him. Only then did he look up in appreciation. We both cut our cigars and lit them in tandem. I pulled out my flask and laced my coffee.

"Now now, don't be a stingy dago." He held out his coffee cup expectantly. I poured a generous dollop. "Attaboy. Hey, Kim just left to pick up some lunch, you want me to call her and tell her to get you a plate?"

"She's not getting sushi, is she?" I only enjoyed sushi on occasion. Kim, his Korean wife, could eat it twenty-four hours a day.

Mick scoffed. "Hell no. We got some good old southern barbecue, coleslaw and cornbread on the way."

Well, it was better than sushi, but I was still going to get heartburn. I nodded and he picked up the phone.

Mick was a fourth generation Irish American and I was a fourth generation Italian American. He loved to argue, I imagined all Irishmen were genetically predisposed to do that, and believed the Irish were superior to Italians, and everyone else for that matter. After thirty years as a fireman, he retired and opened a cigar shop. I was his first customer.

I sat enjoying my cigar and reluctantly went back to listening to my voice mail. Most were junk, but there was one from an old friend, Harvey Wilson. He was a retired sheriff who'd done a lot for me over the years. He answered on the second ring.

"I've been trying to call you for two days now. Where the hell have you been?"

"A nice hello to you too, dick-weed," I responded.

"Okay, enough of the gushy sweet talk. I'm calling in a favor."

"Hello, are you there? Your signal's breaking up." I started making hissing noises.

"What? Oh, don't pull that shit on me. This is important. Well, not really important, but I need to get my wife off of my ass, so it's important enough."

I grunted. "Okay, what do you need?"

"My wife's pastor has a second or third cousin, or something like that. Her husband recently died. Now the final verdict is suicide, but the crazy woman is absolutely convinced it was a murder."

I groaned out loud. "Oh shit, Harvey, not one of those. Do you know how many of those I had back when I worked in homicide? I'll tell you, all of them. Every one of those cases had some friend or relative claiming it was a murder. They were a royal pain in the ass. I can't tell you how many hours I wasted chasing down idiotic leads only to prove what we knew all along."

Harvey chuckled. "Nevertheless, you owe me so many favors I've lost count. So, here's how you're going to repay one or two of them. Go and talk to the lady."

After much arguing, I reluctantly agreed. Harvey had been a great friend over the years and in fact lined me up with several clients after I became a PI.

"I suppose I can meet her." I said it, but I sure wasn't what you'd say enthusiastic about it.

"Excellent. I told her you'd be there at five this evening."

Wonderful, I thought. I'm going to have to deal with not one, but two crazy women today. I got the flask and increased the enrichment of my coffee. "Send me a text message of her name and address," I finally said.

Harvey agreed and hung up. It came through a minute later. After getting directions from my iPhone, I leaned back on the couch and stared at Mick as I smoked my cigar. He sensed me staring at him and looked up.

"What?" he asked.

"I've been thinking about that surname of yours, O'Hara. I'm pretty certain it means butt ugly in Irish."

Mick stared at me. "Just because you ain't getting laid is no reason to take it out on me." He pointed his cigar at me. "Now your name, there's no way in hell your name is Italian." He waited expectantly for a smart-assed response.

"I've explained it before," I replied.

"I surely don't remember it. You must have been drunk at the time."

More likely he was drunk, hence the reason for his amnesia. I knew him well enough to know if I didn't retell the story, he'd pester and nag the ever-loving shit out of me.

"When my great-great grandfather immigrated, he couldn't speak a word of English and had to rely on some other immigrant to act as an interpreter. The interpreter says to him, 'They want to know what your surname is.' He responded, 'Taliferro,' which loosely translated means Ironcutter. That's what the immigration clerk wrote down and it's been our name ever since."

Mick nodded, as if I were making up a big story. He finished his coffee as a car drove into the parking lot. "Speaking of getting laid, you're jealous you don't have a wife like mine to wake up to every day." He looked out of my window. "Here comes my big-breasted beauty now."

I looked out the window. Mick's wife had parked the car and was getting out with a large bag of food. "She dreams about me you know," I said. "She told me so." I got up quickly before Mick threw something at me, hurried over to the door, and held it open for her.

Kim and Mick met when he was serving in the military and was stationed in Korea. They married after a whirlwind romance and have been together ever since. When Mick had enough money, he convinced her to get breast implants. He wanted the biggest ones the doctor could squeeze into her. She was only five feet tall, so the double-d cups really stood out. She smiled when she walked in and gave me a sloppy kiss.

"Happy birthday, handsome," she said before heading over to the coffee table and began spreading out the food.

Mick glared at me. "It's your birthday?" he asked. I gave a noncommittal nod. "Well, why didn't you say so?"

"Do you know what a birthday is?" I asked him. "It's God's way of reminding you you're one year closer to a certain death."

Mick frowned in consternation. "There's a word for that kind of attitude. It's uh…"

"Fatalistic," I said.

He snapped his fingers. "Yeah, that's it. You're fatalistic." He probably would have argued a little more about it, but the food distracted him, which was fine by me. I had no desire to talk about how old I was, forty-four if anyone's interested.

I'd finished eating and was about to light up another cigar when Anna, the stripper, walked in the door. It was then I realized she was the one who'd texted me, not the old woman. She was wearing a well-used pair of loose-fitting jeans that looked like they were going to fall down at any second and a plain white tee shirt. Somehow, she made it look sexy. She walked over and sat down.

"Hi," she said.

"Hello," I replied, and after a long second or two of staring at her like a horny teenager, I motioned toward Mick and Kim. "Mick, Kim, this is Anna. Anna, this is Mick and his lovely wife, Kim." They each said hello, and then there was an awkward silence.

Kim noticed it. She goosed her husband. "Come on, fatso, they need privacy."

They stood up, but before walking off, Mick looked at Anna. "I'm not really fat, I'm just big boned."

Kim shouted for him again and he hurried off.

Anna looked at me somberly. "We need to talk," she said.

I nodded. I assumed when she texted me earlier using the same four words it really meant the same thing, but refrained from a smart-assed remark.

"Duke knows who you are."

I nodded in mock understanding before asking. "Who's Duke?"

Her mouth dropped open. "He's the president of the Baroques biker club. You spoke with him yesterday." Ah, the older one. I figured he was somebody of influence. Anna continued.

"He also owns the strip club. They sat in my section last night and had a long discussion about the lawsuit and most importantly, you," she said.

I frowned. "Why? All I did was serve some silly court papers. It won't amount to anything." Actually, it would. This Duke fellow would be lucky if he didn't have to sell his strip club to pay for the judgement.

"Bull believes you personally dissed him and has convinced some of the other bikers too. Duke said he'll deal with it, but don't ask me what that means." She shrugged. "It could mean anything."

This time, when I nodded, I really did understand. Some men had thin skin and fragile egos. "I appreciate you telling me. You didn't have to say anything to me you know."

"Yes, I really did," she said. I looked at her questioningly.

Anna smiled, somewhat sadly. "When I was twelve, my father was murdered. You were our detective assigned to the case. You caught the guys who did it and put them away. I thought you looked familiar. When I looked at your business card and saw your name, I put two and two together."

I looked at her closely, and only then did I remember her as a skinny twelve-year-old girl with acne and braces. Her father was selling weed and molly out of his house. Two punks decided to rob him. He fought with them, got himself shot, and bled out on the kitchen floor in front of his family. That was ten years ago. Back when I was on top of the world.

"I remember now. You have a mother and an older sister. How're they doing?" I asked.Anna quickly looked away and her face darkened. "Oh, they're shit."

I must have hit a sore spot, so I backed off. I retrieved my flask and took a sip before offering it to Anna. She politely shook her head. I looked at my watch.

"Okay, I really appreciate you giving me the heads up, but I have an appointment in the quaint community of Rockvale at five." Anna nodded in understanding as I stood, but her disappointment was obvious. It seemed to me she wanted my company, and I'd been in short supply of female company for a while. I came to a split decision as she started to get up.

"Would you like to join me?" I offered and gestured toward my car. "It's a pretty day and I have the top down. We can catch up during the ride." She was hesitant only for a moment before accepting the invitation with a friendly smile.

Anna filled me in on her life as I drove. When she turned her head to look at me, the wind would whip her hair around. I caught myself imagining her on top of me, whipping her hair around wildly while she gyrated. I quickly dispelled the mental image and glanced at her again as she kept turning the knob on the radio.

"What's wrong with it?" she asked.

"Nothing. It's a standard AM radio." She looked at me funny, so I explained. "Radios were optional back then."

"Oh. I guess people didn't like music back then," she replied. I laughed. I always thought the music of the fifties and sixties was the best music ever, but instead of arguing about it, I changed the subject.

"How'd you get into stripping?" I asked. She hesitated before answering.

"I had a friend who was doing it. She was making good money and I said to myself, why not?"

I scoffed. "I can think of a dozen reasons why not."

"You're not about to try and lecture me, are you?"

"Nope," I said quickly, thinking I should have kept my mouth shut.

"Good," she replied. We drove in silence for a few miles before she continued. "It's not like I'm going to make a career of it. But it's good money. I paid off my car within a couple of months, and I just took a trip to Vegas with my friends. All paid for in cash. I would never have been able to do so if I had a bullshit job like a waitress or something."

I nodded, but didn't say anything.

"You're being judgmental," she quipped.

"Not at all."

"But you're not saying anything."

"You didn't ask for my opinion." I'd learned over the years if someone doesn't ask for your opinion, it usually means they don't want to want to hear it.

I changed the subject. "Do you have a boyfriend?"

She scoffed. "I used to. He went all psycho on me because I went to Vegas without him, so I dumped him," she grinned mischievously. "He's a cop. You might know him."

"Does he work with Nashville?" I asked. She nodded. I shrugged. "I don't know very many of the younger cops. I haven't worked there for a while now."

Anna looked at me quizzically. "Am I missing something? You're not a cop anymore?" I shook my head slowly. "Why not? Did you retire or something?"

"I resigned," I said.

"Why?" she asked.

I glanced over at her and continued driving. "It's a long story."

She held up her hands and wiggled her fingers at me, like she was casting a spell. "Ooh, the detective is being mysterious," she said with a sarcastic grin.

Okay, she asked for it. "Alright, it goes something like this. I met my wife when she was about your age. Her name was Marcia." I left out the part where I was fifteen years older. "A few years after we got married, she got pregnant. It was unplanned, plus, she didn't want kids. She killed herself, along with our unborn child. Later, I was accused of murdering her. There has been an ongoing investigation, pushed by an Assistant Chief who has a longstanding grudge against me. I wouldn't be surprised if I'm arrested and charged one day." I looked at her. She was no longer grinning. My iPhone's GPS app chimed and advised us in a disembodied voice, you have arrived at your destination.

"Oh look, we're here," I said as I spotted a driveway.

Chapter 3

The long gravel driveway reminded me of my own; curvy and lined with trees. It led to an older, quaint single-story farmhouse nestled close to the base of a hill. It had wooden clapboard siding, which was a couple of years past due for a fresh coat of paint, and the weed-infested lawn was in need of a major landscaping job.

"Do you want to wait in the car?" I asked. Anna had a sudden change of demeanor since I told her about the untimely death of my wife. She nodded her head silently and lit a cigarette. I nodded in understanding.

Rhoda Gwinnette met me at the door with a brown-colored cigarette dangling from her mouth. The main door was standing open, but the screen door was secured with a cheap latch, the kind that's designed more for keeping the door from accidentally blowing open rather than keeping out hostile intruders.

She could not be called an attractive woman. Probably never was. She was in her late fifties, with flaming red hair fixed up in one of those old woman hairdos with lots of hairspray. Crow's feet were deeply etched around her eyes and an extra chin made her look ten years older. The facial ensemble was completed with a mouth permanently shaped in a sad scowl. Her figure was shaped like an oversized pear, which she covered with a plain-looking, rust-colored blouse and a pair of those stretchy pants worn by fat women worldwide. She appeared nervous, even frightened.

"Who are you?" she asked in a harried voice.

"Ms. Gwinnette? I'm Thomas Ironcutter. I'm a friend of Sheriff Harvey Wilson. He asked me to speak to you about your late husband." I went for a pleasant expression, but couldn't quite smile. I didn't want to be here.

"How do I know you're telling me the truth?" she asked uneasily.

I kept myself from rolling my eyes, pulled out my wallet, and showed her my P.I. identification. "I'll wait right here if you'd like to call Harvey and verify who I am."

She looked at me for a moment, and then unlatched the screen door. "Would you like to come in?" she asked. I nodded, and followed her inside to a kitchen which hadn't been redecorated since the sixties. The countertops were a pea-green tile, as were the appliances. I could only imagine how ecstatic a hipster would be if they saw all of this dated décor. An orange tabby was relaxing on the counter, staring at me while flicking its tail. Rhoda motioned me to have a seat at the table.

"That's Tommy Boy," she said, indicating the cat. "He's a mess, but he's all I have left." I nodded in understanding as the cat stared like, you know, the way cats stared when they're plotting to kill you.

"I was just about to brew a fresh pot of coffee. Would you like some?" she asked.

"That would be very nice." I only hoped I wouldn't get a handful of cat hair to go along with it.

She withdrew the filter full of dregs from a well-used Mr. Coffee, threw them into an overflowing trash can and prepared another pot. "My husband liked his coffee strong. I'm thinking you do as well."

This time, I smiled politely when she looked at me. I'd been down this road before. She was the type of person who, instead of getting right to the point, was going to tell me a story. I remembered an interview on a TV talk show. Anne Rule, a famous true-crime author, was being interviewed. She was speaking about female murderers and made a remark about women requiring foreplay in everything they did. It was an apt statement and had forever stuck with me.

As the coffee brewed, Rhoda sat down and lit another cigarette, inhaling deeply before blowing the smoke over our heads. "Everyone thinks I'm crazy with grief, but my husband was murdered, Detective. I will go to my grave believing it."

"Tell me about him," I prompted. I sensed a very long backstory coming, so I prompted her to go ahead and start. I wanted to be home before midnight after all.

"Lester and I met on Christmas Eve of 1980. I was a waitress at a truck stop. It was a cold night and the restaurant was mostly empty. He'd been driving all day and night when he stopped in." She suddenly laughed at some happy memory. "He was such a big talker! Oh the things he said to me. After my shift ended, I took him home with me and we'd been together ever since."

Her eyes glistened as the memories came back. She reminisced while the coffee perked, silently reliving her past thirty-six years. I remained quiet, resisted the urge to look at my wristwatch, and waited. She filled two cups and didn't seem to mind when I produced my flask and enriched mine. After taking a deep drag of her cigarette, she continued.

"For the last ten years, he worked as an independent contractor for Robard Trucking Company."

Now there was a familiar name. I was not a believer in kismet, but there was something going on here. "Robard Trucking Company?" I asked in confirmation.

"Yes, sir. He spoke about the company from time to time, but I never paid much attention. He mostly seemed happy with them. The work was steady, and they always paid him on time." She paused and cocked her head slightly.

"For the past couple of years, he developed an odd character trait. He always told me when he was going on a long haul, and always told me where he was going, with the exception of Canada. He had a hauling job back and forth from Canada. It wasn't a regular job and whenever he did it, he'd never tell me. He'd just tell me he'd be back in a couple of days. I always wondered why he did that." We were interrupted by a gentle knock. Anna was standing on the other side of the screen door.

"May I come in?" she asked. Rhoda was suddenly nervous.

"It's okay, Rhoda, she's with me." Rhoda visibly relaxed then and unhooked the latch. Anna tentatively sat down while Rhoda fixed her a cup without being asked.

"So why do you think he never mentioned Canada?" I asked when Rhoda had sat back down.

"Detective Ironcutter, I believe the Canada haul was something illegal, which is why he wouldn't tell me. He was protecting me in his own way, and maybe he was a little embarrassed to be involved." She lit another cigarette. "It sounds silly when I say it, but it's true."

There was another lapse of silence. I caught Anna looking at me questioningly, like she was about to ask something. I shook my head slightly. Rhoda was going to tell me her story in her own way.

"The last week of his life, something happened; he became very worried. He'd walk around the house back and forth, light a cigarette and then light another one before he finished the first one. He'd also wake up in the middle of the night and walk around the house with the lights off, looking out of the windows. And then, a few days before his death, he came home in a good mood. He was grinning from ear to ear and telling me he was going to retire and we were going to move to Florida."

"Did he have a retirement fund, a savings account, anything like that?" I asked.

She nodded slowly. "But it wasn't much. Lester was always investing in some get-rich-quick scheme, but they never worked out." She sighed. "He was real excited though and made like he was going to be coming into a large amount of money."

"Rhoda, did he have a life insurance policy?" I was thinking about ole Lester. Would he kill himself so his wife would get a payout?

"He had one and it paid out ten thousand dollars." She looked at me. She knew what I was thinking. "Lester wouldn't do that, Detective Ironcutter. He wouldn't kill himself for a measly ten thousand. The insurance agent said they normally didn't pay out on suicides but he'd been a client long enough to be grandfathered in. I guess they were being nice."

I nodded, but it was time to get to the point. "Rhoda, tell me why you think he was murdered."

She started to take a sip of coffee, but it'd grown cold. She looked at it sadly and stood. "My father killed himself when I was younger," she said as she grabbed the pot and freshened her cup. "He was a very depressed man. Lester was never depressed. He liked driving a truck and he liked being around me. He wouldn't have stuck with me for over thirty-five years if he didn't."

She made a good point, but I was still skeptical. "How'd he die?"

"He was shot in the head. And that's another thing," she said. "I don't know whose gun it was. I'd never seen it before. Lester had a gun he carried with him when he drove and had a shotgun for hunting rabbits. The gun he supposedly used was not one of those."

I finished my coffee and suppressed the urge to light a cigar. "The sheriff's department investigated the case, correct?" I asked. She nodded. "And they concluded it was a suicide?" She nodded again. "Were there any witnesses?"

"No, sir." There was sadness in her voice, as if she already knew I wasn't going to believe her. "I came home from church and found him." She nodded toward the area where Anna was sitting. "He was on the floor right there," she said. Anna started squirming a bit. I kept a straight face.

"Would you like some more coffee, dear?" Rhoda asked.

"Oh, no thank you," Anna replied in obvious discomfort now that she knew she was sitting in the same chair ole Lester was sitting in when he took a bullet to the head. I bet she was wishing she'd stayed in the car.

"There is one other thing, Detective Ironcutter," Rhoda said. "Someone broke into the house during the funeral."

I shrugged nonchalantly. "It happens. Unscrupulous neighbors or family members will steal from you during your time of grief."

"That's the odd thing, Detective. I have a few pieces of expensive jewelry, but none of it was taken. The house was completely ransacked, but nothing was taken." She punctuated her statement by stubbing out her cigarette in the full ashtray and lighting another one. I rubbed my face absently, thinking about how this poor, lonely woman couldn't accept the fact her husband had taken his own life.

The next part wasn't going to be easy. "There is a matter we need to discuss before I go any further."

"Your fee," she said plainly.

I nodded. "Some folks believe my fee is quite high."

"I don't have much. Harvey mentioned you like old cars. Lester has an old Buick parked in a shed out back. It's been sitting there for several years."

"What's wrong with it?" I asked wonderingly.

"As far as I know, nothing. He brought it home one day, parked it in there, and never drove it again." She frowned a moment. "For some reason, that car seemed to upset him, but he never talked about it. I can give it to you, and after I sell my home, I should be able to pay the rest." She placed her cigarette in the ashtray and tentatively placed her hand on mine. "Some people said Lester was as full of shit as a Christmas turkey, and it's probably true, but he was good to me, Detective. He was good to me." She started tearing up. With some effort, she stood up and occupied herself with some dirty dishes in the sink.

I looked over at Anna and gestured toward the door. We walked outside quietly. I found the shed, an old wooden remnant of days past. It was leaning to one side and appeared as if it could collapse at any moment. The double doors opened outwardly. The hinges were heavily rusted and groaned loudly in protest as I pulled, but after a brief struggle, the doors surrendered.

I walked inside and stopped suddenly, the hair on the back of my neck standing straight up. Anna bumped into me and grunted.

The car was covered in a thick layer of dust. Nevertheless, I recognized it immediately; a 1967 Buick Wildcat. After a moment of standing there, dumbfounded, I slowly walked around the car. It was getting dark now, so I used the light on my iPhone to get a better look. I found the spots where, years ago, I'd not completely finished sanding the bondo. I made my way to the back of the car and crouched down. The left taillight was broken. There were two distinct round holes in the lens.

I straightened slowly, like the weight of the world was on my shoulders. I'd given up long ago of ever seeing this car again. I stood there, staring at it in the darkness.

Anna interrupted my thoughts. "You act like you've seen a ghost," she said tentatively.

She was right, I was indeed staring at a ghost. My hand found its way in my jacket, retrieved my flask and guided it upward. My other hand fumbled along, and after successfully unscrewing the cap, I emptied it in two swallows.

"Come on," I said, my voice strained. "I'll drive you back to your car."

As we exited the shed, Rhoda was standing behind the protection of her screen door, waiting, like a small child anxiously waiting for their parents to come home.

"I'll take your case," I said to her offhandedly as I walked back to my car. "Let's go," I said to Anna as I got in. She hurriedly followed.

Chapter 4

The drive back was quiet, very quiet. Anna didn't have much to say and I didn't feel like talking. As she lit a cigarette, my mind started drifting back to when I was eighteen.

I was a senior in high school and worked for my father, whom I was named after, at his three-bay automotive garage. He was a strong, overbearing bull of a man, prone to temper tantrums and resolving differences of opinion with a vicious backhand or, on his bad days, his fists, especially when he was in his cups.

He boxed when he was younger and would never let you forget it. He'd often coerce me into sparring with him, eschewing modern boxing gloves and insisting on using old leather mitts, which, as you can imagine, did little to soften his punches. I often ended up with a sore and swollen face. He was the person who broke my nose the first time. I suffered in silence and tried to make the best of it. After all, I had nowhere else to go. At least he paid me.

At the beginning of my senior year, I'd found an old junked Buick Wildcat sitting in the weeds behind a farm house. The owner, an old widow woman sold it to me for twenty dollars on the condition I hauled it off. I obliged and used Pop's tow truck to haul it home. Long after the garage was closed for business, I'd spend hours working on it, painstakingly restoring it a piece at a time, often spending all of my meager paycheck on parts.

It was a week before the senior prom. I had a date with the prettiest girl in school, Lana Hudson, and I was quite smitten with her. The plan was to surprise everyone when I picked her up in my fully restored, kick ass Wildcat. All I had left to do was some minor body work and then put a few coats of paint on it. In its current state, it was a primer gray, and I had plans of painting it a beautiful lacquer red. I came to the garage on a Friday afternoon ready to spend the weekend finishing it up, but it was not in its usual spot.

"Hey Pops, where's my car?" I remembered asking.

"What do you mean, your car?" he replied gruffly. "You don't own any damn car."

He ignored me for a minute, but when I kept staring at him, he spoke again. "If you're talking about that rattletrap Buick you had parked in here taking up room, I sold it to pay some bills." I thought he was joking at first, even though my father never joked. Ever since my mother ran out, back when I was ten, he had been an unpleasant person to be around.

The good part about having a father with a hair-trigger temper was it taught me how to walk on eggshells and to choose my words carefully, never speak impulsively or off the cuff. I became quite skilled at it. But not this time.

"You sorry son-of-a bitch!" I blurted it out before I could stop myself. The look in his eyes was one of shock, but was quickly replaced by a flash of malevolent anger. He walked over and backhanded me with one of his big meaty hands. He'd done it before, more than once. I never retaliated or fought back.

Until now.

Adrenalin coursed through me as I responded with a wild left hook. It connected, knocked him off of his feet and he landed roughly on his backside. He held his mouth a moment and then glared at me with murder in his eyes. I stared back at him, scared shitless, but years of pent-up emotions coursed through my veins like molten metal. This was it. Win lose or draw, I was going to fight back this time.

"So, this is how you want it, boy?" He slowly started rising to his feet, but suddenly lunged at me from a crouch. He was fast for a big man, but I was onto him. I'd seen him use this tactic in a barroom fight not so long ago and I was ready for him. I blocked his attempt to tackle me and circled around, throwing another punch, which he shook off and countered with a couple of his own.

We fought long and hard in that dirty garage. His punches were like sledgehammers and hurt like hell. But, I was giving every bit as good as I got, and I had youth on my side. He was past his prime. The endless cigarettes and years of heavy drinking had taken their toll on him and he was winded within seconds.

I kept circling him, keeping my range, the way he taught me, and peppered him with jabs and combinations every time he tried to press me. My fists were finding their mark and causing damage.

"I'm going to kill you, boy," he growled as he tried to connect with a haymaker. He tried to sound menacing, but he was gasping for breath.

"The fuck you will," I retorted angrily. It was the second time in as many minutes I'd ever cursed at him and it made me smile. He tried another haymaker. I ducked under it and responded with a left into his armpit. He grunted in pain and dropped his right. I seized the opportunity and landed a flurry of punches.

His chin was rock hard. Each punch sent shockwaves through my hands and up my arms, but I didn't stop. I was reveling in my own pain and the pain I was inflicting on him. Each punch I connected with fueled the years of resentment and animosity.

I think my nose was broken again, but I had my rhythm now and my breathing was steady. Pops, on the other hand, was bloody, and one of his eyes was swelling shut. He cursed me and cursed my mother's name. It only made me madder, more determined. I continued punching him, harder and faster now. Mindful of his lessons, I kept my feet moving. He tried more than once to tackle me, but he was now too weak to manhandle me. I'd muscle him off and punch him in the ribs or gut, letting him know who the boss was now.

The rage in his eyes was being slowly replaced with fear. He'd not been on the losing end of a fight in many years, but he was losing now and he knew it. He saw the rage in my eyes and knew. He knew his years of being the tormentor had come back to haunt him in spades on this fateful evening.

Finally, in desperation he grabbed a ball peen hammer and swung it at my head. I grabbed it and the two of us wrestled over it for a moment. His breathing was coming in deep frantic gasps now. He was gassed out and out of strength. We made eye contact.

"Now, I'm going to kill you," I growled, twisted my hips, and threw him to the ground. Throwing the hammer aside, I jumped on top of him and began pummeling him unmercifully. I probably would have succeeded in killing him, but suddenly I was grabbed from behind and pulled backwards. It was my Uncle Mike, a sergeant on the local police department.

"What's all this now?" he asked with worried concern.

I pointed a bloody finger at my father, who was now lying pitifully on the grime-covered shop floor, barely conscious. His face was so swollen and bloody he was hardly recognizable.

"He's hit me for the last time," I spat out. "He's treated me like shit for the last time." My hands were trembling and I realized I was crying.

I shook free from my uncle and stormed out of the garage. Uncle Mike might have chased after me, but his little brother, my father, needed medical attention.

The Army recruiting sergeant found me curled up asleep on the stoop to his office the next morning. My face and fists were bruised and swollen, and all of my worldly possessions were sitting beside me, stuffed into a paper grocery sack. He grinned knowingly; I wasn't the first troubled soul he'd found on the stoop. He interviewed me over breakfast. Finding me a suitable candidate for the illustrious United States Army, he put me up in his house. I shared a bedroom with his young son while I went through the processing. A week later, I was a guest at Fort Benning, Georgia, getting my head shaved learning the fine art of pounding sand.

Anna broke me out of my reverie. "You've hardly said a word."

I glanced over at her as I realized we had arrived back at Mick's Place. I parked beside her car and looked through the plate glass windows. Kim was behind the counter pouring a beer for a customer and Mick was nodding off on the couch. I cleared my throat.

"Yeah, please accept my apologies. I should've never invited you along. We hardly know each other and I'm sure you would've never gotten into the car if you had known about my wife's death."

"It's okay," she said. "It just caught me by surprise. That car, it brought back some memories?"

"Yeah," I responded quietly.

She turned to face me while still sitting. "I can't figure one thing though, why are you suspected of murdering her? Your wife, why are you suspected of murdering your wife?"

I wasn't going to answer her at first. I leaned over toward her. We were inches apart, but if our close proximity made her nervous, she didn't show it. We stared into each other's eyes for a moment, and then I got a cigar out of my glove box. I leaned back, clipped the end, and answered her before I lit it.

"A death investigation begins with a standard premise – any death is a possible homicide. The detectives who were assigned to the case were friends of mine. One might say they ignored the standard premise and instead went through the motions without suspicion. They interviewed neighbors, who confirmed they saw me leaving the house and heard a single gunshot approximately thirty minutes later. They performed gunshot residue testing on me, which turned up negative. They performed it on her and it was positive.

"Everything was cut and dry. And then, about a month later, the Crime Stoppers hotline received an anonymous call by a person who claimed I murdered her. The case was ordered reopened. It was then when they found out my alibi didn't check out."

"Wait, what?" she asked.

"My alibi, it was false, contrived, made up. It was a lie," I said. She looked at me with wide eyes as I lit my cigar. Once I got the tip glowing in a nice reddish glow, I looked over at her.

"Now, you're about to ask me why I did it. Why, if my wife's death was a suicide and not a murder, why did I lie about my alibi? Don't bother asking, because I won't answer."

"Okay," she said quietly.

"So, after the alibi was disproved, I was disempowered. My badge and gun were taken away and I was assigned to desk duty. I was ordered to undergo lie detector testing while my entire career was being dissected. No matter what happened after that, my career was basically over. I realized I had a decision to make and chose to resign."

I've told the story once or twice over the past two years and I didn't know why I kept retelling it. It was getting old. People either chose to believe me or believe I was a murderer. I was past caring.

"I think I'm going to head to a liquor store before they close. Would you kindly do me a favor and tell this Duke fellow to give me a call if he'd like to talk to me?" I asked.

Anna nodded. "Sure. I think it'd be good if you two talk. He's actually pretty level-headed." Anna got out of the car and shut the door. She stood there looking at me a moment. "Are you going to help Rhoda?" she asked.

"I'm going to look at the case," I answered. "But I've no idea if I can help her get closure or not."

"She's a very sad lady. I think maybe you are as well." She walked away before I could respond.

I watched her get in her car and drive off before I got on my phone. I hit the voice command function and said the name Ronald. He answered after a few rings.

"What's up?" he asked.

"I got two names for you; Lester Gwinnette and Duke Holland. Lester was a truck driver for Robard Trucking before he killed himself. Duke is an outlaw biker and he owns a strip bar in the adult district. It's called the Red Lynx, although the business license might be something else altogether." I could hear the typing on a keyboard in the background for several seconds before Ronald spoke.

"Both Lester and Duke have records. Looks like Lester was arrested in the eighties for armed robbery, but that's all I'm finding so far. Duke has served time for a string of crimes. Let's see, weapons, drugs, assault. He was on parole up until a year ago. He's been clean ever since."

I grunted. Ronald was a genuine genius but woefully inept at understanding people. Possibly because he spent most of his life in his parents' basement with nothing but computers to keep him company.

"Just because they've not been arrested doesn't mean they're clean. Work me up a report on each one."

"You got it. I should have it all by tomorrow morning," Ronald said. "Oh, by the way. I have a plan."

"Oh yeah?" I asked.

"Yeah. I want to buy a series of options on the Russell Two Thousand. I figure about ten grand on your end should be enough.

We should have a return of at least fifteen percent within a month." Ronald was a computer genius, and extremely introverted. He loved to play on the stock market, in between all of his meta gaming. Ten grand was going to pretty much wipe out my savings.

"I don't know, Ronald. I've got bills due at the end of the month and I don't know when I'll get paid for the Robard case."

"I'll have it back by then," he promised.

I hesitated, but then came to a decision. "Yeah, okay. Don't lose all of my money." Ronald chuckled and hung up without replying. I headed toward the liquor store.

Chapter 5

Henry and I had an enjoyable but quiet breakfast. He decided not to do the dishes today, opting instead to go outside and leave me a nice present on the front lawn.

"Alright, time to get to work." It was time to get started on the Robard case. I booted up my computer and opened the emails from Ronald. My phone rang as I was printing them off.

"What're you doing?" Ronald asked before I could even say hello.

"Oh, looking at midget porn on the Internet."

Ronald snickered like a little kid. "You don't ever look at porn."

"I'm working on the Robard case, what're you doing?"

"Looking at you in your surveillance camera." I looked up at the camera mounted on the ceiling. My security system was state-of-the-art. Ronald helped me install it, and in doing so, rigged it so he had access to it.

"Pervert."

"Am not," he replied quickly and snickered again, reminding me that in many ways he was still a child.

"Alright, enough spying on me. How're your hacking skills lately?"

Ronald responded with an indignant scoff. "As good as anyone, why?"

"I want to see if the Spieths have any bank accounts at these banks." I gave him the names of the banks I'd noted yesterday. Ronald was quiet now. If it wasn't for the sound of typing on his keyboard, I would've thought he'd hung up.

"Uh-huh," he said once or twice, and there was an occasional, "Oh yeah," but that was our only conversation for the next fifteen minutes.

"Okay, we've hit pay dirt."

"Talk to me," I said as I finished my coffee.

"It looks like they've opened accounts in all five of them. At the moment, all I'm getting are account numbers. I can't tell you how much is in each account, at least not at this time."

"Why not?" I chided.

"Each individual account is password protected. I can breach each one, but it'll take time."

"Nope, not necessary. All I need are the account numbers."

"Okay," he said. "Get on Duck-Duck." Duck-Duck was our code for the dark website created and maintained by Ronald. I didn't understand the reasons for using the dark website over the website AT&T provided for me, but Ronald did, so I went along. After all, hacking into banking accounts was a felony.

I printed off the information and then used the shred function to erase the cyber footprint off of my computer. Ronald no doubt did the same on his end.

"What's all this about?" Ronald asked.

"It looks like they're hiding assets, but I suspect there may be a lot more going on."

"So, that's why they're creating all these accounts? They're hiding money?"

"I think so, but we can't jump to conclusions yet. Some more work needs to be done."

"Okay, cool."

I changed the subject. "How're you doing on groceries and stuff?" I asked him.

"Oh, okay."

"How about your meds?" My friend suffered from occasional panic attacks. The doctor had him on meds. I'd tried to convince him there were self-help groups which he could get involved with, but he wouldn't have any part of it.

"I'm getting low on the Valiums," he answered.

"Okay, call in a refill and let me know when it's ready. I'll pick it up and bring it over."

"Thanks, Thomas."

After hanging up, I concentrated on the trucking company's bank statements Sherman had provided me. They ostensibly showed the cash flow of the company; payments coming in, payments going out. I started by making line by line comparisons of payments. Most of the money was easily traceable. Fuel costs, maintenance costs, and other various overhead payments made perfect sense. But, starting around three years ago, were the beginnings of some unusual transactions. Interestingly, at about the same time, the company had closed their local accounts and transferred them to some obscure bank in Detroit.

"Why in the world did they do that?" I wondered aloud. I looked it up on the Internet and the domain had expired. But, I found their phone number on the Better Business Bureau website. Curious, I called it, but not before using the phone spoof app Ronald had installed so that their caller I.D. would display Robard's main phone line.

After several rings, a man with a gruff voice answered. "Bank."

Well now, I thought, that's no way for a professional bank employee to answer the phone. "Uh, yeah, I'm calling for Tony."

"Tony ain't here, who's this?"

"Ski, down at Robard," I said, trying my best to sound like a beefy truck driver.

"Ski?"

"Yeah."

"I ain't never heard of youse."

"You don't wanna know me, pal. Tell Tony I'll call back." I hung up before he could respond and chuckled to myself. There's always a Tony or a Sal with those mobsters up north.

I jotted everything down and had barely finished when I heard the unmistakable deep throaty rumble of a motorcycle exhaust. My humble abode, a two-bedroom log cabin, sat well off of the main roadway and there was a sign at the head of my drive clearly stating trespassers were not welcome.

So, it wasn't some random bikes driving down the road. I was being paid a visit. I performed a press check on my handgun before sticking it in my waistband. Grabbing my iPhone, I activated the security camera app and watched two motorcycles coming up the driveway. I walked outside, stood on my front porch and waited. It was Duke and the other weasel-looking biker.

They stopped their bikes in front of the walkway leading up to my house. Duke casually removed his helmet, a black turtle shell that looked like it'd kissed the asphalt once or twice, hung it on the handlebars, and looked around, as if he were enjoying the scenery.

"Nice layout. Very secluded, but easy enough to find when you got Google at your fingertips," he said and grinned like he'd scored a major victory over me.

"Yes, I like it a lot. Of course sometimes there are pretentious assholes who occasionally show up uninvited." I motioned toward one of the security cameras mounted on the front eave of my house. "Good thing I have this surveillance system recording everything. I have over a dozen of them hooked up. The live feed goes to a server, or cloud, or something like that. It's stored at a different location. Of course, sometimes things get recorded which you don't want other people to see. Those are easy enough to delete, if you have the administrative rights to do so."

As the two men scowled at me, I glanced again at my iPhone. "Yep, you two are being recorded as we speak. Would you like to see?" I walked over to Duke and showed him the live feed on my phone's little screen.

"Hey, check out this neat function." I drug my fingertip across a scroll bar and made a minor adjustment. I now had a close up of Duke's face on the phone. "Isn't it awesome? The technology available these days, all I can say is, wow." He sat on his bike in silence, the scowl deepening.

"Yeah, very nice," I said and gave them a hard stare. "Now, what the hell are you assholes doing here?"

"You disrespected one of our brothers the other day," he said in a heavy tone as he waved a hand back and forth between him and his friend. I glanced at his fellow biker, a twenty-something wannabe tough guy who was trying his best to mean-mug me.

"You mean Bull?" I asked. Duke nodded. "By serving the papers on him?"

"Yeah, and threatening him with a gun," he replied.

"The papers were business. The gun was survival. Would you take on Bull unarmed?" I asked. "He's pretty damned big."

Duke grunted noncommittally and then briefly pointed a finger at me. "That lawsuit is against my business as well. It could cost me a lot of money."

Yeah, he was probably right. William was representing the pitiful mope, and although he was not yet the same caliber as his grandfather, he was a pretty decent attorney. My first thought was to tell the two of them to piss off before I put a bullet in them, but I instead chose the diplomatic tact.

"Do you have any security video of this guy sucker punching Bull?"

Duke shook his head. "It's on a thirty day overwrite."

"And this thing happened almost a year ago," I said. "That's too bad."

"Yeah, too bad. You sound all tore up about it," he said in a cold tone.

I shrugged. "It's not my problem, big guy. If you'd like, I'll train your crew on proper use-of-force protocol, and how to burn CDs anytime there's an incident in the club. My fee is reasonable." This time, the little tagalong scoffed.

"Yeah, I'll think that one over," Duke replied. "In the meantime, my sergeant-at-arms is very pissed off."

"I'll tell you what," I said. "If it will help any, please convey to him my apologies, and, I believe I can make it up to him."

Duke arched a suspicious eyebrow. "How so?" he asked.

"When I was doing research on him, I found a trailer I believed he was living at. I think you know the trailer I'm talking about, the one up in Joelton." Duke stiffened slightly and continued staring. I continued.

"So here I am, trying to keep a low profile and stake out the trailer. You know, catch him at home so I can serve him there instead of at his place of employment. Save him some embarrassment and what not. But, there was a bit of an issue."

"What kind of issue?" Duke asked suspiciously. His eyes had narrowed at me, much like he did a couple of days ago.

I leaned forward. "Much to my surprise, there were other people watching the aforementioned trailer, if you know what I mean. There was even a surveillance camera mounted on a utility pole pointed right by the driveway. Here, I even took a few pictures of it." I tapped on the screen of the iPhone, found the photos, and showed him.

I watched him as he looked at the tiny photo. His expression was that of suspicion and uncertainty at first, but as I scrolled through the pictures, he began recognizing landmarks. He finally looked up at me, concern etched on his face.

"Narcs?" he asked. I shrugged noncommittally. Duke let out a long string of expletives. He said a few more things under his breath about the carelessness of his fellow bikers and how at least one of them should be castrated. After he got control of himself, he looked at me.

"How bad is it, do you think?" he grudgingly asked.

I shrugged again. "If you're asking my advice, I would advise walking away from it and not go back. Cut bait." He cursed again and gripped the handlebars of his Harley tightly.

My phone rang. It was Ronald. "Would you gentlemen excuse me for a minute?" I walked back to my porch without waiting for an answer. "Hey, Ronald," I said quietly.

"Is that Duke? What's he doing at your house?" he sounded out of breath. The only problem with having a computer geek friend run your surveillance system is he was always monitoring it.

"Yeah, him and his friend. He didn't bother introducing himself. Get a still shot capture of him, we may need to find out who he is."

"Okay, I can do that. So, everything's alright?"

"Well, I guess so, but you should keep monitoring, just in case."

"Okay," he replied and I hung up. I'd been watching Duke and his biker brother as I talked to Ronald. They had their heads together and were in an intensive discussion. The other one was now on his cell phone. They stopped talking when I walked back over to them.

"Well, gentleman, this has been an interesting chat, but I've got work to do. I'm guessing you've got some things to take care of as well." Duke rubbed his hands together, and for a moment I thought he was going to extend one and offer a handshake. He stopped himself and reached for his helmet instead.

The younger Thomas Ironcutter, the hothead full of piss and vinegar, would have warned Duke of the dire consequences if he pushed the matter. The older and wiser Thomas, that would be me, sought out a more diplomatic solution.

"Look, Duke, there's no reason for us to be at odds with each other. Maybe we could talk some more at a later time." I reached into my wallet and pulled out a business card. "Do me the courtesy of calling first. Perhaps next time it can be under more amicable terms." Duke took the card and nodded curtly. They fired up their hogs and tore out.

I watched them leave and called Harvey. "How the hell are you, Sheriff?" I asked.

"I ain't a sheriff no more. I'm more of a gardener and maintenance man for my bossy wife. What'd you think about the Gwinnette thing?"

"Oh, it's probably a suicide, but I'll look into it. Do you know who worked the case?"

I heard him cough up some phlegm and spit. "Nope. When the new sheriff got elected, he fired all of my people and put his own in there. No, wait a minute. You remember Jerry Herndon? He still works there. I think they got him in records. What've you got in mind?"

"I want to speak with the investigating detective and maybe get a copy of the case file," I said.

"I'll give Jerry a call and get back to you," he said and hung up without waiting for a reply.

Chapter 6

I got up early and had a quick breakfast with Henry.

"I've got a busy day ahead, what about you?" I asked him. His only response was to walk over to the door and then stand there expectantly. We went outside and after doing his business, he watched as I hooked up my car hauler to the truck.

"You see, I'm going to go get the car my father took from me. But first, I'm going to meet with the detective who investigated Lester's so-called suicide."

Henry snorted, or sneezed, whatever you call it when dogs do it.

"Yeah, you're probably right, but I've got to try."

Traffic wasn't too bad and I arrived at the Rutherford County Sheriff's Department in a little under thirty minutes. I had a little difficulty finding a place to park, and finally decided on the side of the road leading into the parking lot. I hoped some overzealous deputy didn't think my parking on the shoulder constituted some kind of traffic offense.

After speaking with a lady who was behind bullet-proof glass, I sat patiently in the lobby and waited. I mean, I guess I could have badgered the lady about why it was taking so long, but it wouldn't have done any good. A full forty minutes passed before a back door opened. A man approximately my age walked out. He was heavyset, bald, glasses, square jawed with a slight under bite. There were fresh food stains on his tie.

"Are you Ironcruddy?" he asked with an air of unfriendly indifference.

I stood. "Ironcutter," I corrected. "Thomas Ironcutter." I held out my hand. The detective seemed to debate a moment before whether or not to do so before finally extending his hand.

"I'm Detective Thompson. The receptionist said you're asking about the Gwinnette suicide." The tone of his voice left no doubt he felt greatly inconvenienced and I was interrupting something important, probably his post breakfast nap.

I acted as if I didn't notice. "I am. I've been hired by the widow. She's having a hard time accepting her husband's death. I'd like to ask you a few questions, if you don't mind. Is there someplace we could talk?"

Detective Thompson made a sweeping gesture of the lobby with his chubby hand. "Since this won't take long, right here is fine." He obviously didn't have a high opinion of me and had no intention of spending more than a couple of minutes in my presence.

I ignored the discourtesy and continued. "Okay. Could you give me a run down on how you determined it was a suicide?" I asked.

He scoffed and wiped his nose with the hand I'd just shaken. Very classy. He probably did that often. I hoped I had some hand sanitizer in my truck. "The man was home alone. He stuck a gun up to his head and pulled the trigger. His wife found him when she got home from church. The gun was still in his hand when the ambulance crew got there."

He leaned forward slightly. "Now before you go spouting off stuff you've seen on CSI or some other cop show, we had ballistics testing done. The slug was a match with the gun."

I nodded as if he spoke with deep wisdom. "Was there an autopsy?"

"Of course. How do you think we got the slug out of his brain?" he replied as he made an exaggerated motion of looking at his fake Rolex watch. I'm sure he told everyone it was real, but the tarnished winding stem gave it away.

"Where did the gun come from?" I asked.

"What do you mean?"

"Did you run a trace of the serial number with the ATF?"

Detective Thompson snorted again. "There wasn't no need for that. What difference does it make where the gun came from?"

I ignored his question. A competent detective would already know the answer.

"Would it be possible to purchase a copy of the case file?"

"Absolutely not," he answered quickly. "Case files are confidential."

"So, it's still an open case," I said.

He shook his head and looked at me as if I were an idiot. "No, it is a closed case." He enunciated each word, like he was talking to a child. "It's been ruled a suicide. I already told you that."

"Are you aware, by Federal and State statute, if a case is closed the file becomes public information?"

He rolled his eyes. "So sue me. Are we done here?" He looked at his watch again. I knew it was fruitless to ask any other questions. I may as well have been banging my head against a brick wall.

"Yes of course. I apologize for taking up your time." He started to turn away but I spoke up. "Oh, one more question if you don't mind and I'll be out of your hair, uh, no pun intended." He stopped halfway in his turn and frowned at me. "I'm sure you did an excellent investigation and came to the correct conclusion. But, if I am able to dig up any evidence which would point to something else besides a suicide, would you be willing to listen?"

Detective Thompson glared at me for a brief moment, as if he'd just discovered something undesirable on the bottom of his shoe, but then smiled condescendingly. "Why sure, mister private investigator. If you come up with any information, be sure to give me a shout."

I walked back to my truck thoroughly frustrated. If I wanted a copy of the case file, I was going to have to file a motion with the court. Things like that were not free and Rhoda Gwinnette was a woman of limited finances. It was a quandary. I still thought it was a suicide, but that so-called detective irritated me and I found myself wanting to put him in his place.

As I approached my truck, I saw something sitting in the bed. It was one of those brown accordion folders, capable of holding several documents. I casually scooped it up and got into my truck. There was a post-it note stuck to it telling me to thank the real sheriff of Rutherford County and to turn it in when I was finished with it.

I carefully looked inside it. It appeared to be the master case file of the Lester Gwinnette death investigation. Karma was on my side, for a change. I lit up a cigar as I perused the file for several minutes and then pointed the truck toward Rockvale.

Chapter 7

Try as I might, I was unable to move the Buick out of the shed. The tires were flat and the brakes had seized up, which was common for automobiles when they've not been moved for several years. I tried pushing and rocking the vehicle for several minutes, but my only reward was a sweat-soaked shirt and the beginning of a headache. Rhoda watched me from the secured screen door as she smoked a cigarette. I gave up and walked over to her. The screen door separated us.

"I'm going to have to use a tow truck with a winch. It may be a couple of days before I can get back out here."

Her expression became sadder, which I would have sworn would have been impossible. "Am I going to have to pay the tow bill?" she asked.

"Oh, absolutely not," I said with a reassuring smile. "Don't worry about it at all. I'll take care of it." I pulled a handkerchief out of my back pocket and wiped my face. I desperately wanted to go home and take a refreshing cool shower, but I wasn't finished yet.

"Before I leave, there are a couple of things I want to go over. I have the case file and I want to show you some photographs of Lester. Do you think it would be okay?"

"Okay," she replied with her usual sad tone and unlatched the screen door. I grabbed the case file and went in. She already had a pot of coffee waiting. I accepted a cup, foregoing my usual enrichment process. I reached into the accordion file, pulled out the packet of photographs, and arranged them on the kitchen table.

"These may be unsettling to you, but I need you to look them over carefully," I said. She nodded tentatively.

The crime scene photographs were printed in color, but on regular copy paper instead of photograph quality paper. I had no idea why they. The sheriff's department was either too cheap to upgrade or Detective Thompson didn't care when he created the case file. I'd only made a quick perusal of the file before coming to her house, but it looked scant and disorganized. A bad sign. Rhoda lit another cigarette with trembling hands before looking over the photos. After a moment, she picked one of them up, inspected it carefully, and handed it to me.

"Detective, there's something wrong with this one."

I looked at the picture. It showed Lester lying on the floor, halfway on his left side and halfway on his stomach. There was a gunshot wound on the right side of his head, just behind the ear. A cheap, blue-steel revolver was partially gripped in his right hand. I pointed at it.

"Is that the revolver you told me about? The one you've never seen before?" I asked.

She nodded. "And another thing. Lester has that gun gripped in his right hand, which is awfully strange. Lester's left handed. He broke the index finger on his right hand years ago. He refused to see a doctor and it never healed properly. It was always bent, he couldn't straighten it all the way out and he said he had no strength left in it. He couldn't have shot a gun with it." I was raising the cup to my lips, about to take a sip of her awful coffee, when she told me this information, causing me to spill some on the table.

"Are you sure?" I asked before I thought about it. Yeah, stupid question. She'd been with the man for over thirty years, she'd know if he was left handed.

"Yes, sir," she replied and quickly got up. She found some paper towels and began cleaning up my mess.

"Okay," I acknowledged quietly, waited until she was through and seated again. "Rhoda, have you spoken with any of your neighbors since Lester's death?"

"Yes, they've been really nice. One of them fixed a nice casserole for me and my family, but none of them showed up." Her lip started quivering. I thought she was about to cry.

"Do you know if any of them were interviewed by the detectives? I've not had a chance to completely read the case file yet, but I didn't see any report indicating they had been spoken to."

She shook her head. "No, Detective, not that I'm aware of."

While Rhoda was looking at the pictures taken at the scene, I focused on the close-ups of the gunshot wound. A hard contact wound, or a wound in which the barrel of the gun is in actual contact with the skin, will leave a mark called an abrasion ring. There were powder burns on Lester's head, but no abrasion ring. It was what is known as a near-contact wound, that is, the barrel was not in contact, but held at a close distance from his head. I realized something by looking at those photos.

It was a murder.

My shirt was still damp, and I probably looked like I'd been chasing cows around the barnyard, but I needed to knock on some doors. Back when I was a real detective, we called it canvassing. Something Detective Thompson didn't seem to know very much about.

I didn't have any luck. Immediately across the street was a man a little older than me, dressed like a hippy. He hadn't shaved in years and kept looking at me like I was about to raid his pot-growing operation. The only thing he could say was he thought he saw a dark-colored car exiting the driveway a few minutes before Rhoda got home. He then wanted to talk about the 9/11 conspiracy before I politely excused myself.

I went back to Rhoda's and opted for a large glass of ice water rather than coffee, talked with her some more, and then told her I'd be in touch before leaving.

I had some phone calls to make. The first was to Uncle Mike. I got his voice mail.

"Listen, I have something important to discuss with you. Give me a call in the morning." It was cryptic enough. His curiosity would be piqued and he'd call me as soon as he woke up. I was going to get to the bottom of the mysterious disappearance of my Wildcat and how it ended up in the shed of a truck driver living in Rockvale, Tennessee.

I was about to call Ronald when my phone rang. I looked at my caller I.D. It was from Mick's cigar bar. I hit the answer button.

"Honey, I told you not to call me anymore. I think Mick is growing suspicious."

"Very funny, smart ass," he growled. "I don't know why I'm calling you, but there is a quite attractive young lady sitting here."

Oh boy, I thought, it had to be Anna.

"She started off drinking coffee but now she's on her third beer and she's constantly looking out of the windows. I think she's waiting for you, which means she's obviously a little bit on the retarded side. "

I grimaced at his remark. "You know, there are a lot of people who believe that word is offensive." I heard Mick scoff into the phone.

"Whatever. Anyway, all of the coffee and beer is starting to have effect. She's been to the ladies room twenty or thirty times now. You need to do something before my water bill goes through the roof."

"Oh, dear, the world is coming to an end."

"Are you coming down here or not?"

Well, I was fresh out of cigars. "Yeah, I'll be there in thirty minutes. Have me a box of those Rocky Patels waiting."

Mick mumbled something unintelligible and hung up.

I didn't smell so well, but I didn't think it was going to matter. When I drove up, I spotted her through the windows immediately. I could see her smiling from the parking lot and she even waved. I hastily checked myself in the rearview mirror.

"Hi," she said as I walked in. "I was wondering if you were going to come in or not." She was wearing khaki cargo shorts that barely covered her butt cheeks and a semi-tight-fitting polo shirt which bore the Tennessee Titans logo and color scheme. Several of the regulars were unabashedly ogling. She acted as if she didn't notice.

I shrugged casually. "I was stopping in to pick up a box of cigars. I've been out in the hot sun and probably don't smell too good right now."

Mick cackled. "You got that right. You smell like stale cigarettes too." He grabbed my debit card out of my hand and began ringing up my purchase.

I ignored him. "Anyway, I'm about to head home. What are you up to?"

She hesitated. "Can we talk outside?"

"Sure you can, little lady," Mick said as he handed me back my card and the box of Ashton cigars. "And don't worry about your tab. The dago here paid it."

I frowned at him, as if to silently convey I would get him back at a later time. Mick grinned gleefully.

I walked Anna over to her car and looked at it closer now. It was a Nissan Cube.

"Interesting-looking car," I commented.

"I love it. It's my baby," she said with a proud grin. "I get right at twenty-five miles to the gallon in town and I put in an awesome kick-ass stereo."

"Very nice."

"You don't like it."

"It's not something I'd buy, no," I said. "I'm more into older cars. So, what is it you wanted to talk about?" I asked.

She inhaled and smiled tentatively. "It goes like this. I've not been totally truthful with you."

"Oh, how so?" I asked.

"My older sister, her name's Alicia. She and I were never really close. She moved out shortly after our dad was murdered and kind of fell in with the wrong crowd. Anyway, she's been missing for over a year now. The last place she worked was at the Red Lynx."

"So, that's why you're working there," I surmised. It was a heck of a way to find out what happened to her sister.

She nodded. "I thought I'd get in close with the girls and see if I could find out anything. The trouble is, none of the girls worked there when Alicia was there." I nodded in understanding. "So, anyway, I've always been fascinated by police work, which is your fault. Ever since you solved my dad's murder, I've wondered what it'd be like to be a detective."

I chuckled. "It's not like TV, in fact most people would find it quite boring."

She nodded but was unfazed. "Okay, so here goes; I was wondering if you could help me find her. My sister."

I blinked, took my tie off, and undid the top button of my shirt. "I don't know, Anna."

Anna grabbed my hand and held it tentatively. "I can pay you, and I can even help you with your work. I can be your assistant." I thought it over as carefully as my tired brain could.

"Was there a police report filed?" I asked.

"Yes, absolutely. I made my mom file one, but the case seems to have gone nowhere. I don't think the cops have done anything."

My first inclination was to say no. Sure, she could probably well afford me, but I knew I'd never take any money from her, so that would be two cases I'd be working on without drawing a paycheck. Not a good idea. But, instead of saying no…

"Well, we could talk it over, I guess."

Her eyes lit up and she smiled brightly. Her investment in the braces had paid off, her teeth were perfectly aligned. She reminded me of a young Reese Witherspoon.

"Awesome," she said gleefully. "So, let's talk it over more at your place. Let me get my overnight bag and I'll ride with you. I've had too much to drink and shouldn't be driving."

"Wait, what?" I asked, but Anna had already unlocked her doors with her key fob and was reaching into her back seat. I was trying to object, but she was bent over and those shorts, which were exceedingly short already, well, I had trouble concentrating.

Looking around, I saw Mick watching us through the window. He had a large, shit-eating grin which was impossible to miss. I knew I was going to be catching a rash of shit from him over this, and he'd draw it out as long as he could. Anna moved the accordion file out of the passenger seat as she climbed into the truck.

"What's this?" she asked.

"It's the Lester Gwinnette case file."

Her eyes widened. "No shit?"

"Yeah, no shit," I said.

"Can I look at it?" she asked as she held it.

"When we get back to my place, we can read it together. By the way, are you sure about this? You hardly know me." And I hardly know you, I thought to myself. The part of my brain which fed my paranoia was wondering if she was setting me up. After all, she was a stripper who worked at a joint which was owned by the president of an outlaw biker club.

She looked over at me and grinned. "Oh, you're a good man, Thomas. I can tell." Her smile vanished. "Besides, I'm having problems with my roommate and work. I want to get away from all of them for a little while."

She'd become quiet during the drive, as had I. I don't know what she was thinking, but my thoughts were a jumbled mixture of Lester's murder, sex, my old Buick, sex, Robard Trucking Company, sex, Anna, and sex. My phone chimed. It was an alert.

Anna heard it and looked over. "Do you have a text?" she asked. I didn't explain. My surveillance system had motion sensors. Most of the time, they activated when deer wandered into my yard, and at first I was going to ignore it, but paranoia got the best of me. I pulled over to the side of the road and stopped. Were Duke and his boys at my house, waiting on me?

"Is something wrong?" Anna asked.

I clicked onto the screen. There was a familiar white car in the driveway, and a man was sitting on my front porch smoking a cigarette. I switched to the camera that focused on my porch and zoomed in closer. It was Uncle Mike.

Exhaling in relief, I looked over at Anna. "Oh, nothing. I try not to text while I'm driving."

She grinned mischievously. "No jealous girlfriend waiting?"

"You should have thought of that before you jumped in the truck with me," I said as I checked behind me and drove back onto the roadway.

Her grin disappeared. "I hope you're joking."

We were home ten minutes later.

"That damn dog keeps growling at me," Uncle Mike said gruffly as Anna and I walked up. "He's known me ever since you got him and he still doesn't like me."

"He doesn't like anyone. He doesn't like me and I'm the one who feeds him." Uncle Mike looked at Anna and then back at me.

"Anna, this is my Uncle Mike."

"Hi," Anna said pleasantly. He reached out and shook her hand. Anna noticed the trembling and looked at me questioningly.

He noticed the look. "Don't mind the shaking hand, missy. I've got Parkinson's."

"Oh," Anna said awkwardly. Uncle Mike was diagnosed with Parkinson's a couple of years ago. Lately, it had become more pronounced. There was a moment of awkward silence.

"Nice place," Anna finally said. It was dark now and she couldn't see much. I guess she was being polite.

"Missy, would you mind waiting inside, please? I'd like to speak with my nephew."

"Sure, and call me Anna please." I unlocked the door, turned off the alarm, and she went inside. I saw a couple of lights being turned on and casually wondered if I'd left any dirty underwear lying around.

After the untimely death of my wife, I could no longer live in a home where she had killed herself. I sold it and bought the home I was currently living in. It was a quaint log cabin which was built from a construction kit. It was small, square footage wise, but it suited the needs of a single man. The front door opened into a foyer which led into the kitchen. The only separation between the kitchen and den was a bar-type counter. It had two bedrooms on either side, both of which had its own full-sized bathroom. I had a prefab metal building out back which was almost as large as the house. I'm pretty sure I spent more time in there than in my own home.

I pulled out my flask, wet my whistle, and handed it to my uncle.

Uncle Mike watched her walk inside. "Cute kid," he said. He wiped the mouth of the flask with a handkerchief and drank.

"I'm glad you approve. Did you get my message?" I asked.

He shook his head. "I've had my phone off."

"Well, okay. What brings you out here then?"

"I've been to see your father." I stared at him in the dark. My father, his brother, was not a topic we discussed. "He's not doing so good lately. He actually asked about you today."

I tensed up. The mere thought of him always made me tense up. "Yeah, well the hell with him. How are you doing?"

He took another swallow before speaking. "The meds don't seem to be working very well anymore," he said.

I nodded silently. The disease was slowly but surely killing him.

He took a drag off of his cigarette. "I've got a lot of sins to atone for before I die. I think it's about time I told the truth about that night. Father Anthony thinks so too." Ah yes, Father Anthony. He must be eighty or ninety years old by now. I'd quit going to church years ago.

"It's a moot point now, Uncle Mike." I repressed the memories of the night he was referring to and changed the subject. "You don't need to be driving at night. Why don't you stay here? I've got some things I want to show you and talk about."

I expected him to be stubborn and say no, but to my surprise, he agreed. He finished his cigarette and we walked inside together. Anna was sitting on the couch, one leg tucked under her and drinking a beer. She'd taken the contents of the file and had neatly arranged everything on the coffee table. And to top it off, Henry was lying on the couch next to her with his head in her lap. She looked up and smiled.

"What's your dog's name?" she asked.

"Henry," I replied. "He normally doesn't like people too much."

Anna stroked his head. "He's a sweetheart. Why'd you name him Henry?"

I headed to the kitchen to get some beers. Uncle Mike sat in my easy chair and picked up some of the photographs. His old cop instincts made him curious.

"I didn't name him. He belonged to a neighbor, an elderly widow. She was convinced the dog was the reincarnation of her late husband, Henry. The dog came over one day and told me his master had died, so he's been living here ever since."

She looked at Henry, and then looked at me quizzically. "What do you mean, he told you?"

I came back into the den, wondering where I should sit as I motioned at Henry. "Dogs have their own way of communicating. He was sitting in front of the door one morning. When I came outside, he would start walking away and then stop and look back at me, like he was asking me to follow him. I did. We walked back to his house. I found his owner on the floor. She'd died of a heart attack."

I handed Uncle Mike a beer, started to sit down beside Anna, but then caught a whiff of myself. "I'm going to take a quick shower. You two chat."

I went to my bathroom, stripped, and took a long minute to look at myself in the mirror. Three inches over six feet, two hundred and twenty pounds. Well okay, maybe two forty. I still had muscle, but it was nothing like the physique I had when I was a younger man. My face was not as sharp featured now that I was older, but I still had deep set dark brown eyes, a testament to my Italian heritage. My hair, including my chest hair, had more gray in it than I liked. It begged the question, why would a twenty-two-year-old girl be remotely attracted to me? I didn't have a logical answer, sighed, and jumped in the shower.

Freshly showered, wearing a clean pair of blue cotton shorts and a tee shirt, I walked back into the den. The two of them were chatting like old friends, and the topic of conversation seemed to center around me.

"When he got his detective's shield, I'd never been more proud," Uncle Mike said with a grin.

Anna smiled as well and pointed at a large plate sitting on the coffee table. "I fixed us turkey sandwiches," she said and patted the space on the couch beside her. "Come sit down and eat." Henry was on the other side of her and looked at me out of the corner of his eye. I realized I was famished, grabbed a sandwich and sat down.

Anna looked back at Uncle Mike. "So, how did he get promoted so quickly?" she asked.

"I got shot in the line of duty," I said between bites. "And it wasn't a promotion, more like a lateral transfer."

Anna gasped. "You got shot? What happened?"

Uncle Mike piped up. "I'll tell you what happened. He was chasing a robbery suspect who pulled out a pistol and popped off a few rounds at him. He damn near got himself killed, but his bullet-proof vest saved him."

Anna looked over at me in wonder. "Yeah, I was lucky," I said. "One round put a nick in my shoulder." I pulled up my shirt sleeve and showed her the gouge mark. "It wasn't a serious wound, but it bled like crazy."

"Oh, wow. What happened then?" she asked.

"Heh, Thomas tackled him, took the gun away from him, and beat the shit out of him," Uncle Mike answered with a grin. "He got an award and I got him transferred into homicide."

Anna chugged her beer and smiled. "There's so much about you that is so amazing," she said with wide eyes. I felt my cheeks begin to redden.

She chuckled and stood. "I need another beer. How about you, Uncle Mike?"

"Sure," he replied. She returned a moment later with three cold ones and plopped back down on the couch.

"So, let's change the subject. Have either of you two looked at the case file?" I asked.

"Some of it," Anna replied.

I nodded and looked pointedly at Uncle Mike. "Does Lester's name sound familiar to you?" I asked.

He was about to drink his beer, but he stopped and looked at me warily. "Should it?" This was how my uncle acted when he was being intentionally evasive. He'd answer every question with a question.

"Yes, it should. Are you going to answer me?"

He didn't look at me, instead he took a long sip of his beer and set it down. "It's been a long day for me. I think I'm going to turn in." He got up and walked into the spare bedroom without another word. I heard the door close quietly. Anna waited until the door closed before she spoke.

"I'm missing something, aren't I?" she asked.

I nodded my head slowly. "Yeah, but it's not important right now. Let's focus on Lester's death. Oh, before I forget, I need to lay some ground rules."

"Okay," she said agreeably.

"The death of a human, no matter the circumstances, is a sensitive matter. We, and when I say we I mean you, will not be discussing this case with anyone. Not your stripper friends, not your biker friends, nobody. Do you understand, and do you agree?"

She nodded her head.

"Give me your word."

She turned on the couch, faced me and squared her shoulders. Or pushed her breasts out, however you wanted to interpret it. "I give you my word I won't say shit," she said with a big grin on her face.

I grunted. "I'm thinking I want you to talk like a proper private investigator, and not like you're talking to the riffraffs who hang out where you work."

She gave me a look now, but she straightened again. "Okay, how about this. I promise I will not divulge any information."

I nodded. "Much better. I hope your word is good."

"Of course it is," she replied haughtily.

"Okay. So, I've not even had a chance to read all of this yet, and I need to call Ronald."

"Who's Ronald?" she asked.

"He's a friend of mine. He's extremely good with computers." I punched an icon and spoke Ronald's name into the phone.

He answered after a few rings. "I'm in the middle of a war!" he said hurriedly. "I can't talk now." He hung up without further explanation.

Anna heard and arched an eyebrow. "Your friend is in the middle of a war?" she asked.

I sighed and tried to explain. "Ronald is an island unto himself. He rarely ventures out in public. He lives in the house he grew up in and his parents are deceased. They were killed by a drunk driver going the wrong way on the interstate. He still lives in the basement. He hasn't even cleaned out his parent's clothing. He only eats soup, crackers, and bread, and only drinks water or vegetable juice. The war he's referring to is probably one of the many computer games he constantly plays. One of them is called Eve, or something like that."

"Oh, he's a meta gamer," she said.

I stared at her. "What the hell is a meta gamer?" I asked.

"The Internet has all of these games called massive multiplayer online role-playing games. They're very popular and addictive."

Ah, I guess that explained it. "I'd say you're right on the money, because he's hooked." I gestured at the case file. "So, you've read more of the file than me. Tell me what you think."

Anna looked down at the paperwork and photographs and scrunched up her face. "The reports don't really say much. Nothing but a bunch of, I got called to the scene, I saw a dead body, and then the detective took over. Then the detective's report basically says, I got called to the scene, I saw a dead body, there was a gun, and he killed himself."

I chuckled without humor. "Yeah, I thought as much. Let's give these photos a look." I went through each of them and explained what they showed, especially the close-ups of the gunshot wound. I then told her what Rhoda told me.

She looked at me wide-eyed and took a swig of beer. "So it really is a murder?" she asked.

"It appears so," I answered. "Now, if I were the homicide detective assigned to the case, I'd need to figure out who killed him and why."

"How are we going to figure it out?"

She'd interjected herself into this case rather quickly. I wasn't certain if that was a good thing and wondered if I was simply going along with this so I could get into her pants. I told myself to try not to be a pervert.

"If we were homicide detectives, we'd start by figuring out who Lester really was, what he was doing in his life, and who he may have pissed off enough to either kill him or have him killed. The term used is victimology, the study of the victim."

She continued staring at me wide eyed. "You said somebody may have had him killed. You mean like a hit?"

"It's possible. If he was murdered, someone went to a lot of trouble to make it look like a suicide. Most murderers don't really care. They don't take the time to cover it up." I took a seat at my desk, opened my laptop and waited for it to boot up.

"Alright, here are my thoughts on this. If I can prove to the detective and the sheriff that this is a murder, they'll reopen the case. As far as I'm concerned, my involvement will then be over."

"It will?" she asked.

"Yes." I was going to tell her if Rhoda was a paying customer I'd go further. But, since my only payment was the return of a car which had been taken from me years ago, well, I simply didn't see how my obligation could, or should, extend any further.

"I'm going to need to get to that point before I can even begin to start on your sister's case. You understand that, right?"

Anna nodded after a moment of staring at me.

"Okay, good."

Once my laptop informed me it was good to go and wasn't going to lock up on me, again. I opened a new Word document, this one was a template I'd created for taking notes. Anna saw my empty bottle and carried it with her to the kitchen. She came back a moment later with a fresh beer and handed it to me.

"Thank you," I said with a grateful nod. "I've got a lot of reading to do, so feel free to make yourself at home. I've got satellite TV." She nodded, made herself comfortable on the couch, and picked up the remote control. I started reading from the case file, and within ten minutes, I had a couple of pages of notes.

I spent the next hour scanning the various reports and jotting notes. Anna was right. The official police reports were generically worded and sparse. It was as if Detective Thompson came to the scene expecting a suicide, did nothing to prove otherwise, and hurried through the necessary paperwork.

Anna had stretched out on the couch and had fallen asleep before the movie was over. She was lying in a fetal position with her butt pointed at me and I have to admit, I looked it over for longer than I should have. Henry was lying on the floor beside the couch, his legs occasionally twitching, like he was dreaming of chasing somebody down and biting them, or something.

I was very tired as well. Glancing at the clock, I frowned as I realized it was three in the morning. I carefully put an afghan on top of her, turned everything off and went to bed.

I didn't remember falling asleep, but I remember waking up. Someone was using my shower. Using my powers of deductive reasoning, I was pretty sure it was Anna, and I needed to pee very badly. Henry was lying next to the partially closed bathroom door, watching me studiously. I guess I was going to wait. Thankfully, the water turned off and Anna emerged a moment later. She was wrapped in a towel and brushing her hair.

She saw me and smiled. "I hope I didn't wake you."

"Oh no," I replied and glanced at the clock on my nightstand. It was after nine in the morning. "It's time for me to get up." I stifled a yawn. I could have slept another hour at least. "Do you know if my uncle is still around?"

She shook her head and the towel almost dropped. "No. He left just a few minutes ago. I woke up and saw him reading your notes. When he saw me looking at him, he got up and left."

I nodded. "Are you done in the bathroom?"

She responded with a grin. "More or less. You go ahead."

"You know, there's a full bathroom in the spare bedroom."

"Yeah, but there's no shampoo or toothpaste in there." She started to walk out of the bedroom, but paused. "Do you have any tea here?" she asked. "I'm not a coffee drinker." I shook my head. "Okay. Oh, I almost forgot. Your phone has been going crazy. I didn't answer it though."

"I usually turn it off before I go to bed and don't turn it back on until after noon. I guess I forgot." I waited for her to leave my bedroom and then hurriedly went to the restroom. I got a hot shower going and had my head under the faucet when Anna opened the shower door and poked her head in.

"Wow, look at you. Maybe everyone should be calling you the Italian Stallion." I jerked and turned away from her. Anna giggled and turned toward the steamy mirror. "So what are we going to do today?

"Don't you have a home and job to go to?" I asked.

"I live with two other dancers and there's too much Jerry Springer drama going on right now. I need to take a break from all of it. So, what're we going to do today?" she asked again as she brushed her hair out.

"Well, for starters, you're going to the den and give me some privacy," I replied with no small amount of embarrassed exasperation. Anna giggled again and walked out.

I walked into the den a few minutes later, wearing cargo shorts which were a few inches longer than the ones Anna was wearing yesterday, and one of my older golf shirts.

Anna had on a fresh pair of shorts, just as short as the ones she was wearing last night, and a black tank top. She looked up from my notes when I walked in the den. "No coat and tie today?" she asked. I sat down beside her.

"Nope, going casual today. I'm hungry. What do you say I take you back to your car and then maybe we grab some brunch?" Anna readily agreed and we were soon on the road. I opted to take the truck. It was warm and humid, but it looked like rain was on the way. As we drove into the parking lot of Mick's shop, Anna gasped.

"Oh, no!" she wailed. I saw it too. Someone had vandalized her car.

Chapter 8

"Now who would do something like that?" I asked rhetorically. Someone had taken a sharp object and crudely scrawled the word "WHORE" on her driver's door in big, block letters. I got out of my car and looked over the damage closely. I mentally told myself I had the equipment in my shop to sand it down and repaint it without too much trouble. The car was new enough where a new coat of paint would closely blend in with the existing paint. The question in my mind, did I want to?

"Doug had to have done it," she said as she fought back tears.

"Who's Doug?" I asked.

"My ex-boyfriend. What do I do now?"

"The first thing you should do is file a police report," I said. "We'll see how it goes from there." As we stood looking at it, Mick drove into the parking lot. He got out and walked over.

"What the hell happened here?" he asked.

"Well, one of two things," I replied. "Either Anna has a very upset ex-boyfriend, or Kim Lee is rather jealous."

Mick gave me a pained expression. "Already you're starting?" he asked.

I slowly nodded my head. "Yeah, you're right. Kim wouldn't to it. She doesn't mind sharing me."

Mick threw up his hands in disgust. "Come on, Dago, let's go look at the surveillance video. I got a camera right there." He pointed up as he walked inside. There were four cameras mounted on the exterior of the building. One of them was facing the area where Anna had parked her car.

A few minutes later, he had it. The cameras recorded in color during the day, but changed to black and white after dark. Even so, the clarity of the video made it obvious the suspect was driving a marked police car. It showed the officer driving through the parking lot several times over the course of an hour.

Finally, the driver stopped, got out, and squatted down by the door. He reached toward his duty belt and some type of object appeared in his hand. After he was done, he hurried back to his car and sped off. The resulting vandalism was clear.

Anna watched it with us and verified it was her ex in the video. I gently reminded her to call the police. She complied. After a few minutes of talking on her cell phone, she hung up.

"The dispatcher said it'd be about an hour before someone came out," she said. "She asked me who I thought did it."

"Did you tell her?" I asked. She nodded. "Good, because we've got irrefutable evidence on this idiot."

I didn't tell her about the domestic violence policies in place. This young man will be lucky if he has a job with the department after the investigation was completed. I also suspected if I told this to Anna, she wouldn't file a complaint.

"What's this *we* shit?" Mick said. "I'm the one who got it, and I'm going to burn some CDs of it for you too." He hooked a thumb at me as he spoke to Anna. "This dumb wop has no idea how to work one of these things."

In fact, Ronald and I installed the system, and it was Ronald who trained him how to use it. I declined to point out his error and instead ordered us some lunch from a local restaurant which delivered.

We were eating lamb gyro sandwiches and washing them down with bottled water when a police car drove into the parking lot. At least, Mick and I were. Anna merely picked at hers. A sergeant got out and inspected the vandalism before entering the shop. Anna and I were sitting at one of the small tables. The sergeant looked around and then froze momentarily when he spotted me. We recognized each other. He walked over until he was about ten feet away.

"Hello, Thomas. I haven't seen you around in a while," he said quietly. He didn't offer to shake my hand.

"Hello, Jim. Are you here about the vandalism complaint?" I asked. He nodded. I motioned toward Anna. "This is the victim. Anna Davies. Anna, this is Sergeant Jim Ozment."

He looked at Anna a moment, and then glanced at me as if to say, you sure like them young. "I'm pleased to meet you, ma'am. It's my understanding you're alleging a police officer did this?"

Anna nodded reluctantly. "Yeah, Officer Doug Eastlin. He's an ex-boyfriend. We dated for about a month."

"But how do you know it was him?" Jim asked. "Do you have any proof? A witness perhaps?"

I slid over one of the CDs. "This is a video recording of him doing it. It happened late last night, which I assume was when he was on duty." I glanced at Anna. The look on her face had changed. She was no longer sad, she was now getting mad. Good for her, I thought.

Jim looked at the CD and furrowed his brow. "Shit," he muttered. I shrugged a shoulder in agreement and lit a cigar. "Is it possible to view it here, or do I need to take it back to the office?" he asked.

Mick grabbed the CD and motioned for the sergeant to follow him behind the counter. "You and Thomas used to work together, huh?" Mick asked.

Jim nodded reluctantly, like it was something he didn't want known.

Mick didn't notice. "Are you a dumbass Italian too?"

Jim frowned and looked over at me. I shrugged again and puffed on my cigar.

He watched the video silently with a disapproving frown etched on his face. When he was finished, he took the CD from Mick and walked back over to our table. "Ma'am, may I have this CD for evidence?"

Anna looked over at me. I nodded.

"Excellent," he said. "I'm going to get a report started." He glanced over at me. "We do our reports on our department-issued computers now. Not like the old days. They call it progress but I find it to be a pain in the ass."

"How long before retirement?" I asked.

He rubbed his face. "My youngest one is starting college this fall. It's going to be a few more years." His face clouded a moment. He was feeling his age, and feeling the effects of being a cop for over two decades. I could see it plainly.

He continued. “Anyway, the computer is in the car. Ms. Davies, if I could borrow your driver’s license, it’ll save me from asking you a bunch of questions. I’ve also got to call the precinct commander and notify him about this, and I have to notify OPA.”

Anna fished her license out of her purse and handed it over. “What is OPA?” she asked.

“It’s the acronym for the Office of Professional Accountability,” Jim replied. “They’ll be investigating the case.”

She frowned. “They will?”

“Yes, ma’am,” he replied. “We have policies in place regarding an officer’s conduct in relationship issues. We’ve had one too many incidences in the past and the department has become very strict.” He realized what he was saying and looked at me a little embarrassed.

“Anyway, I’ll be out in my car. Give me a few minutes.” He hurried out.

Anna was confused a moment, before she understood. “He realized he was talking about you.”

“It’s old news,” I said curtly. I wasn’t in the mood to talk about my deceased wife.

I listened to my messages while we waited for Sergeant Ozment. There were some potential clients, Ronald called me back, and Rhoda called. She’d left a message and sounded frantic. I called her immediately.

“Detective,” she said in near panic. “FBI agents are here!”

Chapter 9

Mick located some duct tape and I spread strips of it across the offending word. The three of them watched me quietly. I stood when I was done, stretched my back, and felt vertebrae cracking as they settled back in place. I remembered a time when squatting was a lot easier.

"It's temporary, but it'll do for now," I said. Anna nodded, but didn't say anything.

Jim cleared his throat. "I just spoke with the head of the OPA, he's requesting Ms. Davies to come down to the office and give a statement."

Anna looked at me. "What should I do?"

"If you're asking for my advice, I recommend cooperating with the investigation and meet with the OPA detectives."

"Are you coming with me?" she asked.

I shook my head. "Rhoda is very upset. I promised I'd go to her house right away." She nodded again. "You'll be fine," I assured her.

"I'd be glad to have you follow me to the OPA office if you'd like," Jim offered.

Anna looked at me for approval. I silently assented. She drew a breath. "Okay, I'll follow you." She looked back at me. "I'll call you when I'm done, okay?"

"Sure," I said and watched her as she got into her car.

Jim cleared his throat again. It was becoming annoying. "Hey, listen, I wasn't implying anything in there earlier when I was talking about domestic violence issues."

"No problem," I said and looked at him. He had aged considerably since I first met him. He had a head full of gray hair now and his features were drawn. We used to be friends. Good friends.

"How's life been treating you, Thomas? You still doing PI work?"

"I am. Life's been okay, I can't complain. How about yourself?" I asked.

"Well, I can't complain, I guess. I caught throat cancer about a year and a half ago. Thought I was a goner, but the doctors were able to treat it. I've been in remission ever since. The kids are all grown up now. The youngest turned eighteen last month. You wouldn't recognize them."

I nodded. We'd been in patrol together, but had grown apart when I was transferred to homicide. When my wife died, we'd stopped talking altogether. We probably could have spent a few hours catching up, but right at that particular moment, I found myself with nothing to say. It felt awkward being in close proximity to someone who at one time was a close friend.

I broke the silence. "I guess you'd better get her down to OPA. I have a client who is panicking over something, so I need to be heading over to see her."

He nodded his head, and perhaps there was some sadness behind it, I didn't know.

I hooked a thumb back over my shoulder. "I usually hang out here. If you're ever in the neighborhood, drop by. We can have a beer and catch up."

"Yeah, I'd like that. We're not getting any younger, are we?" He walked back to his car and drove away. Anna dutifully followed.

There was a midnight blue Ford Crown Victoria with heavily tinted windows parked in Rhoda's driveway. I parked beside it and got out. Two people, a man and woman, wearing raid vests with FBI emblazoned on them met me outside as I walked up to the back door.

The female agent was very attractive, with blonde hair pulled back in a ponytail and hazel eyes. The male agent was a handsome man as well, sharp eyes, short-cropped hair, clean shaven. He too had hazel eyes. Both were wearing casual khaki slacks, black polo shirts, sensible shoes. They looked like a Ken and Barbie pair. The woman spoke first.

"I'm Special Agent Ridgeway and this is Special Agent Jeffreys. Ms. Gwinnette advised us you're a police detective. Is that true?" she asked directly with a steady gaze.

I shook my head. "I'm a former detective with the Metro Nashville Police, now I'm doing private investigations work."

She nodded her head in apparent understanding.

"May I ask why Ms. Gwinnette is being investigated by the FBI?"

The man, Special Agent Jeffreys, spoke up. "I'm afraid the investigation is confidential."

I was about to retort but Special Agent Ridgeway intervened. "Mark, she's going to show him the copy of the search warrant as soon as we leave, we may as well tell him." He frowned, but didn't respond.

She focused on me. "We're investigating the trucking company with whom the late Mister Gwinnette worked for. We're looking for certain documents. Mrs. Gwinnette is not suspected of any criminal offense at the moment."

"Oh, what kind of documents?" I asked.

She smiled politely. I was uncertain how genuine it was, but nonetheless it was a pleasant smile with bright white bleached teeth. "I'll have to agree with my colleague on this point. The specifics of the documents are confidential. It's nothing personal, but we don't want to risk jeopardizing the integrity of the investigation. As a former detective, I'm sure you understand." She was very diplomatic, and I suspected she was very smart. Her colleague gave a small, smug expression.

I smiled back at her. "Point taken," I said. "May I ask if the two of you are investigating Lester's death?"

Special Agent Jeffreys frowned again. "Are we investigating his suicide? Of course not," he said with a tone suggesting investigating a suicide was beneath the mighty FBI, and more importantly, beneath him.

I nodded. "I see. Would it be alright to speak with Rhoda? She sounded upset over the phone."

"Sure, we're done here," she said. "We were about to leave when you drove up."

"Well, I'm glad I got here in time. It's a pleasure meeting you both. I'd like to swap business cards if you don't mind." They agreed amicably, but I doubted they'd ever use my card other than to stick it in their case file or pick out tofu from between their glow-in-the-dark teeth. I glanced at their cards and noticed both of them worked out of the Nashville office.

They started walking to their car, but Special Agent Jeffreys stopped and turned. "You said death. When you were talking about Lester Gwinnette, you said death. You didn't call it a suicide," he said it matter-of-factly.

I nodded slightly and tapped my temple with an index finger. "I've got some questions up here I need answered before I'd be comfortable calling it a suicide." He thought over what I said, but offered no comment or opinion. Special Agent Ridgeway smiled courteously but curtly before the two of them left.

Rhoda watched the conversation from behind her screen door. An ever-present cigarette dangled from her lips as she showed me a copy of the search warrant. I read it over carefully. There was no inventory sheet indicating what had been seized.

I looked up at Rhoda. "What did they take?" I asked.

Rhoda shook her head. "Nothing at all. They looked all through the house, asked me some questions, and took some pictures, but that's all. I offered them coffee, but they turned me down."

"Well, that was stupid of them. They don't know what they were missing." For the first time, Rhoda actually smiled. "Why don't you pour us both a cup and tell me exactly what questions they asked you."

Rhoda dutifully fixed us cups of her brackish concoction before sitting down and lighting a fresh cigarette. If nothing else, she was a creature of predictable habits. She inhaled deeply and blew the smoke toward the ceiling before answering.

"They asked me where Lester kept all of his paperwork. I showed them his file cabinet. All it has are the usual things, some receipts, insurance papers, and our tax returns. They took some photographs of it, and put it all back." She took another drag off of her cigarette.

"Then they asked me about our bank accounts and wrote down the account numbers. All we have is a checking account and a savings account. Oh, and they asked me if anyone had visited recently. I told them about you and your friend."

"Has anyone else visited in the past couple of months, Rhoda?" I asked. She shook her head. It was obvious Rhoda and Lester didn't have many friends. She was truly all alone now.

"One last question Rhoda, where are Lester's log books?"

"His log books for trucking?" she asked. I nodded. "He used to keep them in the shed. He kept a double set of books. I asked him why once and he said all truckers keep two sets."

I kept a poker face. "Do you know if they're still there?"

She shrugged unknowingly.

"Did the agents go out there?" I asked.

"I saw the man poke his head in, but it must have been too dirty to go in there." She leaned forward. "Lester would have called him a pretty boy." I smiled and had to agree.

I forced myself to finish the coffee and stopped by the shed to look at my Buick before I left. Curious now, I looked around the shed, but found no log books. I started to walk out and took a last look at the Buick before stopping suddenly.

On a hunch, I opened the trunk. Lo and behold, there they were, wrapped in a piece of scrap tarpaulin and stuffed under the spare tire. I peeked out of the shed to see if anyone was watching me, grabbed them and carried them with me when I left.

I called Ronald as I drove down the road. "How did the war turn out?" I asked.

"Oh, man, it was amazing. I was the FC of a two-hundred-man fleet. We had the perfect amount of DPS, ECM, and logis. My scout lit a cyno deep in enemy space and..."

"Ronald," I interrupted. "I have no idea what you're talking about."

"Oh, sorry. I tend to get caught up in it. So, how's it going? Who's the gorgeous girl you've been with?" he asked.

"That's Anna, and if you're nice, I'll introduce you to her," I said. He tittered nervously.

"Where are you? Your phone GPS shows you're in Rockvale."

I sighed. The little shit had access to my iPhone through his computers and always knew exactly where I was. He'd set it up that way without telling me. When I found out, I was a little irked, but then I reminded myself Ronald was harmless. Besides, if someone were to kidnap and kill me one day, he'd know where my body was. Or, at least, my phone.

"I'm leaving Rhoda's house," I answered. "She was served with a search warrant by the FBI."

"Oh wow, what were they searching for?" he asked.

"I'm not sure. The affidavit of complaint refers to an ongoing investigation into Robard Trucking Company. The wording is very vague, which is probably intentional. It only said they were looking for documentation, journals, and logs regarding his employment with the company. I'm thinking the word 'logs' may be a subtlety meaning Lester's truck driving logs."

"So, what's next?" he asked.

"I'm going to try to figure out what the FBI is up to and look over these logbooks. Say, do you want to do some snooping on this bank up in Detroit?"

"Uh, sure, but it'll be a day or two. My alliance is involved in an all-out war."

I held my tongue. Ronald sometimes lost himself in the fantasy world of computer games. He was too socially inept to physically interact with people in any venue other than cyberspace. I've tried to intercede in the past and get him to socialize more, but it was a futile effort.

"Okay, buddy, do what you can," I said and hung up. My next call was to a number I was now familiar with.

"Hello, this is Thomas Ironcutter. I'm returning your call." It was the older woman who had raised hell about my fee.

"Hello, this is - this is Esther Braxton," she responded in a tone which indicated she was uncomfortable identifying herself. "We've already had a brief conversation, a bit too brief."

"Yes ma'am, I remember you. Before we continue with this conversation, I have two questions to ask you."

She exhaled loudly into the phone, no doubt intended to convey to me she didn't have the time nor patience for trivial questions. "What are your questions, Mister Ironcutter?" she finally asked.

"First, my fee is non-negotiable, so, my first question is, can you afford it? Before you answer, I am advising you once again, I do not waste my time investigating cases of spousal infidelity or any of its variants. I suspect this is exactly what you want to hire me to do. So, my second question is, do you think you're going to try to talk me into changing this policy?" There was a long pause before she answered.

"You have been referred to me by a person whom I trust. I will not divulge the name of this person, but they have a very high opinion of you. They advised me you are very competent and will exercise the utmost in discretion. Now, in answer to your first question, I can very much afford you, although I think your fee is outrageous. The answer to your second question is more involved. I would very much like to discuss it further with you in person." She finished and waited for my response. So, it was a case of adultery after all. I was drawing a breath and thinking of a response, when she continued.

"I will be willing to pay you one hundred dollars to meet with you and discuss my, situation. But it will have to be in cash. All of my business transactions will have to be in cash."I perked up instantly. Cash is good, it was always good. "Very well," I said. "It's getting late in the day. Perhaps we could meet in the morning. Is there somewhere you have in mind?"

"Could I meet you at the Belle Meade entrance to Percy Warner Park? At the top of the hill, there is a picnic table with a scenic view overlooking a quaint community golf course. Shall we meet there tomorrow at ten o'clock?"

"Consider it a date. You'll recognize me by my car. It is a very elegant black 1961 Cadillac convertible. It is the most amazing car in Nashville. Oh, I may have one of my associates with me."

"Very well, Mister Ironcutter. All I ask is discretion. Discretion is vital." She hung up before I could respond. I ignored the rest of my messages and drove home with only my thoughts to occupy me.

Chapter 10

Anna was waiting on me when I drove up. She was sitting in one of the rocking chairs, her legs curled under her and Henry was keeping her company. I was both pleasantly surprised and uncomfortably conflicted. I parked my truck, walked up to the porch and plopped down in one of the other chairs. Her eyes were red and puffy from crying.

"I really like these chairs. It's like they're built to fit your posture. Where'd you get them from, IKEA?"

I snorted. "I bought them from an Amish craftsman. They're handmade and built to last."

"Yes they are," she replied.

"How did it go? I asked.

"It was awful. They questioned me about everything. I mean, we only dated for a short time, but they asked me about everything under the sun. They asked me to describe every illegal activity we'd ever participated in, if there was anyone else involved in our relationship, if there was a possibility I was pregnant, everything. It was unpleasant, I feel violated to be honest. Then they asked if I had a safe place to stay and I thought of you. I hope you don't mind." I shrugged and found myself needing a drink. She continued.

"Anyway, a couple of detectives escorted me downtown in order to take out a warrant and an order of protection, and then we went to my apartment so I could get some belongings, and I will be damned if he wasn't there."

"What happened?" I think I knew the answer, but I asked anyway.

"They handcuffed him and took him away." She tried to light a cigarette, but her hands were trembling. I took the lighter and lit it for her. She took a long drag.

"They said they'd call me when I need to be in court," she said before letting out an involuntary sob. She smoked her cigarette a long couple of minutes before speaking.

"It was a casual thing, Thomas. We met when he came in the club one night. I thought he was cute. We talked, I gave him my phone number and we started going out. It wasn't anything serious. At least, it wasn't for me. I mean, I liked him, but it wasn't anything serious." She finished her cigarette and discovering her hands were a little steadier, lit another one.

"So, my friends and I were hanging out one night and talked about going on a trip. We got online and booked plane tickets and a room in Vegas. It was a spur of the moment thing, you know? When I got back, he was waiting for me at my apartment. He didn't have a key, so I didn't know how he got in at the time. He flipped out and accused me of being unfaithful. I mean, I was like, really dude? Do you have your flask?" she asked.

"Thought you didn't like scotch," I said as I reached into my pocket and handed it to her. She took a small sip and made a face.

"So anyway, there was a big argument and I told him to fuck off. He didn't take it well. And now, here I am." She looked at me with no small amount of anxiety in her eyes.

"As he was being led away, he looked back at me and told me he was going to kill me. There were these detectives standing right beside him, and it didn't even faze him. And, to top it all off, when I was packing my clothes, one of my roommates came in and told me while I was in Vegas, my other roommate slept with him."

I listened in silence. Listening to other people was my strong suit. She took one more sip, more like a big swig this time, coughed, and handed the flask back to me. I'd been neglecting my little silent buddy all day and took a long pull.

"I've been unfair with you, Thomas. I practically invited myself over here last night and I've gotten you involved in my stupid problems. I want you to know I'm very sorry."

"It's okay," I said.

"I've decided I'm going to move out of my apartment. I think I'm going to quit stripping too. I mean, it's good money, but the main reason I took the job was to find out what happened to my sister and that hasn't worked out at all. I've been thinking about it for a while, but I guess this bullshit is the final straw. If you'll be kind enough to let me stay here for another night, I promise I'll be out of your hair tomorrow and I'll find another place to live."

Perhaps it was the heady rush of drinking a healthy gulp of scotch on an empty stomach, but I came to a sudden decision. "Don't be ridiculous. I've got that spare bedroom sitting empty. You can move into it."

She looked at me in surprise, wondering if I were playing a mean joke on her. "Do you mean it?"

"Of course I mean it. But, I've got rules," I said.

"Okay." She took another small sip from my flask. "What're your rules?"

I grunted. "I have no idea, but I have rules and I expect you to abide by them." Anna giggled. I laughed as well. Sometimes I was a real dumbass. "How much did you pack up?" I asked.

"Most of my clothes and my girly things. I've got some furniture and a TV I had to leave behind because my car wasn't large enough to carry all of it."

"No problem. We'll get to it tomorrow and move it all back here."

"That'd be wonderful."

"We'll get to it in the afternoon, but first, I have a potential new client to meet in the morning. I'm sensing she has money to spend, so I'm going to listen to what she has to say. You can come along, but I need you to dress demurely. Do you have those kind of clothes?"

"Demure clothes?" she asked and laughed. "Yeah, I think I can do that."

"Excellent. So, it's settled then. You're now my official roommate and assistant," I said.

"Wait, I'm not your partner?" she asked. I finished off the contents of my flask before speaking. I chuckled.

"You're going to have to prove yourself as a competent PI before you're promoted to partner."

Anna squealed in delight, jumped up, and gave me a tight hug. "Don't worry, I'm a fast learner," she exclaimed. "We'll be partners in no time."

I said something else, but shit if I remember what. All I could focus on were her breasts pressed tightly against me.

Chapter 11

At promptly ten o'clock the next morning, an older but very immaculate black Rolls Royce slowly made its way up the hill and stopped near my Cadillac. The chauffeur exited and held the back door open. I recognized her immediately.

After our phone conversation, I did a brief search on Esther Braxton. She was the wife of Theopolis Braxton the Third. The Braxton family was one of old money. She exited the car with just a hint of stiffness and stood, eyeing us much like Marie Antoinette would have eyed the commoners. I stood beside my car, wearing a suit fresh from the dry cleaners, necktie smartly knotted in a half-Windsor. Anna had been chatty on the drive here, but now sat quietly in the passenger seat. She was wearing charcoal gray slacks and a white blouse and her hair was smartly pulled up in a bun. I thought she looked very attractive, and demure.

Mrs. Braxton made direct eye contact with me before speaking with her chauffeur under her breath. His facial expression indicated he did not like what she said, but he nodded curtly at her order and stayed with the vehicle.

I waited patiently as she walked over and introduced herself. She was a stately woman in her mid-sixties. Her medium-length hair was dyed an austere shade of brown with just the right amount of highlights, I'd guess the salon she patronized was located in Belle Meade and therefore very chic. Her outfit was an off-white pantsuit with a hint of saffron added to the coloring and a black blouse underneath the jacket. It all looked expensive. For her age, she was a handsome woman. She probably would've never won a beauty contest, but I had no doubt she fit in very well with the elite blue bloods.

She glanced over at Anna and frowned. "Who is the tart?" she asked with a touch of southern twang she probably tried desperately to eradicate but never quite succeeded. Her tone left me with no doubt she was used to speaking down to people.

Because I had the top down on the Cadillac, Anna heard the remark clearly. I glanced over and could see her cheeks redden.

"Where is the money you referred to?" I asked curtly. She stared at me a moment down the bridge of her sharply angled nose before retrieving a hundred dollar bill from her purse. I snatched it out of her hand and motioned toward Anna.

"This is Anna Davies, my partner. If you insist on using insulting nouns when referring to her, I will take this money and leave now. If you want to continue this discussion, the first order of business will be an apology, from you, to Miss Davies."

Esther Braxton was not a woman who apologized for anything she did, I could see it. She was the type of woman who would bump into a waitress at the country club and then expect the waitress to apologize. Her facial muscles tightened. I turned to go.

"Wait," she said and looked over at Anna. I could see her composing herself before speaking. "Dear, I apologize for my poor choice of words. I've been under a lot of stress lately. I hope you understand."

"It's okay," Anna replied quietly. It was almost a whisper. I looked at Anna for affirmation. She smiled weakly.

"Very well," I said. "How about the three of us have a seat at the picnic table over there and we can discuss your case." Mrs. Braxton was about to object. It was obvious she wanted to discuss the case only with me. Normally, I would have agreed, but chose against it. I didn't like her insulting Anna. It was kind of my way of bringing her down a notch.

"I presume you've heard of the Braxton name?" she asked once we were seated.

I nodded. After our phone conversation, I put her name through Bing. So, I Binged her. It sounds a lot more weird than Googling someone.

Anyway, the Braxtons were possibly the richest family in the state of Tennessee. Theopolis Braxton Senior was a rags-to-riches coal miner. With an eye for geology, he spotted some foreclosed property that looked promising, put a down payment on it with a forged loan, borrowed some mining equipment, and parlayed it into millions.

Theopolis Braxton Junior was a six-term United States Senator who parlayed the millions into hundreds of millions in various business investments.

Theopolis Braxton the Third had done absolutely nothing. He was a Harvard graduate who'd never worked a day in his life, at least, not in any métier in which a sweat would have been broken. The only thing he was successful at was not squandering the family fortune. I once read an article in a local magazine in which the author speculated he would have to spend over a hundred thousand dollars a day for the next twenty years before the family fortune would evaporate. I assumed they had children, but had no idea if there was a number four. I looked at Mrs. Braxton and waited.

"Yes, well he has been, and continues to be unfaithful," she said. I hung my head, yet another adultery case. She saw my reaction and frowned.

"If I may ask, Mister Ironcutter, why do you detest infidelity cases?" she asked as she stared at me pointedly.

"Because adultery is basically irrelevant in court, especially if you don't have any minor children. You want to divorce him? Fine, in most states, and Tennessee is included, you don't need any kind of reason. You file the paperwork and go forward from there. You'll get at least fifty percent of all assets. Any decent divorce attorney will tell you this." When I finished, she looked at me as if she were about to score a major victory.

"Yes, you have a point. In normal circumstances, you would be absolutely correct. But in this case, you are totally wrong, Mister Ironcutter."

"How so?" I asked. My curiosity was piqued.

"There is a matter of a prenuptial agreement. A prenuptial agreement is a form of a contract as I'm sure you are aware. I signed one before I married Theo, but not before I had an attorney review it and add my own stipulations. After much negotiation, we agreed on the terms and conditions of the prenup. One of those pesky little conditions addressed the issue of adultery. I won't bother with the legal speak, which articulated in detail for several paragraphs the terms and conditions and what would have to occur for it to become null and void. The bottom line, if adultery can be proven, I stand to reap a vastly larger settlement than what would otherwise be obtainable."

I nodded in partial understanding. I'd never been to law school. I had a lot of experience in criminal court and felt I had a pretty good understanding of legal theory in that particular realm, but I was at sea when it came to divorce court, especially when it involved prenuptial contracts and millions of dollars.

"Do you have any particular person in mind with whom he is having an affair with?" I asked.

She had been watching an elderly man teeing off, but now turned and looked me in the eye. "Yes, my former daughter-in-law. In fact, I'm fairly certain she has a child by him."

I looked at her curiously.

"So, you'll take the case?" she asked. I digested what she said for a moment or two before responding.

"No complaining about my fee, agreed?" I asked. She may have nodded, but if she did so, I missed it. "Alright," I said and motioned for Anna. "Anna will take down all of the necessary information."

The conversation lasted for thirty more minutes before the chauffer cleared his throat. Mrs. Braxton glanced at him and stood.

"I must be going," she said. "There is a function scheduled at the country club which I must not be late to."

I stood as well, which caused Anna to stand. "We'll start our preliminary investigation and will be in touch within a couple of days."

Mrs. Braxton looked at me a long moment before walking to her car and leaving.

I was still in disbelief as I drove to Mick's cigar shop. Apparently, so was Anna.

"Oh my God, she believes her husband is sleeping with the ex-daughter-in-law. That's pretty fucked up."

"It reminds me of the old Jack Nicholson movie, Chinatown." Anna looked at me quizzically. I explained. "It was a movie about murder, intrigue, and an incestuous relationship between a father and daughter." The look on her face indicated she'd never seen it.

I shrugged. "Never mind," I muttered.

Duke was sitting on a bar stool talking to Kim when I walked in. He looked over as the two of us walked up. "Well, lookee here. You two have become fast friends it seems," he said.

I ignored the comment as I sat down beside him. Kim gave me a beer and I prepared a cigar. After I lit it, I looked over at him. "You look like a man who doesn't screw around with silly little word games, a man who is up front and to the point."

"I guess you could say that," he replied evenly.

"Alright then. You seem to have taken quite an interest in me the past couple of days. You took the time to find out where I live, and now you're in a place where I like to socialize. I've been hanging out here for the past two years and I've never seen you in here before."

Duke arched an eyebrow and took a drag off of his cigar. He motioned at Kim. "This lady here seems to have a high opinion of you. My attorney knows you too. He seems to have a high opinion of you as well, but he said you're suspected of killing your wife." He looked over at me and arched an eyebrow. "Now, I understand if a bitch deserves to die. Believe me, I understand."

I looked him over closely. "Duke Holland. President of the Baroques outlaw motorcycle club and owner of the Red Lynx. You've got quite a criminal history, but no arrests in quite a while. That tells me you've gotten smart over the years. Smart enough to avoid getting pegged by my former co-workers. Now, do we need to go somewhere quiet, remote, no witnesses, and settle this grudge, or whatever it is you have against me? We can do it right now, no need putting off tomorrow what we can do tonight. And for the record, my wife may have been a little off-center, but she wasn't a bitch."

Duke looked me over, long and slow. "Here I am being friendly and sociable, and you're challenging me to a duel or some shit."

It was my turn to shrug a shoulder. "You're being somewhat elusive, or maybe I'm just dense. Spell it out for me. Are we enemies or what? Define our relationship for me in layman's terms if you don't mind. I want to know where I stand."

Duke laughed now. "I merely came in to enjoy a beer and a cigar. Oh, I guess I'm here to thank you as well. The advice you gave me earlier was very helpful. By the way, why don't you answer your damn phone sometime?"

"I usually keep it turned off," I replied. "You should've left a message."

"Yeah, right," he replied, knowing it wouldn't have made much of a difference.

We drank and smoked in silence for a while. Anna occupied herself by talking with Kim and Mick, but she kept a wary eye on us.

"Would you be interested in doing background checks on prospects?" Duke asked offhandedly. "I'd pay in cash."

"When you say prospects, are you referring to people who are trying to join your biker club?" Duke nodded. "Then the answer is no," I responded.

"Why not? Is it beyond your skill level or something?" Duke chided.

"You know why. You're trying to find a way to determine if any undercover officers are trying to infiltrate your club. I may not be a cop anymore, but to identify one would be a betrayal to my former profession, and if I discover an undercover narc and don't tell you, I'd be betraying you. So, no, I'm not going to get into that quandary."

Duke grunted. "You told me about that little thing in Joelton," he said quietly. He had a point. The surveillance camera was owned by a law enforcement agency, although I had no idea who.

"True enough," I said. "But that was a favor. A peace offering. As far as I'm concerned, the slate is clean. I don't owe you, or any of your buds, jack-shit."

Duke stared at me a second before grunting. "I suppose I already knew the answer before I asked." He sat there, drinking his beer, causing me to wonder why he was still dallying around here. After all, the only reason he had for coming here was to attempt to enlist my services, and I'd turned him down flat.

"Oh say, I didn't get a good look, but I caught a glimpse of a good-sized metal building behind your house," Duke said as he ordered another beer.

"It's my garage and workshop. I tinker around in there."

"Ah, I thought as much. You work on cars?"

I nodded. "Yeah, mostly."

"That's a pretty sweet looking Cadillac you got. You rebuild it yourself?" I nodded again. "Nice," he said. "You ever work on bikes?"

"I rebuilt a '48 pan head a while back for a friend. I can't say I'm an expert though."

"A '48?" I nodded. "FL?" he asked, referring to the larger version of the engine.

"Of course," I said.

"Nice," Duke said and drank his beer. Mick grabbed the remote and found a baseball game. We watched it for several minutes in silence.

"Why'd you become a cop?" he finally asked.

"I went in the Army when I was still a kid. I decided I didn't like being told what to do every waking moment, so when my time was up, I didn't reenlist. My uncle was a cop, he talked me into applying." I looked over at him and grinned. "He's the mean SOB who had the shotgun."

Duke grunted. "I see. You definitely gotta watch those old guys. The young dicks are always underestimating them. Did you like it? The job, did you like it?"

I frowned, took a long slow drink, and worked on my cigar for a minute. The truth was, up until my wife's death, I was flying high. I felt like I was doing good work and honestly felt as though I was making a difference. But, after my wife died, it all went to shit. I answered him with a noncommittal shrug.

Duke grunted and drummed the bar counter with his fingers. "I had this stepdad," he said. "He was mean as shit, especially if he was drunk." It sounded familiar. "He liked to wail on my mother, me, and my little sister."

I looked over at him, surprised at our similarities.

He continued. "One night, he was beating on my mother a little more than usual and I decided I'd had enough. I stabbed him a few times with a paring knife. He lived, but I ended up in juvie." He laughed without humor.

"You've probably never been in juvie," he said, "but let me tell you, it's total bullshit. The black boys outnumbered the white boys and they hated us. We had to stick together just to survive. The leader of our group was the son of a biker. When I got out, I went to live with his family. I got involved with the lifestyle and have been a one-percenter ever since."

"Understandable, I suppose," I said. "My old man was a mean drunk too, we fought frequently."

"Did you ever win?" Duke asked.

I scoffed. "Win? Hell, I lost all of them, all but the last one. The last one was a doozy though. I walked out of the house and didn't go back. If not for my uncle, I'm sure I would have been arrested. Instead, I missed my high school graduation and enlisted in the Army." I thought of Lana. I'd stood her up for the prom and hadn't seen her since. I wondered what ever happened to her. The last I'd heard, she'd gotten married and moved to California.

"So, maybe we're not so different, you and me," Duke said. I thought about it.

"You may have a point," I conceded. Duke held up his beer. I held mine up and clicked his bottle. Kim seemed to think it was a signal and walked over with two fresh ones. I looked over at Anna and winked.

"So, Duke, what're you doing this afternoon?"

Chapter 12

We swapped the Cadi for my truck and trailer and headed to Anna's apartment. Duke and I had Anna's furniture loaded up in no time. The two roommates watched in silence, occasionally whispering to each other, but didn't bother helping. They were attractive, in a trashy sort of way. Both of them were blondes with large breast implants. The only real difference was one of them had her arms tatted up in full sleeves. It was nice ink work, and even though I didn't like tattoos, I had to admit it added to her trashy sensuousness.

"Typical women," Duke muttered. "Lazy as shit." I grunted in semi agreement. I wouldn't say all women were lazy, but these two made no offer to help.

Anna emerged from the manager's office and walked over."It's all taken care of," she said to her roommates. "I've paid my share of rent for the next two months and I'm off the lease."

"Where're you moving to?" the tattooed girl asked.

"None of your damned business," Duke growled at her before Anna had a chance to respond. Tattooed girl pursed her lips and stopped talking. Anna ignored her and hugged the other one, which made me suspect tattoo was the one who had slept with Anna's beau. It was a tearful goodbye, which seemed odd, but I never was an expert on females.

Traffic was heavy, so it took almost forty-five minutes to get back to my house. Anna held up better than I'd thought; she'd stopped crying but she was extremely quiet.

"We have two options," I said, trying to fill the silence. "We can store your furniture in the shop, or if you'd rather, we can move my furniture out of the bedroom and put yours in."

"Whatever," she said. I glanced over at Duke, who shrugged indifferently. The final decision was to keep my furniture in the house and store hers in the shop. After all, I reasoned, when the time came for her to move out, I'd have to move all of my furniture back in. It'd be easier this way. After getting everything sorted, we broke for lunch.

"So, what's happening with this crazy ex-boyfriend?" Duke asked. We were sitting at my kitchen table enjoying some spaghetti Anna had cooked while we had unloaded the trailer.

"The detectives arrested him on the vandalism charge and served the order of protection. That didn't seem to faze him because he threatened me within ten seconds. So, they charged him with violating it. I have court tomorrow," Anna said. "Are you coming with me?"

I looked up and realized she was talking to me. I shook my head. "I've got a lot of work to do. I've not even made any headway on Lester's case and now we have the Braxton case."

Actually, I wanted some time to myself and wondered what the heck I was thinking when I invited her to move in with me.

She looked at me pleadingly with those big blue eyes. "Oh, please come with me," she begged. "It's going to be nerve racking enough. I don't want to go through it by myself." She grabbed my hand and squeezed for emphasis.

I didn't want to. I didn't like going to court anymore. Whenever I went, I'd see people I once worked with. Most of them would pointedly ignore me. Others looked at me like I'd gotten away with murder. I was about to tell her to put on her big girl pants, but she was still looking at me with those big puppy dog eyes and I caved in.

"Yeah, okay," I found myself saying. Anna squealed in glee and gave me a tight hug. Duke grunted and continued eating his spaghetti.

I snapped my fingers suddenly. "I need to call Sherman." I wasn't sure I was ready for Duke to hear the details of the case, especially since I'd signed that contract with the NDA, so I went outside before calling him. The conversation lasted about ten minutes as I told him about the FBI's visit to Rhoda and some of the information Ronald had uncovered.

After dinner, Duke received a series of text messages, thanked us for dinner, and hurried off. Anna helped me clean up the kitchen.

"Thanks," I said and rewarded her with a cold beer while I poured myself three fingers of scotch.

"Is Duke married?" I asked.

"Divorced," Anna answered. "He's friends with benefits with one of the dancers and I think he still sees his ex on occasion."

"Oh, nice."

"Is there anything in particular you want to watch?" she asked as she turned the TV on.

"Nope," I answered and pointed at my desk, which I had positioned in the far corner. "I need to do a little work on the bankruptcy case."

Logging on to my laptop, I perused everything Ronald emailed me, copied it to a CD, and then used a software app to completely obliterate all of the data on my computer.

Anna had been sitting on the couch flipping through TV channels, but apparently became bored. She stood and walked over to my desk. "So, what kind of case is this?"

"It's a bankruptcy case involving a trucking company. Money and other assets are apparently being hidden. My job is to try to find it."

"But, if they're bankrupt, how do they have money?" she asked. I tried to explain the intricacies of Chapter Eleven.

"So, they're not broke?"

"Chapter Eleven is a section in the bankruptcy laws designed mostly for businesses that have run into debt issues, but are still generating revenue and are solvent enough to possibly pull themselves out of debt."

"Okay, I think," Anna said.

"Up until recently, they still had a thriving business. They'd simply overextended themselves and had amassed sizeable debts."

"How?" she asked.

"That's the big question. From what I've seen so far, it looks like money was being siphoned from the business."

Anna frowned, trying to understand.

I continued. "Anyway, they filed under Chapter Eleven in order to stall the creditors while they get their affairs in order and hash out a plan of reorganization. It was all going good at first, but the owners of Robard Trucking dropped the ball and now Sherman has taken control of all or their money."

"I think I see now," she said. "Your job is to find the money."

"Yep," I answered.

"And Rhoda's husband was murdered because of all of this?"

I looked at her and thought about my answer. "At first, I would have said no. But, after looking at Lester's trucking logs and the other stuff he had, I'm beginning to wonder."

"How so?" she asked.

I frowned. "I'm not sure I can answer that question right now." I pointed at the paperwork. "I need to read everything over and I've let too many other things distract me."

Anna sensed I was referring to her issues, which was true, but I didn't want to blame her.

"Oh," she replied. "Well, I guess I'll shut up now and let you get to work."

I'm sure this was the part where I was supposed to say something like I was more interested in talking to her rather than reading over pesky paperwork, but I wasn't going to let my other head interfere. At least, not this time. I mumbled my thanks for her understanding and she went back to channel surfing.

I worked long into the night perusing the printouts, highlighting certain sections, and cross-referencing them with google searches. When I found myself starting to nod off, I glanced at my watch. It was a little after midnight. I put a blanket over Anna, turned the lights off, and stumbled off to bed.

Chapter 13

Anna and I sat together on one of those uncomfortable wooden benches that all courtrooms seemed to have, waiting on the proceedings to get underway. Anna was wearing a nice dark blue pair of slacks with a tight-fitting white blouse and I was wearing one of my better suits, a custom-tailored gray one with small pinstripes and a red print tie with matching gray accents. I was not going to testify or anything, but I wore it anyway. Old habits die hard I guess.

I occasionally glanced over at the police officers, who had a section of pews reserved for them. I only recognized a few of them. The rest seemed to be too young to be wearing a badge. A few of them who seemed to have a lot of testosterone and very little common sense kept ogling the more attractive women present in the courtroom. I got a few sidelong looks as well, but I was fairly certain it had nothing to do with my sexy looks.

Then, I noticed one particularly cocky acting officer. He was wearing a sport jacket, tie and slacks. He was sitting with the other officers, talking and laughing with them. Occasionally, he'd shoot daggers in our direction.

"That's Doug," Anna whispered. So, that was the nefarious Doug Eastlin. He was a handsome man, perhaps in his late twenties, short brown hair. He saw me looking at him and responded with a challenging stare.

"He's a little on the cocky side," I remarked.

"Oh, yeah," she replied. "I thought it was an endearing quality at first, then I got smart."

After sitting for at least thirty minutes, the liaison for the District Attorney walked into the courtroom and approached us with a clipboard in her hand.

"Ms. Davis? Anna Davis?" she asked. Anna looked around and realized the lady was calling out her name. She raised her hand.

"It's Davies," Anna responded. "Anna Davies."

The liaison looked at the preprinted docket and then back at Anna with a slight frown, as if she was offended at being corrected. "Oh. Yes, well. The Assistant District Attorney handling this case is Mister Reichman. He directed me to advise you that at this time there is not enough proof to prosecute this case."

Anna looked over at me in confusion. "What does she mean?" she asked.

I looked pointedly at the liaison as I answered. "It means Diff had not bothered reading the affidavit. If he had, he would've noted the fact that there is a surveillance video recording of the entire incident, clearly showing the defendant committing the act, while on duty and in uniform. And, he threatened Anna with bodily harm while in the presence of two Metro detectives. Please ask ADA Reichman for confirmation, if you don't mind. I'd hate for him to be caught unawares, because this case is not going away. Perhaps the media would like to ask him to justify his unwillingness to prosecute a police officer caught breaking the law."

The liaison, a chubby redheaded woman in her thirties, appraised me coolly for a moment before walking off. I watched as she walked over to the desk where there were two prosecuting attorneys sitting, complaining to each other about their respective caseloads. She bent close to his left ear and began whispering.

"Diff? What's a Diff?" Anna asked.

"That's his name. Diff Reichman. Actually, it's Dilford, but he's very sensitive about it apparently and prefers to be called Diff."

I watched as the liaison spoke to him and then pointed us out. He pushed his glasses up on his nose, flipped through some pages, and, finding the correct case, began reading. A moment later his eyebrows arched up in surprise. Even though he appeared only to be in his early thirties, he was a severely overweight man with the beginnings of baldness. He had a hard time getting out of his chair, stood with no small amount of discomfort on his face, walked over and introduced himself.

"We have a small meeting room in back. Would you please join me there?" We followed him as he escorted us back. Once we were all seated, he began.

"First, please allow me to apologize. I had this case mixed up with another one. And, I want to assure you, Ms. Davies, the District Attorney's Office has every intention of pursuing this case." He was interrupted by a couple of OPA detectives entering the room. By the look on their faces, I'd say they recognized me. One of them pointed an angry finger.

"What in the hell is he doing in here?" he demanded. Diff looked at me, and then the two of the OPA detectives in befuddlement. I was about to make a smart-assed retort when Anna spoke up.

"He's with me, and I would appreciate it if you would be respectful." I held back a chuckle as I saw the detective's jaw tighten, but he said nothing. The younger detective nudged his partner and pointed toward two open chairs. They shuffled in and sat without any further commentary.

Diff spent the next ten minutes discussing the case, but most of the discussion was with the two detectives. I watched and listened in silence. The conversation was interrupted by a knocking on the door and then a man entered without waiting. Shutting the door behind him, he looked at all of us with a smug arrogance before focusing on Diff.

"Good morning, Diff," he greeted with mock pleasantness.

"Good morning, Fletcher," Diff responded. "Everyone, this is Fletcher Wheeling. He's representing Officer Eastlin."

Fletcher didn't bother shaking hands, although he ogled Anna a little longer than I cared for. He was a little man, maybe five-six, and the face of a weasel who overindulges in junk food. He currently was wearing a suit that I guessed was straight off the rack, and therefore didn't fit properly, and a stupid-looking burgundy bowtie with little flowers on it. Fletcher was well known among the courthouse crowd. He was around my age and thought a lot of himself. He had a reputation of hating cops, so I had no idea why he was representing one.

He made a show of tapping his wristwatch with a finger. "Diff, I've got a full slate up on six today, so I'll go ahead and tell the judge were good for dismissal."

Diff held up a hand. "Yeah, about that, Fletcher, it seems as though I misspoke earlier. The state is moving forward with prosecution."

Fletcher gave a pained expression. "Now, Diff, this is really stupid."

"How so, Fletcher?"

"Lawyerism 101, Diff, you need proof and you don't have any," he declared condescendingly. "No offense to this little girl and the two detectives, but it's their word against my client's. I'll make mincemeat of them on the stand." He haughtily eyed everyone for effect. He lingered on me a moment in halting recognition, but he couldn't make the connection. He looked back at Diff and waited for him to concede defeat.

Diff couldn't suppress a smug grin. "Fletcher, we have a surveillance video catching Officer Eastlin in the act, and, he threatened Ms. Davies with bodily harm in front of several witnesses, including these two detectives."

Fletcher was about to speak again, but Diff cut him off.

"Fletcher, you should probably bind it over," Diff said.

"Perhaps we need to speak privately," Fletcher said, as if he knew if he got Diff alone, he'd get his way.

Diff shook his head. "That won't be necessary."

Fletcher caressed his bowtie with his fingers, as if it had some kind of magical powers. "Well then, I'll file a continuance. Who knows what'll happen in the meantime?" He still had the arrogant attitude, but I sensed uncertainty now. To his credit, Diff showed some intestinal fortitude, but I suppose when you have a fifty-five inch waistline –

"You and the judge don't have a very good history, right?" Diff asked.

Fletcher frowned but didn't answer.

"Yes, I believe I'm going to object to your motion for continuance and ask for a prelim to be held first thing this morning. Oh, I'm going to ask for a revocation of you client's bond as well due to his recent threats of violence toward the victim, and perhaps even add a charge of intimidation of a witness. Ask your client if he wants to spend a few months in jail waiting for this to go to trial."

Fletcher Wheeling was no longer smiling. Instead, he scowled. "You're really going to play it this way, Diff?"

Diff nodded his head slowly.

"Okay, fine, I'll bound it over. I'll need a copy of that video," he said, spun on his heel and walked out of the room.

Diff beamed with satisfaction. "I've wanted to do that to him for a while now. I'm glad I had an audience." He leaned forward and used the armrests to push himself upright as he stood. "Okay, all of you can go. Ms. Davies, please make sure the liaison has your correct information so she can contact you when you'll be needed for court."

Anna and I were walking toward the elevators when I felt a hand grab my shoulder. I spun around and instinctively put a hand up, ready to ward off an attack. It was the two OPA detectives.

"It's time we had a little chat with you. You're coming with us," one of them said. He was about two inches shorter than me, in his late thirties and short brown hair with mousse rubbed through it. It made his hair look as if he had not used any shampoo in a while.

"I remember you. A couple years back you were drunk in a bar on Music Row and got your ass whipped. You tried to say a gang had attacked you, but I knew the bartender. He said you started a fight with a guy who was smaller than you and he cleaned your clock. You made a mistake then, and you're about to make another mistake now."

His face turned a deep crimson, but he recovered quickly. "You're coming with us," he repeated. "Whether you go willingly or in cuffs is up to you." He pulled back his jacket, showing the handcuffs hanging from his belt, which I guessed was supposed to intimidate me. I sneered at him.

"If I'm under arrest, you'd better do your duty and handcuff me," I replied rather loudly. There were people walking by and heads were turning. The two detectives noticed, but the loudmouth didn't seem concerned.

The other OPA detective, a clean-cut man in his early thirties was definitely concerned with the unwanted attention. He held a hand up in a peaceful gesture and spoke in a quieter tone. "Thomas, please excuse my partner. He's very much a type-A personality and is a little intense at times. We merely want to talk to you. It concerns some new developments in your wife's death and we'd like your input."

I glanced over at Anna and pointed at the two of them. "This is what you call the good cop, bad cop routine." I looked back at the two of them. "If you really have new information, send me an e-mail. Maybe I'll respond."

"Now, Thomas, you know that's not how we work," the second one said.

I gave him a look. "I have no intention of sitting in an interview room with you two assholes while you try to elicit a nonexistent confession from me. One day, one of you will come to the realization a certain assistant chief is using this personal tragedy of mine to launch a vendetta." I lowered my voice. "The man has a grudge against me and he's using you two as dupes."

The good cop maintained a poker face. The bad cop openly glared at me.

I straightened. "Gentlemen, unless I am under arrest, I'll excuse myself from this conversation and be on my way."

I waited a moment while they stared at me in silence. It confirmed to me they had no arrest warrant, so I held out my arm for Anna and the two of us walked out of the courthouse. The two detectives watched us leave without protest.

Sherman Goldman was seated at his desk, a handmade walnut monstrosity, and grinned when the two of us walked in.

"Sherman, I've never asked, but do you think your desk is big enough for you? Hell, I think you could land a small airplane on it."

Sherman chuckled pleasantly. "It's rather large, I agree, but it was a present from my wife. So, you know what that means."

"It means it's the most wonderful gift you've ever received," I said.

He pointed a finger at me like it was a gun. "Bingo. Now, who is your lovely assistant?" he asked as he stood and walked around the desk with an outstretched hand. I made the introductions.

"It is a pleasure to meet you, young lady," he said warmly. "If the two of you will excuse me for a moment, I'd like to freshen up and then we'll get started." Without waiting for an answer, he hurried off and disappeared behind a door in the back of his office. I suspected it was his private restroom.

"This office is huge," Anna whispered as she looked around.

I nodded in agreement. "Sherman has done well for himself. He's the son of a Jewish immigrant who had survived one of the Nazi death camps. He got an academic scholarship at Vanderbilt and the rest is history." There was a much more involved story regarding Sherman's life, but it would've taken several hours to do the man justice.

"Oh, wow," Anna replied. We made small talk until I heard the faint sound of a toilet flushing. A moment later, Sherman emerged, looking much more relaxed. If Anna wasn't present, I would've made a smart-assed remark about his bowels. Sherman motioned us to a conference table. His eyes went to my accordion file.

"You've made progress, I trust?"

I nodded. "I believe so, yes." This caused his expression to light up in anticipation. I started to say more, but we were interrupted by his phone ringing.

He spoke to the caller for a minute and hung up. "That was Miss Carson. She has advised me there are two FBI agents waiting in the reception area and they are desirous of speaking to me about Robard Trucking Company." Ah, so Simone was here. She didn't greet us when we arrived earlier and I was beginning to have withdrawal symptoms. "I'd say they're the two agents you spoke with yesterday," Sherman opined.

"Yeah, most likely. Let's see what they have to say," I suggested. Simone must have read our minds. The door opened about a tenth of a second after my mouth had closed and she escorted them in.

Upon seeing me, Special Agents Jeffreys and Ridgeway looked surprised, but withheld any commentary as I took the liberty of introducing everyone. Simone didn't acknowledge me as she left the office, which was a little painful. That is, until she walked back in a moment later with the receptionist, who was pushing a cart bearing a coffee carafe, cups, and doughnuts. Without asking, she poured my cup first.

"You are a wonderful woman, Miss Carson," I said with a smile. She was wearing a black dress today. It had little gold threads in it and the hem ended at her knees. I promise I didn't stare at her lean, shapely calves. She looked at me without comment and then looked over at Anna.

"Would you like some coffee?" she asked.

"Oh, no thank you," Anna replied. Simone repeated the question for the two agents, but they begged off as well. Once Simone completed the coffee courtesy, she took a seat beside Sherman.

"Well now, what can I do for the FBI?" Sherman asked.

"It has been brought to our attention you've been appointed the trustee for Robard Trucking Company."

"I have indeed," Sherman replied. "Three months ago, Robard petitioned for relief under Chapter Eleven provisions. They were obligated to perform certain actions within one hundred and twenty days. They failed to do so."

"They didn't file a plan for reorganization," Jeffreys said.

Sherman smiled. "No they didn't." He looked at the two agents. "So, I must ask, why is the FBI interested in a bankruptcy issue?"

Special Agent Ridgeway spoke up. "I cannot go into specific details, but the company is suspected of being involved in criminal activity. Our investigation is active, but confidential."

She then looked over at me and smiled pleasantly. "We know Mister Ironcutter is investigating the death of Lester Gwinnette, and while it is tragic, it is not pertinent to this investigation, and so we must request that he and his associate leave before we can discuss this further." She then looked pointedly at Simone. "And that would go for your assistant as well."

Sherman gazed at her steadily for a long moment before responding. "Your objection to their presence is duly noted, Agent Ridgeway. But, let me be perfectly clear. When you are in my domain, I'll be the one who decides who stays and who leaves. If you find that objectionable, I'm sure you can find your way out."

Ridgeway's cheeks reddened and I thought for a moment she was going to say something harsh to Sherman.

Agent Jeffreys spoke up. "We're merely being cautious," he said. "We want to discuss some sensitive information and would rather not do so in the presence of unauthorized personnel."

Sherman was nonplussed. "Miss Carson is my trusted personal assistant. Thomas and I have been friends for many years. His character is above reproach, and while I have just recently met Miss Davies, she is with Thomas and that's good enough for me.

"Now, the reason Thomas and Miss Davies are here is because I have hired him to assist with the Robard Trucking Company case. Which reminds me." He looked over at Simone. "Please prepare an NDA for Thomas's new assistant."

Simone stood, walked over to Sherman's computer and began typing on the keyboard. Within a minute, the printer was whirring. She retrieved the print out and handed it to Anna.

"We'll need you to print your full name here and sign at the bottom before we can discuss this case in your presence," she said perfunctorily.

Anna looked over at me questioningly. I gave her a nod and she signed it without comment.

Sherman waited until the ink was on the paper before speaking. "As I was saying, Thomas has been hired to assist in this case and we were about to discuss his preliminary findings when the two of you arrived. You're welcome to sit in on this meeting, or," he paused and looked at me in mock seriousness. "Thomas, we're going to be discussing some sensitive information. Do you think we can trust these two members of the FBI should sing non-disclosure agreements as well?"

Agent Ridgeway spoke up. "We will not be doing so," he said. "The FBI is well versed in discretion."

"Oh, well, then. If an FBI agent makes a proclamation, you can take it to the bank," I said with a tone of sarcasm. Simone arched an eyebrow at me. I don't think she cared much for my attempt at wry humor.

"Well, I suppose they should stay," I said. "After all, I have some things they'll want to hear."

"Very well then," Sherman said. "Now, if there are no other objections, let us please begin." He nodded at me. "Thomas, if you will?"

Simone took out a stenographer's pad while everyone else looked at me expectantly. I pulled a legal pad out of my folder, glanced at the notes, took a breath and began my presentation.

"For at least the past three years, Robard Trucking Company has been engaging in the illegal interstate transportation of heroin from Canada to various states, starting in Michigan and finishing in Tennessee. I believe I can also prove they have committed fraud under 18USC152. The current president and his wife have recently created approximately eighteen new bank accounts within sixty days of filing Chapter Eleven. They've also paid off debts to several shell companies within ninety days prior to the filing." I looked at Sherman, who nodded at me. His pleasant grin had returned.

I looked at the agents. "I believe the proper legal phrase is preferential transfer, which violates the tenets of Chapter Eleven reorganization."

Simone paused in her writing and arched her eyebrow again. I didn't know if that was a good sign, you know, like when Spock arched an eyebrow when someone said something profoundly interesting, or if she thought I was ridiculous, like Spock did when some lowly human said something ridiculous.

I then paused a moment and looked at Special Agent Ridgeway. She was wearing navy blue slacks similar to Anna's, a blouse I'd describe as butternut in color, which seemed to fit her nicely, and a jacket which matched her pants. Presumably, the jacket was to cover her duty weapon which I saw peeking out. She was wearing her blonde hair down today, casually resting across her shoulders and enhancing the shape of her face. She'd apparently recovered from Sherman's rebuke and was staring at me attentively. I saw Anna frowning out of the corner of my eye.

I refocused. "And, Lester Gwinnette was murdered when he discovered this operation and then attempted to blackmail someone within Robard Trucking Company."

Chapter 14

Everyone was quiet now, I had their undivided attention and they were staring at me quizzically, with the exception of Simone, she was dutifully taking notes. I sat there enjoying my coffee before continuing.

"I can walk everyone through it, if necessary," I said.

"Can you prove any of this?" Special Agent Ridgeway asked.

"May I call you by your first name?" I asked.

"Certainly," she said and smiled pleasantly. "Teresa," she added.

"Teresa, I believe I can." I stood and emptied the contents of my accordion file folder on the conference table and carefully arranged my printouts and notes.

"Alright, I'm going to start at the beginning, so if you already know this, please indulge me, I'll be quick.

"In 1990, four brothers started Robard Trucking Company." I pulled out a copy of the original Articles of Incorporation. "From all appearances, the brothers ran an honest business and were very prosperous. In 2010, the eldest brother died of a heart attack. The surviving brothers elected to sell the business. A gentleman by the name of William Spieth purchased the business with money he received from an inheritance and a settlement from a lawsuit."

"What kind of lawsuit?" Teresa asked.

"He purchased a new car from a local car dealership and paid for an extended warranty," I said. "The owner of the dealership kept the money and didn't bother turning the paperwork in to corporate. Low and behold, Mister Spieth's new car developed an issue after the normal warranty had expired. It was then he found out he didn't have an extended warranty. Apparently, he went to the dealership one day and caused a big scene. The owner and a couple of his sales reps didn't care for his attitude and gave him a pretty good beating. He spent a few days in the hospital. Long story short, he received a six-digit settlement."

"Why a trucking company?" she asked.

"He used to work at a trucking brokerage firm. I guess he decided to strike out on his own," I replied. She nodded in understanding. "Mister Spieth installed his wife as vice president and their total employee count, not counting the truck drivers, was four."

"So, it was a small-time operation," Agent Jeffreys remarked, and glanced at Teresa. She briefly returned the eye contact. They knew more about this operation than they were letting on.

"Yes, up until a couple of years ago, and then it seemed as though business started booming for them." I briefly looked at my notes.

"Let's see, about October of 2013 is the approximate time when they started the Canada route. By the way, this was a trip lease as opposed to a contract lease. As far as I am able to determine, this is the first time Robard has done business through a trip lease. This is also a route the previous owners never contracted." Before I could continue, Teresa interrupted.

"Excuse me," she said. "But what is the difference between a trip lease and a contract lease?"

"A trip lease is used for a specific, one time trip or load, and there is no brokerage firm lining up the trips," I replied. "This was very much out of the ordinary for Robard, they routinely used brokers, and although there were multiple hauls over the course of the year, they were all being done with a trip lease." She nodded in seeming understanding and scribbled hurriedly. I waited for her to catch up before speaking.

"Lester Gwinnette was one of the drivers who regularly drove on the Canada haul and apparently became curious about why double-bottom trailers were only used on this particular haul. He was also curious about the fact that the trailers had the same pallets of boxes on the ride up as they did on the ride back down. On one haul, curiosity got the best of him. He went somewhere, probably a loading dock where he knew the guy working the midnight shift, and spent an hour or so unloading the pallets. You see, the pallets of boxes were meant to keep prying eyes from looking into the bottom compartments, but Lester had been a trucker for years, he knew all of the tricks. He found several kilos of heroin in the bottom compartment under the pallets." I reached over to the stack of reports and fished out some scanned copies of photographs.

"These are copies of photographs Lester took of the drugs." They all moved closer and looked.

"Not the greatest quality," Jeffreys remarked.

"Yeah, they were taken with a digital camera that uses the JPEG format," I said.

Jeffreys looked at me in puzzlement. "Is that important?"

"JPEG is a common format. For taking normal pictures, it works fine. But, it's known as a lossy image format. When you try to enlarge the photo, it becomes blurry. What format do you use when you photograph evidence?"

"I'm not sure," he reluctantly answered.

"Well, I'd recommend using a tagged image file format. It uses more memory, but it keeps more data." The agent looked at me like he was trying to tell me he didn't need a lesson on digital imaging. I moved on.

"So, the photos show bricks of heroin sitting in the compartments." I pointed. "And Lester used the front page of a newspaper as a way of date-stamping the photos."

"Clever," Jeffreys remarked.

Yeah, Lester was clever, but not clever enough to keep himself from getting killed. I kept that opinion to myself and continued.

"He also kept copies of the bills of laden. If you'll note, this company is called Tag First Distribution. The address under the company logo is a private post office box in Detroit. I've not found much else for this company." That's because the job I was hired for is to find the money. I laid out some more paperwork and walked them through the trip lease hauls, all of which presumably were hauling heroin.

"It's a pretty clever operation if you map it out. Think of the thought, organization, and attention to detail needed to create all of this." I leaned back. "Pretty damned impressive, if you ask me."

"How did you get all of this?" Teresa asked as she waved a hand over the documents. I smiled and shrugged in feigned ignorance. She glanced at her partner, who kept a poker face.

"Okay, we'll come back to that later," she said. "What facts lead you to conclude Lester's death was a murder and not a suicide?"

Before I could speak, Simone stood up and began refilling my coffee cup. I smiled gratefully and this time she actually smiled back.

"In this case, the physical evidence is ample proof of a murder, and not a suicide. The Sheriff Department's investigating detective came to the scene with a mindset of suicide and he chose not to see any facts or evidence which proved otherwise. I have a meeting scheduled with the sheriff later today, perhaps you two would like to come."

Special Agent Jeffreys suddenly leaned forward and fixed me with a stare. "Are you trying to pad your wallet from the widow's life insurance policy? You know, if it's a murder and not a suicide, the payout is substantially higher, right?"

I sipped my coffee and returned the stare. "When the two of you were serving your search warrant, I'm sure you noticed the old car in the shed behind her house. The car is my fee, nothing more." I looked as if a thought had suddenly popped into my head. "Oh, by the way, what prompted you two agents to search the home of a truck driver? I mean, he's a low-level employee of the trucking company. What evidence could he possibly have?" I asked rhetorically. "Perhaps you have a CI who has told you about the blackmail attempt? Perhaps you were looking for whatever Lester was trying to blackmail them with?"

Teresa looked at her partner in surprise. Special Agent Jeffreys ignored my question.

"You're not going to charge her a fee, just an old junk car?" he asked with feigned shock. I nodded. Obviously, he knew nothing about cars, and he was not going to answer my question. I let it go, for now.

"Thomas, how are you going to prove it's a murder?" Sherman asked.

"Proving Lester was murdered will not be difficult. Identifying the murderer will be somewhat of a challenge. I had a brief conversation with the investigating detective two days ago.

Unfortunately, I believe he didn't have much of an opinion of me and had a very condescending attitude."

"So, what are you going to do?" Sherman asked.

"Meet with the sheriff and try to convince him his detective screwed up. If the esteemed members of the FBI would be willing to accompany us to this meeting, perhaps they would be more receptive." I looked pointedly at the two agents. "There might even be some information which will aid in your investigation." I sincerely doubted my last statement, but I was trying to lure them in.

Ridgeway and Jeffreys looked at each other. Teresa looked at Sherman and gave him the same radiant smile she had given me a few minutes ago. "Sherman, is there somewhere my partner and I can have a private discussion?"

At Sherman's direction, Simone escorted the two agents to another room. I hurriedly pulled some printouts out of my file and slid them over to Sherman.

"If someone were to take a look at those, they may find the necessary information for an asset search of certain banks," I said quietly. Sherman did not respond verbally. He took the printouts, walked over to his titanic-sized desk, and stuck them in a drawer. "And then, someone should probably shred those papers," I finished. I didn't need to say it, Sherman knew what to do. Anna looked at me questioningly, but I stopped her from asking questions with an admonishing look.

It took about five minutes before the two agents came back in the room. They sat, and Teresa gave a friendly smile. I guess the earlier rebuke by Sherman was forgiven.

"I first want to say that we really appreciate your cooperation," Teresa said. "And we'd like to work together on this case."

I smiled appreciatively as Sherman thanked them. Inwardly, I knew how the Fibbies operated. They were only interested in their own case. If helping us helped them, they were all in, but if they were open and honest, they'd come right out and tell us they really didn't give a damn about our respective cases, only theirs.

I finished my coffee and stood. "This is great. Shall we go visit the sheriff of Rutherford County?"

Chapter 15

Anna had been hinting how much she'd like to drive my car, so I let her while I checked my phone. One message was from Mrs. Braxton, one was from Duke, and one was from Ronald. The rest were unimportant.

"You really blew them away back there. You weren't bullshitting about all of it, were you?" Anna asked.

"I hope not," I said with a chuckle.

"Well, you made quite an impression."

"Thank you."

"What was on those printouts that you told Sherman to shred after he looked at them?" she asked.

I briefly glanced over at her. "Just some data files," I answered.

"That's pretty vague."

"Yep."

"Data files you don't want me to know about, I'm assuming," she said.

"Yep."

"Why?" she asked.

I glanced over at her again. "I'm thinking when you were a little girl, you constantly peppered adults with questions, and when they answered, it was never good enough, and you always had to ask why."

"Why would you think that?" she asked.

"Yep, I thought so," I said.

Anna turned toward me and wrinkled her nose. It was silent for a few minutes, but I guess she couldn't stand me having the last word.

"You seem to like that FBI agent," she said.

"Who, Mark?"

"You know who I'm talking about."

"Ah, you mean Teresa. Yes, she seems very nice. Special Agent Jeffreys, Mark, he's not too keen on either one of us."

"Why not?" Anna asked. I shrugged.

"Law enforcement people don't like civilians interjecting themselves into an investigation. They consider it nothing more than unwanted interference."

"Blondie doesn't seem to mind you being around," Anna said rather snidely. I chuckled. She continued. "She must be in her thirties." She made it sound like someone in their thirties was really old.

"Yeah, I'd say you're about right," I said.

"She's a bitch. She uses her looks to get what she wants."

"Isn't that what strippers do as well?" I asked innocently. Anna glared at me.

We rode in silence for a few miles before she spoke again. "Sherman's assistant seems nice."

"Yes she does."

"You sure looked at her a lot," she said with that same snide tone. "You looked at both of them a lot. In fact, I'd go as far as to say you were ogling them like a horny teenager." I didn't respond, instead I looked in the side view mirror and confirmed the agents were following us along the interstate.

"Don't worry, blondie's still behind us," she said.

"Ah, good. I was afraid you'd lost them," I responded sarcastically.

"Don't be making fun of me just because I drive the speed limit. I'm a very safe driver." She looked pointedly at me, as if daring me to say something. I responded with a smile.

"So, what happens now?" she asked.

"If the sheriff believes me, he'll reopen the case."

"What if he doesn't?"

"I guess I'll be investigating it on my own, although I'd rather not."

"Why not?" she asked.

I sighed in exasperation. "Oh my Lord you ask a lot of questions."

Anna pursed her lips, but didn't respond. After a minute or two of her giving me the silent treatment, I capitulated.

"A murder investigation is very time consuming and Rhoda doesn't have the money to pay me. So, no, I'd rather not get involved with the case any further than I have already."

"But, wouldn't you want to see justice done?"

"Justice doesn't pay the bills," I retorted.

There was another long span of silence before Anna spoke again. "Can we talk about us?" she asked.

I looked over at her. "Certainly, what's on your mind?"

"Am I temporary, Thomas? Do I need to be looking for a job and a place to live?" She glanced over at me, and I detected the anxiousness I saw in court earlier. Yeah, she was right. I'd been avoiding this issue as well.

"I wouldn't call you temporary," I said. "I'd like to think the two of us are friends."

"Of course we are, but are you going to kick me out at the end of the month? And you never told me what my rent's going to be."

"The Braxton and Robard Trucking cases will pay the bills this month, so we're good there."

"You never said anything about a salary either," she said tentatively.

"No, I didn't. I believe the best way to go about this is to pay you a percentage of the cases you're involved with, but it won't be much."

"Oh," she said simply.

"I won't charge you rent, but if you need to take a side job, I'd certainly understand." I paused a moment. "I'd rather you not get back into stripping though."

"Don't worry, I'm done with it."

"Good, you're too good for that kind or work."

She snickered. "It's funny, I like to say I went through three phases. First, it was a little embarrassing, then it was exciting."

"Exciting?" I asked.

"Yeah, I have to admit, it was exciting having all of those men ogling and lusting for me."

"Oh."

"Even women." I looked curiously at her and she explained. "Women come in all the time and try to hit on the dancers."

"Wow, I didn't know that."

"Yeah. So, like I said, it was exciting at first, and then it became boring, even irritating at times. So, yeah, I'm done with it."

"Okay, good." I paused for another second. "There's something else I've been thinking about. I believe I can fix the door on your car, so you won't need to file an insurance claim."

Anna looked sharply at me with her mouth open and then broke into a big, happy grin. "Really? Awesome! When can you do it?"

"We've a lot of work to do. After these cases, I'll get on it first thing. It might be a couple of weeks though." Anna's smile was replaced with a frown but she said nothing. I sighed. "I'll see what I can do, okay? Besides, we need to get started on your sister's case too," I said. Anna looked at me gratefully.

The new sheriff, Dustin Hatcliff, looked surprisingly young. It was hard to believe he was over thirty. He had a boyish face and a short haircut slicked up in little spikes with mousse. All the young men seemed to enjoy greasing their hair up these days. Back when I was a kid, only the rednecks did it and everyone called them greasers. It has always been my opinion a real man does not use mousse as a hair product, or for anything else.

He met us in the lobby and introduced himself with a boyish grin and an exaggerated southern twang. Unlike Detective Thompson, he eagerly escorted us past the security doors and to his office.

The inner sanctum of the sheriff was not quite what I expected. He had an assortment of toy police cars cluttering his desk and the bookshelves where important-looking sheriff books should have been instead held even more model cars. There were also a couple of model helicopters hanging from the ceiling with fishing line. It reminded me of a prepubescent boy's room. There were plenty of chairs and even a couch. I suspected it was used for afternoon naps.

"Everyone grab a seat," he invited. "Anyone want a cold drink?" he asked and then went on without waiting for an answer. "I'll have a trustee bring us a pitcher of sweet tea." He called someone and placed the order. There was a short conversation before he hung up.

"They just cooked up a bunch of chocolate chip cookies!" he said excitedly. "So, we got tea and cookies on the way. Now, what can I do for all of y'all?" he asked. There was a moment of silence as the sheriff looked around to see who was going to speak first.

I took the initiative. "Sheriff, Agents Jeffreys and Ridgeway are conducting an investigation of a business named Robard Trucking Company. I have been hired to investigate the death of Lester Gwinnette, an employee of the same trucking company. He lived in your jurisdiction at the time of his death."

"Okay," the sheriff said with a blank expression. I glanced at the two agents. They looked back at me questioningly, as if I knew why he was acting like he was lost at sea.

"Detective George Thompson..."

"He works here," the sheriff interrupted.

"Why yes, yes he does. And Sheriff, it's the damndest thing, he's the detective who investigated Lester Gwinnette's death."

"He did?" Sheriff Hatcliff asked.

"He did indeed," I answered. I took the case file off of my lap and put it on the sheriff's desk. "Here is the case file. Have you had the chance to look it over?"

He shook his head slowly. "Is everything alright? Did Georgie do something wrong?"

"Sheriff, is Georgie working? Would it be possible for him to join us? Perhaps he can add some insight to the case," I asked hopefully.

He snapped his fingers. "That's a good idea!" he exclaimed while reaching for the phone. I looked over at my three companions while he made another phone call. From the expressions on their faces, I think we were all wondering about the level of mental intellect of the incumbent Sheriff.

A minute later, Detective Thompson walked in, along with a trustee with a tray of cookies, plastic cups, and a pitcher. George was wearing the same coat and tie he had on the first time I met with him and I detected a faint mark on the tie at the same location of the food stain. He recognized me with a frown, and when he spotted the accordion file, his face turned to a harsh grimace.

The sheriff welcomed his detective. "Hi, Georgie," and then helped himself to a cookie while the trustee filled the paper cups.

"Hello, Sheriff," the detective answered. "What's this all about?" He stood there not knowing if he should sit down or not.

Sheriff Hatcliff pointed. "They're FBI agents and this is Thomas and Anna. Do you know anything about a dead guy named Lester?"

George stood stiffly. "Lester Gwinnette killed himself. I investigated the case." He suddenly noticed the case file sitting on the sheriff's desk and pointed. "Sheriff, that's the case file. It went missing a couple days ago. Where'd you find it?" The sheriff quickly pointed at me.

George scowled. "How'd you get ahold of it?" he demanded.

"I signed it out, like you told me to," I replied with a pleasant, taunting smile. He started to voice his objections, but I interrupted before he had a chance.

"Don't worry, nothing is missing from it and I'm bringing it back all in good order."

"There better not be," he growled as he ruffled through it. "What's going on here, Sheriff?" he asked again.

"I requested a meeting and the sheriff was kind enough to oblige us," I said. He continued giving me the stink eye.

"About what?" he asked.

"We'd like to go over Lester Gwinnette's death. If you have the time, I'd like to go over some of my findings."

"Sure," Sheriff Hatcliff said.

"This ought to be good," Agent Jeffreys mumbled. Agent Ridgeway tried to hold back a grin, but didn't do a very good job at it. Georgie slowly sat down. I reached for the file and pulled out the photographs taken at the crime scene and at the morgue.

"Oh, cool!" the sheriff said and reached for a couple of them.

"The pictures you're looking at, Sheriff, are of the crime scene. As you can see, Lester is lying on his kitchen floor. There is a handgun in his right hand, and what appears to be a gunshot wound behind his right ear," I explained. He looked at the pictures attentively.

"Would you agree with my description, Detective Thompson?" I asked.

He looked at me and then at the sheriff. “That’s right. The victim was found on the floor, exactly the way we photographed him.”

I glanced at him before continuing. “By the way, Sheriff, your crime scene photographer is very talented and took some very detailed close-ups. Look here at the close-up of the wound. The correct phrase for this type of gunshot is a penetrating wound, right, Detective?” I asked. Georgie said nothing, but I noticed a slight tic starting in his left eyelid.

“As you know, Sheriff, a penetrating gunshot wound does not go all the way through the body, as opposed to a perforating wound, which does. So, in this case, we have a projectile still in the victim’s body.”

“Projectile?” the sheriff asked.

“Yes. Most people call them slugs, but the correct term is projectile. A slug is what you find in a garden.” Agent Ridgeway chuckled, which caused the other men to laugh as well. Anna looked at me as if to say, see what I mean?

I continued. “Alright, when a detective investigates gunshot wounds, he or she can look at the wound and make some initial determinations.”

“Really?” he asked. “Like what?”

“The general angle of the gunshot wound and the approximate distance the firearm was from the body when it was fired,” I said.

“You can figure that out from these pictures?” He was full of questions, which was good, but it confirmed to me he’d never conducted a criminal investigation, which begged the question, how was he elected sheriff over a man who had almost forty years of experience in law enforcement? I will always wonder why people vote the way they do.

“Yes you can, Sheriff,” I answered as I reached for a couple of the photos. “What you have here are photographs taken at the autopsy. As you can see, the Medical Examiner shaved Lester’s head around the area of the gunshot wound and then they took a whole mess of pictures.”

“They sure did,” he said. I arranged some of the photos on his desk. “Check these out.”

"What am I looking for?" he asked. It was a question I hoped he would ask.

"In these particular photos, we're looking for evidence which shows the distance of the firearm at the time of discharge, right, Detective?" I looked over at Georgie again. He was as lost as his boss, and the nervous tic was becoming more pronounced.

"How?" Sheriff Hatcliff asked.

"Sheriff, the distance of the muzzle to the target can be grouped into four general categories. They are: contact, near contact, intermediate, and distant. You can also look at the wound and break it down to the relative angle of the muzzle to the target. Take a look at these photographs, Detective. Can you tell the sheriff the distance of the firearm's muzzle from Lester's head at the time it was fired?"

He stared at me balefully before snatching the photograph out of my hand and glancing at it. After a second or two, he scoffed dismissively. "The photos don't show anything really. Lester held the gun to his head and pulled the trigger. That extra hole in his head didn't get there by itself. If you had ever done any real criminal investigations, you'd know it," he retorted with a roll of his eyes and tossed the photograph onto the desk.

I ignored his antics and turned back to the sheriff. "Sheriff, a contact wound, or as Detective Thompson says, Lester holding the gun up to his head and pulling the trigger, will cause the skin to be seared and soot to be embedded into the seared skin. The embedded soot cannot be wiped off or washed away. If you will look closely at the gunshot wound, there is no embedded soot around the wound." They all looked at me in puzzlement, looked at the photograph, and then back at me.

"With this information, a detective can determine this is not a contact wound. Lester did not hold the gun to his head." They all looked closer at the photographs now.

"There's soot there. Look at his hair," Georgie said with growing hostility.

"Yes, you're correct, Detective. There is some soot in the victim's hair. It is on the bottom of the wound and extends forward at a slight angle. It is clearly shown in the photograph taken at the scene. But, as you can see, there is nothing embedded in the victim's scalp. Now, look at the photographs of the revolver. It's a thirty-eight caliber and has a four-inch barrel. Look back at the photo of the shaved scalp. There are no reddish brown spots which is called tattooing, only a small amount of soot deposit which is only on the surface of the skin. Based on this evidence, one can conclude the firearm was held somewhere around three to ten inches away from Lester's head when it was fired."

While they sat there, staring at the photo and attempting to digest what I'd told them, I shuffled through some of the photographs. "Now, have a look at this photo," I directed. The young sheriff took if from my hand and examined it closely.

"The dead guy has a steel rod sticking out of his head," he said and chuckled at his joke. Nobody else laughed.

"Yes, he does. The Medical Examiner did that to give a visual of the projectile's trajectory when it entered poor Lester's head. What do you think of it?"

He looked at the photos and studied them hard. He even held them closely in front of his face and turned them upside down. Finally, enlightenment dawned on his face.

"The bullet went kind of downward, right?" he asked.

I nodded. "Indeed it did, Sheriff. The handgun in question was held away from Lester's head and fired in a slightly downward trajectory."

Detective Thompson scoffed again. "All of that don't prove a murder," he declared stubbornly.

Instead of replying with something profound and witty, like calling him a dumbass, I continued with the other evidence. "I'm sure all of you have seen the photograph of Lester holding the firearm in his right hand. Is this exactly how he was found, Detective?"

Georgie glared at me with sudden suspicion before answering. "Yes," he said quietly, defensively.

I searched through the file and found two handwritten statements. "Yes, the medical personnel wrote the same thing. The handgun was loosely gripped in Lester's right hand. Well then, we have somewhat of a mystery here. Rhoda Gwinnette, that's Lester's wife, has advised Lester is left handed, and he had an old injury to his right index finger which never healed properly.

Basically, he was incapable of squeezing the trigger of a handgun with his right index finger."

I went through the file and found one last report. I held it out to Detective Georgie. "Here is the TBI's gunshot residue test report. I'll summarize, the test result is negative for gunshot residue." I slid another report forward to the sheriff. "This is one of Detective Thompson's reports. It says the test was positive for gunshot residue."

I sat back in my chair and let the sheriff and his incompetent lackey absorb the information. When they looked at me again, I smiled pleasantly.

"Sheriff, the physical evidence you have in front of you should be ample proof that Lester Gwinnette did not kill himself. You have yourself a murder on your hands."

Chapter 16

After my presentation and proclamation of murder, Sheriff Hatcliff said he had a lot of thinking to do and summarily dismissed us. The four of us walked out and met in the parking lot.

Special Agent Jeffreys spoke first. "I must admit, watching you in action today has been quite amusing." He smiled for the first time since I had met him with bleached white teeth, just like Teresa's. Ken and Barbie personified.

I shrugged. "You should see my Elmer Fudd impersonation." They laughed appreciatively.

"I absolutely agree," Teresa said with her own neon smile. "It has been a pleasure watching you operate, Thomas Ironcutter, and I suspect we've only seen the tip of the iceberg." She glanced at her cell phone and showed it to her partner. "We really must be heading back to the office. It looks like Mark and I have several subpoenas to write up."

We all shook hands. They made false promises to share information learned from the subpoenas and I told them I would anxiously await their phone call. They left a moment later. As we walked toward my car, I heard a gruff voice call out.

"Hey you, I want to speak to you!" I looked around and spotted the source. It was Detective Thompson, otherwise known as Georgie. His face was contorted in undisguised anger as he walked across the parking lot like a person with chafed thighs and a bad case of hemorrhoids. I also noticed a few people looking at us out of office windows. I casually reached for my phone and tapped the screen a few times, as if I were composing a text message.

He stopped when he got within mere inches of me. "What the hell do you think you were trying to pull back there, asshole?" he demanded.

"Why Georgie, wasn't it obvious? I proved you conducted a half-assed investigation and incorrectly labeled a murder as a suicide. How can I make it any clearer to you?"

He scowled and pointed a stubby finger at me. It was a hair's breadth from my nose. If I didn't have so many witnesses, I'm not sure I would have stood there doing nothing. But, at the moment, that's about all I did.

"I know your type," he declared. "You've read a few books, watched cop shows on TV, and now you think you know how to be a detective." Anna was not appreciative of Georgie's insults and came to my defense.

"He is a detective, you dumbass. He was solving murders when he worked with Metro while you were, I don't know, writing parking tickets and eating doughnuts."

The detective glared and started to point one of his stubby fingers at her. I moved sideways, putting myself in between the two of them.

"Georgie, you can insult me all you want. But think carefully before you say one derogatory word to her," I warned and motioned at my iPhone. "I'm recording our entire conversation." He looked at my phone, glared even harder at me, started to say something, but stopped himself.

"When you've calmed your ego and get over this denial stage, give me a call and we can discuss the case further. Don't take too long though," I said.

He breathed deeply before speaking. "What's that supposed to mean? Is that a threat?" he asked in a low, hostile tone.

"In case you missed it, those FBI agents are taking an interest in this case. If they take over the investigation, I'll make sure the media knows about your screw up. It could prove very embarrassing for both you and your sheriff." Okay, they weren't interested in Lester's death at all, but he didn't know that. He continued glaring and puffing like he was a Brahma bull about to charge, but instead, he then turned around and waddled back inside.

I waited until we were back in the car before I retrieved my flask. The scotch made a nice soothing burn as it went down. Anna looked over at me as she drove. "You haven't had a drink all day," she said. I nodded without replying. "Where to now?" she asked.

"Back to Nashville, Crieve Hall to be exact. I need to go to the grocery store for Ronald."

"I get to meet the mysterious Ronald? Why are we grocery shopping for him, can't he do it on his own?"

"Yes and no. He has a thing about places with a lot of people. So, we'll get him a few cases of soup and go pay him a visit. Which reminds me," I said and sent Ronald a text message: *We're going to the store & will be there soon. Get cleaned up, Anna will be with me.* I hit the send button and then slapped my thigh at the realization I'd forgotten to call Duke.

"Shit," I muttered, replayed his message, memorized his phone number and dialed.

"You sure don't believe in calling anyone back promptly," he grumbled.

"Yeah, I got tied up." I didn't bother to explain my senior moment.

"Are you going to be at Mick's later? I got a favor to ask you." I looked over at Anna. Duke spoke so loudly she could hear our conversation. She shrugged a shoulder and nodded.

"Yeah, okay. We'll be there in a couple of hours." Duke grunted and disconnected.

I hung up. "Remind me to call Mrs. Braxton in the morning. We really need to get started on her case."

Ronald was standing in the doorway as we parked. He was freshly showered, indicated by his wet hair, and it looked like he'd even put on clean clothes. He helped me unload his groceries as Anna watched.

I whispered to him as we walked in. "Don't be shy, introduce yourself."

Anna must have heard me. She smiled and introduced herself instead. "Hi, Ronald, I'm Anna. Thomas speaks very highly of you."

He had a great amount of difficulty making eye contact with her and mumbled something unintelligible as the three of us walked inside. He was nervous and uncomfortable having a stranger in his home, especially a sexy girl his own age. As much as I was tempted, I didn't tease him.

"Alright bud, I got you enough groceries for a couple of weeks. Is there anything else you need?" He glanced at Anna briefly and then focused his attention back on me. He shook his head.

"Okay, we've got to get moving. Oh, it looks like the Robard case is getting a bit more involved."

His eyes lit up. "Oh, yeah?" He loved snooping into people's personal lives via the Internet. He merely needed someone like me to point him in a specific direction.

"See if you can find a complete list of employees, where they live, etcetera, etcetera. Give me a shout tomorrow afternoon," I said as we started to walk out.

Anna walked over and gave him a hug. "Bye, Ronald," she said cheerfully. I thought Ronald was going to piss himself. She was giggling as we got into the car.

"You embarrassed him," I said. "You did it on purpose."

She giggled some more. "He's so bashful! I bet he's still a virgin." I chuckled. She was probably right on the money.

"How did you two meet?" she asked.

"It's not a pleasant story, I'm afraid."

"What happened?"

"Ronald was an only child, and as you can see, he's very introverted."

"You got that right."

"Yeah, he has Asperger's syndrome, or whatever they call it nowadays, but he's really quite intelligent. He was home schooled and so never developed any real social skills. He lived with his parents and his computers. One evening, his parents went to visit some friends in Lebanon. On their way home, a drunk driver was driving the wrong way on Interstate 40 and hit them head on."

"Oh, how awful," Anna exclaimed.

"Yeah, I was tasked with delivering the death message. He ran and locked himself in a basement closet. I sat there for a couple of hours talking to him through the door before he finally came out. We've been friends ever since."

"So, you've been like a father figure to him," Anna opined.

"More like a big brother. I'm not that durned old," I replied with a huff. Anna giggled.

Duke was sitting at the bar in the same seat as last time. There was plenty of room on either side. At 6'4" and tipping the scale at 300 pounds, nobody seemed eager to crowd him. I grabbed a couple of stools and drug them over beside him. Anna sat beside me.

He gestured with a freshly lit cigar. "Mick here was just telling me you're Italian."

"Did he also tell you about him being cursed with an unusually small penis as well?"

Duke looked over at Mick and let out an uproarious laugh. Mick waved a hand at me dismissively and walked away.

"I got a favor to ask and I want you to hear me out before you say anything."

"Alright," I said cautiously.

"I want you to check a guy out. See if he's legit." I looked at him sidelong. Duke held up a hand and shook his head. "I know he's not a cop, so don't go worrying about that." He slid over a sheet of yellow legal paper. "Here's his information." I continued looking at him for a long minute.

"He proposed to my daughter last night," he said, finally explaining what this was all about. "I'm having a hard time getting my brain around this. I don't know if he's good enough for my little girl."

"How old is she?" I asked.

"She's nineteen," he answered. "He's twenty-one, and he's not a biker." Duke finished his beer and waved the empty bottle at Mick. "He's going to school. He wants to be a real estate broker, like his dad."

"You sound like you know everything about him already," I opined. Duke shrugged as Mick brought him another beer.

I thought about it a moment and then made a decision. "Alright, it doesn't sound like I need to run any criminal background check. I'll do a credit check, see if he's got any court judgments against him or if he's paying any child support, things like that. Good enough?"

"Yeah, I suppose," Duke said.

"I've met him," Anna said. "He's a really sweet guy." Duke frowned and grunted.

"Have you ever considered that maybe it's your trepidation about letting your daughter go and not so much the young man's reputation?" I asked.

Duke eyed me. "If he's not good enough for my little girl, he isn't going to marry her. I can assure you of that." Mick had wandered back up to our end of the bar and was now listening to the conversation. He nodded in understanding, but I frowned.

"What is it, Dago?" Mick asked. "What're you thinking?" The two men looked at me expectantly.

"Oh, I was remembering back when I was a kid and went to Bible study every Wednesday night. There are one or two pieces of scripture that would probably apply to this situation." I realized I didn't have a cigar, got up and went to the humidor. Mick had a sizable selection and I loved trying new brands. I had my favorites but decided to try something different. Choosing a Rocky Patel Century, I walked back to the bar as Mick uncapped a fresh beer for me.

"Well, don't stop in the middle of the story, you dumb Dago," Mick said in exasperation. "Tell us what you're talking about."

"Alright." I sat down. "In the book of Matthew, he tells his version of the Sermon on the Mount. Part of the scripture tells of the baptism of Jesus," I said. The three of them continued looking at me expectantly.

"You see, some religions teach baptism is a sacrament, a symbolic ritual of cleansing your body and soul of sins. But more importantly, being baptized was a manner in which a person would undergo a near death experience. The logic behind it is, a near death experience enables a person to have a fuller appreciation of life and therefore live a more righteous life. Now, during the time of Jesus, there was this man we all know as John the Baptist. He had a little place set up at an oasis out in the desert. He was popular in the act of baptism because he was a good showman and he was very good at having his assistants hold a person down long enough where they thought they were really going to die before pulling their head out of the water. Not very many people drowned when John was doing the dunking."

I took a swallow of cold beer. "Alright, so I've laid the groundwork, now here's the story. One day, John is out there in his little loincloth doing his thing, when along comes Jesus. They say hello, shoot the breeze for a little while, and then Jesus says it's time for him to get baptized and he wants John to do it. John suddenly becomes very anxious. He doesn't want to do it because he doesn't believe he's worthy enough to baptize Jesus. Jesus calms John and explains. He tells John all he has to do is suffer through it, and the act will make him worthy."

I looked over at Duke. "You see, Duke, in your eyes, this young man may not be worthy enough to marry your daughter, but isn't it possible the act itself will make him worthy?"

Mick chortled. "Listen to him, Duke. Even though he's a dumb dago, he knows his Bible." Duke had been staring at me in silence. He grunted once, or maybe it was gas, and drank the rest of his beer in silence.

I looked over at Mick. "Do you know anyone who has a tow truck I might be able to borrow? I need a rollback with a winch."

Mick frowned and scratched his chin. "I don't think so, Thomas. What do you need a tow truck for?" He asked.

"I have an old car I need to tow back to the house. The tires are flat, the brakes are seized up, and there's no way I can get it on my car hauler." I shrugged. "Oh well, I guess I'll pay a towing service to haul it, I was hoping I could avoid doing that. It'll cost a pretty penny."

Duke finished his beer and paid his tab. He mumbled something under his breath and walked out.

Mick chuckled. "You sure got him thinking about it, Dago."

Chapter 17

I was hopeful the damage was only superficial, but when I inspected closer, I could see where the scratches had actually cut into the aluminum.

"Well, this job just got a little harder," I mumbled as I started sanding the door down to the bare metal. I only needed a small amount of bondo and finished applying the first coat of primer before lunch. I sat there on a short stool admiring my work and lost in thought when Anna walked in.

"Where've you been?" I asked. She and Henry were gone when I'd awakened and I was so upset I drank two or three cups of coffee all by myself.

"Henry and I went for a power walk." Henry was standing beside her, panting contentedly. He was a mean old cur, but he'd really taken a liking to her. He even slept in her room. I imagine he would take a piece out of my ass if I tried to tiptoe in there one night.

"I met one of your neighbors. Some old fart named Buford. He was wearing dirty overalls and had a wad of chewing tobacco in his mouth the size of an apple. He wouldn't stop staring at my boobs." She was wearing a pair of short shorts and a tight-fitting bright green tank top with no bra, which left very little to the imagination. No wonder Buford was staring, even if he was over eighty. Anna squatted down beside me and looked at my handiwork.

"Okay, I have a question. If you're only painting the door, why have you covered my entire car with paper?"

"Overspray," I answered. "It'd mess everything up and I'd end up having to buff your entire car. It's a lot of needless work which can be avoided if you prep properly. That's why I have my Cadillac and truck parked outside." I glanced over at her. "You should invest in some of those athletic bras if you don't want horny old farts gawking at you. Or wear a sweatshirt."

She looked over at me and grinned. "Yeah, I guess so."

"Alright, so while you were out walking, I've been doing some thinking. I've decided you will be in charge of the Braxton case."

Her eyes widened. "Really?" she asked.

"Yep. So, turn my phone on and give Ronald a call. See if he's found anything on Theopolis the pervert. Then, call Mrs. Braxton and set up a meeting with her."

She was grinning when I told her to call Ronald. But when I mentioned Mrs. Braxton, her face paled. "I can't call her," she said anxiously. "She thinks I'm some kind of low life."

I looked at her. She had sat on the floor beside me and I actually thought she was going to start crying. I gently took her chin in my hand and turned her head to face me.

"Time for a little story," I said. "A married couple has two kids, a little boy and a little girl. Anytime the little boy would fall down or get a scratch, the parents would tell him to tough it out because he was a brave little boy. Anytime the little girl fell down, the parents would hold her, cuddle her, kiss her boo-boo, and all of that silly shit."

She looked at me questioningly, confused. "What are you trying to say?" she asked.

"Which one of those kids do you think will grow up to be emotionally strong? I'm not going to coddle you and kiss your boo-boo and all of that silly shit. You're a good person. I like you. Hell, Henry likes you, and he doesn't like anyone. There will always be people who dislike you for one reason or another, you simply deal with it and meet it head on. So, if you like hanging out here and you want to earn a paycheck, quit feeling sorry for yourself and toughen up."

I took my hand off of her chin, tapped her nose with my finger, and pointed at the phone. She dropped her gaze and stared tentatively at the phone.

Suddenly, Henry started barking and ran out of the garage. The two of us stood up and walked outside and saw a red tow truck coming up my driveway. Duke was driving. He got out and relit the stub of a cigar before walking over. Henry growled menacingly. Anna stroked his head reassuringly to calm him.

"A parable," he said as he walked into the garage. We followed. He spotted Anna's car, squatted in front of the freshly primed door and began inspecting my work.

Anna looked at me questioningly. I shrugged. At the moment, I was only thinking about the aroma of Duke's cigar, the smell of it was making my mouth water, kind of like Pavlov's dog.

She focused on Duke. "What do you mean a parable?" she asked.

He stood and gestured with his cigar. "What he said last night about the baptism of Jesus and the act making one worthy. It was a parable, a story of familiarity in which a comparison or analogy can be drawn." He waved his cigar around some more. "You ain't the only one who's read the Bible," he said with a scoff and pointed in the general direction where the tow truck was parked. "Alright, I got you a rollback. Where're we going?"

Anna looked at me and smiled. "A parable," she said softly, stared at the phone a moment and then turned it on.

I topped off my flask and grabbed a few cigars before getting into the passenger seat. I looked over at Duke. "Before we go, I have one question. Please tell me this truck isn't stolen."

Duke looked at me innocently. "I borrowed it."

"Yeah, I was afraid of that," I lamented. I handed him a fresh cigar and lit one for myself.

Before we drove off, Anna came running out with those lean shapely legs and her breasts bouncing happily under her shirt. I rolled the window down as she jogged up. She was a little out of breath as she spoke. "I just got off of the phone with Mrs. Braxton. She gave me the name and address of the daughter-in-law and she believes her husband visits her every day during lunch."

"So, what're you going to do?" I asked.

"I'm going to set up a stakeout and try to catch him," she said with a grin.

I nodded. "Wasn't so hard after all, was it," I replied. "I've got a video camera in my desk drawer. The battery may need charging. Use my truck. Oh, and be sure to document your times. I'll show you how to write up a report later."

Anna nodded enthusiastically and handed my phone back to me. "You're right, it wasn't tough at all, but it'd still be nice if you kissed my boo-boo once in a while." She giggled and ran off before I could respond. Duke frowned, but kept silent.

"She was making a parable," I said feebly.

I called Rhoda and told her we'd be there in a half hour, barring any unforeseen catastrophe. She gasped and asked what I meant, but I hung up without answering.

After much sweating and grunting, Duke and I got my Buick loaded up and chained down. When we finished, I pulled out my pewter flask and readily shared it. He tried a small sip and then helped himself to a healthy swallow.

"That's some good shit. What is it?" he asked.

"Balvenie Scotch," I said. I didn't mention how I frequently mixed it with coffee, which scotch connoisseurs the world over would burn me at the stake if they knew. Duke took another long pull and nodded in satisfaction. He rubbed the top off with his shirt and handed it back to me as I looked over at the house. Rhoda was watching us through the screen door. When she saw me looking, she held up the coffee pot.

I looked over at Duke. "Duke my friend, do you like coffee so thick it goes down like molasses?"

It was late. I sat in a metal folding chair in my garage. Once we got the Wildcat back home, I'd been sitting here looking at it, and drinking scotch, too much scotch. I couldn't stop looking at her. It caused my mind to wander back in time. I'd been doing a lot of reminiscing since this car came back into my life. It was obvious why it made me think of my father, but for some unknown reason I kept thinking about my wife as well. Sometimes, I could go a whole day without thinking about her and how much I missed her.

My reverie was interrupted by a presence beside me. It was Anna. Her hair was a bit tousled and I had no idea if she was wearing anything underneath the blanket she had wrapped around her. Henry wandered in behind her, gave me a sniff and then went back outside.

"It's late," she said simply.

"Yeah. How'd the surveillance go?" I replied.

"All I got was some video of him coming and going. I'm going to try again tomorrow. Maybe he'll stick his tongue down her throat or something." I nodded absently.

"What is it about this car?" she asked.

"It's a long story, and like you said, it's late."

Anna looked at me. The fluorescent lighting accentuated her childlike face and blue eyes. "Please tell me," she said.

"Alright, you better pull up a chair." Anna chose the small work stool. When she sat, the blanket parted, causing an ample amount of her legs to be exposed.

"So, tell me," she said again.

I sighed and pointed at the Buick. "It all started with the car." I told her of the events leading up to the fight.

"Oh my God, it must have been awful growing up with him," she said when I'd finished.

I nodded. "He was a very unpleasant man to be around. After my mother skipped out, he developed a really bad habit of taking out all of his frustrations on me."

"What did you do after the fight?" she asked.

"I ran away and joined the Army," I replied and fondly remembered the recruiting NCO, Sergeant First Class Harold Darlington. He was a tall lanky man with skin as black as coal and his wife was almost as tall. I shared a bedroom with their three-year-old son. Mrs. Darlington was a fantastic cook. I almost regretted leaving them.

I refocused. "So, I was staying at the recruiter's home until I could get processed and sent to basic."

"What do you mean, processed?"

"When you enlist, you go through a background check and testing, plus physical and psychological exams to make sure you qualify. It takes a few days. One can't merely walk into a recruiting office and ship out the same day."

"Oh," she said.

"Anyway, there was no way I was going back home, so I stayed with the sergeant and his family while I was being processed. The first night, we were watching the evening news and the reporter talked about how a cop was murdered when he interrupted a robbery. I only caught part of the story, but the police said the suspects sped away in an older primer-colored car that possibly had bullet strikes in the rear."

I pointed at the car. "When I saw the news story, I somehow knew my father was involved and my car was a part of it. Don't ask me how I knew. I just knew. Now, after all of these years, fate has rejoined me with it."

I finished off my flask before continuing. "My father was involved in the murder of a police officer. Is that some shit or what?"

We were both silent then for several minutes. I was thinking about what could have been, while perhaps Anna was thinking of her own childhood and how she'd watched helplessly when her father was murdered.

"Tell me about your wife," she asked quietly.

"You're trying to change the subject," I said. She nodded. I sighed again, heavier this time. "A nice gesture, but my wife was even more of a sore spot."

She snaked an arm out from under the blanket and found my hand. She squeezed tightly.

"Please?"

"Okay, I met her about five years ago. I was thirty-nine and she was about your age." I caught her looking at me funny.

"Yeah, I know, big age difference. She was very pretty. Blonde hair, blue eyes, nice body and a set of breasts she liked to show off. When I first met her, she was singing in a nightclub. I couldn't take my eyes off of her. We dated for almost a year and got married."

"Was it a big wedding?" she asked.

"Nah, we eloped. We found one of those chapels."

"Alcohol was involved, no doubt," she remarked.

"You'd be correct."

"Was it a happy marriage?"

"It had its ups and downs. She had all of these crazy little idiosyncrasies that both drove me nuts and made me crazy for her all at the same time."

"Like what?" she asked curiously.

"Well, let's see. One day we were out running an errand or something. She was driving and had stopped at a traffic light. For some reason, she thought it would be a good time to put some lotion on her legs. I was on the phone and not paying much attention until I heard the incessant honking of a horn behind us. The light had turned green and there Marcia was, rubbing lotion on her legs and not paying the least bit of attention to the traffic light or the horn honking." I chuckled halfheartedly at the memory.

"She was a bit scatter-brained I guess, but it was an endearing quality." I paused a moment. "We weren't planning on children and the pregnancy was somewhat of a surprise." I paused again, remembering. "She'd waited for a month before telling me. I was elated, but for some reason she was – angry, troubled, something. I can't really describe how she was acting, but she wasn't happy. It seemed so uncharacteristic of her.

"Anyway, one night I got a phone call and I had to leave. It wasn't uncommon for this to happen, but for some reason, on this particular night Marcia became very upset about it. I was apologetic and told her I'd be back as soon as possible. Well, you know the rest." I took a long slow breath, remembering that fateful evening.

"I was hopelessly in love with her and I miss her terribly."

"You haven't been with anyone since her?" she asked.

I shrugged. "Nothing worth mentioning."

"Oh, c'mon on, you have to tell me now," Anna begged.

"Well, a couple of months after Marcia's death, I started seeing a fellow officer. She was freshly divorced and didn't want a serious relationship, same as me."

"Friends with benefits."

"Yeah, I guess that's one way of putting it."

"What happened?" she asked.

"It was stupid. We were watching a ball game on TV and drinking. She took offense at some smart-assed remark I made and we got in an argument. It escalated, because we were both drunk and being stupid, but then she called me a wife killer."

"Ouch."

"Yeah, ouch. The next day she called and apologized, but the damage was done." Other than that brief interlude, there were a couple of one night stands, which I regretted almost immediately, but I wasn't going to tell her about those.

I looked at my watch. "It's late," I repeated. She stood and pulled me out of my chair. We walked inside together.

Chapter 18

Somebody must have known I'd forgotten to turn my phone off and was now blowing it up. I tried the pillow over my head trick, but it didn't work. It finally stopped, but I knew it was going to start up again any second. All I wanted to do was sleep for a few more hours, but I knew it wasn't going to happen as long as that damned phone was on.

Crawling out of bed, I sat up and rubbed the sleep out of my eyes. My head was pounding and my mouth tasted like Henry had taken a shit in it while I was asleep. As I knew it would, the phone started ringing again. It took several frantic seconds before I found it hidden under a pile of clothes. I looked at the caller I.D. and saw it was Harvey. I called him back.

"Are you still asleep, Hoss? It's almost eleven o'clock!"

"I had a late night last night. What's up?" I asked.

"That idiot, Hatcliff, had a news conference this morning. They've reopened Lester Gwinnette's case and are now calling it a murder."

I rubbed my temples in an effort to ease the pain. "Let me guess. He's spouting off some bullshit about how they've discovered new evidence and all that."

"Of course they are, and they're taking all the credit. No surprise there, right?" he asked rhetorically.

"Well, I'm sure Rhoda's happy. I'll give her a call later."

"I've already talked to her. She said to tell you thank you, and you have an open invitation to drink coffee at her house anytime." He laughed before saying goodbye.

I hung up, rubbed my face, and looked around. It was pretty obvious I was the only person who slept in my bed last night. Part of me was disappointed, but another part was glad. I was old enough to be her father after all. Standing up, I stretched the kinks out of my back and headed for the shower. I'd mixed beer with scotch, which was always a no-no. It wasn't the first time I'd done it, and afterward I swore I'd never do it again. But, fleeting promises always seemed to melt away at the first encounter of hedonistic temptation.

Feeling a little better from the shower, I put some fresh clothes on, khaki cargo shorts and one of my favorite golf shirts, one with a Masters logo affixed, and headed to the kitchen. There was a plate of breakfast waiting on me, along with a pot of coffee and a post-it note from Anna. She informed me she was dutifully continuing the surveillance of Theopolis Braxton the Third and to call if I needed her.

Very nice, I thought. I turned the TV on and caught most of the midday news as I ate breakfast and was enjoying a second cup of coffee when my phone chimed, this time indicating the motion sensors at the head of the drive being activated. Henry jumped up and ran to the door growling.

I joined him, but held off on the growling part. "Easy boy, it's probably Anna," I said to him. He turned his head sideways at me briefly before I opened the door. Peering out, I saw two vehicles. It wasn't Anna, but I recognized the lead car. It was Special Agents Ridgeway and Jeffreys. They were followed by a similar unmarked car. Two men were in it.

"I wonder what the heck they want," I muttered. I wasn't in the mood for company, but was at least thankful I'd bathed. They were all friendly acting when they walked up to the door, and I greeted them in an equally friendly manner.

"This is our supervisor, Special Agent in Charge Reuben Chandler and this is Special Agent Enrique Hernandez."

I invited them in which caused Henry to retreat to Anna's room, emitting a low growl as he walked off. I sat my guests at the kitchen table and poured them all coffee. I kind of felt like Rhoda at that particular moment, all I needed was stretchy pants and a cigarette dangling out of my mouth. They nodded gratefully and I looked them over.

Reuben Chandler looked more like a lawyer than a cop, which he probably was. If you wanted to climb the hierarchal ladder in the FBI, education surpassed street smarts. I guessed him in his mid-fifties, salt-and-pepper hair cut short, but it looked like one of those fifty dollar haircuts, expensive-looking tailored suit, and spit-shined wingtips.

Enrique was younger than me, maybe late thirties. He had Latino good looks, jet black hair, dark brown eyes, a perpetual three-day growth of beard, and as a famous professional wrestler used to say, he oozed machismo. He had on what appeared to be an expensive Italian suit, but instead of a tie, he wore his shirt with the top two buttons open and a gaudy gold necklace around his neck. I guess his only flaw was his teeth. They weren't pristine white like Mark and Teresa's. There was a noticeable yellow patina. I got the impression he was a heavy smoker and hadn't yet discovered Crest Whitestrips.

"Alright, now that we've gotten all of the formalities taken care of, what's the occasion for the visit?" I asked. I mean, yeah, Teresa looked especially nice today. She was wearing a pantsuit which was a little bit tight across the backside, not that I'm complaining, and she smiled sweetly more than once, but I wasn't in a very sociable mood at the moment. My head was no longer pounding, but there was still a dull throb, and my late breakfast was causing my stomach to grumble.

Reuben, the supervisor, took my cue and started the conversation. "Agent Hernandez has been working undercover with Robard Trucking," he said it matter-of-factly, like it was hardly newsworthy. I looked over at him in mild surprise and he responded with a broad smile.

SAC Chandler continued. "His focus of investigation centers on a racketeering operation operating out of Detroit and more specifically utilizing the services of Robard Trucking."

I slowly nodded in understanding. "I see. Lester Gwinnette had indeed figured it out."

"You are correct, Thomas," Enrique replied with a distinct accent. He sounded like a younger version of Ricardo Montalban. I bet the man had women chasing after him from Canada to Mexico. I also couldn't help but notice Teresa paying close attention to his every word. I didn't like him.

"Alright, I have a question. Why is the FBI investigating a drug trafficking network? I mean, wouldn't an agency like the DEA handle it?"

Enrique smiled pleasantly. "The FBI has seven main investigative arms. They are civil rights, investigative support, organized crime, violent crime, white collar crime, counterterrorism, and narcotics. I am with the narcotics unit."

"Oh," I said. "So, the heroin is coming from Canada."

"Not exactly," Enrique replied and explained. "The raw opium originates from the Golden Triangle. It is processed into heroin using what is essentially slave labor, and is then smuggled into Canada through either air or water. The services of Robard Trucking were then utilized to transport the heroin to various distribution points in the States."

I suddenly understood. "You're the inside man." I pointed at the FBI agents. "You provided them with the information about Lester." I looked at Reuben for confirmation, who acknowledged with a slight nod. "My suspicions were correct then. He was trying to blackmail someone."

"Yes indeed," Enrique said. "Approximately four days before his death, he contacted the president of Robard Trucking and attempted to extort a considerable amount of money from him." He dusted at some imaginary lint on his lapel. "And that brings us to the point of this visit. I am afraid I might have some bad news for you."

I waited for him to continue, but instead he drew out the moment while he drank his coffee silently. Normally, it wouldn't have bothered me, but my hangover was making me irritable. My phone buzzed and I looked at the caller I.D. It was Ronald texting me.

Everything OK?

"Excuse me for a moment," I said and walked outside.

"Alright, you've got to stop watching me all the time," I said to Ronald when he answered the phone. He had a bad habit of monitoring my surveillance cameras. That's why I didn't have any cameras in the bedrooms.

"I was worried," he responded meekly.

I sighed. "Okay, since you're already on them, see if you can get close-ups and still photos of each of them."

"I already have," he responded. "Who are they?"

I looked up at the camera mounted on the front porch. "Well, if it's any of your business, they're government agents. Email me the photos," I said, hung up, and walked back inside. Ronald's snooping caused me to finally lose patience.

"Alright, where were we?"

Enrique held up a finger. I noticed his nails were freshly manicured. He was definitely not a man who worked on cars. "First, I am afraid I have no information which might allow you to identify the murderer. I was sitting in the office with the president of the company and his cronies when Lester's name was brought up. He'd sent a letter to the president with copies of his paperwork and photographs. He demanded one million dollars in exchange for his silence."

"What was the response?" I asked.

"When the president read the letter aloud, everyone laughed uproariously," he said. "We made many besmirching jokes at Lester's expense." He finished his coffee and looked longingly at his cup. Reluctantly, I got up, retrieved the pot, and poured him a refill. He smiled gratefully. I figured it was the only way to keep him talking.

He blew softly and took a sip before continuing. "It was mutually decided to ignore this halfwit, and if he pressed the issue, I volunteered to pay him a visit and smack him around." He leaned forward.

"It never happened, Thomas. I came in to the office a couple of days later and the president was laughing gleefully as he told me of the unfortunate suicide of Lester Gwinnette. I can assure you, Thomas, everyone was convinced he had killed himself. There was no order given to murder him."

He leaned back and sighed. "I am afraid I have some more unpleasant news for you, my friend. We have obtained a search warrant for your residence." Special Agent in Charge Reuben Chandler reached into his jacket and produced the warrant. He handed it over to me without comment.

I retrieved my reading glasses and quickly read it. After a moment, I looked up. "Guys, Teresa, do I understand correctly, the warrant is for Lester's photographs and log books?"

"Yes, my friend," Enrique said pleasantly. I didn't know we'd become friends within a few minutes of knowing each other, but whatever. I took my glasses off.

"Well, you guys didn't have to go through all of this unnecessary paperwork. Everything is sitting right there." I turned and pointed at my desk. The logbooks and photographs were sitting in plain view. They all looked. Teresa's mouth actually dropped open.

Enrique gasped in obvious delight. He motioned with his hand. "May I?" he asked.

"Of course," I replied. He stood and walked over to the table. I looked over at the three FBI agents. They were sitting stiffly, probably in realization of the fact they had wasted a few hours drafting a search warrant and then hunting down a judge to sign it.

I held up the pot. "More coffee?" I asked. They shook their heads in unison. I shrugged a shoulder and refilled my own cup. Enrique had picked it all up, brought it back to the kitchen table, and sat back down.

"This is excellent, Thomas. I believe this will be valuable evidence in the event of a trial." He went into his jacket and retrieved a pack of cigarettes.

I held up a hand. "Hold up, no smoking in the house."

There was what was called a micro expression that flashed across Enrique's face. An expression of contempt, anger. Kind of like, how dare I tell him what to do, but it was only there for a microsecond before quickly changing to an apologetic smile.

"Of course, my friend. Where are my manners?"

I returned his smile. "Why don't we go out on the front porch, I'm having a craving for some nicotine myself."

When I first moved into this house, I got it in my head the front porch needed some good old fashioned rocking chairs. I found an Amish furniture store in Murfreesboro. I originally intended to only purchase one or two, but for some unknown reason, I'd bought four. Damned if I know why, the Amish gentleman was a sour old man with lamentable people skills, bad breath, and a combination of sawdust and food scraps stuck in his unkempt beard.

Anyway, it worked out in this instance. Everyone had a rocking chair to park their ass in. Well, except for me. I grabbed a chair from inside and brought it out. Enrique and I lit up, some kind of smelly cigarette for him and a delicious, aromatic cigar for me.

"Does the FBI still test their employees for marijuana usage?" I asked.

"Of course," Reuben said. "Why do you ask?"

"Oh, I was just curious. Knowing what we know about marijuana nowadays, it seems kind of silly," I said. Reuben nodded thoughtfully, or dismissively, I wasn't sure which. Well, so much for throwing out a wild question in an attempt at getting a read on him.

Enrique looked over the paperwork as he smoked and the rest of us made small talk. "Very nice," he'd say occasionally. He looked it over for a full ten minutes. Stubbing out his cigarette in the ashtray, he lit another one and looked over at me.

"What do you think of all of this, Thomas?"

"Somebody made quite a bit of money," I replied. "I don't think it was only the Spieths though."

"Why do you believe that?" he asked.

"The numbers with the money does not add up. So far, I've only located approximately three-quarters of a million. If you look at Lester's pictures, each shipment could've easily netted a hundred grand or more. They've apparently been doing this for what, three years now? A couple of shipments a week, multiplied times, oh, I don't know, let's say multiply times an even one hundred fifty, that amounts to somewhere around thirty million."

"The bank in Detroit has several million in their coffers," Teresa interjected. Reuben gave her a look, like he didn't want that particular piece of information shared with the likes of me.

I shrugged indifferently. "Well, there you go." I wondered how they knew how much money was in the Detroit bank, but didn't ask.

Enrique stubbed out his second cigarette. "Do we have anything else to pester Thomas about?" he asked. The three other agents shook their heads in unison. "Is there anything I can do for you, Thomas?" Enrique asked.

"So, any suspicions on who may have killed Lester?" I asked hopefully.

He held up his hands and shook his head. "I have no idea, Thomas. I do not believe it was any of the operatives within the organization. It is possible he had an enemy who was a lower-level employee, perhaps a fellow truck driver, but word has not reached me. If you wish, I will make subtle inquiries and call you immediately if I learn anything."

"You're still embedded within the organization?" I asked.

Enrique nodded his head solemnly. "We've not yet issued indictments. Even though the trucking company has filed for bankruptcy, the business continues, as it will always, no?"

I had to agree.

There was more small talk, which lasted for maybe ten seconds before boss man Chandler perfunctorily stood and announced they were leaving. I didn't argue. All I wanted at the moment was for them to be gone and to sit on the front porch and smoke my cigar in peace and quiet. They left me with a copy of the warrant after dutifully noting the log books, photos, and paperwork on the inventory page. Henry joined me on the porch as their cars disappeared from sight.

"Good thing I'd made copies of all that stuff, right?" I said to him. He gave me a brief, approving look before stretching out and closing his eyes.

When the Ibuprofen kicked in, I decided to do something productive and went to work on Anna's car. I spent a couple of hours on it before reaching a point where I needed to let the paint dry before applying the clear coat, so I started in on the Buick.

"Let's see how bad these brakes are." I put it up on jack stands and took the tires off. Just as I suspected, the brakes had oxidized to the point where they had fused together with the drums. They would all have to be replaced, along with everything made of rubber which had dry-rotted. I changed the oil, siphoned out any old gas out of the tank, and tried to crank it up with a spare battery. After a few shots of ether, the engine surprisingly started. I'd rebuilt it years ago, and apparently I'd done a good job. It backfired a few times, and then ran smoothly. I let it get good and warm, and then shut it off. I'd not bothered with filling the radiator so I didn't want it to overheat.

Looking the car over, I created a mental list of everything I would need to do in order to restore it. I also made a decision. Reaching for my phone, I scrolled through the contact list until I found a particular number.

Sammy Wu answered after several rings. "Thomas?" he asked.

"How are you, Sammy?" It'd been too long since I've spoken with my friend. He was another academy classmate. Several of us had become close friends and, as rookies, we often got stuck working the midnight shift in the bad parts of town. We watched each other's backs while we learned the trade.

"I'm doing okay," he replied. "Just counting down the days until retirement. How about yourself?"

"Not too bad, doing PI work and enjoying life," I responded.

"Oh? Got any good cases going?" he asked. Sammy had wanted to be a detective back in the day, but internal politics prevented it. A couple of boneheaded rookie mistakes had resulted in pissing off the wrong people. As a result, every time he had applied for a specialized position he was rejected without explanation. Finally, he was transferred into property and evidence section. He often lamented it was a dull, boring job, but it was possibly the best thing that'd ever happened to him, career wise.

"I have an old case I think I'm going to take a look at," I said. "But, in order to do it I'll need a favor from you."

"Sure, Thomas, you name it. If I can do it, I will."

"I want a copy of an old unsolved murder case file, Rick Martin's case." I heard Sammy whistle and say something in Chinese.

"I've seen the file, Thomas. It's pretty thick." He seemed to think it over a moment. "Yeah, I can do it. I'll get started on it right away. I'll give you a call when I got it, sound good?" he asked.

"More than good, Sammy. Also, I have one other case file I want to take a look at. You may or may not have access to it, it's a missing person by the name of …"

"Eh, you can stop right there. Trotter keeps all of the missing person case files locked away in a file cabinet in the homicide office. Don't ask me to try to get a copy from him. You know how he is."

Indeed I did. Detective Percy Trotter and I had a lot of history together. And yet, he was still an enigma to me and everyone else. I dropped it and we spent the next several minutes speaking about inconsequential things until Sammy hit me with something.

"I totally forgot! I meant to call you. Last week some of the rat squad came in and signed out all of the evidence from your wife's case."

I frowned. "What kind of evidence?"

"Well, let's pull up the log sheet." I heard the sounds of tapping on a keyboard. A moment later he rattled off the itemized list of evidence, all of which I already knew about with the exception of two additional DVDs.

"You said there were three of them?" I asked Sammy, to which he confirmed. I frowned again. One of the videos was of my first interview, and then there was the second one, the one in which they confronted me about my bogus alibi, but I had no idea what the third one was.

"Do you have the dates the videos were first submitted?" I asked.

"Yeah, all of the evidence was submitted on the same date, with the exception of one. It was submitted two weeks ago."

"Sammy, I have another favor. Is there any chance you can copy them for me if they ever turn them back in?"

"You got it, boss. Give me a day or so and I should have everything."

"Thanks, Sammy. I really owe you."

"No, no. You're the one who saved my son's life. He's graduating college in December by the way. I'll always owe you. I'll talk to you later," he said and hung up. I sat looking at the phone as I recalled what he was referring to. Back when his son was in high school, some girl he was smitten with dumped him. He'd taken it pretty badly and tried to kill himself. I found him out in Percy Warner Park, barely alive. He'd taken a bunch of pills and washed it down with alcohol. When Sammy saw me at the hospital, he declared himself to be forever indebted to me.

The memory, which should've been a good one, left me depressed. My hands were grimy and black from working on the Buick. I opted for another hot shower.

Chapter 19

I tried calling Uncle Mike. It went straight to voice mail and the robotic voice advised me the subscriber was not currently accepting incoming messages. I then tried calling Rhoda, but to no avail. It was only two o'clock and I was getting antsy to get out and do something. I resisted the urge to call Anna and see how she was doing. She'd been gone all day, and although I missed her company, I was worried I'd done something inappropriate the night before, and didn't remember it.

"Alright, what are you going to do this afternoon?" I asked myself. "Hang out at Mick's?" I shook my head, I hung out there too much. I thought about it a minute and decided to go pay Rhoda a visit. She was probably not aware of it, but Tennessee had a victim's compensation fund. Since Lester's death had now been declared a murder, she was eligible. Besides, it was a nice day to get the convertible out. I intentionally left my flask sitting on the kitchen counter, locked up the house, and headed out.

In addition to the beautiful day, the traffic was fairly light. It almost made me forget about the terrible coffee awaiting me. A thought occurred as I drove by a grocery store and quickly changed lanes.

"I'm going to bring her some decent coffee," I said as I parked. I headed straight for the coffee aisle and grabbed a couple of bags of Seattle's Best, blend number ten. I called again, maybe she needed some groceries, but still no answer.

The kitchen door was standing open when I drove up, but there was no Rhoda, not even when I tapped my horn. My cop's intuition took over as I absently set the flimsy plastic bag holding the coffee on the ground and moved my hand close to my holstered sidearm.

"Rhoda?" I called out as I simultaneously knocked on the screen door. There was no response. I tugged on the handle and found it unlatched.

"Rhoda, it's Thomas," I said loudly. After all, she may have been sitting on the throne, and that was a sight I'd rather not see. I had enough nightmares. Still, there was no response. I drew my sidearm out and slowly, carefully cleared each room in the small house with the tactical skills ingrained in me when I was in the academy.

Nothing. Not even the cat.

It was possible she'd gone for a walk, or maybe she was visiting with her hippy neighbor and they were sitting around buck naked and getting high, but my intuition didn't agree. While I was clearing the house, I smelled something burning. Returning to the kitchen, I found the source. The coffeepot was still on and it'd burned off the remaining coffee, leaving a brown smoking glob at the bottom of the pot.

As I started to walk back outside, I stopped suddenly at the door and fixated on the screen door. There was a small cut in the screen, right about where the latch was located. A thought suddenly gave birth in my brain. I looked around, and still seeing nobody, I retrieved my own pocket knife, stood on the outside and simulated what I believed had happened.

"Yep," I muttered. Someone had cut a slit in the screen and used their knife to lift up the latch. "There's only one reason why someone would do that instead of just yanking the door open, isn't that right, Thomas?"

Walking outside, I inspected her car. The hood was cool to the touch and nothing appeared out of the ordinary. Wondering where she was, I spotted the shed out of the corner of my eye. One of the doors was partially open. Just a crack, but it was enough to tell me what I needed to know.

That's where I found her, hanging from one of the wood crossbeams. Tommy Boy was crouched in a corner and meowed at me. The little bastard sounded sad, as if it were possible for a dumb cat to feel sad.

I made sure I was the only person in there, besides Rhoda of course, before taking my phone out and snapping several photos. I then secured my handgun in the trunk of my Cadillac and made the 911 call. The first deputy on the scene was a baby-faced but athletic young man whose nametag identified him as Trimble and the little identifier underneath it said he'd been serving since this year. A true rookie. I introduced myself and showed him Rhoda.

"Holy shit," he exclaimed. "Shouldn't we cut her down?"

"No, sir," I responded. "We shouldn't touch anything. Let the crime scene techs do all of that."

"Yeah, okay." He looked around, shaking his head. "You know, I responded to the scene when her husband killed himself. Now, they're saying he was murdered."

"Oh, yeah?" I responded as I heard distant sirens in the background approaching. "What'd you think about it?" I asked as I looked him over.

"It was damned bizarre," he said and then looked a little sheepish. "Just between you and me, it was the first dead body I'd ever seen."

"Don't worry, if you stay in this profession long enough, you'll see plenty."

"Sounds like you've had experience." I nodded and told him of my former profession. The sirens were getting louder.

"Okay, I've already cleared the house, but I want to show you something." I led him to the kitchen door and showed him the slit in the screen.

"Is that significant?" he asked.

"Yeah, probably so. I don't think she killed herself, Deputy. I think someone murdered her."

"And then tried to make it look like a suicide," he finished.

"Yeah, but some of your co-workers may come to a different conclusion. Something for you to keep in mind."

He looked at me curiously as other officers began speeding into the driveway. One deputy actually skidded sideways to a stop, spraying gravel everywhere. The same deputy jumped out of his car, sidearm in hand, waving it around wildly.

Soon, the driveway was jammed packed with cars, both marked and unmarked. I stood off to the side, watching the cluster fuck unfold. I spotted Georgie about the same time he spotted me. He spoke to a couple of other men in suits and the three of them walked over.

"What the hell are you doing here?" he demanded.

"You're really going to start this conversation like that?" I asked. Georgie started to puff up like a bullfrog, but before he could say anything, another one of the detectives put himself between the two of us.

"I don't think we've met," he said with an outstretched hand. "I'm Virgil Smallwood."

There was nothing small about him. He was every bit as tall as me and easily weighed over three hundred pounds. His big meaty grip was firm, like a man who knew he could squeeze down and break your hand, if he wanted to.

He wasn't what you'd call a snappy dresser, he was wearing wrinkled khaki slacks, scuffed brown soft-souled shoes, and a blue polo shirt. Completing the ensemble was a beige fishing vest, size XXXL. It had multiple pockets and it looked like he had something stuffed in every one of them. He sported a flattop haircut, had an easygoing smile and I guessed him to be somewhere in his late thirties.

"Thomas Ironcutter," I replied.

"Thomas, if you don't mind, I'd like to get a statement from you." He gestured around. "We can sit in my car, but then I'll have to repeat everything to my co-workers here." He retrieved a small digital tape recorder out of one of the vest pockets and looked at me hopefully, kind of like how an oversized dog looks at you when you're eating a juicy cheeseburger.

"Not a problem," I said and told them of coming to visit Rhoda and how I found her in the shed. It was apparent Georgie wanted to interject his own opinions about why I was really there, but one look from Virgil kept him quiet. I suspected they'd had previous run-ins and Virgil looked like the type who would've had no problem inviting a co-worker out back to settle their differences.

"They tell me you used to be a lawman," Virgil said when I'd finished my statement.

"That's right."

"What do you think of all this?" he asked.

"I think you probably have another murder on your hands," I answered.

Georgie couldn't restrain himself now. He scoffed loudly and spit on the ground. "And how would you know?" he demanded.

Virgil looked at me pointedly now. "I believe that's a good question, Thomas."

I shrugged. "Well, Virgil, as Georgie would tell you, I'm not a lawman anymore. Just call it a hunch. Once you look things over, maybe you'll think the same thing. Are we through here?"

Virgil gave me a long look, like he wasn't through picking my brain, but he thought over what I said. "I guess you better be going then. Maybe you and me can jaw on this a little more later on," he said. I nodded and we swapped business cards.

I started walking toward my car, trying to figure out how I was going to get out with all of the other cars blocking the drive. I opted to sit and smoke a cigar. It took a little over an hour before some of the deputies finally grew bored and hungry. Three of them left, creating an opening. Just as I started my car, Georgie walked over. Another one of the detectives, one who had not spoken the entire time, followed him.

"I suppose you've heard we re-opened the Lester Gwinnette case," he said. I nodded. There was no need for me to rub it in or anything.

"I'm going to need everything you've got on it." He said it like it was a lawful order.

"Everything I had, you have. The FBI has the rest." I gave him a brief rundown of the log books and the photographs. "I'm sure they'll have no issues with you getting copies."

"Oh, I'm one step ahead of you. I've already talked to them. They tell me you took a car from Rhoda." I didn't respond and instead continued smoking my cigar. I had a feeling I knew where this was going. Georgie pointed his stubby finger at me. I was getting tired of him doing that.

"You took that car illegally. You can either return it or face charges."

"Yeah, good luck with that." I started to drive off, maybe even spray him with a little gravel in the process, but paused.

"Let me help you out, Detective Georgie. That car was stolen from me several years ago. In fact, I still have the title. So, if you try any shenanigans, it'll come back and bite you in the butt." He stared at me malevolently, but had no retort. I drove off.

I called Harvey, got his voice mail, and left a message about Rhoda. Then I called Anna and filled her in.

"Oh my God," she said.

"Yeah." I knew her brain was in the middle of formulating at least three hundred and seventy-one questions to pepper me with, so I took preemptive measures. "Look, I think I'm about to go through a dead spot. We'll talk more when I get home." I then hurriedly hit the end button.

I'd gotten maybe ten miles down the road when the sensation of being watched came over me. I checked the mirrors and then looked in the backseat. Tommy Boy was lying there, staring at me.

"Shit." I did not need or want a cat. Before my mom left, we had a cat. It would sleep all day and then run around the house all night, raising as much hell as it possibly could. After Mom packed up and left, the cat disappeared. I suspected Pops had something to do with it, but wasn't too concerned.

My first impulse was to take him back, but I was in no mood to deal with Georgie again. My second thought was to pull over and throw him out on the side of the road, but I knew I couldn't do something like that. Sighing, I headed for a nearby Walmart.

"You're only getting food and a litter box, no toys," I declared. Tommy Boy stared back silently.

Chapter 20

My throat burned, I was gasping for air, and my sides were cramping up. It was a painful reminder of how badly out of shape I had become. Nevertheless, I finished three miles in a relatively decent time, but only if I was eighty. I did some perfunctory stretching for two or three seconds before dropping in a heap on my front porch. Anna walked out and sat beside me, Tommy Boy and Henry following.

"You're all sweaty," she observed.

"You got a cigar?" I asked. She slapped me playfully on the arm.

We'd talked late into the night about Lester and Rhoda's untimely demise, and, although several beers were consumed, no logical conclusion was reached.

"Oh, you'll never guess what happened yesterday. Theo the pervert took her to lunch with her baby. She left a sippy cup at the restaurant and Ronald grabbed it."

"Ronald was with you?" She grinned and nodded.

"When I left yesterday morning, I went over to his house and sweet talked him into joining me."

I chuckled. It was almost impossible to get Ronald to do any socializing. "Where's the sippy cup?"

"I've got it stored in a paper bag. Ronald said you had a business you used for DNA analysis."

"Yep, but we need something to compare it to."

She grinned. "I'm one step ahead of you. After we left the restaurant, I called Mrs. Braxton and explained. Long story short, she met us at the park with a hairbrush. She said only Theo the pervert used the brush, so we have hair samples."

"That should do it."

"Then we went back to Ronald's and played video games until you called."

I laughed now.

"What?" Anna asked.

"I'm glad you two get along. Ronald desperately needs a few friends his own age."

"He's a grade-A nerd, but he's a sweet guy." She stood and stretched. "What do you have planned today?"

"I'm going to finish your car and later on we'll go to FedEx and mail the evidence to the lab." I stood, a little too quickly, and I got lightheaded.

Anna noticed. "Cigars and jogging don't work out too well, do they, big guy?"

I ignored her dig and motioned toward the garage. "C'mon, let's take a look at your baby."

Looking it over in satisfaction, I carefully removed the tape and paper from the area around her door.

"Alright, let's back it out into the sunlight," I directed. Once we'd done so, I pointed at the door. "Okay, what do you think? Can you see any color difference?" We both looked closely.

"It looks the same," she said after a minute.

"Yeah, I believe you're right. Okay, it's ready for me to apply the clear coat. Drive it back in and get the tape and paper back in place while I get my paint gun ready. There's some extra tape on the workbench if you need it."

Anna grinned. "Okay."

"How are you going to do this?" Anna asked as she started taping.

"Two coats, the first coat is applied thinly, where it looks a little wet. We wait for it to dry and then apply a second, slightly thicker coat." I grabbed a tack rag and began wiping the surface of the door in order to get any remaining dust off.

"How long will it take?"

"A couple of hours," I said. "But I want to let it dry overnight before you drive it." She looked at me and bit her lip, like I was telling her she couldn't wear her favorite pair of panties.

"I know you want your car back, but have a little patience. We want the clear coat nice and hard before you get out on the road." Anna nodded in understanding and watched as I applied the first coat.

"Alright, we've got to wait about thirty minutes before applying the second coat," I said as I took my mask off.

Anna took hers off and inspected my work. "Are we going to go to Rhoda's funeral?" she asked.

"If there is one," I replied, wondering if her family would go through the trouble.

"I think we should conduct our own investigation," she said.

I nodded thoughtfully. Maybe she was right. Maybe I needed to pursue both hers and Lester's murder. They had to be related and I had no confidence in Georgie, but maybe that big country boy, Detective Smallwood, would do a better job.

"Yeah, maybe so, let me think on it."

I went inside, got a large glass of water, and turned my phone on. I currently had only one message. It was from Sammy. I called him back immediately. He answered after one ring.

"Hold on just a minute, honey," he said. I heard some distorted noise, as if he were putting his hand over the little microphone on his cell phone, and then I heard some muffled conversation. "It's my wife, Sergeant. She needs to talk to me about something. I'll be outside if you need me." I heard some movement and the sound of a security door opening and closing before Sammy started speaking.

"Hey buddy, I got some heavy shit to lay on you," he said. He seemed anxious and there was a distinct note of tension in his voice.

I involuntarily stiffened. "What's wrong, Sammy? I didn't get you in a jam, did I?"

"I'm fine, Thomas, it's you who's in a jam. The two rat squad detectives were here this morning. They turned the evidence back in and I overheard them talking. They've got a warrant for your arrest, Thomas. They're charging you with murder!"

Oh shit. My chest tightened. Although I knew it was probably going to happen one day, it didn't make the moment any easier. I cleared my throat and tried to think. "Have you had a chance to look at the other video?" I asked.

"Yeah. It's an interview of a woman who claims she was with you and helped you murder Marcia. She said the two of you were lovers and you coerced her to help you and make it look like a suicide. Then she goes on to give a detailed description of the inside of your house."

"Who the hell is she?" I asked.

"Her name is Brittany Long. I ran her history, but it doesn't look like she's ever been arrested in Nashville. Thomas, there's something not right about this," Sammy said.

"You got that right, buddy." My mind was racing. "How long ago did you see them?"

"Two hours ago. When they were leaving, I heard one of them calling the SWAT commander."

Damn, I didn't have much time. This was a good argument for leaving my phone on at all times. "Okay, let me think. Did you get copies of those interviews?"

"I've got everything, Thomas, but they're coming to get you. There's no way I can get this stuff to you in time."

I snapped my fingers at Anna and motioned her over as I worked the phone. "Sammy, I've got you on speaker phone now. I'm here with a friend of mine. Her name is Anna."

"Hi, Anna," Sammy said anxiously. Anna looked at me questioningly.

"Alright, listen. You can trust Anna with everything. She'll have my phone with her so you can contact her at any time. If you can't get in touch with her, call my attorney, Sherman Goldman."

"Okay, big guy. I've got to get back to work. I'll give Anna a call after my shift ends and make arrangements to meet. But, Thomas, I want to help if I can."

"I appreciate it, buddy, but I don't want anyone finding out about our friendship. You keep a low profile and if you can find out anything about this Brittany Long person, call Anna or Sherman."

"You got it, buddy. I don't think you have much time, so I'll let you go." I thanked him and hung up.

"Thomas, what's going on?" Anna asked.

"Let me call Ronald and I'll explain to both of you at once," I said. I tapped an icon on the screen and spoke his name into my phone. He answered almost immediately.

"Ronald, don't ask questions, just listen for now. The police are going to show up at any minute and arrest me for the murder of my wife. It'll probably be the SWAT team they send in. Get on the surveillance system and record everything. I want you to get close ups of everyone. Oh, and turn the audio on, I want everything they say recorded as well." Ronald started breathing heavily. He was prone to panic attacks. I tried to calm him.

"Now don't panic on me, buddy, I need you. Just listen to me. It's all going to be alright, but there's going to be a rough stretch. You and Anna have got to stick together, okay?"

"Okay," he said weakly. I heard him fumbling around. "Okay, I've got control of all of the cameras. Uh, Thomas, there's a black SUV parked on the side of the road near your driveway. I can't see who's inside it, the windows are tinted and they're too far away."

"Okay, they're already here. They're staging somewhere nearby and will be coming in anytime now." I tried to think. I was sweaty and dirty, but there was no time for a shower. My mugshot wasn't going to be very glamorous, and I had no idea why I was thinking about something so insignificant at this particular moment.

"Alright, Ronald, I'm going to give the phone to Anna, and she is going to go inside and lock all of the doors." I looked at Anna. "Get on a three-way with Sherman. If he answers, tell him everything. If he doesn't answer, leave him a message and then call William. Got it?"

Anna nodded her head nervously.

"Good girl. Now get inside and lock the doors."

Anna hurried inside.

There was nothing else left for me to do. I walked around in the front yard until I found a suitable spot in which Henry had not visited in a while, sat down and waited. It didn't take long.

A helicopter came in low and slow over the tree line, shortly followed by the SWAT team's armored vehicle rumbling down my drive. I rolled over onto my stomach and stretched my arms out. I hoped Ronald was manipulating the cameras properly, because I was having a bad feeling.

The officers piled out of the back door of the armored vehicle while a disembodied voice shouted out of a loud speaker attached to the roof of the vehicle. "This is the police! Do not resist! You are under arrest! Do not resist!" He kept repeating the mantra over and over. I did not move. I wanted nothing to be misinterpreted as a sign of resistance. Turns out, it didn't matter.

The first SWAT officer ran up to about two feet away from me and pointed an M4 assault rifle at my head while yelling at me to not move. I'm sure it sounded good, but anyone with half a brain would have noticed I'd not moved a whisker since they drove up.

A second officer ran up, dropped down beside me, and rammed a knee into my ribcage. I let out an involuntary gasp. The hardened plastic knee pad he was wearing caused a lightning bolt of pain to shoot through me. I forced myself to remain immobile.

"That was for my buddy, Doug, you piece of shit," he growled as he began handcuffing me. I assumed he was talking about Officer Eastlin, Anna's crazy ex-boyfriend. This one was a hothead, it was going to be easy to get him going.

"Doug Eastlin? Is he your lover? Is that why you're so upset?" He responded with another expletive and several punches to the back of my head. He thought he was being clever by not hitting my face, which would have cause visible injury. His padded gloves protected his hands from hitting my hard head. He didn't knock me out, but I felt an intense headache already forming.

"Wow, dude," I exclaimed. "You hit like a girl. You must be the wife in the relationship." He responded by punching me some more.

"Acevedo! That's enough!" I looked around as I was being pulled to my feet. All of them had their black ski masks on, but I recognized the sergeant who chastised Acevedo.

"Sergeant Trent, good to see you. I hope you'll act accordingly to the unjustified use of force," I said.

"You shouldn't have resisted arrest, Ironcutter," he retorted with no amount of friendliness. "Whose side do you think I'm on? My fellow officers, or a poor excuse of a man who kills a woman and her unborn child?" I assumed they were rhetorical questions and therefore I didn't bother with a response. There was a microphone on the camera mounted on the eve overlooking the front yard. I hoped we were close enough for it to record the dialogue. When they rolled me over and stood me up, the first thing I saw was a body camera on his tactical vest. Acevedo saw me looking at it and smiled through his mask.

"I think my camera's battery is bad. Too bad for you, right scumbag?" I looked over at Trent. He made brief eye contact before turning away.

Chapter 21

After the SWAT team took me into custody, I was unceremoniously shoved into a squad car and transported downtown. My temporary custodians were two patrol officers, a training officer and her rookie. I didn't know either one of them. The rookie kept turning around and looking at me, as if he were looking for character traits which would help him identify murderers in the future. I ignored him, attempted to find a comfortable sitting position that caused the least amount of pain in my ribcage, and tried without success to enjoy the view as we rode toward downtown Nashville.

Like I said, I knew this was eventually going to happen and had mentally prepared myself for it. Still, I felt humiliated.

The media and their cameras were present when we arrived. Instead of going directly to booking, the officers parked on Third Avenue South, right where the media were waiting. Someone had made a phone call.

"Looks like you're going to be on the evening news," the senior officer said with a strong hint of joyfulness in her voice. The rookie looked back at me with an unsympathetic grin.

"Schadenfreude," I said to him. His grin turned suspicious, like I'd called his mother a dirty name. I explained. "It means deriving pleasure from the misfortune of others. It's a character trait a good police officer should never have." The senior officer retorted with a derisive snort.

Once we parked, I looked around and spotted the culprit of this dog and pony show. Assistant Chief Raymond Perry was standing at parade rest on the sidewalk, his class-A uniform crisply pressed, trying to look as austere as his effeminate face could muster. He was an old adversary of Uncle Mike.

Under his watchful eye, I was assisted out of the patrol car by the two officers and they started to escort me up the steps into the side entrance of the Criminal Justice Center. Perry raised his hand, stopping them. The members of the media watched in rapt silence as the Assistant Chief walked up to me and looked me in the eyes. Actually, he had to tilt his head upward since he was several inches shorter than me.

At sixty-eight, he was well past his prime and should have retired years ago. Uncle Mike was a couple of years older than him, and was once his sergeant. He detested my uncle, and therefore felt the same about me.

He waited until everyone was silent before speaking. "Justice is being served today for the heinous murder of Marcia Ironcutter, a woman who loved you unconditionally, and yet you killed her in cold blood. It was a cowardly and despicable act, and I'll see to it you receive the full brunt of the law." He said it loudly and clearly. I can only imagine him rehearsing the words all morning to make sure it sounded good when it was replayed on the evening news.

"Hey, Ironcutter," a voice shouted out. "What do you have to say about murdering your wife?" I didn't bother acknowledging. Even if I had answered, I would've been drowned out by the sudden onslaught of questions by the rest of the media.

I let Perry stare balefully at me a moment longer before taking the initiative and started walking up the stairs. The two officers hurried after me. When I reached the top of the landing, several of the day shift detectives had gathered, staring coldly and saying nothing. One of them used his key card to open the door and held it for me as I walked inside.

"Take him to interview room one," he told the patrol officers. They looked confused. They had no idea where the interview rooms were.

I cleared my throat. "Follow me," I said and walked directly to the room.

I was intimately familiar with this room, having spent many hours in it, interviewing suspects and witnesses alike. It was generic in appearance and fairly small, about twelve feet by ten feet. The walls were painted a dull blue, matted carpeting of undetermined color scheme, and a plain table with four chairs surrounding it. The camera was surreptitiously mounted in a box designed to look like the HVAC thermostat, which only fooled drunks and morons. The recording equipment was located in a room down the hallway.

I helped myself to a chair, tried to find a position in which my ribs didn't hurt too much, and sat patiently, waiting.

Several minutes passed before my two friends from OPA entered the room. It was a purposeful act, making me wait, a psychological ploy designed to stress the suspect. Oscar and Jay walked in together, looking somber.

"Hello, Thomas," Jay said and sat beside me while Oscar took one of the chairs on the opposite side of the table. It was a common tactic. Jay was going to play the role of the caring, concerned detective.

"Thomas, we know you're aware of interview procedures, so I won't pretend we're not being recorded." He looked at his watch. "For the record, the time now is thirteen hundred hours. We are presently in an interview room at the Criminal Justice Center with Thomas Ironcutter. My name is Detective Jay Sansing and with me is Detective Oscar Marson." He paused and opened his file folder. I caught a glimpse of a copy of the warrant.

Jay looked at Oscar, who nodded. They'd been rehearsing this moment and they wanted it to be flawless, magnificent. I understood, detectives should always prepare and rehearse before conducting a formal interrogation. I still found it amusing though. If I weren't cuffed, I might have given them a golf clap.

"Thomas, I have a copy of the warrant for your arrest. I am going to read you the affidavit, but first I would like to formally advise you of your rights." I nodded silently. I'd memorized the Miranda warnings years ago, but he was going to go by the book. There was no need to interrupt him.

"You have the right to remain silent. Anything you say can and will be used against you in a court of law. You have a right to speak with a lawyer and have him present during questioning. If you cannot afford an attorney, one will be appointed to represent you, if you desire. If at any time you decide to stop answering questions, this interview will cease." Jay looked at me somberly. "Thomas, do you understand your rights?"

"Indeed I do," I answered. Satisfied with my response, Jay then read the affidavit for the probable cause. It was perfunctory and to the point. In it was one sentence stating they had an eyewitness to this alleged murder. It piqued my interest and I wanted to know more about this witness, but it was going to have to wait. Once he'd read the affidavit, there was a pregnant pause, and then Detective Marson joined in. He leaned forward looking contrite and sincere.

"Thomas, I want to start by apologizing for my attitude toward you in court the other day. It was unprofessional of me to let my emotions get the better of me."

So, he was going to try the good guy approach as well, but his tone was spurious, oily. He sounded like a used car salesman telling you the car you were about to buy was in pristine shape, all the while knowing the engine was on its last legs.

He continued. "We sincerely want to hear your side of this story. Perhaps this is all a terrible misunderstanding, but the only way we can hear your side and get to the bottom of this is if you agree to speak with us and perhaps answer some questions."

I lowered my head as if in deep thought, like I was on the verge of confessing all of my sins. "I guess you make sense," I said quietly.

Suddenly, Jay stood. "Oh, where are my manners? You used to be one of us after all." He motioned for me to stand. When I did so, he removed my handcuffs. I smiled obligingly and rubbed my wrists, the same way every suspect I'd ever arrested did when I removed their cuffs. In truth, my wrists didn't hurt. My ribs were in agony though and I could have desperately used some extra strength Tylenol. And my flask.

Oscar stood then. "I'm a little thirsty. Jay, Thomas, would you two like some coffee?"

"I believe I would," Jay replied. "How about you, Thomas?"

"Yes, I believe I would too. Black and hot please, Oscar." He feigned a smile at me before walking out of the office.

Jay stretched back and sighed. "You know, Thomas, this job has some tough days, but I'm sure you've had more than a few of your own tough days during your years with homicide, am I right?" I silently nodded. This was the part of the script where he was going to bond with me and reduce my resistance. Oscar was probably in the monitor room watching, waiting for his cue to reenter the room.

"During your career, how many of those cases have you had in what seemed to be a no-win situation, so you just did the best job you could?"

"Oh hell, Jay, I've had a few of those, more than I cared for. But, like you said, you do the best job you can and hope for the best."

"Yeah, I can see that in you. I've read your personnel file at least a dozen times. You've had a distinguished career. I must admit, I am somewhat envious. You've cracked some difficult cases and have some impressive arrest statistics."

It took a lot of self-control not to laugh at him. If he worked it much more, he was going to need some Vaseline and tissues.

"Thank you, sir," I said humbly. I had some other witty retorts, but was mindful of the video camera.

I rubbed my hands together and exhaled, as if I had come to a decision. "Jay, I mean Detective Sansing." I gave a short sigh. "You know, I've been calling you and Detective Marson by your first names. Maybe that's not appropriate. I apologize."

Jay held up his hand. "Listen, don't worry about that, Thomas. We're all on a first name basis here," he said with a placating smile. I returned his smile with a timid, hopeful one of my own.

"Okay, great." I cleared my throat. "Uh, before we get started, I'd like to ask some questions of you and Oscar, if you don't mind."

"Of course," Jay said. "We'll just wait for Oscar and we can answer together, would that be okay?" I nodded in agreement and mentally started counting down from ten. When I got to one, Oscar entered the door with three Styrofoam cups of coffee.

"Sorry I took so long, I had to find some cups." I nodded gratefully when he handed me one of them. I started to take a sip and then stopped suddenly.

"What's wrong, Thomas?" Jay asked.

"Uh, you guys aren't trying to slip me a roofie or something, are you?" Actually, I was wondering if Oscar had spit in my coffee. I caught him frowning, before he quickly smiled condescendingly, as if I were being paranoid.

"Here, let's swap," Jay said. I smiled gratefully and swapped coffee with him. I drank slowly and took my time, occasionally pausing and acting like I was trying to form a question, but would stop before speaking. I embellished my act with a masterful display of a conflicted frown.

"Take your time, Thomas, we're in no rush," Jay said. I gave him an appreciable gesture of understanding, finished half of my coffee and finally spoke.

"I know you two are assigned to the Office of Professional Accountability, and you've recently been assigned the task of investigating my wife's death. I guess I'm wondering why wasn't this case assigned to the homicide unit?" I asked.

"Well, since you were once a member of the homicide unit, it was decided to assign this case to the OPA in order to eliminate any perception of possible bias," Oscar said.

I nodded. "Well, that certainly makes sense. Please forgive me for saying this, but I only know a little about you guys and the quality of work the two of you do." I held a finger up to my face and tapped it once or twice. "Wait, that's not entirely true. I remember a couple of cases the two of you had. There was a sergeant who was soliciting minors through some kind of online chatroom, you two had that one, correct?"

"Yes we did, Thomas," Jay said. "It was a difficult case emotionally, but we had to act according to the law."

"Oh, I agree. And, there was one case I remember where a rookie officer beat the crap out of a smart-assed kid during a traffic stop." Jay nodded at this one as well.

"Another difficult case," Oscar added. I nodded thoughtfully, and the sat for a full two minutes staring at a speck of dirt on the wall before one of them spoke up.

"Thomas?" Jay asked. "Is there anything else you want to talk about before we get started?"

"Oh, I'm sorry, I must have zoned out for a minute. I think I'm suffering a concussion."

Jay's jaw suddenly tightened and he slowly turned in his chair. "What are you talking about?" he asked suspiciously.

"When I was taken into custody earlier, I was brutally beaten by an officer named Acevedo. I think I've got a concussion and some broken ribs. Would it be possible to go to the hospital? I'm not feeling so well."

Chapter 22

A new pair of officers transported me to one of the local emergency rooms. X-rays revealed two broken ribs. A CAT scan revealed no internal trauma to my brain, a testament to my hard headedness, but the doctor, a no-nonsense looking African American woman, commented about several knots on the back of my head. I asked her to please notate it on her report. She agreed without comment.

"May I ask one other favor from you?" I asked. "It may sound like an odd request." She arched an eyebrow questioningly. "Would it be possible for you to order blood work and test for drugs and alcohol?"

She stared at me for several long seconds before responding. "Are you scheming, Mister Ironcutter?" she asked.

I tried to give her my friendliest smile. "Certain people will sometimes make claims which aren't true. Claims like, the suspect was high on drugs and very combative. Claims like that." She continued staring at me a moment and then left the small room. One of the officers overheard what I said. I recognized him, but we had been acquaintances only. He saw me looking and winked. I guess that meant my secret was safe. A minute later, a nurse came in and drew blood.

It was a typical visit to the ER; two hours of waiting for about ten minutes of face time with the doctor. When I was discharged, I was escorted directly to the booking room this time. The media was no longer present. They'd lost interest and moved on to their next story.

"I'm surprised the detectives aren't here waiting on me," I said out loud. One of the officers chuckled.

"Your attorney has already spoken to them. No interviews. We're to serve the warrant and book you in." I nodded in understanding.

My bond was set at a million dollars. It seemed ridiculously high, as if somebody had made a phone call to the magistrate and asked for a favor. The patrol officers handed me off to the Davidson County deputies, who ran the jail. They took my mug photo, printed me and then had me shower, which was nice. Well, with the exception of two of them watching me soap up, and then a trustee issued me an oversized orange outfit, complete with matching orange shoes. I looked ridiculous. A deputy with sergeant's stripes on his sleeves approached me as I was being issued a blanket, pillow, towel, toothpaste and a child's sized toothbrush.

"Due to your injuries and past employment, you're going to be kept in isolation. You'll be let out for thirty minutes every day to shower and shave."

"Sounds good, Sergeant," I replied.

He snorted. "After a couple of days, you'll be going stir crazy."

"So, throw me a paperback if you're inclined, I promise you won't hear a peep out of me." He eyed me a moment and then led me to my temporary home, a very small cell with a combination sink and toilet made out of stainless steel and a concrete pad with a thin foam mattress thrown on top of it.

"Roll on four!" he shouted. A second later, a reinforced steel door with a large black number four stenciled on it began moving and slammed shut with a loud bang. I set the blanket and pillow down and sat wearily. There was no way I was going to be able to raise enough money for bail, so I was stuck here, probably until the jury trial, which could take as long as a year or more before the case was heard.

"Well, this sucks," I muttered as I looked around at my new home. I was pondering my situation when I heard footsteps outside of my cell door. There was a small rectangular piece of reinforced glass at about eye level, but I didn't bother getting up to see who it was. A moment later, a paperback book was shoved through the slot in the lower portion of the door. I stood and saw the sergeant looking through the thick glass at me. I nodded in appreciation.

Retrieving the book, I read the title. It was A Tale of Two Cities. I'd read it before, several years ago, and I didn't much care for it. But, beggars can't be choosers. I made myself comfortable and turned to the first page.

After a while, I stood and stretched. Pain shot through my side and I grimaced. My ribs were going to be a severe detriment if I had call to defend myself. A fellow inmate may be harboring a grudge against me specifically, or, more likely it'd be a case of one of these thugs with a hatred of cops, even ex-cops, and looking to improve their rep. I hoped I wasn't going to be released into the general population anytime soon.

About an hour into my first day, I heard a buzzer. Little did I know how many times I was going to dream about that damn buzzer over the next few years, but at this particular moment, I had no idea what it meant. I stood and looked out of the window. A wiry trustee with lots of tatts, long stringy hair and equally long beard was pushing a dinner cart around to each cell, pausing to push a tray through the slots in the doors. When he got to my cell, he looked at me a long moment before pushing the tray in. My meal consisted of a sandwich, a small scattering of potato chips and a carton of milk. I noticed the trusty was still staring at me. He looked a little bit like Charles Manson, but without the idiotic swastika carved into his forehead. He motioned down toward the slot. I cautiously leaned down to see what he wanted.

"Duke said the two of you are friends. That true?" he asked through the slot.

"I'd like to think so, yeah," I answered. It figured Duke had acquaintances in lock-up and would already know about my arrest.

"No talking to the inmates, Flaky." A deputy who was monitoring the meal distribution admonished the trustee. Flaky stood, looked at me a moment longer and then continued on to the next cell. He came back a couple of minutes later and shoved an extra carton of milk through the slot.

It was not until the next morning when I received a visit. But instead of Sherman, it was William. I really wanted to speak to Sherman, not his grandson.

"How's it going, big guy?" he asked.

“I’d be a lot better if you and the old man can get me out of here,” I replied, but from the look on his face, I knew it wasn’t going to happen.

“The judge denied our motion for reduced bond. The preliminary hearing is set for the day after tomorrow.”

“Seems quick,” I commented. William nodded.

“Normally, it would be, but Anna and that little nerd have come up with all kinds of stuff. Did you know they got ahold of a copy of the original murder file?” I nodded but offered no explanation. “Yeah, and that’s just a part of it. They’ve found some really significant information. Gramps is feeling confident.”

“So, why isn’t he here?”

William shrugged apologetically. “The last time he visited an inmate, he caught pneumonia. He’s avoided jails and prisons ever since. He said you’d understand.” He waited for a response. Instead, I acted like I was going to sneeze. I would’ve followed through with it, but any sudden movement caused my ribs to cry out in agony.

William stared at me warily. “Anyway, let me show you a picture.” He reached into a manila folder and pulled out a mugshot. It was of a rough-looking woman, about my age. “Do you know her?” I shook my head. “Positive?” he pressed.

“I suppose it’s possible I’ve come into contact with her during the course of my duties, back when I was a cop, but I couldn’t swear to it.”

“Never had a relationship with her?” William asked.

“Oh, hell no,” I replied. Seemingly satisfied with my response, he put the photograph back into the folder.

“Okay, Gramps said to tell you not to tell anyone about this picture. It’s going to be a surprise,” he said with a cryptic smile.

“Is she the mystery witness?”

“Yeah, but don’t worry about that. We’re going to make mincemeat out of her.” He chuckled, like it was an inside joke.

“Tell me about Anna,” he suddenly asked.

“Uh, not much to tell. She’s a typical twenty-something-year-old. A little aimless at the moment, but I’m sure she’ll figure it all out.”

“She said she had some trouble with an ex-boyfriend.”

"Yeah, he's been arrested. Don't know when it's going to trial."

"So, she's single? You're not dating her, are you?"

"I'm not dating her, and no, I'm not sleeping with her. Now, can we focus back on my case?" I asked with growing exasperation.

William responded by snapping his briefcase shut. "The old man has it all planned out," he said standing.

"Is that supposed to make me feel better?"

"We've got it covered," William said, grinning. "Trust me." He started to shake my hand, but then his grin vanished and he quickly pulled it back. I guess he was thinking about germs and pneumonia.

Chapter 23

Sherman Goldman was well known in the legal community. He'd been practicing law since before most of them were out of diapers. He seldom appeared in court anymore, but in his day, he was highly respected for his deep knowledge of the law and his courtroom skills. He'd started out in criminal defense. That led to being hired as a junior associate at a well-established law firm which specialized mostly in contract law but needed someone like Sherman to round out their portfolio. Sherman became a senior partner within five years.

None of his children went into the legal profession, preferring other endeavors. One is a neurosurgeon, one works on Wall Street, and, as far as I know, William's mother quit working the day she got married. William was the only grandchild who followed in Sherman's footsteps, so he'd become Sherman's de facto shining legacy. He was good, a little too arrogant at times, but he was smart enough to listen to his grandfather whenever the man spoke.

It'd been three days since my arrest. The sergeant who was in charge of the segregation unit took pity on me and let me have another paperback, an old Sherlock Holmes novel. He even allowed Flaky and I to talk, which was nice. Sitting in solitary was enough to drive a man crazy.

Finally, on the morning of the third day, the door clanged open and a deputy informed me I had court and to get my ass moving. Several of us were lined up and walked through various security doors and through a corridor that led to a secure holding room adjacent to the courtrooms. I got several looks, some curious, some hostile, but I ignored them all. I didn't make eye contact, but I watched every one of them, wary of a possible attack.

"It's a crowded house today, gents," one of the deputies said when he came through the security door from the courtroom. It was a given the media would be in attendance for the preliminary hearing, so William filed a successful motion for me to be able to wear a suit during the proceedings. There wasn't a changing room, I had to put it on in front of all of my cellies. There were a couple of snide comments, but I ignored them.

The judge entered the courtroom precisely at nine o'clock. The holding room was noisy, but when the bailiff called the court to order, the inmates became quite. We all listened to the calling of the docket. Inmates were shuffled in and out as their case came up. There were some plea agreements reached, and there were some rescheduling requests made by defense attorneys who like to use this strategy. It forced victims and eyewitnesses to take another day off of work to come to court. If they got it continued enough times, most people quit coming back and the case would be dismissed. It was a shitty tactic, but they all used it and the judges allowed it.

I was finally escorted into the courtroom by two burly deputies a little after ten o'clock. All eyes in the courtroom turned toward me, which meant all noses were pointed at me. I imagined I felt a collective exhalation and a memory of the Dickens character Charles Darnay came to mind when he was being tried for treason.

I was pleasantly surprised to see both Sherman and William present. I'd originally believed only William was going to be representing me. He was up to the task, but still, seeing the old man raised my spirits exponentially.

I pointedly ignored the crowd and cast a quick glance over at the prosecution table as I sat down. The Deputy District Attorney himself was sitting there, along with two subordinates, one of them being the fat guy, ADA Diff Reichman. He glanced at me briefly, but when he saw me looking, he hurriedly buried his nose in his legal pad. I wondered which one of them would actually be presenting the State's case.

"Hello, Thomas, how are you?" Sherman asked with a warm smile as he shook my hand. William greeted me next. I knew they were acting for the news cameras that were currently pointed toward us. I went along with it.

"I'm okay," I responded and gave them a confident smile.

I heard someone loudly clear their throat and looked behind me. It was Anna and Ronald. They must have come early and found a spot on the front row. Anna had on a very nice dress, and even

Ronald was in a well-fitting suit. It looked new, but he was wearing one of my ties. Anna did a good job dressing him. He was pale and looked like he was as nervous as a long-tailed cat in a room full of rocking chairs. I almost turned back around when I saw Simone, quietly sitting in the back row. She gave me a small, hopeful wave. I must admit, it made me feel giddy inside.

Reluctantly, I turned back to Sherman. "How's it looking?" I asked, keeping my voice low.

Sherman looked around the courtroom and waved pleasantly to several people before answering me in the same low voice. "Look at those three over there. They're all so very smug, aren't they?" he asked, but didn't wait for an answer. He made a subtle gesture toward the head District Attorney. "I still remember when that scrub was struggling through law school." He turned toward me now and gave me a light-hearted slap on the back.

"Your two partners behind you have done some magnificent field work," he said with a hint of admiration in his voice and leaned toward me. "Now you sit back, relax, and watch the master in action." He winked and grinned like a mischievous school boy. Our conversation was cut off by the court officer beginning the proceedings with a harsh bellowing of the announcement of the case.

"Case number fifteen dash four, zero, zero, seven. In the matter of the State of Tennessee versus Thomas Ironcutter, the charge being first degree murder. All parties intending to testify step forward so you may be sworn!"

I watched as four people stood and stepped forward. Two of them were Oscar and Jay. The third was a woman who was dressed in scrubs. Doctor Holly Gross, a pale ginger about my age, looked like she rarely went out in the sun. She'd been working with the Medical Examiner's Office for the last ten years. We knew each other well, but today she avoided eye contact.

The last person was the woman I saw in the photograph. She was close to my age, maybe slightly younger, but the years had been rough on her. Her dyed black hair was tied up in a bun, I assume it was supposed to make her look prim and innocent, along with the new dress she was wearing. But, it didn't look right, like the dress knew it didn't belong on her. She might have been attractive once, but those days were long gone.

I instantly knew she was Brittany Long, their key witness, and I was certain now; I'd never seen her before.

Holly testified first. At the direction of Diff, she stated she was the person who performed the autopsy and confirmed Marcia had died of a single gunshot wound to the head, and then the fetus died as a result of oxygen deprivation. Her testimony lasted less than ten minutes and Sherman chose not to cross-examine her. She stood and walked out without even looking at me.

Detective Oscar Marson was next. Once he was seated, Diff took a deep breath. He hastened another brief glance at me, gathered himself and then attempted to put on a stately air before beginning his questioning.

"Please state your name and occupation."

"My name is Oscar Marson. I'm employed with the Metropolitan Nashville Police Department and I am currently a detective assigned to the Office of Professional Accountability."

"Detective, in May of this year, were you assigned to investigate the death of Marcia Breedlove Ironcutter?" Diff queried.

"That is correct," Oscar answered.

"Would you please describe to the court the facts and circumstances of this action? And, if you will, start from the beginning."

"To begin, on the night of February 1st, 2014, police were called to the scene of a shooting. The location was a residence located at 4779 Front Runner Road. The house was a two-story, single occupancy home located in a residential neighborhood. The decedent was located in the den of the home. She had sustained a single gunshot wound to the head. The decedent was identified as Marcia Breedlove Ironcutter, the wife of the defendant, Thomas Ironcutter Junior. An investigation was conducted by members of the homicide unit. As a result of their investigation, they concluded the probable cause of death was a suicide."

"I have a series of photographs of the scene. Could you identify them please?" The District Attorney handed copies of the photographs to Sherman and then walked up to the stand and placed the original photos in front of Judge Watling. Watling looked them over and nodded. Diff then handed them to Oscar.

"Yes, these are the original photographs. The crime scene technician and the detectives signed the back of the photographs. In addition, they were also downloaded and stored electronically at 0300 hours on February 2nd of 2014." The questioning stopped a moment while they went through the process of entering the photographs into court exhibits. Diff waited patiently until the bailiff was finished before continuing.

"So, the original detectives concluded the death of the victim was a suicide."

"Yes."

"What, if anything, changed?" he asked.

"Approximately six months later, an anonymous tip came in through the Crime Stoppers hotline. The tipster advised the suicide was in fact a murder." Oscar looked over at me smugly. "I happened to have been the detective manning the hotline on that date. I took the call."

Diff retrieved a piece of paper from the table. "I have the original Crime Stoppers tip sheet. Will you inspect it and confirm this is the sheet you filled out?" Diff approached the witness stand and went through the similar motions as he did with the photographs. The other Assistant District Attorney handed over a copy of the tip sheet to William. Sherman barely acknowledged it while he sat with his fingers interlaced.

"It is one and the same tip sheet I filled out." The tip sheet was dutifully admitted into evidence.

"Detective Marson, what happened, if anything, as a result of this tip?"

"The case was reopened and a fresh investigation was conducted," Oscar said.

Diff continued his questioning. "And during the course of this investigation, were there any new details learned as a result of this investigation?"

"Yes, during the first investigation, Thomas Ironcutter advised he was at his office during the time of his wife's death." This was hearsay, and I wondered why Sherman or William wasn't objecting. They didn't, and I suppressed the urge to kick one of them in the shins.

Oscar continued. "As a result of the secondary investigation, it was proven that in fact, Thomas Ironcutter was never at the office during the time frame in which the death occurred. He made a false statement regarding his alibi." A small murmur ran through the crowd at this tidbit.

"In fact, Thomas Ironcutter had no alibi as to his whereabouts during the time period when his wife was shot to death. Would that be a correct statement, Detective?"

"It would," Oscar replied.

"Has Thomas Ironcutter ever provided a credible alibi for his location on the night and time of his wife's death?" Diff asked.

"Not to my knowledge, sir," Oscar responded.

"How did the investigation proceed after this discovery?"

"Detective Ironcutter was disempowered and relieved of duty. When he was asked to undergo a formal interview and polygraph testing…"

William shot to his feet. "Objection! Your Honor, the state is attempting to interject immaterial evidence and testimony into this proceeding." He looked pointedly at the prosecution table. "They are playing to the cameras, your Honor."

"Objection sustained." Judge Watling peered over his bifocals at ADA Reichman. "Be very careful with your line of questioning, sir. I expect nothing but professionalism from you."

"I'm sorry, your Honor," Diff said glibly. "I'll rephrase the question. Detective, did Thomas Ironcutter cooperate with the ensuing investigation?"

"No, sir," Oscar replied quickly and looked pointedly at me.

"In fact, rather than face any further questioning, he resigned from the police department, is that correct?" Diff asked.

"Objection!" William said again. "Unless Detective Marson can prove he is a mind reader, his answer would be purely speculative as to the defendant's state of mind."

"Sustained," Judge Watling said curtly.

Diff acted as if the question had never been asked. "Detective, what happened then, if anything?"

"Unfortunately, very little. The few investigative leads that were available were pursued, but they were all dead ends. The case languished."

"I see. Now, have there been recent events in this investigation? Events which led you to obtain a warrant for the arrest of Thomas Ironcutter?"

"Yes," Oscar answered.

Diff held his palm up. "Please explain."

"A person came forward and admitted to being present when Thomas Ironcutter murdered his wife." There was a collective gasp in the courtroom and now the murmuring became louder. Judge Watling pounded his gavel for silence.

"It is my understanding both you and Detective Jay Sansing interviewed the witness extensively, correct?"

"That would be correct," Oscar responded.

"As a result of your interview, did you determine how she knew the defendant?"

"Yes."

"How?" Diff asked.

"They met one night in a bar, became friends and the friendship led to an illicit affair."

It was a clever way of circumnavigating the hearsay rule. William was about to stand and object, but Sherman put his hand on William's arm. For some reason, Sherman wanted that information to come out. Why, I had no idea because it was a lie. The old man was definitely up to something.

"I see. Now, Detective, in the course of your investigation, did you do anything to confirm the credibility and veracity of this witness?"

"Yes. A competent detective will corroborate any and all information provided by a person who claims to be an eyewitness to a crime, especially murder."

"And did you do so with this lady?"

"We did," Oscar said.

"How?"

"One of the things we did was to have her write a statement, including a detailed description of the Ironcutter home. We also asked her to draw a diagram of the house. This was done to, among other things, test the veracity of her statement. Every detail she wrote about was correct, right down to the color of the sheets on the bed. I have her handwritten statement here. It is signed by the witness and notarized." Detective Oscar Marson removed several sheets of lined paper out of his file while ADA Diff Reichman nodded in gloating satisfaction.

"If it pleases the court, I would like to now call this person, a Miss Brittany Long." Diff turned toward the audience, specifically the cameras, with an air of smugness. Oscar stood and started to walk off of the witness stand.

"Sit back down, Detective," Judge Watling boomed. He had a deep resonating baritone voice and sounded like James Earl Jones with a southern twang. "General Reichman, if you are through questioning the witness, he will now be available to the defense for cross-examination. Then, and only after I dismiss the witness, may you call another witness."

Diff turned beet red at the admonishment. He cleared his throat. "My apologies, your Honor." He turned toward us briefly. "Your witness," he said.

Sherman stood and walked to the podium which stood in between the counsel tables.

"Good morning, Detective, my name is Sherman Goldman. I am representing Thomas Ironcutter."

Oscar didn't bother to respond and merely stared at Sherman. Sherman was nonplussed and held up a finger.

"I want to go back a little bit. You were not involved in the original investigation, is that correct?"

"Yes," Oscar answered in a tone suggesting Sherman was wasting his time.

"In fact, the two original detectives have since retired, is that correct?"

"Yes. One is now living in Belize, the other is deceased."

"I see. So, this case is now under the purview of yourself and Detective Jay Sansing?"

"Yes, that's correct," Oscar replied.

"Please describe for the court the object you have brought with you to the witness stand."

Oscar looked a little confused, and then he realized Sherman was referring to the thick notebook sitting on the stand before him.

"Are you referring to this?" Oscar asked, holding up the notebook.

"Yes," Sherman answered.

"It is a copy of the case file."

"Excellent," Sherman said and paused a moment. "You mentioned earlier of the actions a competent detective would take. As a competent detective, you have thoroughly reviewed the case file, correct?" Sherman asked.

"You are correct and I have done so, many times." Oscar responded.

"Excellent. Before I continue, I'd like to ask you, Detective, since you've already mentioned competency, would a competent detective, one who has been assigned a very important case, would said competent detective take detailed notes of all things pertinent to the investigation?" Sherman asked.

Oscar paused and stared, wondering what Sherman was up to.

"Yes, if it is pertinent to the case." He looked at the judge. "But a detective cannot be expected to be bogged down taking notes of minutiae."

"I understand, Detective, so I won't be bothering with minutiae, we'll stick with the important information. As you testified earlier, you are in fact the person who answered the anonymous Crime Stoppers tip two years ago. How is your memory regarding that call?"

"Pretty good. I wrote down everything he said. Everything the caller said."

"Oh, you just answered my next question, the caller was a male?"

"Well, yes. But as a matter of policy, we do not ask any questions which might identify the caller, nor do we notate any information which might possibly identify the caller."

"I understand. Very good. We'll talk about this male caller more at a later time. Let's now concentrate on what you testified to earlier. You advised a person came forward who is alleged to have firsthand knowledge pertaining to the death of Marcia Ironcutter, is that correct?"

"Yes."

"What is her name?"

"Her name is Brittany Long."

"I see. Please go to your first report regarding this person identified as Ms. Brittany Long." Sherman waited while Detective Marson found the report. He held it up and waited expectantly.

"Are your investigative reports detailed and accurate, Detective?" Sherman asked.

"I'd like to think so," Oscar replied.

"Excellent. I would like for you to read aloud to the court, from your investigative report, how exactly you or Detective Sansing first learned of the existence of Brittany Long," Sherman directed.

Oscar looked concerned and shuffled through his reports for a long minute. "I don't believe I have that with me." Oscar's voice was a bit quieter now.

"Why, Detective, that information is important, is it not? She did not magically appear out of thin air one day. Or, did she? Is she an imaginary character, Detective?" Sherman asked facetiously.

"I can assure you, Counselor, she is very real," Oscar said.

"But is she credible?" Sherman asked and then held up a hand. "Don't answer that just yet. Let's get back to my original question. We have agreed, you and I, a competent detective compiles thorough documentation of the information learned and the actions taken in an investigation. And yet, you have neglected, either by ineptness or by intentional design, to memorialize how it was discovered that a woman who identifies herself as Brittany Long had intimate knowledge of an alleged murder." Sherman stared pointedly at Oscar, who stared back silently.

"Very well, even though you have not documented this important information, please tell the court how you learned of Brittany Long."

"Brittany Long contacted police personnel and stated she had information about the murder of Marcia Breedlove Ironcutter," Oscar exclaimed. "We made contact with her and conducted a series of formal interviews. This is when we learned that not only was she intimately involved with the defendant, but she was present when he murdered his wife."

"Who are these police personnel she originally contacted? What are their names?" Sherman asked.

Detective Marson hesitated and looked over at the prosecution table.

Diff stood. "Your Honor, I must object. This is irrelevant to the case."

Judge Watling looked at Sherman. Sherman held out his hands. "Your Honor, it is very relevant. I am attempting to establish a foundation of the alleged eyewitness evidence, or perhaps a lack thereof. This goes not only to the credibility of Detective Marson's testimony, but the credibility of the charges altogether."

"Overruled," Judge Watling said evenly.

Sherman looked back at Oscar. "Please answer the question, Detective."

"We were referred to Brittany Long by the Commander of the OPA, Commander Bartlett."

"And how did he learn of this information?"

"What do you mean?" Oscar asked.

"Did Ms. Long make the initial contact with Commander Bartlett? Or perhaps someone contacted Commander Bartlett on behalf of Ms. Long? Please don't waste the court's valuable time, Detective. You know exactly what I'm getting at. Where did Ms. Long come from and who inserted her into this investigation?"

Oscar inhaled and let it out slowly before answering. "Commander Bartlett, my immediate supervisor contacted Detective Sansing and me. He informed us of the existence of Brittany Long. We proceeded from there."

"Ah yes, and based upon your communication with Commander Bartlett, please tell the court how he learned of this alleged witness."

"Counselor, I have no firsthand information to give you an answer without supplying hearsay information." I'm sure Oscar thought he was being very clever with that statement, but he was clueless.

"Ah, I see. Well then, please go to the case file and find the report from Commander Bartlett which documents the facts and circumstances of how he learned of Miss Long."

"There is no report," Oscar said in a tone of irritation.

"Oh? Commander Bartlett did not write a supplement report about this?"

"No."

"I see," Sherman said and looked over at his grandson.

William handed Sherman a couple sheets of paper. "Detective, I am holding a copy of Procedural Order ninety-seven dash one. It is an order establishing the Metro Police policy of report writing. You are familiar with it I assume?"

"Yes," Oscar answered.

Diff stood. "Relevance?" he asked.

"Goes to credibility," Sherman replied.

"Overruled," Judge Watling said.

"I'll hand you a copy of the policy if you need it," Sherman said. "But I think you are familiar with it enough to answer this question. Did Commander Bartlett violate departmental policy by not documenting information he learned of a possible eyewitness in an alleged murder? Yes or no, Detective." Sherman had changed the tone of his voice now. Gone was the pleasantness.

"I wouldn't know how to properly answer that question. He is my superior officer after all."

"You're a detective in the Office of Professional Accountability. You investigate officers when they violate departmental policies, correct?" Sherman pressed.

"It depends upon the nature of the violation."

Sherman nodded at William, who handed him some more paperwork.

"Detective, I am holding in my hand a disciplinary action of an investigation recently conducted by you. This is an investigation of an Officer Craig Schmittou. He apparently neglected to complete a supplement report in an unrelated case. Do you remember it?"

"Yes," Oscar responded and impulsively wiped his face.

"As a result of your investigation, this officer was in fact suspended for five days without pay, correct?"

"I believe that's correct," Oscar said after a moment's pause.

"Has Commander Bartlett been disciplined for his policy violation, the exact same policy violation in which Officer Schmittou received a five-day suspension?"

"No, not to my knowledge."

"Of course not, that would ruin the framework of this conspiracy, correct?"

"Objection!" Diff shouted as he jumped to his feet as quickly as his pudgy body would allow.

"I'll withdraw the question, your Honor. Maybe I'll readdress it in the future." Sherman returned to his pleasant disposition.

"Detective, I want to now ask you about this person who has identified herself as Brittany Long. My first question is: have you vetted her?"

"Yes, of course," Oscar answered quickly.

"Is Brittany Long her real name?" Sherman asked.

Oscar had been holding up fairly well during Sherman's cross examination, now his jaw dropped. "I believe she was married once, but this is her name now."

"What is her original, legal name?" Sherman pressed.

"Her maiden name was Simpson, but that was many years ago. She kept her husband's surname after her divorce."

"Has she ever been arrested?" Sherman asked.

Oscar shook his head. "Negative. We ran her credentials. She has no record in the United States and has never obtained a passport. She has never been arrested."

"Under the name of Brittany Long, you mean," Sherman said.

"Not under Brittany Long nor under Brittany Simpson. I checked personally," Oscar said adamantly. He felt like he was regaining control. I looked over at the prosecution table. They were whispering to each other now, trying to determine what Sherman had up his sleeve.

"Did you take her fingerprints?" Sherman asked.

"Of course not, there was no reason to," Oscar answered. He didn't see the trap Sherman was laying for him. I wondered if anyone else did.

Sherman smiled pleasantly. "Both you and Detective Sansing interviewed Brittany Long, correct?"

"Yes."

"Now, you mentioned earlier the measures you used to corroborate her statement and allegations, correct?"

"Correct."

"And I believe you stated you had her write a statement detailing the interior of the Ironcutter's home, and you even went as far as having her draw a diagram of the home, correct?" Sherman asked.

"Yes, correct," Oscar said. He was feeling comfortable again.

"Would you please go now to that particular section of your case file, Detective?"

Oscar turned a few pages. "Okay, I have it here."

Sherman remained at the podium. He had no notes in front of him. I've known the man for years and I've always been impressed with his memory and focus.

"Very good, sir. Now, if you would, look at the crime scene photograph of the back door." Oscar looked at him but then searched until he found the photo. "Please place the photo on that device beside you which allows the court to see it."

Oscar did as he instructed. The photograph was now visible on a projection screen mounted on a wall of the courtroom. The picture being displayed showed the back entryway of my former home. The doorway led into the kitchen. There was a flower pot lying askew on the floor with a sprinkle of dirt beside it.

"Direct your attention to the flower pot which appears to have been knocked over and describe what is shown," Sherman directed. Oscar tried to act casually as he looked at it.

"Okay," he said. "There is a generic clay flower pot. It looks like some kind of plant is in it. It appears to have been knocked over and there is a small amount of dirt on the floor, presumably having come from the flower pot when it was knocked over." He stared at it a moment longer and then looked questioningly at Sherman.

"Detective, please leave the photo on the view screen and direct your attention to the transcript of Brittany Long's first statement. Go to page four please and read aloud to the court the sentence in which Ms. Long describes the flowerpot."

Oscar turned to the appropriate page and began reading aloud. "After Thomas shot his wife, we hurried out of the back door. I guess Thomas wasn't paying attention because he accidentally kicked over a flower pot that was sitting by the door. I was careful where I stepped because I didn't want my shoeprints in the dirt." Oscar was about to continue reading, but Sherman stopped him.

"Detective, look at the photograph again please, specifically, the pattern of the dirt which was cast out of the pot upon the pot being kicked over. In which direction is the pattern of the dirt?" Sherman asked.Oscar paled in realization of what he was seeing.

"The dirt appears to have scattered out of the flower pot toward the interior of the kitchen."

"Someone knocked over the flower pot when they entered the residence, Detective, not when they were leaving. Would you agree with my assertion?"

Oscar instantly shook his head. "Not necessarily," he countered. "There could have been other variables involved, other scenarios."

Sherman frowned and cupped his chin in his hand before continuing. "How about this scenario, an officer is dispatched to the home of a fellow officer in which a woman is deceased. In the officer's haste to enter the residence, he accidentally knocks over a flower pot which had been placed by the door in order to catch the afternoon sun rays. Would that scenario be plausible, Detective?"

A few beads of nervous sweat had suddenly appeared on Oscar's brow. His lips moved, as if trying to formulate an answer, but no words came out.

Diff stood. "Your Honor, the question calls for speculation," he said.

"Sustained," Judge Watling said.

Sherman furrowed his brow. "Yes, I believe you're correct, it's a speculative question. Perhaps I can help Detective Marson so he does not have to speculate." Sherman turned and faced the audience.

"Officer Boone, are you present?" Officer Boone, who had been sitting on one of the side benches where officers sit, stood and waved slightly. There was a folded sheet of paper in his hand.

Sherman turned his attention back to Oscar. "Detective, do you see Officer Boone?"

"Yes."

"As I'm sure you are aware, Officer Boone was one of the first responding officers on that fateful night, would that be a correct statement?" Oscar looked puzzled.

"I'm not sure."

"In fact, Officer Boone wrote a detailed supplement report regarding his response and his actions at the scene. In the report, he even documented his faux pas when, in his haste to enter the house, he accidentally knocked over the flower pot. You should have a copy of it in your case file. Would you look for it please, sir?"

Oscar hurriedly scanned through the case file. He finally looked up and looked over at the District Attorneys worriedly before answering.

"I can't seem to locate it."

"Did someone remove it?" Sherman asked. Oscar didn't answer.

"Who did you get the case file from, Detective?" Sherman asked.

Oscar tugged at his tie and cleared his throat. "I made copies of the original, which was loaned to me from Commander Bartlett."

The courtroom again burst out in loud murmuring. Judge Watling pounded his gavel and the court officer demanded quiet.

Diff stood, again. If he kept it up, by the end of the day, he was going to be ten pounds lighter. "Your Honor, we object. The witness rule has been applied. Officer Boone has been sitting in the courtroom during the entire testimony."

Sherman listened attentively to Diff's objection and then turned toward the judge. "Your Honor, the state neglected to subpoena Officer Boone. I requested his presence merely as a possible rebuttal witness."

Judge Watling motioned. "Counsel, approach." The Goldman duo and the three District Attorneys approached the bench. There were several minutes of hushed discussion before they returned to their respective tables. Sherman returned to the podium. He turned and faced Officer Boone

"Officer, you are now scheduled to testify. Would you be kind enough to wait out in the hall, sir?" Officer Boone nodded, winked at me, and walked out.

Sherman waited for him to leave before resuming his cross examination. "Detective Marson, I now want to direct your attention to page sixteen of the same transcript."

Oscar looked hard at the District Attorneys before turning to the appropriate page.

"There are a series of questions directed toward Ms. Long and why she took so long to come forward with these allegations," Sherman said. "Do you see the section I am referring to?"

"Yes," Oscar answered. His tone was wary, suspicious. He sensed yet another discrepancy was about to be pointed out. I hoped he was stressed so much sweat was running down his butt crack.

"As a result of your questioning, what did you learn was her reason for withholding the information for so long, and for now coming forward?" Sherman asked.

"Objection, hearsay," Diff said.

"I am asking about information from the case file, your Honor. The case file which Detective Marson has brought to the witness stand."

"Overruled."

"Please answer the question, Detective."

"She was apparently in fear of her life. She believed Thomas would cause her bodily harm if she came forward, but her conscience finally got the better of her."

Sherman nodded. "I see. She gave no other explanation?"

"No, sir, it was explanation enough," Oscar said.

"Okay, now direct your attention to the next page..." Sherman was interrupted by Oscar.

"Excuse me, but how do you know what's in this case file? You haven't even filed discovery yet. This is a confidential file."

Oscar was in disbelief. He didn't want to believe a co-worker had more loyalty to me than to him or the department.

Sherman wagged a finger at him. "Now now, Detective. You know better than to ask questions from the witness stand. You are here to answer questions. Now, where were we? Oh yes, the next page of the transcript. You specifically asked Ms. Long if she had told anyone else about what she had allegedly witnessed on the night of February 1st, 2014, is that correct?"

"I did," Oscar replied tersely.

"That was an excellent question, Detective. What was Ms. Long's response?"

"Objection, hearsay," Diff said as he rose. "Ms. Long has not yet testified. Perhaps Mister Goldman can save these questions for her."

"Your Honor, during ADA Reichman's direct, he elicited hearsay information from this detective multiple times. He can't have his cake and eat it too."

"I'll allow it," Judge Watling said. "But, keep it to a minimum, counselor. And by minimum, this should be the last one."

Sherman nodded and refocused on Oscar.

"She stated she had kept it to herself."

"But, she finally divulged this information to someone, correct?"

"Yes," Oscar answered.

"Who was the first law enforcement personnel that she told?" Sherman asked quickly.

"It is my understanding she is a family friend to Assistant Chief Perry."

"I see. So, it was Assistant Chief Perry who identified Brittany Long as a witness in this case?"

Oscar instantly realized he'd been tripped up by Sherman. He'd been trying hard to keep Perry's name out of it. I'd bet a dollar to a doughnut he was told to do exactly that, but he messed up. I bet his crack was like Niagara Falls now.

"That is my understanding," he reluctantly admitted.

"Okay, perhaps we need to address that in more detail later, but I must admit you have confused me, Detective," Sherman said. "You earlier testified a male made the call to the Crime Stoppers hotline a little over two years ago, the very phone call you handled, and yet, Ms. Long stated, during a formal interview, she told no one about what she had supposedly witnessed. Since you yourself said you're a competent detective, I've no doubt you discovered this little discrepancy. My question to you is, how have you resolved this blatant contradiction?" Sherman looked expectantly at Oscar.

The amount of sweat on Oscar's brow increased, as well as his fidgeting. "Perhaps she told someone and forgot about it," he finally replied.

"Did you, or did you not follow-up on this discrepancy, Detective?"

Oscar didn't immediately answer. His eyes appealed to the DA's for help, but there was none forthcoming.

"No," he finally conceded. Of course you didn't, you incompetent bastard.

"Who directed you to swear out this warrant against the defendant?" Sherman asked quickly.

"After a meeting, I was directed by Commander Bartlett to obtain the warrant."

"Was Assistant Chief Perry present at this meeting?" Sherman pressed.

"Yes."

Sherman paused for a long ten seconds, his hands clasped behind his back. Judge Watling finally cleared his throat. Sherman looked at him and smiled.

"Your Honor, I have no further questions at this time." Sherman turned to make his way to his chair and sat.

Judge Watling turned toward the prosecution. "Redirect?"

They conferred in a huddle for a long ten seconds before Diff stood.

"No further questions."

The judge was about to excuse Oscar when Sherman suddenly stood. "Your Honor, at this time I would like to move to keep this witness available for further questioning."

"On what grounds?" Judge Watling asked.

"After the state rests, I possibly intend to recall Detective Marson." Oscar looked stunned at first, but then he could barely contain a baleful scowl.

The judge nodded. "Detective, you are to remain available for possible further testimony. You may remain in the courtroom, if you desire."

The prosecutors exchanged glances, wondering what Sherman was up to. I think they knew him well enough to realize he wasn't playing games, he had something up his sleeve.

Chapter 24

After Oscar's testimony, Judge Watling called for a thirty-minute lunch recess and returned to the bench precisely at twelve o'clock.

After court was called to order, the judge looked at ADA Reichman. "If there are no matters to discuss, you may call your next witness."

Diff turned toward the bailiff. "The state calls Brittany Long to the stand."

I had expected Jay Sansing to testify next, but they opted to not to. Perhaps they opted to keep him in reserve, depending on what Sherman did to Oscar.

The courtroom, which was even more crowded than before lunch, was deathly silent as Brittany entered through a side door and took the stand. I stared hard as she walked to the witness stand. She had freshly applied lipstick, but I caught the heavy odor of cigarette smoke as she walked by. I still did not recognize her and was fairly convinced I had never come into contact with her under any circumstances.

The opening questions were roughly the same as with Detective Oscar Marson. He asked for her to state her name, how old she was, where she lived, and then dived in to the main questions.

"Ms. Long, I direct your attention to the defendant." He paused and pointed a finger at me. "Do you know him?" he asked.

"Oh yeah," she replied. "We were lovers. I know him real well."

Diff paused for dramatic effect, letting this bombshell sink in. I knew I was being stared at by many members of the audience and possibly at least one TV camera, so I kept my composure. But, mentally I was wondering why this woman was lying. I may have spoken to someone one night while I was heavily in the cups and never remembered them, but I remembered every woman I'd ever had a relationship with. There weren't very many, and she wasn't one of them. Of that I was certain. The questioning continued.

"Good. Now, on the night of February 1st, 2014, do you recall the events of that night?"

"I most certainly do," Brittany replied quickly and then made a big show of shuddering. She'd never win any academy award.

"Please tell the court your memories leading up to that night."

She took a deep breath before responding. "Well, he'd been very upset with his wife and told me all kinds of nasty things about her. One night, we was lying in bed at my place and he started talking about her again and going on and on about how she was an evil bitch. I said he should go ahead and divorce her, but he said it'd cost him too much money. So we talked some more and he said he wanted to kill her, but he needed my help to make it look like a suicide."

It was more hearsay, all lies of course, but it was damaging. I wondered why Sherman was allowing it.

"When did this conversation occur?" Diff asked.

"It was a week before he killed her," Brittany replied. I glanced at Sherman. He remained stoic. I started to write on his notepad, but he placed his hand on top of mine and subtly patted it. I wasn't sure what was going on in his mind, but I sure hoped he knew what he was doing.

"Alright, how did he convince you to go along with his plan?"

"He said he needed me because it was the only way he could get away with it. He was going to park his car a few miles away and he wanted me to drive him back and help him in case something went wrong." She made a show of how the memories were troubling her, poured herself a glass of water and slurped some of it down before continuing.

"I didn't want to do it and I told him so. Then he told me he'd kill me if I didn't help him." Brittany finished her sentence with another dramatic shudder and then dabbed at her dry eyes with a tissue.

Diff continued. "So, what happened then, if anything, on that fateful night?"

"Well, on that night, he had me meet him at a Walmart parking lot a couple of miles away from his house. He drove up at about eight o'clock. He jumped in my car and told me to drive down a street where there was a house with all of the lights off. He told me he knew who lived there and they weren't home. So, we parked and got out and walked through his back yard and in through the back door. When we walked in, she was sitting in a chair in the den. She saw us and got real scared, she must have known something was wrong. She got up and tried to run. Thomas ran after her and grabbed her in a bear hug. She must have fainted or something because she went limp. He put her in the chair. He held her with one hand and pulled his gun out with his other hand." She wrinkled her eyes up now, as if the memory was traumatic.

"He shot her in the head."

"What happened next, if anything?" Diff asked gently.

The shuddering stopped as quickly as it came upon her. She seemed to have regained her composure rather quickly as she answered the next question. "He put his gun in her hand. Then he took his holster off and dropped it on the floor beside the chair."

Diff directed the court officer to place one of the photographs on the projection screen. It showed my beautiful wife, sitting in one of our easy chairs, blood and brain matter oozing out of her head. A handgun was loosely grasped in her hand and the holster was lying on the floor beside the chair. It was the first time I had a look at any of the photographs of the scene. Once I'd discovered my wife, I was in shock. I refused to look at her and instead walked outside and called 911. I'd never viewed the photographs.

Until now.

Like a moth to a flame, I subconsciously leaned forward and looked closer at the pictures. The projection screen enlarged everything. It enlarged the handgun held in my wife's hand. I had always assumed at some point in time someone would ask why I had left my duty weapon at home when I supposedly went out on a police matter. I'm glad they didn't. The next picture was of my deceased wife, bigger than life, on the projection screen. I watched intently as Diff went through the photographs, asking this woman if this is what she saw on the night of my wife's death.

As I looked at the view screen, a slow explosion erupted throughout my soul and I tried to remain calm as I had an epiphany of how wrong I'd been, like a corrosive poison slowly coursing itself through my body. I slowly put my hands in my lap so nobody could see them trembling. I felt myself zoning out and reliving that night.

"What happened afterward?" Diff asked, jerking me back to reality. If he had asked any other questions, I didn't know.

"Well, it was kind of a blur for a few days after that. He said when things cooled down we were going to take a trip to Vegas and get married. We saw each other a few more times. Then, when he resigned from the police force, I started seeing less and less of him."

"When was the last time you saw him prior to today?" Diff asked.

"I guess about three months after he killed his wife. He'd stopped answering my calls, so I went to his house one night. He was there with another woman. He told me to get the fuck out of his life, excuse my French, and if I ever told anybody about what we did, he'd kill me. So, I didn't breathe a word about it until recently." She looked at the judge. "I've been trying to get closer to Christ, so I knew I had to do the right thing." She gave her best angelic expression when she said it. It almost sounded convincing, but only if you were an imbecile.

"This must have been very stressful for you," Diff said consolingly. She nodded.

"Have you ever told anyone about this?" Diff asked.

She nodded. "Yeah."

Diff waited for her to elaborate, but instead she stared at him blankly. He finally took the cue. "Whom have you told about this terrible crime?"

"Well, I met Raymond a few years ago."

"Are you referring to Assistant Chief of Police Raymond Perry?" Diff asked.

"Yeah. He seemed like a good man, so when I decided to tell what I knew, I instantly thought of him, so I called him," she said.

"Have you told anyone else?"

"It's possible I have mentioned it by accident. I can't tell you who or when, but it's possible," she said.

Someone had coached her during the lunch break. I glanced over at Oscar. He was staring straight ahead.Coaching a witness to intentionally lie. What bullshit. Any ideations I'd previously had of this man simply trying to diligently perform his duties to his utmost abilities went out the window. This man was dirty.

Diff conferred with his colleagues for a moment. "Your witness," he said confidently.

Sherman stood stiffly, not unusual for an elderly man who'd been sitting in an uncomfortable chair too long, and walked to the podium. "When ADA Reichman asked you to state your name, you replied, Brittany Long. May I call you Brittany?"

"If you want," she replied.

"Is Brittany Long your real name? Your legal name?"

A hint of a scowl was starting on her face. "Yeah, it is. Why?"

"Please madam, I know you've been coached extensively, I hope they mentioned you do not ask the questions when you are on the witness stand, you answer them."

Diff stood stiffly, in much the same way Sherman had, but he was at least thirty years younger than Sherman. "Your Honor, who is playing to the cameras now?"

"I'm sure you can prove him wrong on redirect, General. Continue, Counselor," Judge Watling said.

"Have you ever been arrested?" Sherman asked.

"No," she replied a little too quickly. Her wary scowl was back, and it did nothing to enhance her looks.

"You are aware that you are under oath, I trust?"

"Yeah, so?" She was scowling with more intensity now.

"So, madam, in the short time you have been on the stand, you have perjured yourself from the start. Let's start with the simple things. What is your legal name?"

Diff stood again. "Your Honor, counsel is badgering the witness. He has asked the question, and she has answered it."

Judge Watling looked at Sherman. "Counselor?" he asked.

"Perhaps I should rephrase my question," Sherman said and looked over at Diff. "Thank you for helping." He then turned to William, who in turn handed Sherman two files.

"May I approach?" Sherman asked.

"Approach," Judge Watling said as he motioned for Diff to come up as well. Sherman whispered something and handed Judge Watling a manila file folder. The judged perused it and then handed it to Diff. There was some more whispering and then the two men walked back to their respective positions.

"For the record, I have just handed ADA Reichman a file containing the criminal record of a woman named Sherry Ann Simpson."

I looked over at the prosecution. All three of them were looking at the file.

Sherman refocused on Brittany Long. "That record is of you," he said. "So, here we are, Miss Simpson, Miss Sherry Ann Simpson."

She scrunched up her face like she was confused.

"Are you still refusing to admit your legal name is Sherry Ann Simpson? I have mug photos of you right here, along with your fingerprints. It'll be a simple matter to resolve this, if you like. We can bring a fingerprint technician in here. They can compare your prints to these prints of Sherry Simpson and have an answer rather quickly."

"That's not me anymore," she contended.

Sherman was not amused. "Really? What name did you have it changed to, Sherry Ann Colemont perhaps?" Sherman glanced at his copy of the file with his bifocals and looked at Sherry. "That seems to be one of the several aliases you've used when you were arrested."

Sherman glanced at the file again. "Quite the list of arrests here. Drug charges, prostitution, theft, the list is lengthy. So Sherry, please clear the air. State your full legal name for the record."

"Okay, it *was* Sherry Simpson, but I had my name legally changed. I've started my life over since I've been saved and accepted Jesus into my soul," she retorted. There was a hushed guffaw from somewhere in the audience.

"Where did you have you name legally changed? There is no record of it. In fact, the only records we've been able to find are these." Sherman held out his hand to the waiting papers in William's outstretched hand.

"I have a birth certificate and a marriage license for Brittany Ann Simpson. The marriage license indicates she married a gentleman with the surname of Long. And," he turned to the last page. "This is a death certificate for Brittany Ann Simpson Long.

It appears she was the victim of a fatal car accident." Sherman now focused a steely eyed stare at the woman on the witness stand. "How long have you been illegally using your deceased sister's name, Miss Simpson?"

"I don't know, a little while, but it's not illegal, she's dead," she said.

"Yes, I can see how much her death upsets you," Sherman quipped. He turned toward the prosecutors, which also gave the news cameras a good profile shot.

"We have now identified two lies you have told, Ms. Simpson. You lied about your name, and you lied when you stated you have never been arrested. Let's move on to another statement you made. You testified earlier that one week prior to the death of Marcia Ironcutter, you were lying in bed with Thomas when the two of you conspired to murder his wife. Is that correct?"

"Yeah, but there was no conspiring, Thomas planned it all and made me go along." There was another chuckle in the back of the courtroom. Judge Watling glared at the offender.

Sherman continued. "And let's see, when you were interviewed by Detectives Marson and Sansing, you told them you were in fear of your life, and so you never told a soul until your meeting with the Assistant Chief of Police, Raymond Perry."

"I said I don't think I told anyone," she retorted.

Sherman shook his head in admonishment. "You were recorded, madam. You said specifically you never told a soul. But, no matter, let's move on. They asked you to write a statement describing the house, along with drawing a diagram."

"Yeah, and I may have been wrong about the flower pot," she volunteered. Now Judge Watling cast a baleful stare at Oscar, who remained stoic, but the beads of sweat on his forehead were magically reappearing.

"I'm sorry, madam, what flower pot are you talking about?" Sherman asked innocently.

"The flower pot that was knocked over. I thought Tim had knocked it over, but I think I overheard someone say it was knocked over and just figured he'd done it when he ran out of the house."

"I see. Are you aware the defendant's name is Thomas and not Tim?" Sherman asked. There were added guffaws in the audience now, but the only response from her was a confused expression, like Sherman had revealed to her the earth wasn't flat.

"Detective Marson thought you may have been confused. I'm certainly glad he helped you clear that up," Sherman said glibly.

She nodded. "Yeah."

"You also told them you had never been arrested. You lied to them, and you have lied in court. I want to know why? What would it have mattered?"

"Because he said nobody would believe me otherwise," she blurted.

"Who told you that, dear?" Sherman asked.

"Raymond. I mean, Chief Perry." She frowned and pointed at Sherman. "You're trying to confuse me and twist my words around."

"Not at all, madam, I'm trying to get you to tell the truth," Sherman replied.

"I am telling the truth," she said forcefully.

"Are you? Let me ask you, Sherry, where were you lying in bed with Thomas Ironcutter on the night the two of you allegedly plotted to kill his wife?"

"We were in my bed," she said.

Sherman pressed. "Where were you living then?"

"I was living – I don't remember exactly. I've moved around a lot over the years."

"But it was somewhere in Nashville?" he pressed.

"Yeah," she said and looked at Oscar, as if he'd tell her what to say next.

"And it was exactly one week to the day before the murder?"

She nodded her head. "Yeah, I remember positively."

"Hmm, I am a little confused, madam. Perhaps you can clear it up for me. How could you have been in bed with Thomas Ironcutter one week before the death of his wife, when he was in Miami, Florida interviewing a murder suspect?"

While she sat there looking dazed and confused, Sherman looked over at the District Attorneys. "My very able grandson has a copy of the video in which our client is interviewing a young man in the Dade County jail if you need it. It has a date and time stamp on the recording."

He didn't wait for a response and turned back to Sherry Simpson, Brittany Long, whatever the hell her name was. "Please answer the question, madam."

She looked over at Oscar again. He was staring at a spot on the wall behind her and refused to acknowledge her. "I may be a little off on the exact date," she stammered.

"Ah, some more confusion when confronted with the truth." Sherman looked pointedly at Oscar. "Perhaps you had poor coaching in that little fact." There was a small murmur in the crowd, which made me want to believe they were on my side now.

Sherman paused. He looked around, looked at me and smiled in a fatherly kind of way. I wished right then he was my father. Sherman then looked at the witness. She was shaking slightly.

"I want to go back to a statement you made earlier in your testimony. You said approximately six months after the death of Marcia Ironcutter, you went to the defendant's house and confronted him. You asked him why he was ignoring you."

"Yeah, that's the night he threatened to kill me." She glanced toward me and stared at me as if she were a woman scorned. "And he had another woman in there with him."

"Was it his house or your apartment you were at?" he asked.

"It was his house, the same house where he killed his wife. I already said that."

"Madam, would it interest you to know, Thomas sold his home two weeks after the death of his wife? He wasn't living there at the time you claim to have confronted him." Sherman looked at the woman for a long minute. She stared back, still defiant, but I could see her throat reddening.

"Madam, you are claiming, under oath, that you took part in a murder, a murder which did not happen. Why?"

Her resolve was weakening. "It's the right thing to do," she said with a slight tremble in her voice.

"You have testified you were an accomplice in an alleged murder, do you realize you could go to prison?" he asked pointedly.

She shook her head vigorously now. "Oh no, he made a deal with me," she declared and pointed at the Deputy District Attorney.

Sherman shook his head slowly. "You've been caught in several lies, madam. You have perjured yourself, starting when you gave a fake name. He is now under no obligation to keep his promise of any kind of deal he might have made with you. If you notice, he's not jumping up and down in protest." Sherman sighed. "Dear, tell us why you're telling this wild story. Tell us the truth."

She looked wildly around. Seeing no hopes of rescue, she stood, knocking over her glass of water. "I'm taking the fifth!" she blurted.

Sherman stared at her for a couple of seconds, puts his head down, and turned toward the judge.

"Your Honor, may it please the court, the maxim: *fraud vitiates all transactions* nullifies any pretrial agreement with the District Attorney General as to any testimonial evidence, transactional or otherwise, by this witness adduced in this matter. Also, this witness invoked her Fifth Amendment privileges *after* her testimony."

The judged listened attentively to Sherman, and then turned to the prosecution's table. "General?"

Diff stood. "May we have a moment?"

Judge Watling nodded. "Five minute recess," he said, hit the gavel, and left the courtroom.

After the five minute recess, which in fact lasted a little over ten minutes, Judge Watling returned to the bench. The bailiff called the court to order. Judge Watling didn't say anything, merely looked at the three prosecutors.

Diff slowly stood. "The state rests," he said simply.

Judge Watling nodded and spoke. "Counselor, do you have any witnesses for the defense?"

Sherman took his cue. He stood again, looked at the DA and then at Judge Watling.

"I would like to recall Detective Marson."

Diff had almost gotten his rotund bottom back into his seat until Sherman spoke. "On what grounds?" he demanded as he stood.

"I believe I was quite clear earlier; I intend to show Sherry Ann Simpson's testimony has had a detrimental effect on Detective Marson's previous testimony."

"We object," Diff said.

"What do you intend to show?" Judge Watling asked Sherman.

"I am confident I can demonstrate inconsistencies in Detective Marson's previous testimony."

"I'll allow it, but please proceed carefully, Counselor," Judge Watling said before Diff could argue the matter.

"The court recalls Detective Marson," the bailiff said loudly. Oscar stood and returned to the stand. "You are reminded that you are still under oath," he advised Oscar. Oscar responded with an irritated nod.

"Detective," Sherman started. "Detective, let's take a moment to count the discrepancies that have been discovered during the course of this preliminary hearing." He held up a finger.

"One: this so-called eyewitness consciously and with aforethought used a fake name.

"Two: this so-called eyewitness claimed she never told anyone about this incident until she recently met with Assistant Chief of Police Raymond Perry, and yet there is a Crime Stoppers tip that came in from a man almost two years ago.

"Three: this so-called eyewitness, in an attempt to lend credibility to her story, claimed that immediately after Thomas Ironcutter shot his wife, he knocked over a flower pot in his haste to leave his house.

"Four: members of your chain-of-command have interjected themselves into this case, but have blatantly violated departmental procedure regarding, among other things, documenting their actions."

Sherman was interrupted by Diff standing. "Your Honor, is counsel asking a question or giving a closing argument?"

"Counsel, your response?" Judge Watling asked.

Sherman nodded thoughtfully. "General Reichman makes a good point, so I will ask a question." He focused on Oscar. "Detective Marson, why have you not addressed these issues?"

Oscar fidgeted in his seat. He was lost at sea. He glanced at the District Attorney, silently pleading for them to come to the rescue.

"Do you have an answer, Detective?" Sherman asked.

"The investigation is ongoing," he finally said. William, sitting beside me, scoffed loudly. The judge glared at him.

"Alright, Detective, perhaps that is a satisfactory explanation for you. Perhaps you believed it was perfectly acceptable to go along with Sherry Ann Simpson's false identity and even allow her to perjure herself in court with this false name, would that be a correct statement?"

"I was not aware until today she was using an alias," he replied evenly.

"Okay, we'll chalk that one up to an oversight rather than incompetence or, worse, perpetuating a conspiracy to destroy a man's character." Sherman paused and let his statement sink in.

"When Sherry Simpson claimed to have been with Thomas Ironcutter exactly one week prior to the victim's death, why did you not even attempt to verify this? You would have found at least one inconsistency to Ms. Simpson's claim."

"We could have, but she may very well have been mixed up on her days. As you said yourself, she has a history of drug charges. Drug addicts aren't always accurate in their dates and times."

Sherman held up a finger. "Detective, you make an excellent point. A person with a history of drug abuse is quite capable of forgetting dates, times, even events." Sherman looked at Judge Watling. "Your Honor, the court has already received a copy of Sherry Simpson's criminal record. May I approach the witness and hand Detective Marson an identical copy of said record of Sherry Ann Simpson, lately known as Brittany Long?"

Judge Watling responded with a singular nod of his head. "You may approach."

"Thank you, your Honor." Sherman walked over, handed the rap sheet to Oscar and returned to the podium.

"Detective, we are clear, are we not, Marcia Ironcutter died on the night of February 1st, 2014, correct?"

"Yes, yes we are," Oscar said. The wariness and uncertainty was plain to see now. Sherman continued.

"And this witness, who has admitted to the court her true identity is Sherry Ann Simpson, testified she was present when Marcia Ironcutter died, correct?"

"Yes, Counselor, it's what she claims."

"Take a close look at her arrest history, Detective. I believe you will see something quite shocking." Sherman placed his hands behind his back again and waited with a calm demeanor while Oscar looked at the paperwork. After a moment, he wiped his brow with the palm of his hand and absently rubbed it on his jacket. His face was pale when he looked up.

"Why, Detective, you appear to have seen a ghost. What is it? What do you see?"

Oscar stammered. "It appears that Sherry Ann Simpson, who we also know as Brittany Long, was incarcerated in the Davidson County jail from January 28th until February 15th of 2014."

"In fact, Ms. Simpson could not have been anywhere near 4779 Front Runner Road at the time of Marcia Ironcutter's death, correct?" Sherman demanded loudly.

Oscar looked pleadingly at the prosecutors.

"Correct?" Sherman demanded again, louder than before.

"It appears to be correct, yes," Oscar said in resigned tone.

Sherman nodded curtly and returned to his normal courtroom voice, although all pretense of friendliness was gone.

"Detective, has there been any form of communication between yourself and any supervisor within the Metro Police Department regarding how you are to conduct this investigation?"

"Yes," Oscar replied softly.

I almost felt sorry for him. Almost.

"In fact, this is nothing more than a conspiracy to destroy Thomas Ironcutter, correct?"

Now Oscar scoffed. "There is no conspiracy, Counselor," he proclaimed coldly.

"Detective, let's go back to the arrest of Thomas Ironcutter. You are aware, are you not, that Thomas Ironcutter was brutally beaten by members of the SWAT team when he was arrested and even required medical treatment?"

"Objection, relevance," Diff said without even bothering to stand.

The judge was scribbling furiously now, about what, I had no idea. He didn't bother to look up when he responded. "The detective opened the door when he earlier testified about the arrest. Overruled."

"Please answer the question, Detective," Sherman directed.

Oscar gathered himself now and stared hard at both Sherman and me. "I think you may be over exaggerating. As I testified earlier, Thomas, the defendant, was drunk and belligerent. He actively resisted arrest and had to be subdued. Unfortunately, he sustained minor injuries. Injuries which could have been prevented had he not resisted arrest. The arresting officers advised us the defendant appeared to be intoxicated at his time of arrest."

Sherman returned his own glare at the detective. "Do you really want to perpetuate those lies, Detective?"

"It's the stone cold truth," Oscar said vehemently.

Sherman stared at him for another long five seconds. "Very well. Did you and Detective Sansing attempt to interview Thomas Ironcutter immediately after his arrest?"

"Yes," Oscar replied.

"Do you remember it well?"

"Absolutely."

"Did you memorialize the interview in any fashion?" Sherman asked.

"Yes, the interview attempt was recorded, and in addition, Detective Sansing and I wrote a detailed report regarding the attempted interview."

"Excellent, please find those two reports in your case file." Sherman waited while Oscar flipped through some pages.

"Okay," he said. "I have them right here."

"Please point out to the court where you notate Thomas Ironcutter's state of intoxication."

Oscar was stone faced. "I didn't," he replied and looked smug again. "I was doing him a favor by not pointing out his apparent alcoholism."

"I see, how nice of you. Did Thomas Ironcutter make any incriminating statements during this interview attempt?"

Oscar shook his head. "No. He fumbled around for a few minutes, and then demanded to be taken to the hospital."

"And the reason for his need to go to the hospital was due to the fact that he was beaten during his arrest, correct?" Sherman asked.

Now, Oscar couldn't suppress a grin when he answered. "Like I stated earlier, your client was drunk, or high, or something. He chose to fight the SWAT team instead of complying with their lawful commands."

"Tell me, Detective, did you interview any of the SWAT members in an effort to see if Mister Ironcutter made any incriminating statements?"

"I spoke with them. They confirmed your client was very belligerent, shouting profanities, and was combative."

Sherman stared at him coldly. "Detective, are you sure you don't want to rethink that answer?"

"It's the truth," Oscar contended.

"Very well, have it your way." Sherman stared at the detective a moment longer before turning toward the bench.

"Your Honor," Sherman said. "With the court's permission, I would like to play a video recording of my client's arrest. This video will show Detective Marson has wrongly testified about the facts of the arrest and is in fact attempting to perpetuate the ongoing conspiracy against Thomas Ironcutter."

Diff started to stand. He was going to object to the admissibility of the video. Judge Watling waited for the objection, but Sherman held a hand up.

"I believe I know what ADA Reichman is about to say. He wants to question the foundation of the evidence. I have two eyewitnesses here in the courtroom who are ready to testify, or," Sherman smiled pleasantly, "the prosecution can expedite the issue by agreeing that the court may take judicial notice of the admissibility of the video on the grounds of relevance."

The fat man looked at his boss for guidance, who reluctantly nodded. "No objection," Diff said and sat down heavily. I swear to God, the legs of the chair actually bowed out a little bit.

William handed a DVD to the court officer, who uploaded it and the projection screen came to life. Ronald had handled the cameras expertly. There was a nice close up of that Acevedo idiot kneeing me in the ribcage and then punching me repeatedly in the head. The ensuing dialogue was crystal clear, leading me to believe Ronald may have used his expertise to enhance it a little. The video ended with me being stuffed into a patrol car.

The audience was talking to each other loudly now and another admonishment to the gallery was bellowed by the bailiff.

"I also have a copy of Mister Ironcutter's medical report on the day of his arrest, your Honor," Sherman said as William handed it to him. "It will show my client was, to use a couple of adjectives the detective just used, stone cold sober on the day of his arrest." Sherman provided a copy of the report to the court and prosecution. This time, they barely glanced at it. With Judge Watling's permission, Sherman handed a copy to Oscar.

"Tell me, Detective," Sherman said, "how are you going to lie your way out of this one?"

Diff stood and objected.

"No further questions," Sherman said. He took his seat and waited.

The closing arguments were brief. In fact, Diff did not even bother giving one. Sherman's was short, but very eloquent. He knew we'd won and chose not to belabor the point. He moved for dismissal of all charges.

Judge Watling stared somberly at all parties. "I find no probable cause exists to substantiate the charge of murder in the first degree. This matter is dismissed. I will draw the order." When the gavel struck, the courtroom erupted. Judge Watling quickly left the courtroom, as did Detective Marson and the District Attorneys.

Chapter 25

"I had a little chat with the members of the press during the lunch break," Sherman said. "We're going to hold a press conference outside,"

"Did you talk any of those fools into betting you'd get an acquittal?" I asked.

Sherman looked at me and grinned like a mischievous school boy. "As a matter of fact, I did. Three of them owe me twenty dollars each."

I shook my head, even though I wasn't surprised.

"Perhaps it would be wise if I did all of the talking," he added.

I smiled and nodded in understanding.

"Excuse me, Mister Ironcutter."

I looked around to see one of the deputies speaking to me.

"You'll need to come with me for out-processing."

"You know what you can do with your out-processing," I retorted and fixed him with a stare.

The deputy shook his head. "It's a requirement, all I'm going to do is have you sign for your property. You know, the clothing you were wearing when you were arrested."

"The hell with your requirements. As far as I'm concerned, you can throw all of it away. You're going to have a fight on your hands if you think I'm going back into that foul-smelling holding area voluntarily."

The deputy held my gaze for a second or two before turning and walking off.

Sherman watched the exchange with amusement and then gave me the eye. "Like I said, let me do the talking." For some reason, he thought I'd make a few smart-assed comments. I have no idea why.

William had been chatting with the court reporter and getting some paperwork. Now he walked over and shook my hand vigorously.

"This was awesome," he exclaimed.

"Your grandfather still has it," I said.

"Yes, he does. Hey, do me a favor, Anna has invited Gramps and me over to your house. Please tell her I'm sorry, but we can't make it and I'll call her later."

"Sure," I replied.

"Okay, I've got certain papers to file. I'll see you later," he said with a big grin and took off. I dutifully followed Sherman as he walked casually, acknowledging his lawyer friends who insisted on shaking his hand and congratulating him. I was mostly ignored, that is, until we exited the front doors.

There was a massive crowd of journalists assembled and each one was shouting, attempting to be the first to ask their questions. Sherman stopped in front of them and held up a hand. The din of verbal diarrhea, which was often in excess with members of the media, died down immediately.

"Ladies and gentlemen," Sherman began. "What you have seen here today is the culmination of two years of a concerted conspiracy. Individuals in the police department took a personal tragedy of Thomas Ironcutter and used it to harass him, ruin his brilliant career in law enforcement, and ultimately violate his civil rights when they convinced a misguided woman to fabricate an outrageous story. Today, Thomas Ironcutter has been vindicated."

"Is there going to be a lawsuit?" one of the reporters from the audience asked.

"Even as we speak, the necessary paperwork is being filed with the court clerk's office," Sherman replied. Ah, now I knew what William meant when he said he had papers to file.

"How much are you suing for?" another reporter shouted out. I glanced at Sherman, I wanted to know the answer to that as well.

Sherman held his arms out. "Tell me good people, what is the proper amount of compensation for the deliberate assassination of one's dignity and good name?"

Sherman said a couple of other things, and then I was being bombarded with questions. My first inclination was to tell them all to go fuck themselves, but I held my tongue. All I wanted was to get the hell out of there. God must have read my thoughts. I heard a horn honking and saw Anna's familiar blue Cube stopped in the middle of Second Avenue.

I whispered to Sherman I was leaving, sprinted through a gap in the crowd and out to the car before the reporters had a chance to react. I jumped in the back seat and Anna floored it.

"Where to, handsome?" she asked cheerily. Ronald was sitting in the passenger seat, grinning like a little kid. I leaned forward, gave her a peck on the cheek and ruffled Ronald's hair. When we stopped for a traffic light, Anna reached into her purse and retrieved my cell phone. I had to smile. I never thought I'd miss that damned electronic contraption.

"We've got beer sitting on ice back at your house and Duke is smoking a few racks of ribs," she said.

"Um, not that I'm unappreciative, but is there a lot of people at this shindig?" I asked. It was the last thing I wanted.

Anna shook her head. "Just a few. Mick, Sammy, Duke, William, Sherman, and Uncle Mike." I guffawed silently. One could only imagine the conversation Uncle Mike and Duke were having.

Anna glanced back at me. "Is that okay?"

"Sounds perfect," I said. "You two seemed pretty confident I was going to be set free,"

"Mister Goldman said you would be," she said.

"Yeah. Oh, William said he and Sherman wouldn't be able to make it, and maybe he'd call you if he didn't have anything else to do."

I watched as she looked in the rearview mirror and smirked.

"Man, he kicked ass in there," Ronald said. "It was beautiful."

I nodded in agreement. It *was* beautiful.

I sat back and enjoyed the ride as Anna chatted on and on, but I didn't mind. I missed her. My ribs still hurt and the back seat of her car was not quite large enough for my six-foot three-inch frame, but the view seemed so much better than when I saw it a few days ago.

When we turned into my driveway, the sight of my house did something to my emotions I cannot quite describe. I was glad to be sitting in the back seat. The stress and anxiety of the last few days had suddenly pounced on me and I felt my eyes watering up. I quickly wiped them away as Anna stopped the car and wiggled my ass out of the back seat before she even got it in park.

I thought I'd regained my composure, but Henry, my adopted cur, mean and ugly, came bounding up and knocked me down, sending a jolt of pain through my ribcage. He was running around in circles, jumping on me, licking my face, and whining with joy all at once. I couldn't stop the tears then. Anna walked up and sat down beside me. She hugged me and started crying as well. Ronald stood there awkwardly, not knowing what to do. He finally sat down beside us and patted us both on the back. The rest of our guests waited politely until I'd composed myself and then took turns welcoming me home. Even Tommy Boy wandered up and rubbed up against my leg.

I took a long, very long, shower. I wanted the stench of imprisonment off of me. After several minutes, when the hot water ran out, I came out feeling like a new man. Ronald and Anna were in the kitchen cooking something and chatting amicably. I walked out the back door and saw Duke sitting in front of the grill, beer in hand. Mick and Sammy Wu were sitting in chairs nearby with their own beers. Sammy chuckled as Mick kept giving cooking instructions to Duke. He was frowning, but looked up and grinned as I walked outside.

"Well, did you get married while you were locked up?" he asked.

I chuckled. "Still single, I guess I'm too old and ugly. Those ribs smell wonderful."

"I'd say about another thirty minutes and they'll be done, but only if Mick gives the say-so," he said with a look. I laughed again and looked around. Duke caught my eye and gestured toward my shop. I found my uncle sitting on a stool, staring at the Buick Wildcat, his left leg quivering involuntarily.

He sensed my presence and looked around. "Where did you find it?" he asked quietly.

"Parked in Lester Gwinnette's shed." I walked up to him and put a hand on his shoulder. "What happened, Uncle Mike?"

He sighed and rubbed his face with a shaky hand. "I don't have much longer for this world, Thomas and you're all I've got left. You and your father."

Uncle Mike never had kids and his wife had died years ago. If I were to nitpick, I'd remind him he had a niece, but it wasn't important.

"Please tell me what happened," I repeated. "It's time for me to know the truth." He looked at me a moment, fumbled through his shirt pocket for a pack of cigarettes and lit one.

"I was a patrol sergeant when it happened. It was supposed to be an easy job. I knew of a numbers bank being run in a shotgun house over in north Nashville. On Fridays, they were rumored to have as much as a million dollars in that rat-infested claptrap. The plan was for me to get all of my men eating dinner together a few miles away. Your father and Lester were going to rob the house and use your car to do it."

"Why?"

"It was an older car, so people would have a hard time recognizing the make and model. You'd rebuilt it and your father said it was fast as hell, and you were going to repaint it that weekend. Nobody would've been able to identify it."

It made sense, I suppose. I waited for him while he took a long draw in his cigarette.

"There was only supposed to be one person there, an old boozer who wouldn't put up a fight. It was going to be foolproof. But, there was this one rookie." Uncle Mike shook his head ruefully. "Full of piss and vinegar. He was one of those men who wanted to set the world on fire."

"Rick Martin," I said.

Uncle Mike nodded. "Yeah, he was on his way to meet us. He was running late because he'd stopped a car for an expired tag or some silly nonsense. He saw two white men going down a dead-end street in a black neighborhood. He parked nearby and watched the two of them pull ski masks over their heads as they went inside the house. He called it in, but didn't wait for back up. He confronted Lester and your father as they exited the house. Your father chose to shoot it out. As they drove away, Rick fired a couple of shots."

He pointed at the two bullet holes. "It looks like his aim was little a bit off. He described the car to the first officer who arrived on the scene, which was me, and then he died." Uncle Mike looked at me now. It was a look of a man who'd harbored a truckload of guilt for many years.

"They panicked. They were supposed to drive right back to the garage, but instead, they hightailed it to Lester's house. After everyone calmed down, it was decided to keep it in Lester's shed for a while until things could be sorted out. Your father was supposed to get it back to you one day, but you know how that panned out."

Uncle Mike, a man whom I admired, loved, and trusted, sighed deeply. "You know what the take was? Two hundred stinking dollars." He reached into his back pocket and retrieved a handkerchief to wipe the tears from his face.

"I've let you down, nephew. I don't know what else to say."

I had no response. We sat in the garage for several minutes in silence.

Our thoughts were interrupted when Duke stuck his head in the door. "Supper's ready," he said and ducked back out.

"So, what now, nephew?" Uncle Mike asked.

I patted his shoulder. "Let's go eat. We can talk about it later."

Uncle Mike nodded his head slightly and stepped on the cigarette butt before standing. He and I both knew we were never going to talk about it again.

The ribs were wonderful. Anna had fixed an assortment of side dishes and even made some tomato soup for Ronald. Plenty of beer was consumed and everyone was having a good time. When we couldn't possibly eat anymore, we sat around in the back yard by the picnic table. Duke, Mick and I enjoyed some fine cigars. Anna and Uncle Mike had cigarettes, and Ronald sat at the picnic table doing something on his laptop. After dinner, Sammy begged off, gave me a hug, and went home. There was a couple of minutes of a peaceful quiet, and then Uncle Mike cleared his throat.

"I have something to say," he said. Everyone looked at him. I'm sure they thought Uncle Mike was going to give a small speech welcoming me home and all that, but when I saw the somber expression on his face, I knew it wasn't going to be anything like that.

"That's not necessary, Uncle Mike," I said.

"I think it is, so respect your elder for a minute and be quiet." He stared pleadingly at me for emphasis. I reluctantly nodded. I didn't want him to admit being an accomplice to a murder, but what he had to say next was not what I expected.

"I've made mistakes in my life. Back when I was a younger man, I married my high school sweetheart. It was a good marriage until she had a miscarriage and she had to have a hysterectomy. I still loved her, but things changed. We no longer shared the same bed. If I were a more honorable man, I would have dealt with it, but my soul was weak." He paused a minute. Everyone was quiet and attentive. Even Ronald was listening.

"I began having an affair with a married woman, who happened to have been married to another police officer." Anna gasped.

"It was that assistant chief's wife," she blurted.

Uncle Mike nodded. "Yes. It'd been going on for a year or two, off and on. One night, we met at an out-of-the-way, no-tell motel. We'd used it frequently, which was another mistake. Two armed men broke in on us. They pistol whipped me, robbed us and took turns with her while they made me watch."

"Oh, my God," Anna said under her breath.

Uncle Mike nodded again. He was looking off in space, his face a dark mask of sad memories.

"So, after they were finished, they took all of our clothes, money, and my car. There was only one person who I could trust, my nephew. I guess all of you can figure out what happened next. Thomas came to our rescue and kept my secret."

They were all looking at me now. I guess they expected a response, but I had nothing to add.

"As you can see, my actions, my selfishness, caused more damage than I could have possibly imagined."

There was a long silence, but then Duke spoke up. "What ever happened to those two boys?" he asked. I looked at him sharply. "Well, I mean, were they ever caught or anything?"

"I found them and took care of them," Uncle Mike replied before I could speak up. "Now, all of you know the truth. Thomas was with me on that night. There was no possible way he killed his wife. Thomas threw away a career to keep my secret. I let my nephew down."

There was a stunned silence. I was looking at the ground, but I could see everyone looking at me, as if there was something deep and profound I could add to the conversation.

I had nothing.

Uncle Mike threw his cigarette butt in the yard and stood. "I'm very tired. I think I'll go home."

I stood with him, walked him to his car and helped him get in. "Why don't you stay the night?" I suggested.

Uncle Mike shook his head. "I'll be alright, I just need to go home and rest." He sat there staring at a spot in the distance. "I've often wondered how things would have been different if I'd had a son," he finally said. "Maybe a son like you."

"You've been more of a father than your brother ever was," I replied. The old man shook his head.

"No, I could have been, but I was selfish." He turned in his seat and looked at me. "Come here," he said. I bent down and he grabbed me in a hug.

"I'm sorry, son," he said, his voice husky with regret.

"It's alright, Uncle Mike. Hey, how about I come by tomorrow? Maybe we can go fishing or something?" My uncle didn't answer. He nodded somberly, closed his door and drove off.

It was late. I'd drunk quite a few beers and was feeling lightheaded. Everyone had left except Ronald. I sat on the couch with Anna, hardly able to move. She was leaning on my shoulder with her arms intertwined with mine.

"Oh, I've totally forgotten. Simone said she had a previous commitment with her daughter, that's why she didn't come, but she insisted you give her a call when you're ready."

"I believe I'll do that," I said.

Anna squeezed my arm. "I've missed you, Thomas. I worried so much when you were locked up. My stomach was constantly in knots."

"It seems to have all worked out. And I must admit, I've missed you too." I kissed her on top of her head and looked over at Ronald. He was at the kitchen table, still on his laptop.

"I've missed you as well, Ronald," I said over my shoulder. Ronald looked up distractedly and nodded. I chuckled.

"So tell me, what have the two of you been up to while I was locked up?" I asked.

"Ronald hacked into your database and we looked over any open cases you have." I looked back at Ronald. He looked up briefly, shrugged a shoulder, and went back to whatever was fixating him on his laptop. "We searched your Rolodex and found the business you use for DNA testing and submitted the evidence. The results should be back any day now," she said with a smile. She couldn't stop hugging me, as if I may disappear at any minute.

Chapter 26

I sat in the parking lot of the Good Samaritan Home for several minutes. Resisting the urge to get my flask and fortify myself, I instead steadied my nerves with a few deep breaths and checked myself in the mirror. Satisfied, I got out of my car and walked in the front door. The receptionist was a seventy-something-year-old woman with a cheery personality who greeted everyone with an oversized smile.

"Hello, I'm here to see my father, Thomas Ironcutter Senior."

She was a bit surprised when I told her who my father was, I guess he never told anyone he had children. She recovered quickly and led me to the day room. I spotted him before she pointed him out. He was sitting in a wheelchair, off to the side and away from the rest of the residents. The rest of the elderly were gathered around a big-screen TV watching Ellen DeGeneres. He was staring off into empty space.

He was a shell of the man I remembered, probably fifty or sixty pounds lighter than he was on that fateful day many years ago, and his once wide, powerful shoulders were now drooped, as if all the air had been let out of him. His jowls were sagging, whispers of hair on his sun-damaged scalp, scattered and disheveled. His deep brown eyes, which I'd inherited, were now cloudy and vacant. He wore an old pair of pajamas, slippers, and a threadbare bathrobe. I think he had a diaper on too, but I didn't care to look any closer than I had to. I walked over to him, pulled up a chair, and sat down. The lady looked at us both in awkward silence.

"Hello," I said simply. He looked up slowly, silently. It took a moment before I spotted a dim spark of recognition in his eyes. Half of his upper lip wiggled a bit, but he made no sound.

"Mister Ironcutter has had a couple of strokes. It's very difficult for him to talk," the lady said. My father glared at her and mumbled something that sounded like 'fuck off.'

"I'll leave you two alone," she said while smiling politely. I waited until she walked away before speaking.

"It's been a few years, Pops," I said. He responded with a quiet grunt. "Uncle Mike told me he's been keeping you caught up on my life over the years, so I won't bother reminiscing." I looked around to make sure nobody was listening in, leaned forward until I was inches from his face, and spoke quietly.

"He finally admitted to me what the three of you did. You, him, and Lester Gwinnette."

Pops didn't respond. He merely stared at me with an unreadable, almost vacant expression. The only acknowledgement was his upper lip faintly twitching. I continued.

"You murdered a cop," I said and stared closely at him a moment longer. His breath was rancid, but the only sound coming from him was a slightly raspy breathing. I sat back in my chair, longing even more for a cigar and a drink.

"Over the years, I'd often wondered what'd happened to my car. You remember it, the Wildcat. I figured you sold it because you were a mean bastard that never did anything nice for his son." I pointed offhandedly at him. "You were, are, a selfish, evil little man. You were abusive to everyone who loved you. No wonder mom ran out on you."

Pops worked his mouth. "Bitch," he muttered in a quiet rasp.

"Oh, so she was a bitch, eh?" I pointed again. "I can only imagine how much agony you put her through before she finally worked up the nerve to leave." I looked him over. A touch of drool was forming in the corner of his mouth.

"Did you know the cop you killed had a family? Yeah, he was married and they were expecting their first child." My tone was of disgust. "Of course you didn't know, but hell, you wouldn't have cared anyway."

I shook my head in contempt and looked around the room. There were a couple of younger people visiting their relatives. They were all smiling and treating their older kin with affection. It saddened me.

I took a deep breath and focused back on my father. "And now, there's something I have to tell you. It's the only real reason I came to see you. Uncle Mike, your brother, ate his gun last night."

My father looked at me in puzzlement.

I tried to explain. "That damned disease was tearing him apart, so maybe it's for the best. He left a note with specific instructions to be cremated with no service. I'm going to honor his request."

There were a few more things I wanted to get off of my chest. I wanted to vent. I wanted to list the multitude of inequities the man had inflicted upon me and how I'd harbored every one of them inside for years, like a dark, festering disease I could not rid myself of. He was speaking now, but it was all gibberish. I listened in silence.

Sometimes, I could go for days without thinking about him or my childhood and the crap he put me through, but then something would happen. An insensitive comment by someone, a knucklehead cutting me off in traffic, little things would set me off and bring the memories back.

Yeah, I wanted to tell him about all of it. I wanted to point out to him all of his flaws and all of the rotten things he'd done to people he allegedly loved, but as I sat there looking at this pitiful man, I realized I was wasting my time. I got up and left without looking back.

I sat in my Cadillac with a cigar clenched tightly in my teeth. I left the flask untouched, secure in my glove box, swearing I wouldn't drink from it until at least after sundown.

I thought of my mother and sister. I hadn't seen either of them in thirty years. After I'd become a detective, I had considered finding them. But, in the end, I chose not to. Yes, my mother left because of my abusive father, but she'd also abandoned me, and I was resentful. I guess you could say I had both Daddy and Mommy issues.

Uncle Mike's house was a quaint, small home located in an old established neighborhood off of White Bridge Road. Walking inside was like walking back in time. He and his wife had decorated it when they first moved in, sometime in the late sixties, and it had never been remodeled. Since his wife died, he didn't see the need to keep the house clean and it reeked, mostly of stale cigarettes.

He had a lazy boy sitting in the den. Kind of like mine. This one was heavily patched with duct tape and there was a small galvanized garbage pail sitting beside it. Looking in it, I could see possibly five years' worth of butts. The TV was probably from the eighties.

The kitchen was more of the same; dirty dishes in the sink, old newspapers stacked on the table, a full ashtray beside them.

I made my way downstairs into the basement. There was a pile of clothes beside the washer and dryer, along with several suits, still in the dry cleaner plastic, hanging up on a makeshift clothesline. Since the house was on a hillside, the basement door exited to a patio.

This was where he did it.

He'd sat in a lawn chair on the patio and blew his brains out with his first duty weapon, a Smith and Wesson Model Ten. After the scene had been processed, a thoughtful officer had washed it down with a garden hose, but there were still some small telltale stains.

I looked over his backyard. His wife, my aunt, used to have a small garden. It was overgrown now. Nothing but weeds.

I went back upstairs, washed out a coffee cup and got the old percolator going. Sitting at a kitchen table watching the percolator, I wondered about life, and wondered about Uncle Mike.

I'd only been to this house a few times over the years. When Aunt Sharon was alive, she was not a person who liked entertaining guests. After she died, Uncle Mike wasn't very sociable either. Whenever he felt like company, he'd come to my house.

"Hello?" It was a voice coming from the front door. I walked over and saw a young Hispanic man standing there tentatively. He introduced himself as a neighbor, Roberto Ramirez. Uncle Mike had hired him to cut his grass and he was the one who found him.

"He was a nice man," Roberto said sadly.

"Thanks, Roberto. Is there something I can do for you?" I asked. He shrugged.

"He owes me for cutting the grass last week. I was hoping..." he didn't finish the sentence. I nodded in understanding and fished some twenties out of my wallet.

"Thank you, sir."

A thought occurred to me. "Do you live nearby?"

"Yes, sir. I live down the street with my wife and family."

I thought it over for all of five seconds. "I've some work I'd like to hire you to do, if you're interested."

Roberto was agreeable and we made arrangements for him to watch the house and keep cutting the grass until the realtor sold it. He also agreed to help me give the house a thorough cleaning.

Chapter 27

Doctor Holly Gross left me a rather perfunctory message advising me the autopsy had been completed. She stated Uncle Mike had died of an apparent self-inflicted gunshot wound, no surprise there, and his remains were available for retrieval. I didn't bother returning her call. Instead, I called a funeral home owned by family friends and made the necessary arrangements. He was to be cremated immediately and the obituary requested in lieu of flowers, donations be made to the Parkinson's Disease Foundation.

"Let me go ahead and write a check," I said to one of the owners, who also happened to be a local judge. Fortunately, Uncle Mike had no small amount of money in his savings account, which he'd bequeathed to me. Otherwise, I had no means of paying this bill anytime soon.

We were sitting in one of the back offices of his business. The décor, paint colors, everything, was subdued, it was a funeral home after all. I could hear the faint sounds of an organ playing somewhere in the background. I was hopeful the man did not want to talk about my recent episode with the judicial system.

"My father and your uncle were pretty good friends, back in the day," he said as I handed him the check. "Oh, yeah? I didn't know that."

"Yeah, they were drinking buddies. There was a group of them, they were all very close at one point. They would come over to the home and hang out. Mister Mike is what I called him. He was an incredibly funny man." I nodded in understanding.

The judge laughed at a memory. "He talked me into a practical joke one time. I guess I was eight or nine. Anyway, the grownups were preparing a big meal and my mother was making her infamous broccoli casserole. I told Mister Mike it was really good but I never ate it because it made me fart all night. So, he talked me into taking a sewing thimble, fill it with peanut butter, and stick it down my pants."

"Uh-oh," I said. The judge nodded with a grin.

"Yeah. Then he told me to have extra helpings of that casserole. After dinner, all of the grownups are sitting in the den, drinking and carrying on. The kids had been ordered to stay in the playroom, but when the moment arose, I casually walked into the den and let out an enormous fart."

He laughed again. "So, as we'd rehearsed, your uncle says, damn son, I think you may have shit yourself. Well, I get this concerned look on my face, reached down into my pants and stuck my finger in that thimble of peanut butter."

"Did you do what I think you did?" I asked. He nodded.

"Yep. I pulled my finger out, licked it real good, and said, I believe you're right, Mister Mike, I did shit myself. The men started laughing uproariously but my mother puked everywhere." We both cracked up. "Daddy tanned my hide good for that one."

"I really liked Mister Mike," he said, much more quietly this time.

I sat in a different lawn chair, one without bloodstains, drinking coffee and smoking a cigar while I watched Roberto cut the yard. I had a million things running through my mind. After much internal deliberation, I got my phone and scrolled through my contact list. I still had the number, but it'd been a while since I'd spoken to him. Hell, he'd probably had his number changed two or three times since we last spoke, but he answered after a few rings.

"The caller I.D. tells me it's my old friend calling," he said without fanfare.

"Hello, Percy," I replied. "It's been a while. How are you?" My question was answered with a sudden loud banging noise.

"Damn, I just killed a roach. This damn office is full of bugs."

Even though we'd not spoken in a few years, I understood immediately. Percy Trotter and I had been friends a long time. We were in the same academy class and worked together in the homicide unit before I resigned. I knew him well enough to understand he was telling me the office was bugged. I wondered if his phone was tapped as well.

"That has to be an awful inconvenience," I responded. "You'd think Metro would spend some money and hire an exterminator.

Well listen, you sound really busy. Shout at me sometime and I'll buy you a cigar. I'm heading over to my favorite smoke place now, in fact."

"You got it." He hung up without another word. He knew about Mick's place and what I was suggesting, but I had no idea if he would meet me. But, he arrived approximately ten minutes after I arrived. I looked over at Mick.

"My former co-worker, who is about to come through the door, is a little paranoid. He might take offense if you were to listen in on our conversation." Mick responded with an indignant look.

"I never eavesdrop," he contended in mock indignation. I arched an eyebrow at him. "Okay, fine. You guys sit over there. I'll leave you two alone." He pointed at the far corner of the store where there was a high table and two chairs. I nodded my head toward them when Percy walked in.

He hadn't changed much over the years. There was a little gray in his hair now, maybe the lines in his face were etched a bit more deeply, but his sapphire blue eyes were still razor sharp, penetrating, the kind that could see right through you. And he still moved like a lion moves along the savannah. Confident, afraid of nothing. At six foot, four inches, Percy was an inch taller than me. The loose-fitting sports jacket concealed a muscular torso. We shook hands; neither of us were the type to hug. I offered him a cigar as he sat.

"You're looking good, still working out I see," I said. He nodded nonchalantly.

"The private eye work seems to agree with you," he responded. "I'm sorry to hear about your uncle, he was a good man." I nodded in silent gratitude.

"I hate funerals, but I'll go to his."

"No funeral," I replied. "He didn't want one." He wasn't surprised.

"You want to talk," he said, changing the subject and getting to the point. He never was one for superficial conversation.

"I've been stupid," I declared. Percy grunted as he worked the cellophane wrapping off of the cigar.

"You finally realized your wife was murdered," he said nonchalantly.

I think my jaw dropped open. "How'd you know?"

"I took a long hard look at the case a few days after her death. I figure you either killed her or you were in denial. If you didn't kill her, you would have eventually figured it out. The arrest must have given you a wakeup call."

Percy clipped his cigar, lit it and took several puffs. "That's a good cigar, been waiting to smoke one all day. We can't smoke on duty anymore," he said off-handedly.

I stared at Percy for probably two or three minutes. I remembered working out with him back when we were both younger men. He was a beast in the weight room and a very skilled martial artist. Many people underestimated him. Even I was guilty of it a time or two. He knew I was staring at him, but ignored me.

"So you knew all along it was a murder?" I asked. Percy nodded with a slight dip of his head. "Why didn't you say something?"

Percy looked at me and stared with those penetrating eyes. "I didn't see any reason to." He looked around, spotted Mick who was busying himself behind the bar and spoke up. "May I have a large cup of coffee?"

Mick acknowledged him and quickly brought two cups over, along with a carafe. He pointed at Percy. "Did you pay attention to how polite he is? You could learn a thing or two from him." He scoffed at my perceived lack of social graces before walking away.

Percy enjoyed his coffee and cigar while I pondered what he said. I kept looking at him. His presence brought back memories, some of them good, some not so good, some downright disturbing.

"You've always seemed to know things nobody else does, it's almost like you're clairvoyant," I said. He shrugged without comment.

"Would you be willing to take a look at the case?" I asked.

"For you? Sure. Do you want it official, or on the down low?" Percy asked.

"I don't want you catching any shit from it, so keep it on the down low, at least, for now," I replied. Percy agreed with a slight nod. "I might talk it over with Jay Sansing," I said tentatively.

Percy looked at me sharply. "He's in OPA," he said.

"Yeah, but I don't think he's a bad kid. His heart seems to be in the right place." He stared at me a long moment before taking a sip. If he had any thoughts or opinions about my logic, he kept it to himself.

"I've got one other request," I said tentatively. Percy set the carafe down, stared at me and waited.

"I've hired a kid as an assistant. She has a missing sister."

"What's the name?"

"Alicia Davies," I replied. Percy grunted in recognition.

"Yeah, that case was fucked up from the get-go by one of our former co-workers. You remember Daugherty, right?"

Oh, boy, did I. Daugherty was transferred into homicide because he was a friend of the chief. He was a braggart, blowhard, five pounds of shit in a one pound bag. Any of the aforementioned descriptions was an accurate testament to his character. He loved to talk about himself. I don't know why, he was shit for a detective. Eventually, he was caught submitting one too many fraudulent overtime vouchers. It cost him his job and his pension.

"The sister's name is Anna, isn't it?" Percy asked. I nodded. "Yeah, I've looked into it. Nothing much to go on at the moment. Do you have any new information?" I shook my head.

"I'll get you a copy of the case file. Maybe a fresh set of eyes will help."

"I appreciate it. How're things going with you otherwise?" I asked.

Percy cast a quick, brief glance at me, inhaled deeply, and let it back out. "I got my own share of problems. Maybe I'll get some advice from you about it sometime." He finished his coffee and suddenly stood. "I'll see you." He stuck the cigar in his mouth and walked out as I got to my feet. I watched him through the windows as he paused near his car and got on his cell phone.

As if on cue, dumb and dumber, also known as Detectives Sansing and Marson, drove into the parking lot. Percy was looking at me through the plate glass window, and then I realized he was also watching them via the reflection of the glass. He made eye contact with me and mouthed the word 'bugs.' So, the rat squad had a wire in the homicide office. I wondered what was going on and what Percy had gotten himself into.

I watched as they got out and approached Percy. Percy hung up his phone, glared at the two of them, and then got in his car without saying a word. He nearly struck Oscar as he backed out of the parking spot.

Oscar was still full of himself as he shouted something indiscernible and glared balefully at Percy's disappearing car. Jay was the opposite. He appeared to be apprehensive, looked around, and saw me watching them. He said something to his partner, who directed his attention to me and the two of them walked inside.

Jay held his hands up pleadingly once they entered. "It wasn't our idea. We've been ordered to come here." Sansing glanced at his partner, who glared at him for making such an admission.

"Why?" I asked.

"Why do you ask?" Oscar rejoined. "Are you hiding something?"

I looked at him in disgust and shook my head. "You really are an idiot, aren't you?" I paid my tab and walked out.

Jay followed me outside. "I'm not trying to start any trouble. We were ordered to come down here and see why you two were meeting." Before I had a chance to say anything, Jay continued. "I know, it was stupid, but like I said, we were ordered."

I stopped and looked him over. He was wearing light gray slacks, starched white shirt, and a navy blue blazer. His black loafers were freshly polished. He was a good-looking young man and I wondered why he was in the rat squad. He saw me glance disdainfully at Oscar who was inside, watching us through the plate glass window.

"I told him to stay inside while I spoke to you. I know you don't like him."

"He's a dirty cop, Jay. He's on the verge of ruining his career and he's going to drag you down with him."

Jay stared at me in puzzlement. "What the hell are you talking about? You call Oscar a dirty cop and yet you're friends with Percy Trotter. Oscar's not dirty, he's got his quirks, but he's not dirty. Now, Percy Trotter is a different story."

I started to get in my car, but stopped and stared at him. "You are absolutely oblivious."

"So, enlighten me," he said.

I was going to ignore him at first and drive away, but after a moment, I changed my mind. "Percy is quite possibly the best detective I've ever known. Did you know, when he was a rookie cop, he caught a man who was about to kill his wife and was shot in the line of duty?"

"You were shot in the line of duty as well," Jay added.

I nodded. "Yeah, just like I was. Back then, if you were shot in the line of duty, you were allowed to choose where you wanted to work. Both of us chose the homicide unit, but at different times. On Percy's very first night, he solved two murders. A man killed his wife and confessed to Percy he killed his first wife a few years previously and buried her in the garden. There are many more examples. The man is downright uncanny when it comes to solving cases."

I pointed at his partner. "In direct contrast is your buddy, who is nothing more than an egotistical idiot."

"I think you're forgetting a few things," Jay said. "Let's see, back a few years ago, Trotter was dating two girls at one time. One of them killed herself by slitting her throat with a shard of a broken mirror in his apartment and the other one disappeared. To this day, nobody knows what happened to her."

He waited for me to comment. What he said was true, but I had nothing to say on the matter. He continued.

"You remember when Captain Cheek was a homicide detective?"

I looked at him like he'd offered me a shit sandwich. "Yeah, I remember. He wasn't very good at it. In fact, he was downright incompetent. I guess that's why he got promoted." Cheek was as bad as Daugherty, but he didn't get fired. He eventually climbed the ranks to his present position of captain.

Jay nodded. "I wouldn't know anything about that, but he made a complaint with OPA a few years back accusing Percy of murdering a man"

"Yeah, I know about it. Like I said, Cheek was incompetent. Still is." I glanced inside at Oscar, who was drinking coffee and chatting with Mick. Mick was looking at him like he had a bad case of body odor.

Jay looked through the windows as well. "Well, I'm not supposed to discuss any cases, but I can say Percy has been investigated several times."

"And you guys have never found anything on him, so I'm not sure how you can call him dirty."

"He's made a lot of good cases over the years," Jay conceded. "But, if I were allowed to, I could show you many cases in which there is simply no way he knew some of the facts about a case unless he was somehow a part of it. Whenever he was interviewed, he denied it of course, but he also couldn't give plausible explanations for how he knew certain things."

"That's what makes him so good. He has uncanny talents and he doesn't concern himself with the Quixote windmills certain personnel, like your pussy-face assistant chief keeps seeing."

Jay looked at me perplexed for a long minute. "Well, he certainly is an enigma," he finally said. It was one of the first things the man had said that I agreed with.

"Think of him in this perspective; he's an outlier. If you take a long hard look at the command staff of the department, you'll find all of them are company men and women. The problem with that type of mindset is that they believe if you don't think exactly like them, you're an enemy. Even the chief is like that, with a couple of exceptions."

"Percy," he said. I nodded.

"He'll never be promoted, but he's the best there is." I looked at him pointedly.

"Now, in regards to your pal standing there staring at us through the window, if you're smart, you'll heed my advice," I said. "Separate yourself from him. Oh, and here's something else for you." Jay looked at me expectantly. "That Crime Stoppers tip back a couple of years ago, you know the one I'm talking about?

"I believe so."

"Perry is the one who called in the tip. Think about it."

Jay watched as I drove off.

Chapter 28

I spent most of the next day cleaning out Uncle Mike's house. The clothes went to the Goodwill. I also had an entire truckload of trash. This went into a dumpster of a nearby business on White Bridge Road. About the time I threw the last of it in, a Korean woman emerged from the back door of her business and really tore into me in a mixture of English and her native language. I assume she was displeased about dumping garbage in her dumpster and not trying to solicit her business, an express laundry. I pretended I didn't understand what she was ranting on about and drove away before she thought to call the police.

I'd done a lot of thinking after meeting with Percy and then running into those two knuckleheads. I made the decision while I was grocery shopping, the decision being I was going to have a long talk with Detective Jay Sansing. Sitting in my truck, I pulled out his business card and called his cell phone.

"So, what are you and your idiot friend up to?" I asked.

There was a light chuckle in response. "The usual I suppose. Today's case involves a young officer who has been accused of staring at a woman's breasts after stopping her for running a red light, and then calling her a pretentious cunt before writing her a ticket."

"Yeah, sounds very serious. You might have a civil rights violation going there," I said, and fumbled with the phone while I attempted to light a cigar. Sansing responded to my quip with another light chuckle.

"So tell me, Thomas, why are you calling? You're the last person I ever expected to receive a personal call from. After all, you're about to sue us for millions, am I right?"

"Oh yeah, you got that right. But before I answer your question, I have one of my own. Are you as dirty as your partner?"

There was a moment of silence. "I'd like to think I'm a good cop," he replied levelly. "I had nothing to do with that stuff in court. In fact, I told him it was a really bad idea. I told them all it was a bad idea. But I want you to know something. I still think your wife was murdered."

"Fair enough," I responded. "I agree." There was a stunned silence on the other end of the phone line before Jay responded.

"I guess my hearing is not so great these days, could you repeat what you just said?"

"Oh, you heard me clear enough. If you want to talk more about it, bring the case file and meet me at my house. How about in an hour?"

"Why don't you come down to the office?" he responded. He heard me scoff. "Okay, bad idea, I'll be there."

"Don't bring the Oscar Marson wiener with you. He won't fare so well if he shows up at my house." I tapped the appropriate icon, ending the call, and dropped my phone in my lap before getting my cigar properly lit. Once that task was completed, I started my truck and headed home. My flask was calling my name, but I ignored it. I needed a clear head.

Jay arrived promptly on time. I was sitting on the front porch waiting for him with a cup of coffee and a freshly lit Ashton. He got out with the thick file and looked around warily before approaching.

"You sure enjoy those cigars," he commented as he stood on the sidewalk.

"Ever since I got out of jail, they taste better than ever for some reason. Are you going to stand there all day or are you going to take a seat?"

"I want you to know I've informed my supervisor that I am meeting with you," he said as he walked up on the porch and stood before one of the rockers. I nodded in understanding. "There is no subterfuge, Jay. I'm not trying to set you up and extract vengeance. I merely want to discuss the murder of my wife." I motioned with my hand. "Please, have a seat. I have a fresh carafe of coffee here. Decaf, would you like some?"

"Sure." Jay sat down and looked me over as I poured, two fresh cups. Jay dumped in several full spoons of sugar before having a taste. I watched in displeasure, but said nothing. The two of us sat enjoying the coffee in silence a moment. It was a pleasant day for

August, the temperature was in the low eighties and the shade trees I had surrounding the house kept the sun off of us. Jay broke the silence.

"I imagine you want to look over the case file. I'm not sure I can let you," he said.

"We'll get to that, but first I have a story to tell you." He looked at me and nodded.

"As you know, I got hired on after getting out of the Army, like Percy did, by the way. We went through the academy together." Jay nodded in acknowledgement. I'm sure he'd already read this in my personnel file.

"Anyway, I eventually found myself as a detective in the homicide unit, where I really came into my own. I was good at it, very good. I once considered myself a cut above the rest, the cock of the walk. The only person I considered even close to my skill level was Percy Trotter. I was constantly trying to one up him."

I chuckled a little and sipped some coffee. "On the other end, Percy was not competitive at all. It came naturally to him. He was amused at my behavior and it actually enhanced our friendship." I paused. "Let's see, I can't remember the exact year, but he married a very pretty woman who worked at one of the local TV stations."

"That was soon after the one girl killed herself and the other one disappeared," Jay remarked. "What do you know about that?"

I took a sip of coffee. I knew Jay was going to add the information to Percy's file and was cautious with my answer.

"How old are you?" I asked.

"Thirty-three."

"Let's see, Percy was twenty-two, I think when he first joined the department. Full of piss and vinegar, like all young men. So, he was a rookie officer. He and his training officer…"

"John King," Jay said.

"Yes, John King. There was a serial purse snatcher working the parking garages in the downtown area. John and Percy were staking out the garages."

"That's when he got shot, right?"

"Yeah. A disgruntled husband ambushed his wife in a parking garage Percy was staking out. Percy intervened and took a shot that nicked his ear."

"Yeah, I've read that. He killed the man."

"Yes, but what's not in his file is what happened that night. King took Percy to a titty bar and got him blind running drunk. That's the night he met the two strippers."

"Ah."

"So, they hook up. I don't know how he did it, but he was dating both of them at once."

"What happened?"

I frowned. "I don't know the exact details, but one of them apparently had a bad drug habit. Percy called her on it and broke up with her."

"Is that what supposedly caused her to kill herself?" Jay asked.

"Probably, I'm not sure."

"What about the other one, the one who went missing?"

"According to Percy, she was pretty devastated about the other girl's suicide. She moved away with the intention of starting over."

"You know she's never been located, right? They wanted to interview her about the suicide, but never found her." Jay stared at me, hoping to get some insight.

I shrugged. "Percy didn't kill her." I said it, I wasn't sure I believed it, but kept that opinion to myself.

"Anyway, he started dating Chelsea shortly after, and they eventually got married."

"She left him, right?" he asked.

I nodded. "I don't know the reason why, he never discussed it, but somewhere in all of that, Percy changed. You may not believe this, but at one time he was a friendly, gregarious person." Jay looked at me skeptically. I smiled. "Yeah, hard to believe. Anyway, something changed with him. I asked him about it one evening while we were enjoying some grilled steaks and beers."

"What did he say?" he asked.

"He never answered. We were having an enjoyable dinner, but when I asked him that seemingly innocent question, his mood changed abruptly. I apologized immediately for it and said the only reason I asked was because I was concerned about him. He shrugged it off and changed the subject, but the damage seemed to have been done." I paused for a moment to take another sip of coffee.

"His wife left him shortly after that and our friendship drifted. In fact, he alienated himself with all of his friends." I sighed, and finally gave in. I pulled my flask out and fortified my coffee. I didn't bother offering any to him.

"Tell me about the fight," Jay requested.

"Ah, yes, the fight. A lot of tall tales have been told regarding that fight. Most people's memories of it have been lost in time, but there were actually two fights."

"Two fights?"

"Oh, yeah. You see, the people that keep retelling the story seem to forget that little fact."

"I'd love to hear about it."

"Well, it goes something like this. We had an after-hours party one night at a bar. Everyone was having a good time, perhaps a little bit too much alcohol was consumed, nothing unusual for a bunch of off-duty cops. But this one officer got a little out of control with a waitress."

"Animal," Jay interjected. I nodded.

"Yeah," I answered. "Alan "the Animal" Hayes. The waitress was very flirtatious. She was only doing what waitresses do, trying to hustle more tips, but Animal was drunk and got it in his head that she was hitting on him. He started making advances. She laughed it off at first, but he started becoming more aggressive. I think she told him to back off, I can't remember exactly, but you get the idea. Animal became enraged and slapped her. Percy intervened." I took a sip of coffee before continuing. "So, Animal is like a fifteen-year veteran and well-known karate badass. He's one of those guys who would give demonstrations of breaking bricks and boards with his bare hands."

"But it didn't intimidate Percy."

"Nope," I replied. "Not a bit. Percy tried to be diplomatic, but Animal turned on him and landed a haymaker. Now, here's where Animal should have paid attention. A lesser man would have been knocked unconscious, but not Percy."

"Oh? What happened then?"

"Percy stood there, rubbing his jaw. I guess he was a little dumbfounded that a fellow officer would have hit him for no reason. Then, Animal tried to hit him again, which was a big mistake. Percy ducked and unleashed a flurry of punches in the blink of an eye. I think Animal was out cold after the first punch but Percy hit him four or five more times before he collapsed."

I chuckled. "You had to be there to fully appreciate it. Percy's punches were lightning fast. Animal never stood a chance."

"So, that was the first fight," Jay surmised.

"Yep, that was the first fight."

"And there was another fight?" he asked.

I nodded again. "Animal was a big man with a fragile ego. Other officers started teasing him, not to his face of course, but little things like a comment or two written on the bathroom wall. He was beside himself. He started telling everyone Percy sucker-punched him, which was bullshit, but some people actually believed it. Then, he started telling anyone who'd listen he'd wipe the floor with Percy if they ever squared off in a fair fight." I shook my head. "What a stupid, vain man."

"Is this the fight at the police academy?" he asked.

"Yep. It took place on a Sunday evening. The place was packed and even the academy staff was there. It was touted as a martial arts competition."

"So, what happened?" Jay asked.

"It wasn't known to very many people, but Percy was, and is a very skilled martial artist. He trained religiously in a dojo run by an old Japanese man nobody ever heard of. Percy never competed, so nobody knew the extent of his skills. Animal on the other hand had won several professional fights and often bragged about it. He was very arrogant, as were his buddies."

"The story is Percy had a pair of brass knuckles hidden under his gloves," Jay said.

I shook my head. "I heard that one too. Not true. I'm the one who wrapped his hands and put the gloves on him."

"So, how'd he win?"

"Percy weighed in at about two-forty back then, but he moved like Bruce Lee. I never knew a big man could move so fast. The fight started quick. Animal, who outweighed Percy by about twenty pounds, charged Percy and tried to take him down with that haymaker right. Percy wasn't fooled this time. The match was only one round, a last-man-standing type of match. Percy systematically destroyed him. When it was over, they had to call an ambulance. Animal was comatose for three days after that."

"I heard he died."

"No, he didn't die," I said. "But, he suffered some extensive brain damage. He never policed again. The last I heard, he's living in an assisted care facility. He can't even say his own name anymore without spittle flying."

"Holy shit."

"Yeah. So, you know how it went after that. Some people were on Percy's side, others felt he went too far. Anyway, enough about Percy Trotter, let's get back to my story."

"Alright."

"One cold February night, I received a phone call. This person, whom I will not name, had gotten themselves into a predicament and needed my help. I agreed, kissed my wife and left my home. The thing I had to take care of lasted several hours. It'd stressed me out pretty bad and I wasn't in a clear state of mind when I got home. When I walked inside, I found my wife dead and my duty weapon lying beside her." Now, I had to take a swig from my flask.

"The sight of her, blood and brain matter, I think you get the idea." I stopped for a few seconds and collected myself. Jay looked at the ground and didn't say anything.

"Well, as you can imagine, it was devastating. Looking back, I don't understand why I didn't go into detective mode and start evaluating the evidence before me.

"I went into shock, I guess. I stumbled back outside and called 911. My buddies, my co-workers, may have been a little biased when they investigated the death. They concluded within minutes it was a suicide and then went through the motions."

I looked at Jay. "I never looked at the case file. I never examined the photographs. I never looked for that one anomaly which would provide a clue of what really happened."

I had to pause again, drink some coffee, and clear my throat. "Fast forward in time to my arrest and preliminary hearing. I'm sitting there watching the dog and pony show, when one of the crime scene photographs is put on that damned projector screen.

Everyone in the courtroom got to see my wife in her final repose. And then, I saw it."

"You saw what, Thomas?"

"The anomaly," I said.

"What anomaly?" Jay asked.

"Have you ever had any training in gunshot wound evidence?" I asked. As I suspected, Jay shook his head. Well, what did I expect? He was OPA, not homicide. I'm sure he'd been to many schools learning how to fuck over a police officer, but none pertaining to homicide investigations.

"Well, I suppose I can give you a quick lesson. Pull the photographs out of the case file and look for yourself." He did so and waited for me to explain. "If you'll notice, that picture you're holding shows some petechial hemorrhaging to her eyes."

"Can't a close-contact gunshot wound cause hemorrhaging?" he asked.

"Sure, but it's not a close-contact wound. Look for yourself."

Jay looked at me in befuddlement. He then opened the case file and began closely examining the photographs. Henry walked up and sniffed him while he looked at the pictures.

"You see, I have a case involving a man named Lester Gwinnette." I gave Jay a brief summation of Lester's death.

"The photos reminded me of Lester's death," I said. "I saw some of the same discrepancies.

"I think someone choked her out and then tried to make it look like a suicide. If you look closely at the gunshot wound, you'll note that the bullet hole is oval-shaped, not round. I believe she was not fully unconscious, or had partially regained consciousness and tried to pull away immediately before she was shot. Or, maybe for some reason the shooter flinched when they pulled the trigger. I don't know the cause, but I'm certain she didn't do it to herself."

"Son of a bitch," he exclaimed. "This is the evidence we've been looking for and it's been right under our noses the whole time. I mean, if we were aware of this we…" he cut himself off before finishing the sentence.

"You would have possibly gotten an indictment against me and I'd still be in jail looking over my shoulder at every waking moment."

"May I ask why you refused to take a lie detector test and ultimately resigned?"

"Because at the time, I had foolishly believed my wife had killed herself. Her mood was mercurial at times, so I thought the worst. I was in a quandary. If I told the truth, more people's lives would have been ruined, and my wife would still be dead. I chose a path I believed prudent at the time. If I had known in fact she'd been murdered? I might have acted differently, but I doubt it."

Jay sat silently for a moment, digesting the information. After a minute, he pointed a finger in the air and waved it slightly.

"We've confirmed your duty weapon fired the fatal shot," he said. "Why didn't you take it with you when you left the house?"

"I was armed with a… with an alternative weapon."

"A throw-down gun?" he asked. I didn't answer. "Are you ever going to tell where you went to that night?" Jay asked.

"No," I responded.

Jay scoffed. "Your loyalty is laudable, Thomas, but I'm afraid it has ruined you."

I shook my head. "I'm doing okay, Jay. Without my wife and child, all I have left is my word, my honor and my integrity. I still have those." My voice cracked a bit at the last sentence. The flask beckoned me loudly now. I fished it back out of my pants pocket and rewarded my taste buds with a long, slow swallow. He watched me, but said nothing.

"Thomas, if you didn't do it, who did kill your wife?" he asked. I put the flask away and worked my cigar a moment before answering.

"I have no idea." He looked at me questioningly. I shrugged. It was the truth.

"More coffee?" I asked, got the carafe without waiting for his response and refilled our cups. My hands were a little unsteady, causing me to spill a little. Jay pulled a reporter's notepad out of the accordion file opened it, and spent the next ten minutes furiously scribbling notes. I remained quiet until he finished.

"Detective Sansing," I said quietly. "I need your trust and your discretion in this matter."

He looked at me squarely before responding. "I'm a man who goes by the book, Thomas."

"I understand. I'd like you to look at it from this perspective, you can still be a by-the-book man and delay reporting everything to your supervisors."

He picked up his coffee cup and blew into it. "What did you have in mind?" he asked warily.

"I've asked Percy to investigate the case. He'll need access to the case file." Jay's jaw dropped and he almost dropped his coffee. "I've got everything up until whatever you people have done recently, so he'll need copies."

"Thomas, I'm not sure that'll fly," he finally said, and drummed his fingers rapidly on the wooden armrest for a long minute before speaking quietly. "I'll deny that I ever said this, but there is a list, a secret list and…"

I held up a hand. "I know all about it. It's a black list. Certain people are on it and OPA rats are tasked with finding any possible dirt on them to hang them."

Jay looked at me incredulously. "Only a few people know about that list," he exclaimed. "How did you find out about it?"

"I'm not going to say. So, Percy's on the list? I figured as much."

"Okay, so you know about the list," Jay conceded. "So, you can see why I can't have anything to do with him. It'll be my ass otherwise." He fidgeted nervously. "Why don't you have someone else investigate the case? Me, for example?"

I looked at him. "I want to know who murdered my wife. Percy Trotter can find out. He doesn't need the case file, but it'll save him a lot of time if he has access to it."

Jay started shaking his head worriedly. I slapped my armrest a couple of times to get his attention. "Let me put it to you this way. Why do you think Percy is still a detective and hasn't been transferred to some bullshit job like the impound lot? It's because even those limp dicks up on the third floor grudgingly admit he's the best in the department.

"The chief will never say it, but whenever there's a tough case which has a lot of potential to embarrass the department and needs solving immediately, he sees to it that Percy gets the case."

Jay nodded slowly. "I've heard the same thing, but I can't be seen with him unless I'm investigating him and I can't simply loan him this case file."

"Well then, why don't you go check out the car I'm working on in my garage for a little bit," I suggested. "I think you'll be so interested you'll look it over for an hour or so."

Jay was confused at first, but after a couple of seconds he realized what I was suggesting. "Yeah, I'd like that." He got up, freshened his coffee and walked to the back of the house, leaving the file sitting on the porch.

It actually took me only about thirty minutes. Somebody had created backup CDs of everything, so it was simply a matter of burning duplicates of the portions of the file I didn't already have rather than using the Xerox for the multitude of paper reports.

Afterward, I found Jay sitting in the driver's seat of my Cadillac.

"This is a fantastic ride," he exclaimed. "Did you restore it yourself?"

"Yeah, it took me a while, but it was worth every minute."

"It's really nice," he repeated and looked at the accordion file. "Oh, did I leave that lying around? How foolish of me."

"I'm sure it's exactly like you left it," I said and handed it to him.

"So, what's next?" he asked.

"I'm going to meet with Percy and then get back to you. Do me a favor and don't discuss this with anyone, especially Marson. In fact, I want you to convince Bartlett to take Marson off of the case."

Jay nodded again. "That shouldn't be too hard. I'm afraid Oscar is not in good graces with the command staff at the moment."

Jay looked at me and paused a moment before speaking. "What's going on with you and Perry?" he asked.

"Ah yes, Assistant Chief Raymond Perry. He and my uncle are bitter enemies. I'm surprised they hadn't killed each other years ago."

He snapped his fingers and looked at me in sudden understanding. "That's who called you the night your wife was murdered," he said. He began nodding, as if he'd discovered a major clue. "Your uncle called you for help."

I ignored his declaration and walked back to the front porch. He and Henry followed me.

"Your honor is important to you, so I'm betting you're loyal as well. It was your uncle, it had to be." He looked at me for a response, which was stupid.

"I would prefer it if we didn't talk about my uncle."

"Oh, yeah, I understand. Sorry." Jay furrowed his brow in deep thought. "Okay, I'm going to have to go back to square one on this, I suppose. Be advised, Commander Bartlett expects a full report when I get back to the office."

"I'm sure he will. Are you going to tell him about the gunshot evidence?"

Jay thought for a moment and shook his head. "I'll have to tell him. There's no way around it unless I lie through my teeth. It'll get back to Perry." He looked at me. "He'll probably insist on presenting it to the Grand Jury."

"I'm sure he will, but you should be the voice of reason. Tell them you want to build a solid case first without that crazy woman's testimony. If they don't agree, remind them of the pending lawsuit."

"Yeah, about that. Why am I being named as well?" he asked in puzzlement.

"Civil law 101, you sue everyone involved. You'll be covered, don't worry. Well, let me qualify that. Don't lie in the deposition."

"You won't have to worry about that," Jay said.

"Marson lied in court and I have no doubt he'll lie in the deposition. He's going to hang himself. And, you better damn well believe I'm going to make sure Perry pays through his ass."

Our conversation was interrupted by Anna driving up. She walked up to the porch and stood there in surprise.

"You're one of the assholes who had Thomas arrested," she said when she recognized Jay. She looked at me. "Why is he here?" she demanded and looked at Henry. "And why haven't you taken a bite out of his ass?" Henry sat, looking at her indifferently.

"Anna, this is Detective Jay Sansing. He is going to be helping in the investigation of my wife's murder." Her eyes widened and she dropped her purse.

"Wait, what?"

I explained.

Chapter 29

I finally finished refurbishing the brake system on the Wildcat and was putting the last tire on when my phone chimed. I frowned and looked at Henry.

"I'm not expecting anyone, are you?" Not getting a satisfactory answer from him, I tapped an icon and activated a camera. It took me a moment before recognizing the car. I grabbed a shop rag and wiped my hands as I walked out to the driveway.

"Well, well," I said as William parked and checked himself in the rearview mirror before getting out.

"Good morning," I said as he walked up.

"You didn't answer your phone. I figured you were here and decided to drive out." He looked around.

"How are you, Thomas?" he asked. Good question. Life hadn't been easy the past few weeks, but I wasn't one to complain.

"Doing better, how about you?"

He looked around again before answering. "Doing okay. Is Anna around?"

I eyed him. "Is that why you came out here?"

"Oh, no," he answered quickly and held up his briefcase. "I have the questionnaires for the depositions. I thought we might go over them."

I nodded, even though I knew he had ulterior motives, and gestured toward a picnic table I had sitting under a hickory tree. "Let's sit over there."

William frowned. "It's a little hot out," he complained. "Can't we sit inside with the A/C?" William was wearing a navy blue suit and I could already see beads of moisture on his brow. I was already soaked in sweat and pretty grimy from working on the car. Besides, if we went inside, he'd probably find some way of snooping through Anna's panty drawer.

"Nah, the fresh air will do you good. Besides, I want to smoke." I chuckled as William sighed. He walked over to the table, dropped his briefcase and took his jacket off. I lit a cigar as he got himself situated and opened his briefcase.

"Has everyone been served?" I asked.

"Yep, everyone."

"Even that Brittany woman?" I asked.

"Yeah, I served her myself, but I wouldn't count on her showing up," he said. I nodded in agreement. "Doesn't matter, we got her bullshit on record in the preliminary. It'll be enough."

"Where's the old man?" I asked. William glanced at his watch.

"I'm guessing he's starting on the back nine at the country club right about now."

"Ah, I should've known. Do you play?" I asked. William shook his head.

"Never got into it. Gramps says you're pretty good."

"I'm out of practice and these ribs are going to keep me from playing for a while," I said as I absently rubbed my side.

"Still sore?" he asked.

"Yeah, a little, but getting better every day."

William snapped his fingers. "I almost forgot. Sherman spoke to the mayor, who's currently on vacation in Aruba, but he's promised when he returns, he'll personally speak to the chief."

I nodded. "It's a start."

"So," he said as he arranged some papers. "I'm pretty sure I've got everything in order, but Gramps insisted I go over it with you."

"I appreciate that," I said, put on my reading glasses and started in. I made a few notations over the hour it took me to read them all, but overall, William had done a good job. I told him as much.

"You think so?" William asked.

"Oh, yeah."

He grinned. "We're going to rip them a new one."

"Definitely."

He shuffled through the papers and handed me one. "You'll be deposed last, Thomas. The whole process will take an entire day, maybe two." I nodded in understanding. "I imagine they're going to be extremely hard on you. They'll try everything they can to get you to lose your temper."

"I can handle it."

William looked at me a moment. I guess he was wondering if I could indeed handle it.

"I've put together a list of possible questions you'll be asked," he said and tapped his pen at a section he had highlighted. "You can count on them asking multiple questions about your alibi issue."

"And I'm going to refuse to answer them." I said it like a proclamation, although it felt more like I was being a rebel without a cause at this point.

"Correct," William answered. "Rule Fifteen of the Civil Rules of Procedure will allow me to object."

"How're they going to respond to that?" I asked.

William shrugged. "They'll probably do exactly what we're going to do if and when any of them refuse to answer our questions. We'll contact the judge and ask for a motion to compel you to answer. Keep in mind though, this is tricky ground. They may try to use it against us and file a Motion for Dismissal."

It was something to think about. Uncle Mike was dead now, if I went on record about what happened that night, it wouldn't hurt him. Not anymore. I surely wanted to discuss it with Sherman, but, he had better things to do. I hoped his golf score sucked.

William interrupted my thoughts by suddenly laughing. "You want to hear the latest thing they tried to pull?"

"I'm all ears," I said, wondering if their antics were ever going to end.

"Yesterday, they sent a newly sworn attorney to the office this morning to offer a low-ball settlement," he said. "I wasn't there but Gramps told me about it."

"Is that wrong?" I asked, perplexed.

"Not wrong, per se, but it's a way of telling the opposition that the case is not important to them."

"What did Sherman do?"

"Oh, Gramps being Gramps turned the tables on them," he said with a big grin. "He treated her like royalty and during their conversation he asked her all about herself. You know, how she got interested in law, who's her family, yada yada yada. So, it turns out Gramps knows her grandparents."

"Yeah?"

"Yeah. They go to the same Synagogue. He offered her a job on the spot, with a considerably higher salary, but only if she resigned from Metro immediately."

"Oh, yeah? What happened?"

"Well, according to Gramps, she called her parents for advice and then took the offer." He shook his head derisively. "She still lives at home with her mommy and daddy."

"How's she look?" I asked.

"I haven't met her yet," he answered. I chuckled knowingly.

"What?" William asked with a frown.

"Your grandfather is scheming."

He narrowed his eyes. "How so?"

"Oh, he stuck it to Metro Legal alright, but he's also looking for his favorite grandson to settle down and get married."

William stared at me. "You think he hired this little girl for the simple fact of fixing me up."

I shrugged. "A nice Jewish girl who's a lawyer, I think he wants some great grandbabies before he dies."

He snorted. "That's my sisters' job."

"Come on now, you know you're his favorite."

He frowned at me but didn't respond. Instead, he put the questionnaires away and came out with a fresh set of papers from his briefcase.

"What've you got there, a new case?"

"The Robard case," he said.

"I thought we were done with that," I said. "Sherman, or you, or whoever, has seized all of those bank accounts we found. The rest of it's in the Feds' hands now." William responded by shaking his head.

"Oh, I don't know if you've heard. When the FBI conducted the raid of that bank in Detroit, Robard closed down. Sherman is in the process of filing the proper paperwork for a plan of liquidation."

"Ah, the business is done for," I said. "I figured it was only a matter of time."

"I'm afraid so. The burden now is recovering as many assets as we can find."

"Won't the FBI be doing that?" I asked.

"Gramps is worried they'll keep any assets and file forfeiture warrants. They don't give a damn about the creditors."

"Okay, I can see that."

"So, he wants to recover and secure as much as we can. Once under his control as the trustee for the bankruptcy court, the FBI won't be able to seize it."

"He can do that?" I asked.

"He believes so and that it's a matter of who gets their hands on the assets first. He takes his duty as the trustee very seriously."

"So, he wants me to locate and recover."

William nodded. "There are literally hundreds of thousands of dollars out there in trucks, trailers, and other sundry equipment. I have an inventory list." He handed me a set of papers in a spreadsheet format and looked at me smugly. "You think you can handle it?"

I looked at the fresh stack. It was various registrations to trucks and trailers, along with several spreadsheets of the company's inventory. "Well, there's a lot of stuff to read here."

He pointed at a notation. "That'll be your commission," he said as he stood. "I guess I'm going to miss seeing Anna. Tell her I said hello."

I muttered something in response, and we shook hands.

After William left, I sat back down at the picnic table and began looking over the paperwork as I smoked my cigar. After about an hour of scribbling some notes on the back of one of the printouts, I came up with yet another brilliant plan. Okay, maybe not very brilliant, but I was pretty sure it would work. I called Sherman.

"How'd you play?" I asked.

"Oh, so-so," he replied. That usually meant he had to use a few mulligans in order to improve his score. "Have you spoken with William?" he asked.

"I have and that's why I'm calling." I went on to explain my plan. After some discussion, Sherman agreed and gave me the greenlight. I hung up with him and called Duke.

Chapter 30

"How's it going, Mister Detective?" Duke drawled over the phone.

"Going better than ever," I replied. "I have something to ask you."

"What's on your mind?" he asked.

"Does any of your crew have experience in driving big rigs?" I asked. Duke was silent a moment.

"Yeah, I believe so, why?" I briefly explained the situation.

"Sounds like some good old fashioned repo work," he said.

"Yeah."

"Yeah, okay. Let me speak with a couple of my boys and see if they're interested. Where're you at?"

"I'm home, at the moment."

"You want to come by the club later?" he asked.

"It's tempting, but watching young naked girls dance around a brass pole depresses me. I'll be at Mick's place about three. Swing by if you're not doing anything. I'll buy you a beer."

I'd no sooner parked my butt on the bar stool when the throaty rumble of a few hogs announced their arrival.

"I wish you'd say something," Mick said in a low voice as he placed a beer in front of me. "Duke's alright, but if all of them start hanging out in here, it's going to be bad for business." He gestured toward two men who had paused in their conversation to look at the approaching bikers.

He was probably right. Maybe I should have gone to the strip club instead of meeting them here. Turning, I watched them walk in. Duke had Bull and Flaky with him. I was actually happy to see Flaky, not so much with Bull. Even though Flaky looked like, well, he looked like a flake, my time with him in lock-up resulted in me getting to know him and taking a liking to him.

He was a peculiar fellow. Whenever he spoke, he'd look at you with a wild, half-sane expression, making one think he was sizing you up for a human sacrifice. But, once a person got to know him, they'd find an articulate, thoughtful young man who was an avid reader and quite knowledgeable about philosophy.

"When did you get out?" I asked as I shook his hand.

"Two days ago," he replied. "I took a plea. Time served plus three years on probation." He glanced at Bull, who was in the humidor sniffing around, before looking at me tentatively. "I need an honest job for a while. Duke said you might have something."

I nodded. "Do you have a CDL?" I asked.

Flaky immediately pulled his wallet out of his back pocket and retrieved his license. Bull walked out of the humidor with a nice fat La Gloria Cubana and snatched Flaky's license out of my hand.

"I've got one of those too," he said, tossed it back on the table and light-heartedly slapped Flaky on the shoulder with his big meaty paw. Flaky winced. "Flaky and I work as a team," he declared. "You got a problem with that?" I looked at Duke. He shrugged. I then looked at Flaky.

"We've always been a team," he said and then gave a sidelong look at Bull. "I even took a charge for him." Bull looked at his partner long and hard as he lit up his cigar. Flaky stared at him for a second or two before breaking eye contact. It sounded like a sore topic and I had no interest in talking about it.

"Okay, fine by me. This may be a silly question, but can either of you hotwire a semi?" Bull and Duke responded with indignant scoffs. Okay, I guess it was a silly question, asking a couple of outlaw bikers if they could steal something.

"Alright," I said. "Let's grab a table and I'll explain everything."

"So, what you're saying is, we can steal all of these rigs legally?" Bull asked suspiciously as he slurped a beer.

I nodded. "Sherman is going to have court orders drawn up for every piece of equipment. You'll have the paperwork with you at all times. If you get stopped by the cops, you show them the court order."

"And they won't arrest us?" Flaky asked.

"Nope. This is all perfectly legal. If some cop arrests you anyway, you'll have the best attorney in the state representing you."

"He's the one who represented you on your murder charge, wasn't he?" Duke asked. I nodded again. He chuckled. "He must be pretty good."

"How much do we get paid?" Bull asked. He'd been argumentative at first, but was slowly becoming more receptive to the idea.

"Two percent," I replied.

Bull scowled. "That doesn't sound like very much."

"A rig with a trailer is worth somewhere around a hundred grand, give or take. If you recover it, you'll get roughly…"

"Two thousand," Flaky finished and looked at Bull. "That's not bad money."

"Yep," I said, "and there are seventeen of them still out there." Flaky whistled in admiration and looked at Bull.

"We could make some good money, bro," he said. Bull was interested, but he wasn't quite convinced.

"What are you getting out of it?" he asked me.

"I'll be getting paid a fee separate from your commission. An escrow fund has already been set up and you guys will be getting paid with a good check immediately upon delivery." I had insisted on this with Sherman. These weren't the kind of men who would be satisfied waiting six months or more before getting paid.

"Any other questions?" I asked.

"Yeah," Flaky said. "I'm in, but how do we find all of this stuff?"

"That's where I come in," I replied. "I'm working up a list of all of the former drivers for Robard and their home addresses. I'm betting some of them have kept the rigs for themselves. Also, the trucks have GPS systems on them. Most have been deactivated, but," I pulled out a piece of paper and handed it to Flaky. "This one is still pinging. I've looked up the location on Google Earth. It's a truck stop in Birmingham, Alabama."

I waited for them to look over the Google printout. "It's about an eight-hour round trip. Bring it to this address." I opened the folder and pointed to an address on the paper. It was a truck dealership located off of Hermitage Avenue. "They'll inspect the equipment, secure it in their yard, and fill out one of these forms." I showed them a dozen preprinted forms. "Get the form filled out and signed, turn it in to Simone Carson at Sherman's law firm, and she'll immediately write out a check."

"Well, hell's bells, what are we waiting for?" Bull said. His suspicions seemed to be gone now, replaced with greedy enthusiasm. "We can head down there tonight and be back by morning."

I held up a hand. "The court orders aren't completed yet." Bull scoffed and stood. Flaky stood too.

"We'll worry about those later." He reached for the paperwork but I yanked it back. He glared and gave me a challenging look.

"I've got one other stipulation," I said and looked at the two men. "This is important. Don't hurt anyone." Bull scoffed again.

"Listen, I'm serious. If someone gives you any shit, don't hurt them, back off. We'll deal with it later." Bull put his hands on his hips and I was concerned his temper may get the best of him. Flaky gave him a look and held out his hand.

"Nobody will get hurt, Thomas," he said. I handed him the paperwork. They fired up their bikes and left without paying.

"It looks like you're picking up the tab," Duke said with a chuckle.

Chapter 31

My phone gave that little signal indicating a text message. I rubbed the sleep out of my eyes and looked at it.

Are you awake? We got something important!

It was from Flaky. After reading the text, I looked at the time. Two in the morning. Oh, sure, Flaky, I'm always awake. Instead of returning the text, I called him directly.

"What's up?" I asked.

"We got the truck and a trailer," Flaky said. He sounded nervous, but it was probably due to me only being half-awake.

"That's good, Flaky. Turn it in to the truck lot like we discussed and we'll get the paperwork squared away tomorrow."

"There might be a little problem," he said, with that same nervousness in his tone. Uh-oh, I thought as I instantly became fully awake.

"What kind of problem?" I asked suspiciously.

"We kind of bumped into the dude who had the truck."

"Yeah?" I had a bad feeling with the way he said that.

"Yeah, well, Bull thought it'd be a good idea to bring him with us."

I sat up suddenly. "You kidnapped him?"

"Well, uh, yeah, I guess so."

"Where are you?" I demanded.

"We're over at the truck lot."

"I'll be right there. Don't move."

The good thing about my Cadillac, she could really move. I hopped on the interstate and had her up to one-twenty in no time. Exiting the interstate once I got downtown, I maneuvered the side streets and arrived at the truck business in ten minutes flat.

A red Peterbilt with Robard Trucking emblazoned on the side doors was parked at the entrance to the lot. Flaky and Bull were standing outside of the repossessed semi. Bull stared at me with his beefy arms folded across his chest like he was expecting a confrontation. I knew I had to be careful with my verbiage, Bull seemed to have a propensity for violence and I had enough going on right now.

"Okay, where's he at?" I asked. Bull hooked a thumb toward the semi.

"We got him handcuffed back in the sleeper." I looked at them both in exasperation.

"Guys," I exclaimed in a loud whisper. "You can't do this. Get him out of there right now, I mean it." Bull glared at me a second before looking at his sidekick and motioned him to the truck. Flaky hurriedly got in and emerged a moment later with a heavyset black man about ten years older than me with close-cropped salt-and-pepper hair and matching goatee. I waited while Flaky took the cuffs off him before offering my hand.

"Hello, sir. My name's Thomas. I'm afraid there's been a terrible misunderstanding."

"No shit," he answered as he eyed me suspiciously. "You a cop?"

"Tonight, sir, I am your personal chauffeur for your ride home." I gestured toward my car. "Are you ready?" He rubbed his wrists and continued to stare at the three of us.

"How do I know you're not taking me somewhere to kill me?"

"May I ask your name?"

He stared at me suspiciously several seconds before answering. "Herman. Herman Alsup."

"Herman, you have my word of honor I will not allow any harm to come to you and I'm going to get you home safe and sound."

He was nervous, I could see it. I mean, hell, if I'd been kidnapped, handcuffed, and taken a couple of hundred miles away from my home I'd be nervous too.

I tried another tact. "Do you smoke cigars, Herman?"

"Every once in a while, why?"

"I've got a small travel humidor in the glove box. There're a couple of cigars in it. Help yourself." He eyed me for a couple more seconds before walking over to my car. When he was out of earshot, I focused on the two bikers.

"What the hell, guys?"

"He's got info about Robard," Bull said. "We thought you'd want to talk him. Excuse the hell out of us for trying to help you out."

I took a deep breath before speaking in order to keep any tone of contempt out of my voice. "Okay, I appreciate the effort, but we've got to stay within the law when we do this. Alright?" Bull glared at me, but finally relented.

"Yeah," he answered. "I'm going to turn in this damned truck. You two girls do whatever." He stormed off, like a spoiled child who didn't get his way.

"He'll be alright," Flaky said. "I told him not to do it though."

"Why did he?" I asked.

"When we started to take the truck, Herman ran outside and claimed the Spieths gave him the truck. When we asked why, he grinned real big and said he had incriminating information on them. Bull demanded to know what it was, but he refused to answer and started putting up a fuss. The next thing I know, Bull throws him on the ground, handcuffs him, and here we are."

"Damn," I muttered. "Okay, I'll get him back home and try to keep him from pressing charges. Get the truck turned in and get your overgrown friend home. Have you two got a ride?"

Flaky nodded and pointed at a car parked behind the semi, a rough-looking Toyota that'd seen more than a few fender benders. "We rode down in my car."

I got in my car with Herman, who'd looked at me nervously, like he was waiting for me to pull a gun with a silencer attached, or something. If the situation wasn't so serious, I'd be tempted to mess with him a little bit, but this wasn't the time.

"Herman, I've got to get a fresh tank of gas and some coffee, then we'll get on the road, okay?"

"That big guy put his hands on me and threatened me," he said.

"Yeah, he's like that. I'm really sorry for his actions."

"He had no call to do that. I should call the police. I bet my wife's already called them."

"It's certainly your prerogative," I said casually, but inside I was in knots.

"You don't seem too worried about it," Herman observed.

In fact, I was. Those two could be arrested on Federal charges. They kidnapped this man and took him across the state line. And yeah, I could get caught up in it as well. I sighed casually.

"Those two mean well, but they pulled a boneheaded move. If I had gone with them, I can assure you this wouldn't have happened."

He digested what I said, wondering if I was telling the truth or not, and finally gestured at the glove box. "You said I can have a cigar, right?"

I nodded. "Help yourself." He opened it and pulled out a leather travel case that held four cigars. Looking them over, he spotted a Monte Cristo, took it out and smelled it approvingly. He then spotted my flask. He held it to his ear and shook it slightly.

"It's scotch," I replied. "You want a taste?"

"Are you going to drink any?" he asked as I drove into a Delta Express and stopped at the pumps.

"I'll most likely put a little dab in my coffee."

"You gettin' coffee?"

"Yeah, I like mine strong and black. Would you like one too?"

"You payin'?" he asked. I nodded. "Yeah, I want one."

The bad thing about my Cadillac, especially when speeding down the interstate at over a hundred, was it drank gas like a thirsty sailor, and she took premium grade. Two immediate things worried me. First, I hoped my debit card wouldn't be declined, and second, I hoped Herman wouldn't rabbit. Both worked to my favor; my card was accepted and Herman was still there, puffing away merrily.

"Nice car," he commented when I got in. "I was going to run, but a couple of things stopped me."

"Oh yeah?"

"I want to ride in this baby and I'm too old and fat to run with a cigar in my mouth." He gestured at his prize. "Cuban, right?" I nodded. "Yeah, I thought so. It'd have been sacrilegious to throw this bad boy away without smoking all of it." He motioned with the cigar. "Alright, let's get going."

"How long have you been a truck driver?" I asked after we'd gotten the first ten miles behind us. Herman sure liked my scotch, he took healthy swallows in between sips of coffee.

"About thirty years. Been doing it ever since I got out of the Army."

"Oh, yeah? I was in the Army too." It was an opening I was looking for. A common denominator between the two of us. We spent the next hour talking about our days in the service and swapping stories. The cigars and scotch certainly helped out with mellowing his disposition.

"You know, Thomas, you ain't a bad dude," Herman said about an hour into our trip.

"Thanks, Herman, you seem like a pretty good guy yourself."

"I'm telling you now though, if I ever see that big overgrown biker or that Charles Manson lookalike again, I'm going to shoot on sight."

I laughed now. "I can't blame you, my friend." Damn, I sounded like Enrique.

"Are you going to tell me why they did this to me?"

"They weren't supposed to," I said and tried to explain as I motioned for him to give me a cigar. "They had strict instructions to only repo the rig." Herman got one out, and even clipped the end before handing it to me. I nodded in appreciation and lit it before speaking.

"So, you see, I'd given them strict instructions, but the big one was convinced you had some kind of valuable information."

Herman was silent for a little bit before speaking. "Well, I guess I can see how he thought that."

"They said the Spieths gave you the rig," I casually remarked in a subtle query.

"The woman did, Leona, she gave it to me."

"Why in the world did she do that?" I asked.

Herman chuckled loudly. "Because I caught her in *flagrante delicto*, and not with her husband, if you know what I mean."

"Holy shit," I exclaimed as I laughed along with him. I waited a minute before asking.

"Who was she doing it with?"

"A dude named Javier."

"Who's he?" I asked.

"He works in the main office. He's the logistics manager, or something like that." I had a brain spark, jammed my cigar in my mouth and got my phone. I tried to keep it between the lines while I tapped and scrolled until I found the surveillance photo of Enrique, the one Ronald had sent me. I handed the phone to Herman.

"Is that Javier?" Herman frowned and looked at the photo a second before nodding.

"Yeah, that's him. The next day, the two of them approached me in the lot and offered me the rig if I forgot what I saw."

"Wow."

"Wow is nothing. Before they left, Javier told me if I knew what was good for me, I'd keep my mouth shut, or else." He took a long swallow. "You know, while the woman was offering me the truck, that Javier dude was switching back and forth from staring at me to looking around the lot to see if anyone else was around." He took another long pull from the flask.

"I've been around some cats who'd straight up kill you for looking at 'em wrong, and you know what? I think he was thinking about killing me."

I glanced over at him. "Oh, yeah?" He nodded. "What do you think stopped him?"

"Two things," Herman replied. "One, I don't think he wanted the Spieth woman to witness it."

"What was the other reason?" I asked.

Henry chuckled. "He spotted the Glock I had stuck in my waistband." He thought some more and grunted. "I'm gonna tell you something else. If I had my baby with me earlier tonight, there would've been two dead white boys in the parking lot of that truck stop."

It was a lot to think about. Enrique was something else. By dipping his wick in Leona Spieth, he jeopardized his case and was in fact risking his career. I thought he was smarter than that.

"Do I get my rig back?" Herman finally asked.

"I'm sorry, Herman, Leona didn't have the authority to give it to you in the first place."

He sighed deeply. "Yeah, I thought as much." He took a big swig and then chuckled again.

"She may have screwed me over," he said with a big shit-eating grin, "but I'll get the last laugh." I looked at him. "They don't know it, but I took a video."

Herman was quite drunk by the time we drove into his driveway. It was a good thing, because the cops were there. And, it was a good thing Herman was a happy drunk. He was laughing uproariously at one of my tall tales and actually had to be helped out of the car.

"It's all a misunderstanding," he slurred to his wife and the cops.

His wife was pissed, the cops were skeptical, but without a prosecuting victim, there was nothing they could do. They took down my information before leaving. I got the video from Herman and even an unexpected bear hug from him while his wife glared at the two of us.

"Okay now, if I find any Robard trucks, I'm going to hold you to that commission," he said.

"You have my card," I replied. "Just call."

All in all, it worked out far better than I ever expected.

Chapter 32

Ronald called about the time I was backing out of Herman's driveway. "I found some good stuff," he said as soon as I answered.

"Alright, I'll bite, what did you find?" I asked.

"The Spieth woman had a secret email account and she used it a lot but never sent any emails with it."

"That's kind of confusing, bub. What do you mean she used it a lot but never sent emails?"

"Two of them were using it, Leona and an employee of the company. They'd communicate by writing something and then saving it as a draft. The other person would log on, read the draft, and respond by posting his own draft. Leona was having an affair."

"Okay," I said.

"Yeah, lots of graphic stuff about their sex lives, but these two also wrote in detail about the drug-smuggling operation going on."

"Ah, now that is something. What was his name?"

"Javier," he answered. Bingo, I thought as Ronald kept talking. "Get on Duck-Duck. Use the Robard password. That'll open the PDF file. After you've printed it off, delete and shred it."

"Will do."

"Okay, I've got to go." Ronald hung up before I had a chance to thank him.

The sun was shining brightly in the morning sky as I headed north and the interstate was starting to fill with traffic. Although I'd had very little sleep, I felt it was time to pay a visit to the Spieths. I stopped at a Waffle House, had a quick breakfast and got a large cup of coffee to go. Telling my iPhone the address, I proceeded back on the interstate and arrived at the Spieth residence well before noon.

I must admit, when Leona Spieth opened the door, she was not at all what I expected. She was a deeply tanned, auburn-headed beauty with nicely accentuated curves, wearing a next to nothing bikini whose fabric was being strained to its limits by a store-bought rack, and a black silk sarong, which I'm sure she'd purposely left untied. I'd say she was somewhere in her early forties, but it was hard to tell. Her face was beginning to show the telltale signs of sun damage, but there were no wrinkles, Botox most likely, and her body was as taut as any twenty year old.

She eyed me coolly. "Yes?" she asked.

"Hello, I'm Thomas Ironcutter. I'm working for the Goldman Law Firm in regards to the Robard Trucking matter. Are you Leona?"

She gave me the once over before turning around and walking back into the house, leaving the front door open and affording me an ample view of her backside. I hesitated a moment, and then stepped inside, closing the door behind me. I found her in the kitchen watching a Latina woman slicing oranges and putting them in a pitcher.

"I was about to fix myself a Mimosa, would you like one?"

"Certainly," I said.

Leona uncorked a bottle of champagne, spilling some of its contents on the counter. She ignored it as she poured it into the pitcher which contained fresh-squeezed orange juice with a few slices thrown in for good measure. She finished it off by pouring a few shots of Triple Sec, stirred it with one of those long-stemmed spoons, handed me the pitcher, and then brushed by me.

I picked up two champagne flutes and dutifully followed as she walked outside through a set of French doors. Pausing at the doors, I hastily looked around. The house was nicely furnished, expensive stuff. I caught a glimpse of the maid as she cleaned up Leona's mess. From the look on her face, I got the impression this was a common occurrence.

The in-ground pool I'd spotted back when I first got this case was how I imagined it, beckoning crystal blue water and surrounded by a concrete patio and wrought iron fence. There was a fountain at the far end displaying a statue of a nude cherub with water spurting out of his diminutive penis. Very classy.

Leona was making herself comfortable in a chaise lounge. I sat in a chair next to her and poured us two drinks. She put on a pair of oversized sunglasses, drained half of the flute in one swallow, and looked me over once more before reclining and closing her eyes.

"What did you say your name was?" she casually asked.

"Ironcutter, Thomas Ironcutter."

"What's on your mind, Thomas?" she asked. It was a good question. There were several things on my mind as I looked her over, and I think she knew it. I wondered about her and her background. She was definitely not shy, she knew she had a nice body and didn't mind flaunting it. I wondered whether or not she had any kids, what made her tick, and why she was seemingly oblivious while the business was going in the toilet. I stuck with business.

"I've been hired to recover the assets of Robard Trucking."

"Why?" she asked. If her eyes were open, she'd have probably seen a look of incredulity on my face. I took a small sip of my Mimosa.

"I'm sure you're aware, the company is in bankruptcy status."

"I'm not involved in any of that. That's my husband's job."

"You're listed as the vice president," I said. She responded with a quick flick of her hand.

"In name only. My husband runs everything."

"Is he home?" I asked.

"No, he's out of town," she said and then stretched provocatively. "I'm all by myself." The tone of her voice had changed and took on a tone of pent-up sexual tension. I forced myself to concentrate.

"You never had any day-to-day involvement with the business?" I pressed, knowing good and well she was actively involved.

"I told you, Thomas, no. My husband did it all." She eyed me as she took another long sip of her drink and motioned for me to refill the glass. I knew what she was doing. The fecal matter was about to hit the oscillator and she was already laying the groundwork for the plausible deniability defense.

"Tell me about Javier."

"Who is he?" she asked in feigned ignorance.

"He's the man you're having an affair with," I answered.

Leona swirled her drink with her finger and then made a show out of sticking it in her mouth and sucking the juice off. "I have no idea what you're talking about."

"I talked to Herman Alsup," I said.

"Who's he?"

"He's the man who caught you two in the act one evening, and you gave him a truck in order to keep him quiet," I said.

"And you're taking him for his word?"

"Well, yeah. Oh, and the video he took of you two doing the nasty," I replied. I saw her face tighten ever so slightly, but I had to hand it to her, she was good.

"I think you're full of shit." She tried to sound flippant, but there was a faint trace of stress in her tone now. I pulled my chair closer, and hid the screen a moment until I opened the video. As I turned it toward her, she stared at me hard a moment until she looked at the screen.

"That fucking nigger," she snarled. Yeah, what a comeback. I was seeing her true colors now.

"Not a nice thing to say," I said.

"Oh, don't try to lecture me on any politically correct bullshit. The bastard was blackmailing me."

She made a good point, good old Herman was indeed blackmailing them, but for some reason, I believed she threw that particular disparaging word around casually and frequently.

"Tell me about Javier," I repeated. She reached over to a table where a pack of cigarettes were lying and lit one. She inhaled deeply before speaking.

"He started working for us about three years ago."

"What was his job?"

"I wouldn't know."

"Bullshit, you were having an affair with him."

"Maybe I still am," she answered.

"Why?"

"Because he has a big dick and knows how to use it," she answered glibly. She took another drag of her cigarette. "And, before you start, spare me any judgmental opinion."

"I'm not judging," I said. This time she gave a short laugh.

"Sure you are, and you're also wondering what it'd be like to take me right now, right here by the pool." She stared at me steadily while she took a drink and intentionally stuck her tongue down into the glass and licked it. I took a small sip of mine and forced myself not to look at her breasts.

"I think you know a lot more about Javier than you're letting on," I said.

"How about you start by deleting that video and then maybe I'll tell you. Maybe we can even get to know each other a little better," she suggested.

It was too bad she didn't know about my friend, Ronald. He'd set my phone up to automatically send everything I downloaded, recorded, or photographed to a dedicated cloud server. So, even if my phone were stolen, destroyed, or anything was deleted, it wouldn't matter. I doubted she had a clue, even to the fact I was currently recording her.

I nodded in seeming agreement, scooted even closer to her, and queued up the video. We watched it together. The angle of the video suggested Herman was peeking through an open door. It started with the two of them aggressively embracing. The level of sexuality progressively increased until Enrique, AKA Javier, had her bent over a conference table and was violently ramming her from behind while she screamed in a furious orgasmic bliss.

When it was over, I dutifully deleted it.

"I can see why Javier was so attracted to you," I remarked, hoping the compliment would make her more forthcoming.

"Are you worked up, yet?" she asked as she playfully dragged her fingernails across my crotch. I gave her a smile, putting on my best James Bond lady's man persona.

"Hard not to be. So, you were going to tell me about him."

"You sure are curious about Javier, are you gay?"

I wasn't sure how to answer. I certainly wasn't gay, but maybe if she thought so, it'd get her talking. I shrugged and offered my best sheepish grin. She laughed.

"What do you want to know?"

"How in the world did he interject himself into Robard Trucking?" I asked. She grunted and sat back in the lounge chair.

"Bill and I were at Swingers one night, have you heard of it?" she asked with a playful grin. Indeed I had heard of it. It was a nightclub for swingers, couples who liked to share.

"It's aptly named," I replied. She continued smiling.

"He came over and introduced himself. We were having an interesting conversation. He told us his profession was transportation logistics, and Bill told him we owned a trucking company. It went from there."

"So, you two hired him."

"Yeah, he convinced Bill he could expand Robard and make millions."

"How?" I asked.

"By hauling heroin," she said plainly and held out her glass. It was empty again. Taking the hint, I refilled it. She didn't bother thanking me and took another drink.

"He suggested it right from the get go?" I asked.

"Not at first. I'd guess about a week or two after he started working for us."

"I'm not sure I understand, wasn't Robard doing well, financially?"

Leona responded with a scoff. "We were only paying ourselves a hundred grand a year. Who the hell can live on that?" I hid my scorn. This woman was something else.

"So, how'd he set it up?"

She lit another cigarette. "Do you know anything about trucking?"

"A little bit."

She blew smoke out and waved it away. "A big company, like United Steel, simply doesn't look up a trucking company in the Yellow Pages. They go through a brokerage agency. That's how we did business."

I knew this already, so at least she wasn't lying to me. "Did Javier change it?"

"Yeah," she answered. "Well, he modified it. He created a bogus trip lease system for backhaul loads out of Detroit."

"And the backhauls were the loads of heroin?"

"You got it," she said.

"How long has it been going on?"

"The affair or the hauls?"

"Both, I guess," I said.

"Somewhere around the first or second month after he started working for us," she replied. So, Enrique had been carrying on an affair with her for some time now. I wondered what he was thinking. It was bound to be discovered at some point. How were his superiors going to react when they find out he was sleeping with one of the suspects in a narcotics ring? I know how it would've panned out if I'd done it when I was still a detective. I'd have been fired post haste.

"Are you aware the Feds raided the bank in Detroit?"

If this was news to her, she didn't show any surprise. "Not my problem," she said indifferently.

"All of the accounts you and your husband have are frozen," I said. This time a small smile escaped.

"Not all of them," she replied.

I filed that tidbit away for future investigation. "You don't seem too concerned," I remarked.

She finished her cigarette, threw the butt on the ground and finished her second Mimosa.

"The Feds are most likely going to pursue charges against your husband and you."

She lit another cigarette and blew it out. "Not likely, not against me anyway," she declared casually.

"You seem pretty sure of that," I said. She held her glass out to me, but then saw the pitcher was empty and my flute was still half full. She'd gone through it rather quickly. I offered her mine. She took it and sucked it down before handing the flute back to me.

"I've got an attorney. He's got a plan where I'll turn state's evidence." She then smiled smugly. "Bill and Javier may be going to prison, not me. Go tell Rosita to make us another pitcher."

"Just one more thing," I said. She looked at me in irritation. "What do you know about Lester Gwinnette?"

"Who?"

"The truck driver who found out about the heroin."

"Oh, him. What is it about truck drivers and blackmailing?" she asked rhetorically. "That idiot thought he was going to get a million out of us."

"He's dead."

"Yeah, I heard." She chuckled at some inside joke or something. There were alarm bells going off inside my head now. Was it possible...?

"Did Javier have anything to do with it?" I asked with as much casualness as I could. She looked at me coyly.

"Why don't you ask him? Go get us another pitcher," she said, and readjusted herself on the recliner.

I walked through the French doors and spotted the maid. She made eye contact with me briefly and then left the room. I followed her into a utility room, where she was putting wet clothes into the dryer.

"Hello," I said. "I'm Thomas." She didn't answer. She was an older woman, perhaps mid-fifties, and had a look borne of a person who had cleaned up after other people all of her life. "May I ask you a question?"

She looked at me warily. "No se," she replied with a shake of her head. I doubted it. I bet she understood English perfectly.

"I'm thinking you haven't been paid in a while." She continued staring at me. "Chances are, you won't be. I wish you luck," I said and handed her the empty Mimosa pitcher.

I didn't bother saying goodbye to Leona. As I drove down the road, I digested what she'd told me. I picked up my phone and used the talk-to-text function.

"Do you have time to fish?" I waited for about a minute before I received a reply.

One hour.

I nodded to myself and drove toward a cemetery located on the western end of the county.

Davidson County, Tennessee had a history going back many years. The first people known to inhabit the area were living here about a thousand years before the time of Jesus. After them came the Mississippian people. Both of those groups once had settlements on the banks of the Big Harpeth River. Right about where I was currently sitting.

Now, the property was a large cemetery for the Veteran's Administration. I was sitting on a park bench admiring the view, smoking a cigar, waiting for Percy. He arrived precisely sixty minutes from the time he sent me the text. He got out of the car, casually scanned the area, and then walked over.

"Cigar?" I asked as he walked up.

"Maybe later," he said. Get to the point, was the unspoken message.

"I've got a hypothetical theory I wanted to run by you and get your input."

"And you didn't want to talk about it over the phone," he said. I nodded. "Alright, give me a cigar."

I smiled and obliged. By asking for a cigar, it was an indicator he was willing to sit with me and listen, at least until he finished smoking, which would take an hour.

"I think I've stumbled upon a dirty Fibby," I said. Percy responded with a slight nod. I don't know who first started calling FBI agents Fibbies, but it seemed to fit. Every agent I'd ever interacted with seemed to have a condescending view of local law enforcement. And, they would lie at the drop of a hat when they wanted something from you.

"He's embedded with a company called Robard Trucking Company, working undercover."

"That's the bankruptcy case you're working?" Percy asked. I didn't know how he knew that, but it was Percy. I didn't bother asking.

"Yeah. He's working a trafficking case in which Robard was being used to transport heroin from Canada and down into Tennessee."

"Okay," Percy said noncommittally.

"The thing is, I think he's the one who instigated the whole operation." I told him of my meeting with Leona Spieth and explained how he began working for them.

"So, according to this woman, it was this agent's idea to use the trucks to haul and distribute the heroin."

"Yeah, that's the way I understand it," I said.

"And he's sleeping with her."

"Yeah." I paused. "She's a good-looking woman, and she puts it out there, guess I can't blame him for that. But, there's something more. After talking to her, I got this lingering suspicion he's the one who murdered Lester Gwinnette."

Percy nodded quietly before responding. "What's your evidence?"

"A few circumstances and a gut feeling," I responded.

Percy gave another small nod.

"Yeah, I know, not a hell of a lot to make a case out of. I was thinking about going to his supervisor. At the very least they should know the peculiars of Robard."

"It's possible they already know," Percy said. "If they do, they're either in on it, or they're setting him up." He made a good point.

"Any suggestions?" I asked. Percy tapped some ash off of his cigar.

"Stick with the bankruptcy issue. Let the Feds handle the drug trafficking."

"And Lester's murder?"

Percy looked at me for a long moment. A very long moment. "I know you well enough to know you want justice for him, but if it were me, I wouldn't worry too much about it." He looked away and fixed his gaze on the river. "Things have a way of working out sometimes."

We talked more about it before Percy's phone rang. He spoke to them a minute, then said he had to leave.

"I have to get back to work. Let me think on this and we'll figure something out."

"I appreciate it," I said.

"In the meantime, be careful," he said with a wink.

Chapter 33

Detective Jay Sansing arrived unannounced approximately thirty minutes after I got home. I met him at the door and appraised him. His tie was loosened and he looked fatigued. I guess he'd had a long week and I felt really bad for him. Yeah, I liked jock itch too.

"So, the mayor gets home from his vacation this morning and apparently one of the first things he did was call the chief," he explained. "All of a sudden your brutality case is a top priority."

"Yeah?"

He nodded. "Acevedo and Trent have been disempowered and we've been tasked with having the investigation completed by tomorrow."

"You could have simply called," I suggested.

Jay shook his head in frustration. "I wish it were that simple. I've been told to obtain formal statements from your two friends before I go home," he said as he stifled a yawn. "Thanks, buddy. I was planning on a nice dinner with my family."

I shrugged. "Don't thank me. You guys should have moved on this a week ago, you know, as soon as the video became public."

"Yeah, I guess so," Jay responded with a frown of agreement. "Is Anna home?"

I nodded and motioned for him to follow me inside.

Anna was in the kitchen, setting the table for dinner. She looked up in surprise when she saw Jay. "I didn't know we were having company," she said with a note of suspicion.

I shrugged and explained. Anna gave Jay a shrewd stare.

"Is this a snow job, or are you guys really going to do something about it?" she demanded. Jay cleared his throat.

"They've already been disempowered. It's my understanding warrants will be obtained and served on Officer Acevedo and Sergeant Trent first thing in the morning. They are also going to be fired," Jay said. "The mayor plans on holding a press conference for noon. So, as a part of this investigation, I'm going to need to obtain statements."

"We're busy right now," Anna retorted. "We're about to have dinner. You'll have to wait." Jay looked crestfallen, but nodded his head. I finally took pity on him.

"Jay, why don't you join us?" I suggested. "We've made Caesar salad, a mouthwatering three-cheese lasagna, and garlic bread. Dessert will most likely be something along the lines of alcohol. You can do the interview afterward."

"Well, it sounds really tempting," he said hopefully.

Anna frowned at my invite, but acquiesced and got another plate out of the cabinet. Jay sat down tentatively.

"I must admit, as soon as I walked in my mouth started watering," he said with a sheepish grin.

"So, Trent's going to be charged as well, huh?" I asked. Jay nodded. I sighed. Trent and I were friends at one time. But, he didn't do anything when one of his men was attacking me, so I was less than sympathetic.

"You didn't hear this from me, but Trent and the chief are Masonic buddies, that's the reason for the inaction. It was hoped you'd let the matter drop and it'd all go away."

"Fat chance," I replied.

"Yeah, they figured that out when the mayor called."

The interview was quick. Each of us gave a statement and the only time Jay spoke was to ask a couple of clarification questions. Jay seemed surprised when Anna told him how I had prepared for the arrest. After he turned his digital tape recorder off, he focused on me.

"You knew how it was going to go down when they arrested you," he declared. I nodded as I finished my plate. "May I ask how?"

"The arrest could have been done by the numbers, but you've got to understand a few things. First, people who are drawn to SWAT duty are natural hard chargers. When they're tasked with something, they view it as a military mission and collectively get themselves into a certain mindset."

"Yeah, I understand that," Jay said.

"Now, that's not necessarily a bad thing, but there's always a knucklehead in every bunch who goes overboard. Like Acevedo. When he gets himself psyched up, he's thinking he's doing God's work, because he's stupid. As you should know by now, he and Doug Eastlin are friends. He knew about Anna's situation and my apparent involvement."

"Yeah," Jay repeated.

"So you see, he's a knucklehead, a dumbass. He thinks it's his God-given duty to administer a little street justice. I can assure you he honestly believes he did the right thing. Now, not only is his career ruined, he's going to bring down Trent too." I paused a minute to let it sink in.

"I hope by now you've figured out your little buddy Oscar is on the same level of arrogant stupidity as Acevedo and his equally stupid friend, Doug Eastlin. If you stay partners with him, you run the risk of ending up like Sergeant Trent."

Jay looked thoughtfully before speaking. "So, what do you suggest?"

"Get as far away from him as possible," I said without hesitation.

Jay frowned. "We're friends," he said. "I can't simply turn my back on him."

"Let me ask you something, when the whole Brittany Long fiasco was being manifested, did you voice any objections or misgivings?"

"Well, I had some opinions," Jay said.

"And he ignored you, didn't he?" I asked. Jay didn't answer.

"Yeah, little Oscar thinks he's smarter than you, he doesn't value your opinion."

"I'm not sure I'm ready to agree with that sentiment."

"Oh, trust me, when he looks in the mirror, he thinks he's seeing the smartest guy in the room. It's only a matter of time before he steps on his Johnson in a major way. When he does, and I assure you he will, anyone around him is going to suffer.

"There's a term for a person like Marson. They call it the Dunning-Kruger effect," I said and took a sip of water, waiting for a response.

"I don't believe I've ever heard that term," he said.

"What, Johnson?"

Anna giggled as Jay smiled. "I think I know that one. The Dunning-Kruger effect, I've never heard of it."

"Look it up, I believe you'll find it an apt description of your partner."

Jay nodded in contemplation and was silent for a minute. He finally wiped his mouth with his napkin and stood.

"It was a wonderful dinner," he said while looking at Anna. "Thank you for your hospitality and cooperation. I must be getting over to this Ronald character's house and getting his statement as well."

I stood with him. "I'll call him and let him know you're coming. Otherwise, he won't answer the door." I had no sooner gotten the words out of my mouth when my phone rang.

"Speak of the devil," I said as I looked at the caller I.D. I answered quickly and lit into him. "What did I tell you about eavesdropping on my conversations in the privacy of my own home?"

"Uh, well, I thought it was important," he replied. I looked up at the surveillance camera and glared at him. "We'll continue this discussion later. In the meantime, Detective Sansing is coming over there. He's going to ask you to give a formal statement about how you recorded the arrest. I expect you to cooperate."

"He doesn't get to look at my computers," he replied quickly and hung up before I could respond.

"Ronald is a little eccentric," I said.

"How was he aware of our conversation?" Jay asked. I pointed at the surveillance camera mounted on the kitchen ceiling.

"Oh," he said in understanding and then snapped his fingers. "So, that's how you got such a good video of the arrest."

"Yep, Ronald can monitor them from his home. Do me a favor and be easy on him. He's the nervous sort, and he knows I'm upset with him, so he's going to be a little more nervous than usual."

After Jay had left, the two of us cleaned up the kitchen and were now sitting on the couch watching a movie. I patted my belly in contentment. "Dinner hit the spot."

"It was wonderful," Anna replied.

"Why don't we go out to a nice restaurant this Friday, what do you think? Do you have any other plans?"

"I've heard great things about a new restaurant on Music Row. I'll try to get us a reservation. Maybe I can talk Ronald into going with us."

We sat for several minutes in silence watching the movie, a rather gaumless romantic comedy that was supposed to have won an award or two. I've never cared anything for this particular genre, they were always predictable and filled with cheesy humor, but Anna seemed to be enjoying it, so I kept my mouth shut and pretended to like it.

At some point, there was one scene where the inept alpha male character made a clumsy pass at the sexy, girl-next-door type who seldom bothered wearing a bra. She rebuffs his inept advances. No surprise there. The rest of the movie was filled inane comedy in which said alpha male sets out to win the girl of his dreams, even though she's turned him down repeatedly. In the end, she suddenly discovers he's the man for her after all.

What a bunch of horse shit. Anyway, sometime during this, Anna shifted on the couch and gently nudged my knee.

"Thomas," she asked. I glanced over at her. "Why haven't you ever made a pass at me?"

I started to chuckle, but realized she was being serious. It was a hard question to answer.

"Well, for one thing, I'm a little bit older than you." Hell, who was I kidding, I was old enough to be her father. Just barely though; like two or three weeks. She gazed at me steadily, which made me feel like I needed to keep explaining.

"I bet you want to get married and have kids one day. I'm too old to be starting a family, so a long-term relationship wouldn't work, I don't think."

I cleared my throat again and shrugged. "I don't know how to explain it. It's not that I find you unappealing, you're a beautiful, vivacious woman, but it just doesn't seem right. Does that make sense?"

She gazed at me a moment longer and smiled. "I'm glad you feel that way. I was wondering how I was going to handle it if you tried it."

I responded with a shrug, not really knowing what to say. I mean, she basically said she didn't find me appealing, but in a nice way. Oh well.

"You're a good man, Thomas, do you know that?"

"There are several people who would disagree with you."

"I don't think you care too much what other people think about you."

"Oh, that's mostly true," I said.

She smiled again before reclining on the couch and putting her feet in my lap. "Are you going to hook up with that FBI woman?" she asked playfully, but with a slight edge in her voice.

"I'm pretty sure that option isn't on the table, but even if it was, I kind of got an inkling as to what you've been saying about her."

"She's a manipulator," she said matter-of-factly.

I didn't disagree. I had an odd intuition about her. Not like with Anna. In the short time Anna and I knew each other, we'd become pretty damn good friends. Something told me Teresa and I would never be friends. My phone buzzed, indicating an incoming text message. The caller I.D. indicated an unknown number.

Have a pot of coffee waiting in the morning. We'll talk about the dead and the missing.

"Who's calling you at this time of night?" Anna asked. "Teresa?" she teased.

"It's Percy," I said. Anna sat up quickly and waited for me to explain. "He's said he's coming over in the morning. And if I know Percy, he'll be pulling in the driveway sometime around six."

"Why so early?" she asked.

"It's just the way he is," I replied. Anna grabbed my phone and read the message.

"That's a rather odd message. How do you know it's Percy?" I responded with what you'd call a guffaw, or maybe a snicker. Hell, I don't know what you'd call it. Kind of like something between a short chuckle and a snort.

"Oh, trust me, it's Percy." Anna looked at me oddly. "He's a little on the paranoid side, so he tends to be cryptic when he sends text messages." I looked at the clock and stood. "I'm going to head to bed. It's likely to be a long day tomorrow."

"I have something to tell you before you go," she suddenly said.
I looked at her questioningly.
"William has asked me out."
I groaned and headed to my bedroom without responding.

Chapter 34

I watched as Percy drove down the driveway promptly at six.

"Some of your habits are still predictable," I said as he walked up. Percy didn't respond immediately and looked around. Henry eyed him warily and backed away.

He was dressed simply, a pair of khaki slacks and a starched, dark-blue, button-down shirt, tucked in tightly. Nonthreatening clothing. Even so, he emitted an aura of danger. Smart men felt it and reacted accordingly. Others somehow sensed it as a challenge to their manhood and took an instant disliking to him. Percy's attitude was what the younger crowd called zero-fucks-given.

"Where's the coffee?" he asked. I led him inside. Anna was wearing yoga pants and an oversized T-shirt. She'd heard Percy drive up and was pouring our coffee when we walked in. She stopped what she was doing and looked at Percy curiously. Percy did the same with her.

"Anna, this is Percy Trotter. Percy, Anna."

"Good morning," she said and handed him a cup of coffee.

Percy took it and nodded gratefully. "Good morning, Anna. It's a pleasure to meet you."

"We cooked up a big breakfast," she said. "I hope you're hungry."

"I'm always hungry," he replied and sat down. We already had the food on the table, consisting of a large skillet full of scrambled eggs, a plate of bacon along with toast, butter and grape jelly. Anna had a large glass of orange juice while Percy and I stuck with coffee. Each of us dug in.

"I've got some information," he said between bites. He gestured toward Anna. "Some of it is about your sister and," he gestured at me, "some of it is about your wife." He paused now. "The information about your wife may be a little sensitive."

I read the unspoken signal. “Anna and I are partners in the business, and more than that, she’s my friend. You can speak in front of her.”

Percy nodded.“Alright, let’s start with your wife.” He put his hands on the table and looked at me. “Marcia was twenty-two when you met her.”

“Yeah, we dated for about a year and then got married.”

“She was from Canada if I remember correctly.”

“She moved down here about six months before I met her.”

“Any particular reason?” Percy asked.

“She was an aspiring country music artist, but it didn’t work out.” I left out the part where she was sleeping with her so-called manager. He’d promised her fame and fortune, but ended up marketing another woman he was sleeping with. The last I heard, she had a dozen platinum albums and they’d gotten married.

“Do you have any contact with her family?” he asked. I shook my head.

“Her parents adopted her when they were both in their fifties. They’re deceased. She had an older half-brother who set out to see the world one day. Nobody seems to know where he is.”

“Okay, so after her country music stint…”

“That’s about the time we met and she got the job with the insurance company. She started out as a receptionist, but soon became certified to sell policies.”

“Yeah, the company she was working for carried the policies for Robard Trucking. That’s the company you’re currently investigating, right?”

I nodded in surprise.

“Yeah, that’s what I thought. Marcia’s the one who had the account.” He took another bite while I digested this information. “Did you know that?”

“No,” I said. “I mean, one day she told me she’d landed a big account, but she never told me who it was. It seemed insignificant at the time. The only thing important was she was getting a nice commission.”

“Did she have a computer?” Anna asked. Percy looked up and then looked at me.

"Yeah, she had a company-issued laptop," I answered. "I never could find it and figured she'd left it at work. Since it was company issued, I assumed they kept it."

Percy nodded, finished his breakfast and deftly dabbed his face with a napkin. "I'll ask if they ever got it back."

Percy sat for a minute looking at the view out of my window before speaking again. "A lady who worked with her suspected she was having an affair."

In spite of my suspicions, when Percy said it, it hit me like a ton of bricks and I dropped my cup of coffee. Anna stood and hurriedly grabbed a dish towel. As she wiped up my mess, she glared at Percy.

"You're not a very nice man, Percy," she said.

Percy shrugged. "No, ma'am, I guess I'm not. But Thomas is a big boy and he deserves the truth."

"Do you know who it was with?" I finally asked. Percy shook his head.

"The woman, who seems to be the office busybody, said she answered Marcia's desk phone one day. She said Marcia had stepped away and she was trying to be helpful. She was more likely being nosy, but anyway, she said a man with a distinctive voice mistook her for Marcia and began talking about meeting later before she could correct him. When she asked to take a message, the man declined and hung up." He paused and then added. "She spoke about another co-worker who saw her getting out of a strange car in the parking lot a day or two before she died."

I nodded. "And too much time has passed to pull phone records," I said belatedly. Percy nodded in agreement, watched as Anna took his plate away and looked around.

"This is a nice place," he said.

I had never invited him out here. By the time I'd moved here, our friendship was already on the downhill slope.

He pointed at one of the cameras. "Nice surveillance system. Did you have one at your old house?" I shook my head. "Pity," he muttered and refilled his cup. He took a few sips and continued staring at his cup while he dropped another bombshell on me.

"So, I'm thinking we should get a DNA analysis of the fetus."

Anna gasped when she understood the implication and glared at Percy. “Within thirty minutes you’ve accused Thomas’s wife of having an affair and implied she was pregnant with someone else’s child,” she admonished.

Percy looked at her levelly. “I admit I’m not a very tactful person at times, but I don’t believe Thomas is interested in me sugarcoating anything.” He looked over at me. “If I make the request, it might raise suspicions.”

“I’ll make a phone call to Sansing,” I said quietly.

“That’s about all I have at the moment. I have some ideas I’m going to work on and will let you know how it goes.”

I nodded in understanding.

Percy focused again on Anna. “I have some information about your sister that you may find unpleasant and I’d like to think I can speak to you candidly.”

“Go ahead, I can take it,” Anna said defiantly.

“Alright. Your sister’s name is Alicia Davies, correct?”

“Yes, Alicia Grace Davies,” she replied.

Percy nodded slightly at the confirmation. “Her stage name was Ecstasy, which coincidentally was her drug of choice. I found a couple of the women she used to dance with and had a good long talk with them. They said most of them had bad drug habits at that time, including your sister.

“She also had a boyfriend who was her dealer. He went by Ray-Ray. Ray-Ray was a two-bit drug dealer and car thief by the name of Rashawn Sumners. On the night of her disappearance, Alicia worked a half-shift and left at about nine. This was about a month before Duke Holland bought the place. One of her dancer friends said she was preoccupied with a lot of text messages back and forth with someone before telling the manager she had to take off early. That was the last time anyone saw her.”

“I never knew Ray-Ray, has anyone ever spoken with him?” she asked.

Percy shook his head.“He was shot a few days after Alicia went missing while selling woo in the Napier housing projects.”

“Woo?” Anna asked.

“Slang for fake dope,” Percy explained. “That murder is unsolved. I’ve asked around, but apparently, Ray-Ray was not very well liked. Everyone I've spoken to gave the same general answer; good riddance." Percy looked at both of us before continuing.

"Her car was abandoned in the parking lot. Apparently, nobody thought of its possible evidentiary value. A private towing company hauled it off. Nobody ever came to claim it, so the towing company eventually sold it at an auction."

Anna frowned and bit her lip. "Yeah, my mother was supposed to go pick it up, but she never did."

Percy acknowledged the information with another brief nod. "In any event, if there was anything of evidentiary value in the car, it was lost. There is a surveillance video of the parking lot." He pointed at the kitchen camera again. "But, it's nothing like what you have. It was in black and white and very grainy. All you can see is her getting into a light-colored, four-door sedan type of car which was parked beside hers. They sat motionless for several minutes before driving off. Rashawn had a similar looking car, but there is no way you can match the two."

"Can you see who is inside?" I asked.

Percy shook his head. He stared at his coffee cup for a moment, as if thinking over something important before looking at Anna. "I'm thinking it was Ray-Ray. They were in some kind of argument, it got out of hand, and he killed her. He probably dumped her body somewhere and it hasn't been found yet. But, that's just my opinion. Take it for what it's worth."

Anna nodded impassively. She refilled our cups with an unsteady hand. She spilled a little bit and set the coffee pot down. "Excuse me," she said and hurried off into her bedroom.

Percy watched as she closed her door and then turned to me. "Sorry," he said quietly.

"Have you checked to see if she had any bank accounts?" I asked. "I mean, if you haven't, I can get Ronald to check. He's good at that."

"I've checked and haven't found any under her name, but by all means, have him check as well. I might have missed something. In fact, I've not found anything under her name, like a credit card or car loan, nothing like that. She had no credit history whatsoever." He lowered his voice to barely above a whisper. "That's not so unusual with girls in that type of profession. Believe me, I'm speaking from personal experience."

"Up until recently, Anna was a dancer as well," I said in the same hushed tone.

"I'd heard. Had she been doing anything on the side?" he asked.

I looked at Percy in astonishment.

He held up a hand. "Don't take me wrong, I'm not passing judgment."

"I think I can safely say she didn't get involved in anything like that."

Percy nodded and sipped his coffee. "Good. It's good you got her out of that work. Stripping is not a good profession, especially for a sweet girl like her."

I said nothing but agreed with him. At my suggestion, the two of us went out to the front porch to enjoy some more coffee and smoke a morning cigar. It was a pleasant morning, in the low-seventies with a slight mist in the morning air as the dew was burning off.

"I have a, well, call it a hunch," Percy said.

"Go on," I urged.

"It was someone with Robard, maybe even that Fibby you told me about."

I looked at him. "Are you referring to the person Marcia was having an affair with?" I asked.

Percy nodded. "Don't ask me why I think that, I just do."

I digested the information in silence. I wanted to ask more questions, but I kept for some reason I couldn't.

"Well, he's having an affair with Leona Spieth, I suppose he could be having an affair with her as well, although I don't see how he had time for both," I said.

"Let's change the subject a minute," Percy suddenly said. "I've always meant to apologize to you."

"For what?" I asked.

"For our friendship drifting the way it has."

"Well, I've always wondered what happened."

"It wasn't you. I have some personal things going on," he paused for a few seconds. "I can't really get into it, but I didn't want anyone else to get involved."

"Do you want to talk about it?" I asked. "It'll be just between us."

"Thomas, you're probably the most honorable man I know and your word is as good as gold, but if I told you anything, I'd be putting you in a situation I don't want to put you in."

"Buddy, it sounds pretty serious."

Percy spoke in barely above a whisper now. "Yeah, you might say that." He stood suddenly. I guess he had a habit of doing that when he was ready to leave.

"I've got to get going. I'll let you know when I find out who killed her. Both of them." He said it with certainty. It wasn't his ego talking, it was his way of saying he was going to solve both cases. I nodded gratefully. He extended his hand and we shook.

"You're always welcome here, Percy."

"Thanks, brother. Tell Anna bye for me." He turned and left.

Anna walked outside as Percy drove away. She had changed into a set of warm-ups and sneakers. She tried to hide it, but I could see she'd been crying.

"Would you mind cleaning up the kitchen? I'd like to go for a walk and think."

"No problem, kiddo," I said and gave her a hug. She smiled gratefully and then walked down the driveway as she put her earbuds in. Henry followed faithfully.

Before cleaning up, I had some phone calls to make. Sitting in the rocker, I called Detective Sansing. He answered after the fourth ring.

"Hello?"

"Are you in a position where you can talk and nobody can overhear our conversation?" I asked. There was a moment of silence and some movement before I heard a door being closed.

"Alright, go ahead."

"I'd like for you to obtain a DNA sample from Marcia's fetus and compare it with my DNA." There was a long moment of silence. "Jay, are you still there?"

"Holy shit, Thomas, do you suspect the child isn't yours?"

"It's a possibility." I briefly explained what Percy had learned. "You should have no problem getting a request through with the

Medical Examiner's Office. Let me know when you want to meet and you can get a cheek swab from me."

"I'll have to let the boss know about it," he said.

"I understand. I don't think they'll question your actions, but if they do, tell them you're exploring another angle to the case. It's the truth after all."

"But they'll interpret it differently. They'll think you killed her because she was having an affair."

"Yeah, I'm sure they will."

"You're okay with that?" Jay asked.

"I'll work it out somehow."

Chapter 35

"You are not going to believe this," Anna said when I came in from the garage.

"What's going on?" I asked. She held up a large manila envelope.

"It's the results of the DNA testing on Theo the pervert."

"No shit? What's it say?"

"It says Theopolis Braxton the Third is the father of his former daughter-in-law's child," she said with a triumphant grin. It was good to see her in a good mood. After our talk with Percy a couple of days ago, she'd been a little sad, but she was doing better.

"Wow," I exclaimed. "Good job, partner." I held up my dirty hand for a high five. She slapped it joyously.

"Okay, boss, what do I do now?" she asked.

"You prepare a copy of the case file for Mrs. Braxton, along with a bill, and then set up an appointment for a meeting. Remind her that she declared she was going to pay us in cash, but be subtle about it."

"Okay, and it's Friday by the way. You promised me dinner."

"Sure, let me grab a shower. Is Ronald going with us?" Anna rolled her eyes and shook her head.

"He said something about a major battle his alliance had scheduled and he expects it to last all night."

"Well, that's Ronald for you. I'll be ready in thirty or forty minutes."

Apparently, I was not moving fast enough. She was waiting for me when I shut the water off and stepped out. I hurriedly grabbed a towel.

"I wish you'd stop doing that," I said. "I like privacy you know."

Anna ignored my protests. "We're meeting her in an hour at the same spot in the park."

"Okay, fine. Now go wait in the den and I'll get dressed." Anna made a face at me and left my bedroom. We were on the road fifteen minutes later.

"How do you think she'll take it?" Anna asked.

"I think outwardly, she'll be as cool as a cucumber. Inwardly, I think it's going to tear her up."

"So, she's going to divorce him and get his money," she predicted.

I chortled.

"What?"

"I'd bet a dollar to a doughnut she won't divorce him."

Anna looked at me. "Why do you think that?"

I shrugged. "Old rich people, especially extremely rich old people, do things a little bit differently than everyone else."

She looked at me in puzzlement.

I shrugged. "Time will tell, but it won't be our problem. Let's go get our money."

Mrs. Esther Braxton was waiting on us when we arrived. Anna explained everything, and when she was finished, presented a copy of the case file, including the certified letter confirming the DNA match, along with the bill. Mrs. Braxton was quiet during the entire presentation, looked at the bill, and dug into her purse. She came out with an envelope containing fifty one-hundred dollar bills and handed it to Anna as she looked at me.

"Your protégé has performed exceptionally well," she said, stood without waiting for a response and walked back to her Rolls Royce. The chauffeur obediently held the door open for her and the two of them drove off a minute later.

"Wow," Anna said. "Not the reaction I expected." She sighed in disbelief, moved some hair out of her face and focused on me. "Okay, I have reservations set for five, and then maybe I'll treat you to a cigar later, if you're nice."

"I'm always nice," I said. She called Ronald and tried to convince him to join us, but as expected, he declined, saying he couldn't let down his fellow online nerd friends.

I chose to park the car myself rather than let the valet. I didn't care for a perfect stranger behind the wheel of my baby. Anna had a small, knowing smile on her face as we walked along the sidewalk.

"What?" I asked.

"We might have some company, I hope you don't mind." I started to ask who, but learned the answer as we walked in the door. Simone and a younger version of her were standing in the lobby. She was wearing one of those sexy summer dresses colored in an abstract pattern of different tones of mauve, ending above the knees, and a pair of high-heeled shoes. Her daughter was wearing a Nashville Predators polo shirt and shorts. Anna waved and walked over. Seeing no alternative, I followed.

"Hi," Simone said sweetly and kissed me on the cheek. She then gestured at her young standing beside her. "This is my daughter, Madison." Madison was a cute, teenage girl, a spitting image of her mother. She grinned and said hello to us.

So, if my mathematical skills were correct, Simone had her daughter when she was somewhere around college age. I wondered where the sperm donor was these days.

"We've already got a table," she said and led off. Anna gave me a wink as I walked by.

Anna ordered wine, I held off on the alcohol and ordered water.

"Mom said you were a homicide detective," Madison said.

"Once," I replied. "Now, I'm a private investigator."

"That sounds like really cool work," she said. I responded with a shrug. "Did you ever investigate a serial killer?"

"Nashville has had a couple of them over the years."

"What's the most interesting case you've ever had?" she asked. I used to get asked this question a lot. One of my former co-workers loved this question. It opened the door for him to tell all of his war stories, most of them wildly embellished. I was the opposite, it didn't seem right to tell tall tales about somebody being brutally murdered.

"It's not easy picking out one case," I said. "All of them have an interesting aspect." The waiter brought our drinks and I grabbed my water.

"Give us an example," Madison pressed. The three of them were looking at me expectantly.

"Well, okay. One of my co-workers named Percy Trotter had a good one. On his very first night as a homicide detective, a man called the police and proclaimed he'd killed his wife. Percy went to the scene and found the woman lying on the kitchen floor."

"Oh my God, what happened?" Madison asked.

"He had stabbed his wife to death. She didn't cook dinner properly, or something like that."

"Wow."

"So, Percy took him back to the office. During the ensuing interrogation, the man gave a frank confession, describing how he stabbed his wife to death. Then, he confessed to another murder. Apparently, years ago, he'd killed his first wife and buried her out in the back of his house in the garden." All three women now looked at me wide-eyed. I took a swallow of water.

"So, the lesson is, be careful who you marry, especially if you're not a very good cook. I'm famished, what's good here?"

Simone looked at me oddly, Anna rolled her eyes, and Madison burst out laughing.

"Good one," she said and paused a moment while she looked me over. "How old are you?

"Forty-four," I said. "And you?"

"Fourteen," she answered with a grin. "Are you married?"

"Nope, how about you?" I asked. Now she giggled. It was a harmless teenage game with her, but I didn't mind, I could do it all night.

"Okay, enough with the personal questions," Simone admonished Madison. She then gave me a slight smile. "We're vegans, but I understand the chef here specializes in prime rib."

A woman after my heart, I thought as I smiled.

"That was nice," Anna said after we'd left the restaurant and said our goodbyes.

"Yes it was." Simone had left me with a simple handshake, but there was pointed eye contact. It was confusing.

"Simone was nervous," Anna remarked.

"She was?"

"I think she was worried about what Madison thought of you."

"Oh." Well, that explained the brief peck on the cheek. My thoughts were interrupted by an incoming text.

Dinner was wonderful. Perhaps we could do it again? Soon?

Hmm, I thought a moment before typing out a careful reply.

For you, every night is free. You tell me when.

It took about two minutes before my phone chimed again.

Sunday. I'll pick you up at six.

I started smiling, but then I caught Anna looking at me and grinning like a little kid who made a big boom-boom in their diaper.

"What?" I asked.

"Nothing," she said, but kept grinning.

"When are you and William supposed to go out?" I asked, changing the subject.

"Tomorrow night. Why, do you and Simone want to go on a double date with us?"

I glanced over at her. She had the same mischievous smile.

"Um, no."

"Suit yourself," she said. "It'd be fun."

"Maybe some other time. I hope Mick's isn't too crowded."

"I like crowds. You know, all of the regulars in there think we're sleeping together," she said.

"People like to gossip," I replied. "If there weren't any crowds, there wouldn't be any gossip."

"Was that true about Percy?"

"Yep, he solved two murders on his very first night as a detective."

"Wow, everyone must have been real proud of him."

"Some were, but there were others who were jealous," I said. Anna looked at me as we got in the car.

"Why would detectives be jealous of a co-worker who'd solved two murders? That doesn't make sense." I grunted in agreement as I merged into traffic.

"The law enforcement profession is a magnet for people who crave attention and glory. When someone else gets it and they don't, they become jealous."

"Were you ever like that?" Anna asked with a teasing grin.

"I don't think so," I answered. "Percy definitely wasn't. He hated the limelight. Even so, his success created enemies." And it was the same with me. The first time I'd won detective of the month, I had laid the plaque on my desk and went back to work. When I came back at the end of the shift, someone had stolen the plaque. I never found out who.

"Alright," I said, changing the subject. "Let's go smoke a cigar."

"So, you cracked your first case, huh?" Mick asked. Anna nodded proudly. "Well, good for you, sweetheart," he said with a grin and looked over at me. I was contentedly puffing away on a Rocky Patel. "You got a little Miss Nancy Drew here, Dago."

"I do indeed," I replied pleasantly.

She leaned over and whispered in my ear. "Who's Nancy Drew?"

I choked back a derisive chuckle. "She's a fictional amateur detective. Lots of books written about her."

"Oh," she replied, but there was still a hint of confusion on her face.

"So, what's next for the dynamic duo?" Mick asked. I tapped the ash off of my cigar.

"We've had a couple of potential customers contact us this week, but no contracts yet. So, in the meantime," I pointed my cigar at Anna, "you're going to study for your PI's license."

"I need a license?" she asked. I nodded.

"In Tennessee, to practice private investigations requires a license. Otherwise, it's a criminal offense." She looked at me incredulously.

"I broke the law?" she asked in astonishment. I nodded casually. "Why'd you let me do that?" she implored. "I could've been arrested!" I scoffed dismissively.

"Nah, I would have taken care of it. Besides, I needed to see if you were any good at this stuff before investing the time to train you."

"Oh." She looked perplexed for a moment. "What does it involve?"

"It's not difficult. You fill out an application, submit a fingerprint card, they run a background check, you take a written test, and then you pay an overpriced fee for a cheap laminated plastic license."

"Does Ronald have one?" I shook my head, which brought a grin to her face. "Good, he and I can do it together." I chuckled as she pulled out her cellphone and began texting.

"Good luck with that, I've been trying to get him to do it for a while now."

"What about all of them missing trucks?" Mick asked.

"And what about Lester's murder?" Anna added. I shook my head.

"Still working on the trucks, but our involvement in Lester's murder is done. It's now in the hands of the esteemed detectives with the Rutherford Sheriff's Department."

"You mean that arrogant prick of a detective?" Anna asked. I nodded. "That guy couldn't solve a tic-tac-toe puzzle," she said with a huff. I shrugged.

"Just because he's incompetent, don't judge the rest of their detective unit. Some of them are pretty good, I'm betting. They'll figure it out."

"I'm very dubious," she said. I looked at her. "What?"

"Dubious?" I asked.

"I'm working on expanding my vocabulary. Look," she said and showed me her phone. "It's an app that sends you a new word every day."

"Ah." I had no idea when she'd decided to do that, but I didn't tease her.

"I can download it to your phone, if you want."

"Ah, maybe later," I said. Much, much later.

"Have you talked to Percy lately?"

"Not in a couple of days." I checked my watch and opted to try and call him. He answered on the fourth ring.

"How are you?" I asked.

"Just got through working out," he replied. "I've been meaning to call you. Well, I've been meaning to call Anna. Are you two at home?"

"At the other place," I responded. I had no idea if there was a Title III wiretap on his phone, so I was intentionally being a little vague.

"Stay there," he said and disconnected. Anna looked at me.

"What was that all about?" she asked.

"Percy is either going to join us or break in to my house. I'm not sure which." She eyed me questioningly, but I merely shrugged and ordered another beer. Percy joined us fifteen minutes later. He was freshly showered, wearing jeans and an oversized, light-blue polo shirt. It effectively hid his physique and the duty weapon on his hip. He motioned Mick for a beer and then gestured at his car.

"The rats have a GPS tracking system hooked up to it. None of them work past five, so we won't be getting any visitors. Even so, we need to ride in your car." He finished his beer quickly.

I looked at Anna. "Looks like we're going for a ride."

Percy wanted to drive. Although I loved my Cadi, I acquiesced.

"This is a nice car," he commented, otherwise he was silent about our destination. We soon ended up on a lonely road in the northern part of Nashville known as Joelton. I caught Anna looking at me a couple of times as we rode, as if to say, ask your friend where he's taking us. It was fully dark now when he stopped on the side of the road. There were no houses nearby, no streetlights, only trees and weeds. He got out and pulled a small flashlight out of his pocket.

"Do you have an extra one?" he asked. "It'd help." I retrieved one out of my trunk. Percy looked at it.

"Mine's bigger," I deadpanned. If Percy caught the double entendre, he ignored it and began walking into the woods.

"Where are we going?" Anna finally asked.

"To your sister," Percy replied over his shoulder, without slowing or waiting for a response. We dutifully followed and walked for about twenty feet before stopping. Percy shined the flashlight around, found a stick, and used it to move some leaves. I used my own flashlight and aimed it at the spot on the ground just about the time Percy uncovered a skull. Anna gasped.

"I'll get the forensics team out here in the morning and recover the remains."

"It's my sister?" Anna asked. Her tone was of disbelief, as if Percy were somehow playing a cruel joke on her. Percy didn't bother answering. "But, how?" she begged.

"That piece of shit boyfriend killed her and dumped her here. I'm pretty sure he shot her to death in the parking lot of the strip club. His car had blood in it, but everyone assumed it was his when he was found murdered." He looked over at me. "There were swabs taken, so I'll get some DNA tests run, which means I'll need some samples from her mother."

"But, how do you know it's her?" Anna asked in bewilderment.

"It's her," Percy responded. He offered no other explanation.

I cleared my throat. "If Percy says it's her, it's her," I said. "You should understand, he doesn't always tell how he knows things such as this."

Anna took the flashlight out of Percy's hand and squatted down in front of the skull. It was obvious she was having a hard time digesting this and continued staring at the skull in disbelief.

"I'm sorry to be crass," Percy said, "but the rest of her skeleton will be scattered around here due to animal activity. I'll do my best to get it all recovered in the morning."

"So, she's really dead," Anna said.

"Yes," Percy responded matter-of-factly. "I know this is hard to take, but I wanted you to see it firsthand."

"And you're sure her boyfriend is the one who killed her?" she asked.

"Yes," he replied. We continued staring at the skull for a long, awkward, five minutes.

Anna turned the flashlight off and stood. "I want to go home."

Chapter 36

"Why did he do that?" Anna asked. After we had dropped Percy off, Anna hugged the passenger-side doorknob and wept quietly the entire drive home. She didn't speak until I'd parked my car and turned the engine off. "I mean, why did he do it like that?"

"He wanted you to see it firsthand rather than finding out by watching it on the evening news."

"But, how did he know?" she pressed.

"I have no idea." Henry greeted us and we walked inside. Anna walked over to the couch and Henry jumped up and sat beside her before I could even sit down. I opted for my easy chair.

"What do I do now, Thomas?"

"There will be a big ordeal tomorrow. The media will be out there and the department will not say anything other than an unidentified set of skeletal remains were discovered. The DNA test usually takes between one and two months, but it'll confirm it's your sister. By then, it'll only be a byline."

"Then what?"

"Percy will brief his superiors about his investigation. There will be questions and suspicions, but eventually they'll accept his explanation and the matter will be closed." I paused for a moment.

"At some point, you should think about funeral arrangements. I'll help you out on that if you'd like."

"Yeah, I'd appreciate it. I think I'd like to be alone now, Thomas, if you don't mind."

"Not at all," I said, stood, and kissed her on the top of her head before I went to bed.

The morning news headlines were about what I'd predicted. All stations had a news team at the sight. There was crime-scene tape along the side of the road and forensics personnel could be seen in the background. Anna watched the TV in rapt attention for a few minutes before she saw me staring at her. She used a tissue to wipe her eyes.

"How are you?" I asked.

"I'm okay," she responded. She didn't look okay, she looked like she hadn't slept the entire night. Her eyes were red and puffy and her hair was a mess.

"Alright, consider this an order. Get in there," I said, pointing toward her bedroom, "and take a long hot shower. I'll get breakfast going."

"I don't think I can eat anything," she said quietly.

"Then, after you get out of that shower and have a bite to eat, lay down and take a nap."

"It's seven o'clock in the morning, it's too early for a nap."

"Something tells me you didn't sleep much during the night." She didn't answer directly and instead looked at me sadly.

"I think I should be the one to tell my mother," she said. I nodded in understanding.

"You want to call her or go see her in person?" I asked. She thought about it for a moment.

"I guess it'd be best if I told her in person." And then, of course, she looked at me with those sad blue eyes.

"Will you go with me?"

"Of course," I answered. She sighed and stood.

"Okay, a hot shower sounds good. Be sure to feed Henry," she said. I nodded. Henry looked at me expectantly.

While I waited for her, I sat in front of my computer, looking at my notes and thinking about Enrique. I was getting a bad feeling, a very bad feeling. Not only about his possible involvement with Lester's death, I had a feeling about something else. I fished through the business cards I had stacked on my desk and found his. He answered on the fourth ring.

"Hi, Enrique, it's Thomas."

"Thomas?"

"Ironcutter, Thomas Ironcutter."

"Ah, how are you, Thomas?"

"I'm doing fine. Have I caught you at a bad time?"

"Not at all, Thomas. What can I do for you?"

"I've got a quick question concerning the insurance policies for Robard." I left it at that and waited. Enrique didn't respond. I waited several seconds.

"Hello? Are you there?" I asked.

"Yes, I'm still here, Thomas."

"Robard's insurance carrier was Tri-State. Its home office is here in Nashville. Did you know that?"

"I was unaware of that," he said curtly. "Why are you asking?"

"Who at Robard would be responsible for the insurance?"

"I would assume the president of Robard, or one of his employees." There was another long pause. "Why do you ask, Thomas?"

"I can't really go into details right now, but it appears there may be a connection between Robard Trucking and my wife's death." I rapped the table with my knuckles. "Hey, somebody's at the door. I'll fill you in later." I disconnected the call before Enrique had a chance to respond and turned off the recording function. I then called Percy.

"We're going to go meet with Anna's mother in a little bit."

"You want me to meet up with you?"

"Do you have any other plans?" I asked.

"Nothing that can't wait."

"Okay, because after we deliver the news, I want to meet with that co-worker of Marcia's who took the phone call from the mysterious man."

Heather Piper Davies was an older, rougher version of Anna. She still had her youthful figure, but her complexion had seen better days, her hair was over processed, and her teeth were yellowed from too many cigarettes and too few visits to the dentist. She might have been forty or sixty, it was hard to tell. She stood in the doorway of her apartment looking at the three of us like we were travelling Mormons.

"Hi, Mom," Anna said.

"Hi yourself, where've you been hiding out lately?"

Anna ignored her question and turned toward me. "This is Thomas, I'm working with him now. And this is Detective Trotter with the homicide unit."

"Homicide unit?" she asked, glaring at both Percy and me before glaring back at Anna.

What the hell have you gotten yourself into now?"

Anna's expression was like a small child who'd been unfairly scolded. I found myself bristling and was about to reply, but Percy beat me to it.

"Ms. Davies, there have been some recent developments in regards to your other daughter, Alicia," Percy said. She stared, waiting. "There have been some skeletal remains located in the northern end of the county. Although the tests have not yet been completed, it's tentatively believed the remains belong to Alicia."

"It went better than I thought it would," I said as the two of us drove down the road, following Percy in his unmarked car. "Don't you think?"

"The bitch didn't even shed a tear," Anna replied quietly. Coldly.

"People handle grief in different ways," I offered.

"Yeah, she was so grief stricken she needed money to make her feel better."

It was true. Anna's mother stared at us with no emotion and asked us who was going to have to pay for the funeral. She never invited us in, but as we were leaving, she pulled Anna aside. Percy and I waited by the car, but we could hear the ensuing conversation where the bereaved Anna's mother tried to finagle rent money from her daughter.

"That's why I distanced myself from her. When I got the job dancing, she thought I was making all kinds of money and would hit me up for a loan whenever she saw me." When she said loan, she made quotation marks with her fingers. I understood what she meant. Anna's mother was taking advantage of her daughter's generosity with no intention of ever paying her back.

"The thing is, you did the right thing and told her about it in person," I said. "It may not seem like much, but sometimes the only thing you have to hang your hat on at the end of the day is knowing you did the right thing."

"Yeah," she said quietly and looked out of the window. "Where are we going?"

"I just want to do one thing and then I'll get you back home where you can kick back and relax."

"How about just answering my damn question?" she said irritably and then sighed. "I'm sorry, Thomas. I'm not doing so well today."

"No problem, kiddo." I glanced over at her. She looked tired, beat down. She needed to rest. "In answer to your question, we're going to my wife's place of employment and speak to one of her co-workers. It should only take thirty minutes, tops."

"Oh, okay. I'll sit in the car, if you don't mind."

"Okay," I said, exited the car and met Percy at the entrance to the insurance company.

Marcie Crownover was on the cusp of morbid obesity. I don't know if she had a health condition or self-control issues, but she looked swollen, bloated, a little like the Michelin man would look if he had big mushy breasts, which she was showing off with a low-cut top. She eyed me warily as Percy introduced us.

"Yeah, I remember you from the funeral," she said. I nodded, but damned if I remember her attending. In fact, since Marcia had gotten the job at this place, I'd never been introduced to any of her co-workers.

"I've told Thomas about the phone call you accidentally received," Percy explained. Marcie acted like it was a painful memory, but, in truth, she was basking at being the center of attention. She glanced around, insuring at least one co-worker was looking at us, wondering what she was up to.

"Oh, yes. You see, everyone was always confusing me with Marcia and vice versa. I guess it was because our names were so similar and we both had big tits," she said and giggled like a schoolgirl. Neither Percy nor I smiled. Marcie was easily a hundred and fifty pounds heavier than my late wife. Nobody in their right mind had ever confused them for each other.

"So, anyway, one day she asked me to mind her phone while she stepped out." She made eye contact briefly to see if we were buying her story and decided she needed to embellish. "She was expecting an important phone call and she couldn't roll it over to her cell phone."

More than likely, the lard ass was being nosy, but I kept my mouth shut and let her continue.

"It was about noon, a couple of days before she, well, you know."

"Did you know who was calling?" I asked.

"No, I'd never talked to that man before. I would have remembered."

"Why's that?"

"Because he had a very distinctive voice. I'm very good with voice recognition."

"Marcia didn't say who it was?"

"Oh, no." She drawled out the two words, hinting strongly there was a reason Marcia didn't want anyone to know who it was. Marcie was gazing at me now, practically begging me with her eyes to press it. So –

"Percy mentioned you believed she was having an affair," I said. Boom, her eyes lit up, but she did a good job at acting as though she found gossiping distasteful.

"Well, not me so much," she said in a hushed voice. "That's Scotty." She gestured toward a man sitting in the back of the office, currently sitting in front of his monitor engrossed in a spreadsheet of some type. "He's a notorious gossiper, you know how homosexuals can be," she proclaimed in a whisper so low I could barely hear her. "He told everyone she was seeing someone."

"Did anyone actually see her with anyone?" I pressed. Marcie stared hard at me now, before looking toward the opposite end of the office.

"We should talk with Scotty," she said, and motioned for us to follow her.

Scotty was a pleasant man with a warm smile and thinning hairline. He didn't strike me as the gossiping type. "I'm pleased to meet you," he said, shaking both of our hands. Percy told him why we were there.

"I don't want to speak ill of the dead," Scotty said. He started to say something else, but I cut him off.

"Okay, you two," I said. "Let's not beat around the bush here. You both know I was recently arrested for her murder and the case was thrown out."

"Because it was a suicide," Marcie said.

"Because they had the wrong man," Percy said. The two of them looked at us in surprise and then looked at each other.

"So, she was murdered?" Scotty asked in almost a whisper.

"We believe so," Percy said. "And, we'd really like your honest input." Scotty took a couple of deep breaths.

"What is it, Scotty?" I asked.

"I came to work early one morning." His breath caught momentarily before he continued.

"This was two days before she died."

"The same day of the phone call," Marcie interjected.

I acknowledged her and focused back on Scotty. "Go on," I pressed.

"Marcia's car was parked in her usual spot. There was one of those fancy black sports cars parked beside it. I didn't think anything of it, but as soon as I walked in the office, I saw her get out of it and come inside. She seemed upset, but she didn't say anything and I didn't ask."

"Did you see who was in the car?" Percy asked.

Scotty shook his head. "The windows were tinted and whoever was in there drove off rather quickly."

I turned to Marcie. "You mentioned previously to Detective Trotter this person you spoke to had a distinct voice."

She nodded. "Oh, yes he did. He had some kind of accent, Italian I'm thinking. He sounded very sexy."

"Would you recognize it if you heard it again?" Percy asked.

"You better believe it," she declared. I pulled out my iPhone and played the conversation I had with Enrique. As Marcie listened, her eyes widened.

"You know him?" she asked incredulously.

"Yes, is it the same man?" She nodded dramatically.

None of them knew the whereabouts of Marcia's company-issued laptop. The office manager coolly informed me she'd assumed I'd kept it and that was why she had deducted the cost of it from Marcia's final paycheck.

Percy and I tacitly agreed to wait until we got to the parking lot before discussing it, but before we could, there was another matter to tend to. Anna was sitting in my car, pointedly trying to ignore some street punks who were standing beside her window, harassing her. She was already upset, and now she looked like she was on the verge of crying. I was already in a mood, and seeing them bothering Anna did not help matters.

"Can I help you gentlemen with something?" I asked in a not-so-friendly tone as I walked over. The three of them stared at me balefully. If they only knew what kind of mood I was in, they would have run. The biggest one was my height, but young, I guessed him at no older than seventeen. His left hand was grabbing his groin, which I guess served a dual purpose of holding up his sagging britches and reminding himself he wasn't a little girl.

"What'chou think you gonna do, old man?" he challenged.

At another time, I would have ignored this punk, got in the car with Anna, and driven home. But, in the past few minutes I'd confirmed what I had only recently begun to suspect; my wife had been having an affair, she was probably pregnant with her lover's child, and her lover probably murdered her. I was torn, conflicted, devastated. This young punk had unknowingly succeeded in pissing me off more than I'd been in a very long time.

"You should learn to respect your elders," I said in a low voice as I took a step toward him. He responded with a haymaker right.

He was quick, I'll give him that. His fist scraped across the top of my head as I ducked. I responded with a two-punch combination. He stumbled back, a look of surprise on his face. The fight was on now and I didn't let up. Stepping forward quickly, I peppered him with a flurry of punches. He threw a couple back at me, but they were weak, ineffective.

He was addled now, probably seeing a covey of Tweety Birds circling around. I put a solid right against the base of his jaw. His knees buckled and he went down. I dropped a knee on his chest. The air went out of him as I gave him one final punch, sending him into sleepy time.

I looked up at about the time Percy landed a lunging side kick to the face of one of the other punks. A handgun went flying out of his hand as he hit the asphalt. The third one took off, running like a track star. He was damned fast. He and I made brief eye contact before he disappeared around the side of a fast food restaurant. I quickly frisked my guy, and sure enough, found a snub nose thirty-eight shoved down in his crotch.

I held on to it while Percy used his singular pair of handcuffs to cuff the two men together. He stood and gave me a look to confirm I was okay.

"Looks like I owe you," I said. Percy gave me a small, almost indiscernible smile, and gestured at Anna.

"Why don't you take her home? I'll take care of these two." He was interrupted by the chirp of a siren. We turned to see a squad car driving quickly into the parking lot. A portly officer wearing sergeant's stripes heaved himself out of the car.

"Why, lookee here, it's the two world renowned homicide detectives," he said jovially as he ambled over.

"Hello, Dickie," I said as he held out his hand.

"I ain't seen you in a month of Sundays, Tommy. How've you been?"

"Doing okay, Dickie. How about you?"

"Can't complain, and even if I do, my wife tells me to shut up." He laughed at himself and looked over at Percy.

"Well now, Detective, what the heck have these two ne'er-do-wells done to endure your wrath?"

"One of them took a swing at Thomas," Percy answered, and showed the two handguns. "They were armed."

Dickie reached for one of them. Percy unloaded it and handed it over. "Boy, that's a nice piece," Dickie said as he unloaded it and inspected it. "I bet it's stolen."

"Likely," Percy answered.

"I'll call for an officer to come over and transport," Dickie said. "Who's prosecuting?"

"I am," Percy said. "I appreciate it, Dickie."

Dickie nodded and looked around. Spotting Anna, he grinned and walked over to the car. "Why, hello, sweetie. I'm Dick Durbin, but everyone calls me Dickie-Do, on account my belly sticks out farther than my dickie do." Dickie laughed loudly now. Percy and I'd heard his joke more than once over the years. "You weren't hurt, were you?"

"No, I'm okay," Anna responded. Dickie pointed at the two of us.

"We were rookies together," he continued. "Boy, the stories I could tell you about 'em."

"I bet," Anna said.

"What's going to happen to those two idiots?" Anna asked as we drove down the road.

"Percy will charge them with assault and unlawful possession of a firearm," I answered.

She thought it over for a moment. "Good," she said perfunctorily.

The drive home was very quiet. It hadn't been a good day for either one of us, and it wasn't even noon yet.

Chapter 37

"You look fine," Anna said. She'd walked in on me while I was checking myself in the bathroom mirror for the umpteenth time. I'd changed shirts a couple of times before settling on a burgundy-colored button down to go with a pair of khaki pants and casual loafers.

"Remember what I said, she doesn't care much for cigar smoke," she chided.

I gave her a look in the mirror. "Yes, Mom, you've reminded me a dozen times already." We walked into the den at about the time my phone gave the alert chime. "She's here," I said.

"Where are you two going?"

I shrugged. "Dinner somewhere. She didn't say." I walked toward the front door and Anna followed. I stopped and turned.

"Don't wait up," I said with a grin and walked out, shutting the front door before she could follow me.

Simone was driving a white Hyundai Elantra. It was spotlessly clean, but otherwise it fell in the category of dull. I kept my opinion to myself.

"New car?" I asked when I got in and buckled up.

"Yes. My first choice was a Porsche," she answered with a grin. "But the price was right and it has a great warranty. I hope you're hungry."

She drove to a restaurant in Berry Hill whose specialty was vegan plates. I had a vegan barbeque wrap, which was surprisingly tasty. It didn't compare to real barbeque though.

"How do you like it?" Simone asked.

"It's wonderful," I answered, wishing for a cold beer. "So, tell me about yourself?" I asked as I drank my glass of water. "Where are you from, originally?"

"A small town called Trenton, have you heard of it?"

"Trenton, New Jersey? There's nothing small about that city."

Simone laughed. "No, Trenton, Tennessee. It's near Jackson. My father's deceased, but my mother still lives there."

"Is that where Madison's father lives?" I asked, hoping I didn't appear too terribly nosy.

"No, he currently lives in Chicago. We met at Middle Tennessee State, that's where we both went to school."

"I see."

"Long story short, we got married when we were both seniors in college. It lasted for twelve years before it went to hell. It wasn't a pleasant divorce."

"Oh, I'm sorry to hear that." I was curious to know why the marriage went bad, but now was not the time to ask such a personal question. "Is it still good between him and Madison?"

Simone shook her head. "Other than a few phone calls on occasion, they hardly have contact. We divorced two years ago and he's only seen her once." She gazed steadily at me. "I've tried to be a good mother, but it's been very trying at times." She ate a morsel of something that looked like a weed and then smiled.

"You know, she's had trouble accepting her mother dating, but you're the first one she seems to like. She actually said you're pretty cool, for an old guy."

"I'm not sure how to take that," I said, laughing.

Dinner was filled with more pleasant conversation and I realized I was enjoying the heck out of myself.

We made our way into the parking lot, hand in hand, and when we got to the car I was about to go in for a kiss, but then I was rudely interrupted.

"Hello, Thomas."

I looked around quickly. It was Enrique. He was smiling, but it wasn't a pleasant smile.

"What the hell are you doing here?" I asked with no amount of friendliness in my tone.

"Oh, it's amazing how, when you're thinking of someone, you just happen to bump into them. Did the two of you enjoy dinner?" he asked, and looked at Simone. "Was Thomas a gentleman, or a crass drunkard, like he normally is?"

"You're out of line, Enrique," I said.

"Yes, you are," Simone added.

"Oh, I do apologize then," he said with an arrogant smile. "I was just leaving. Have a pleasant evening, Miss Carson." He gave her a wink before walking off.

"Is he a friend of yours?" Simone asked as we watched him get in a black Dodge Charger and drive away.

"Just the opposite. C'mon, I'll explain everything on the way home."

Chapter 38

I was distracted. Enrique had pissed me off last night, which was his intention. I had absolutely nothing on him other than a few pieces of circumstantial evidence and my gut feeling.

And it was killing me.

He must have spoken to Leona, and now he knew I was onto him. I really wanted to pursue it, but it would have to wait because the depositions were scheduled for today.

Sherman had offered his office for the endeavor, but opposing counsel would have none of it, so we were now sitting in what was known as the two-two-two building. It was the abbreviation of the address, 222 2nd Avenue North. The official name of it was Washington Square, but nobody ever called it that. The building housed a number of offices for the Metropolitan government, along with the District Attorney's office and it was where the Grand Jury met. I'd been here many times in the past, but not lately.

Since I was the one doing the suing, I was allowed to sit in on each deposition. The experience was going to be kind of like getting a colonoscopy; a pain in the ass, but necessary. The only good thing about it was Simone was going to be present. She was responsible for running the video-recording equipment and taking notes for Sherman. We exchanged smiles when she and Sherman came in.

Opposing counsel was a fortyish-year-old man by the name of James Hensley. He was maybe six feet, narrow shoulders, wide waist, and he had a peculiarly large head. It was odd looking. Birthing him must have been difficult for his mother. He pointedly ignored me as he asked Sherman various legal questions which he should have already known the answers to. After taking some notes about who knows what, he suddenly wagged a finger at Sherman.

"By the way, that move you pulled last week was dirty pool. You should be ashamed," he said. Sherman arched an eyebrow. "Stealing away a promising young attorney from us, that was below the belt."

"Had your eye on her, did you?" Sherman asked with a wry grin. "Maybe a romantic interest?"

James reddened, and then scoffed. "Don't be ridiculous," he said, but his reaction seemed to indicate Sherman was right on the money.

"Allow me to give you some free advice," Sherman continued with an easygoing smile. "The next time you try to play games with me, it'll cost the taxpayers a few more zeroes on the judgment, and I'll make sure my friend, the mayor, knows why."

He looked over at me. "I contributed a sizeable amount of money to his campaign. He's an imbecile, but he'll listen if I tell him the head of his legal department is not fit for the job," he said with a wink.

Counselor Henson furrowed his brow and started to retort, but instead buried his nose in his paperwork, furiously scribbling more notes.

William walked in fifteen minutes later carrying a latte from Starbucks. "Sorry I'm late. I had some last minute work at the office."

Sherman stared coolly at him a moment as William sat down beside him. One thing about my father, a firm slap to the side of the head one day when I was late to work cured me like nothing else could. Perhaps I'd suggest it to Sherman.

The first part of the deposition was a mere formality. Officer Acevedo and Sergeant Trent entered the room with their attorneys. Neither made eye contact with me. By prior arrangement between all of the attorneys, immediately after being sworn in, both men formally stated they were invoking their Fifth Amendment right and therefore were not going to answer any questions. Once their declarations were recorded, they quietly left.

As we'd discussed, Jay Sansing was deposed first. Sherman and I were convinced he would be the most straightforward, and besides, I wanted Perry to sit in the hallway and stew all day while everyone else went ahead of him.

Jay was indeed honest and forthcoming with every answer. Unfortunately, his testimony revealed nothing we didn't already know. Jay testified he'd never had direct contact with Perry, that it was Commander Bartlett who had directed the course of the investigation and had given the information about Brittany Long.

Oscar was next to be deposed and he didn't let us down. His manner was arrogant, condescending, and he attempted to interject his own opinions to almost every question asked. Sherman made him look like a fool, but fools seldom realize when they're being made a fool of.

He made one monumental slip up in our favor. He stated he'd had an elevator conversation with Perry regarding the murder investigation and had assured Oscar that Brittany Long was credible.

After lunch, the commander of the Office of Professional Accountability was deposed. Sory Bartlett was a handsome black man who looked like he may have played sports in college, which indeed he had. Cornerback for UT, if I remember correctly. He was in his mid-forties, but looked ten years younger. At the moment, he was wearing a very expensive-looking, oxford-gray pinstripe suit which was custom tailored to his athletic physique. If you were to see him walking down the street, you'd think he was a hotshot lawyer or something, not a cop.

That was the extent of his professionalism. He answered Sherman's questions with the vagueness and double-speak of an oily politician. An oily politician wearing a five hundred dollar suit.

"Commander Bartlett, how were you made aware of the alleged eyewitness known as Brittany Long?"

"I believe Detectives Marson and Sansing discovered her during the course of their investigation," he replied with a straight face.

"Would it interest you to know that both detectives have advised in sworn statements it was you who provided them with this person?" Sherman countered.

"Did I?" he said.

"Are you avoiding answering the question?"

"Not at all, Counselor," Commander Bartlett replied.

"I'll make it simple for you and phrase the question where it can be answered with a simple yes or no. Did you inform either Detectives Marson or Sansing of anyone who identified themselves as an eyewitness to the alleged murder of Marcia Ironcutter?"

"I might have, but I honestly don't recall," he said. Sherman paused a moment and tried a different tactic.

"Did Assistant Chief Raymond Perry ever have a discussion with you about the alleged murder of Marcia Ironcutter?" Sherman pressed.

"Of course, it is my duty to keep my chain-of-command informed of all of our investigations."

"Did he direct you and your office to conduct an investigation?"

"As far as I recall, we discussed the case and decided it was prudent to conduct an investigation."

"Based on what facts?" Sherman asked.

"I don't recall the specifics," Bartlett answered glibly.

"Did you ever have any discussions with the Chief of Police regarding the woman identifying herself as Brittany Long?"

"I don't recall."

"You seem to have a problem with your memory, Commander Bartlett," Sherman said. Bartlett smirked, as if he had scored points.

Sherman sighed. "Very well," he said as he nodded at William, who quickly stood and walked out of the room. "I'm going to call for a recess at this time."

"What for?" James asked.

"So that William can contact the judge."

"So, I can leave?" Commander Bartlett asked as he started to stand.

"Oh, no, Commander, you are still under subpoena. And, in approximately one hour, I will be presenting you with a Motion to Compel." Sherman leaned forward. "We expected you to behave in a dishonorable manner and planned for it. The motion is already typed up and sitting on his clerk's desk, merely awaiting a signature. I can assure you the motion will be granted, and you will be the one to bear the brunt of the costs associated with obtaining the order."

Commander Bartlett frowned at Sherman a moment before looking at James. "Can he do that?"

James nodded. "I'm afraid he can, if he's successful in obtaining the motion."

I felt like it was time to jump in. "James, why don't you and Sorry, I mean, Sory, go somewhere private and you can explain to him why he's not being as clever as he thinks he is."

"That is an excellent suggestion, Thomas," Sherman added. "Perhaps we all need a break." Simone didn't have to be told twice. She hurried out of the door and made a beeline toward the restroom.

James motioned to Sory and the two of them headed toward the door. Sory gave me the stink-eye briefly as he walked out.

"So, tell me what this is all about," I said when I was sure nobody could hear us.

Sherman explained. "When one is being deposed, it is expected that the person will answer the questions honestly and to the best of their ability. According to Rule Thirty-Seven of the Rules of Civil Procedure, evasive or incomplete answers are viewed as a refusal to answer. The Motion to Compel is a way of pointing this out and directing the deponent to comply."

"But, what if he simply continues acting the same way? Refusing to comply, and doing the same stupid dance?"

"There are a couple of options, including being found in contempt of court," Sherman replied. "I'm sure James is explaining it to the commander."

Surprisingly, it didn't take an hour. While William was getting the motion, James and Sory walked back in the conference room. Sory took his seat and stared like he was a VIP member of some secret society; James plopped down in his seat heavily.

"William should be back within the hour with the motion," Sherman said.

"I've explained the issue with Commander Bartlett," James said.

"And?"

"We'll wait on the motion," Sory said curtly. His mouth was compressed into a taut angry line and he stared at us like it was the showdown at the OK corral.

Sherman and I ignored him and discussed golf for the next fifteen minutes before William walked in and slapped some papers in front of James.

"The Motion to Compel has been signed and hereby served," he said.

"Excellent," Sherman responded and nodded at the stenographer. "For the record, a Motion to Compel has now been served to the deponent. Let's proceed." He focused on Sory.

"Commander Bartlett, have the specifics of a Motion to Compel order been adequately explained to you by counsel?"

"I believe so."

"Good, do you intend to comply with the order or continue with vague and nonresponsive answers to my questions?"

"Ask your questions, lawyer," he replied sourly.

"Alright, now let's start over. Were you directed by Assistant Chief of Police Raymond Perry to open an investigation into the death of Marcia Ironcutter?"

"Yes."

"Under what circumstances did this occur?"

"The subject was brought up during a meeting," he replied.

"When was this meeting and what was discussed?"

"I don't recall the specific meeting when this case was first brought up." Sherman stared at him. I could see Sory's jaw muscles tightening. "You must understand, we have regular meetings, multiple meetings, and during the course of those meetings, a lot of topics are discussed," he quickly added.

"Ah, I see," Sherman said and nodded in seeming understanding. "And in these meetings an inordinate amount of information is discussed?"

"Exactly," Commander Bartlett replied.

"Would it be safe to say so much information is discussed, it would be difficult to remember everything?"

"Yes, absolutely," Sory said quickly.

"So, during these meetings which entailed so much information, did you ever take notes?" Sherman asked innocently. I saw where he was going. Notes, whether they were formal, typed reports, or handwritten scribbles, were discoverable material. Commander Bartlett seemed to understand as well.

"It's possible," he said, cautiously.

"Oh, come now, Commander Bartlett. Are you attempting to assert you don't remember if you ever took notes in a meeting with members of your chain-of-command?" Sherman asked. Sory stared at him, wondering how to answer. Sherman helped him.

"A professional, which I'm sure you purport yourself to be, would undoubtedly take notes when he is in a high-level meeting with his superiors, especially when discussing sensitive matters such as police misconduct. Or, maybe I'm wrong about you. You don't care about your profession?"

"I most certainly do care about my profession, Mister Lawyer," Sory retorted. "Don't dare doubt it."

"Excellent, so you did take notes during these meetings?"

"From time to time," he reluctantly answered.

Sherman looked over at his grandson William, who retrieved a thick stack of paperwork from his briefcase.

"For the record, defense counsel is now being duly served with subpoenas for discovery of all notes, recordings, emails, and any other correspondence, both professional and personal of Commander Sory Bartlett," William said, as he handed it to Hensley.

Sory exploded. "You can't do that!"

"Of course I can," Sherman replied and sighed. "Commander Bartlett, did you really believe you could come in here today and lie your way out of this?"

Sory launched out of his chair so hard it slid backwards and smacked the wall. He directed his attention to Hensley.

"You've got to stop this. We have at least three sensitive investigations underway. There is no way we can make any of that information public!" It was no act, he was actually angry now. James didn't respond.

Sherman leaned back in his chair and stared balefully at the man. "Commander, I've been doing this longer than you've been alive. No matter what antic you attempt, I've encountered it before."

Sory stared at him with undisguised contempt before motioning at James. The two men once again stepped into the hallway where we could overhear a tense, hushed argument. They came back in the conference room a few minutes later.

"Commander Bartlett is prepared to turnover copies of his notes and emails specifically relating to the case of Marcia Ironcutter, but for the record, I am vehemently objecting to the other demands in this motion," Counselor Hensley said after we had all gotten seated.

"That would be a good start, James," Sherman replied. "I will look over what is provided and then reevaluate the motion for discovery." Sherman looked at his legal pad a moment.

"Let's focus all of the meetings between Assistant Chief Perry and yourself concerning Thomas Ironcutter."

"Yes?"

"Did you take notes during these meetings?" Sherman asked.

"I was specifically directed by Assistant Chief Perry to take no notes of any of our meetings regarding Thomas Ironcutter," he replied, and after pausing for a moment, continued talking. "However, I may have taken notes after each meeting, just in case."

I saw Sherman's eyebrow arch. "Is Assistant Chief Perry aware you took notes?" he asked.

"No, I don't believe he is," Sory answered.

It was a breakthrough we'd been hoping for, and now the questioning began in earnest. To my surprise, Sorry Sory began providing detailed answers to Sherman's questions. The questioning about Perry's involvement in the case lasted for the next two hours. Ultimately, Bartlett placed the blame all on Perry and chose the theme of merely following orders.

His change in demeanor reminded me of an old sergeant I'd worked with in patrol. He was full of Yogi Berra-like euphemisms, one of which was: when the ship is sinking, it's every rat for himself. It seemed apt in this instance.

"Okay, Commander, I am now going to direct your attention to the day of Thomas Ironcutter's arrest," Sherman said.

"Okay," Commander Bartlett answered warily.

"I am certain you are aware of my client being injured in an unprovoked assault during his arrest, and please don't claim ignorance." Sherman said.

Bartlett shifted in his chair. "Yes, I'm aware of it," he answered, and then volunteered to add to the topic.

"Once being made aware of the video of the arrest, an investigation was begun. Officer Acevedo and Sergeant Trent have been disempowered pending the outcome of the investigation."

"Why did it take so long to launch an investigation?" William asked.

"There was no undue delay," Sory answered.

"On the day of the arrest, Thomas Ironcutter was transported to the hospital to be treated for the injuries he received as a result of the beating. Yet, the formal investigation was not begun until three days ago on orders of Mayor Schoenfeld, correct?"

"I'm uncertain of the exact timeline," Sory answered.

"And he didn't order the investigation until days after the video was made public, correct?"

"I'm not sure," he answered again.

William kept at it. "Is it true that Sergeant Trent is in the same Masonic Lodge as the chief of police?"

"I wouldn't know the answer to that question."

"And this is the result of the delay in the investigation, correct?"

"Again, I wouldn't know the answer to that question," Sory said.

"Commander Bartlett," William said with a pointed stare. "Now that you are aware of this information, information which would show an act of impropriety by the Chief of Police, do you intend to open an investigation?"

"We don't start investigations just because a lawyer says so," Sory retorted.

"I am a citizen of Nashville, Tennessee and I am making you aware of wrongdoing within the police department," William pressed.

Sory stared back at him with undisguised loathing. "So?"

"Very good," William said. "We now have you on record, disregarding allegations of wrongdoing. I am certain the Department of Justice will be very interested in this."

"I never said I'd refuse to investigate," he said quickly. I shook my head in disgust; the man was unbelievable.

"What more do you people want?" Sory said in almost a shout. "Those two men, who are damn good officers, are in all likelihood going to be arrested and fired from their jobs. You should be happy."

"Why hasn't it been done already?" William fired back. Sory glared, but didn't answer.

Sherman spoke up. "Commander Bartlett, are you waiting for the conclusion of these depositions before completing the investigation?"

Sory looked pointedly at me. "Yes."

I knew what he meant. He was waiting until I was deposed. They desperately wanted something to come out during my deposition which they could hang their hat on and close the case. And by closing it, I mean they wanted to find something to blame everything on me and exonerate themselves.

The questioning of Commander Bartlett took another hour, but nothing more of significance was gleaned out of him. It was going to come down to whatever his notes revealed. And, whatever Raymond Perry had to say. Sherman concluded his questioning of the esteemed OPA Command and leaned back in his seat. William nudged him and pointed at his watch.

"My co-counsel has pointed out it is after five. I believe we have concluded deposing Commander Bartlett at this time." He looked at James. "Counselor, shall we begin again at eight tomorrow morning?"

Hensley nodded in agreement and then held up a finger. "As far as I know, all attempts to contact Miss Long have been unsuccessful. That only leaves Assistant Chief Perry and then your client." He looked at both Sherman and William. "Unless you're going to surprise me with some more subpoenas." Sherman shook his head with a pleasant, but tired, smile. I realized this had been a long day for the old man and suddenly became concerned.

William excused the stenographer. She gathered up her equipment and left quietly. Commander Bartlett stood to leave and gave me a long hard look before walking out.

"He doesn't seem to like you very much," William observed.

"We have a bit of history," I said, but didn't elaborate. I silently gestured toward Sherman, who had taken his glasses off and was rubbing his eyes.

William nodded. "Gramps, why don't you go home, I'll take care of everything here." He then looked at me. "Tomorrow is going to be very interesting, I'm thinking."

I spoke with William a few more minutes and then walked Simone to her car.

"How does it look from a third party perspective?" I asked.

"Looks pretty good, but I'm biased," Simone answered.

"Oh? On whose side?"

Simone eyed me and smiled. "When are you taking me out again?"

"How about tonight?"

She shook her head. "Madison and I are going to a hot yoga class."

"What about tomorrow night?"

She shook her head again. "Madison has dance class."

I rubbed my chin. "I see. Well, why don't you call me when you have no class?"

Now she laughed. "Only you could find a Rodney Dangerfield quote out of all of this."

"Rodney was a little before your time, I'm thinking."

She gave me a playful punch in the arm. "My father loved him. I remember watching him as a kid."

"Okay, I'm lost here. When's a good time?" I asked.

"I'll call you, okay?"

"Sure."

She was standing at her car door now. "Come here," she said quietly.

The kiss was wonderful. Some of her perfume rubbed on me and it smelled intoxicating. It smelled so good, it kept me from smoking a cigar. I was so enamored, I almost missed the black car following me.

I exited the interstate, entered a nearby shopping center, and rode around the parking lot. The car dutifully followed.

"Well, I know how to take care of this nonsense," I muttered and sped behind a Target store and parked beside their dumpsters.

I'd gotten my forty-five out of the lock box mounted under the seat about the time the black car slowly came into view. The windows were tinted, but I knew who it was.

Enrique.

Chapter 39

I kept my forty-five down below my open window, ready to bring it up quickly and fire, and waited. Enrique slowly drove past me, and once he got to the end of the building, made a U-turn and drove back. He stopped, his driver's side even with mine, and rolled down his window.

"What the hell do you want?" I demanded.

Enrique stared at me for several long seconds before closing his window. The dark tint hid his facial expression as he slowly drove off.

I worked the heavy bag long and hard. Although Enrique never said a word, his message was crystal clear. This was twice now he'd popped up. He was tacitly telling me he could find me anytime he wanted.

I made it to almost four full minutes before I had to stop and catch my breath. Sometime during this, Anna had snuck in the garage and was now watching me.

"Are you training for the Olympics, big guy?" she asked with a grin. I pulled the mitts off and stretched while I caught my breath. When I did, I told her about Enrique and the little game he pulled.

"I'm thinking I want you to start carrying a gun," I said.

Anna shook her head quickly. "I don't like guns. If it weren't for guns, my father might still be alive."

I wasn't going to argue the point with her, at least not yet. We went inside and fixed ourselves sandwiches.

"We need to start eating better," Anna remarked as I washed down a mouthful with a swig of milk. I looked at her, but didn't say anything. I thought I *was* being more health conscious as I took another drink of milk. I mean, I usually washed my dinner down with beer.

The deposition with the Assistant Chief of Police, Raymond Perry, began the next morning. He walked in fifteen minutes late with an air of arrogance.

"Let's get started, my time is limited," he announced. I snorted in disgust. He glared at me in return. At sixty-eight, the man was well past his prime. He should have retired years ago, but when a man did nothing but ride a desk and delegate, I suppose he could continue working as long as the chief of police allowed it.

After he was sworn in, William led the questioning. "Please state your name and current occupation for the record."

"My name is Raymond Walker Perry. I am currently the Assistant Chief of Police for the Metropolitan Police Department."

"Mister Perry…" Before William could complete the question, he was interrupted.

"You will address me by my proper title, young man," he said a little indignantly.

William was unfazed. "Mister Perry, please state for the record your personal feelings regarding Thomas Ironcutter."

Perry briefly glared at me with undisguised hatred. "He is a murderer. He is a scourge on the department and deserves to be in prison, sitting on death row."

And so, the tone of the entire deposition was set. He denied everything, even when confronted with Commander Bartlett's testimony. His lies were blatant and obvious. I hoped he did the same thing when this was tried in front of a jury. As the questioning came to a conclusion, he began pointedly staring at me.

Sherman noticed it. "Is there something you would like to say to my client, Mister Perry?"

He leaned forward in his seat, looking at me with the same earlier expression of hate. "This is your uncle's fault. His death is just desserts, as yours will be."

I stared at him coldly as he leaned back and actually smiled with his thin wormy lips. The man was delusional. He believed he was on the winning side. It was incredible.

William started to speak again but Sherman patted him on the arm.

"It's alright, William," he said. "We've gotten what we wanted."

Sherry Simpson, or Brittany Long, or whatever the hell she was calling herself these days, did not appear for the deposition. No surprise there. So, I was next.

Counselor Hensley looked at Perry. "I believe you are through being deposed," he said. "You're free to leave."

Perry didn't move. "Oh, no, I am going to stay and listen to the lies this person is about to spew out." He continued eyeing me, like we were two cage fighters about to get it on. It would have been nice to reach across the table and bitch slap him, but leave it to the mores of society to prevent such things.

James looked at Raymond Perry for a long moment before reluctantly nodding in agreement. I guess he wanted an audience for what he was about to do. I was sworn, and then Hensley looked across the table at me like he was a great white shark circling the waters. I'm sure he thought he was going to wipe the floor with me.

"State your full name for the record," Hensley began.

"Thomas Ironcutter Junior," I replied. I didn't like identifying myself as a junior. Whenever I identified myself as being named after my father, I felt like I was disgracing myself.

The first thirty minutes consisted of mostly background questions. It was a complete waste of time as I could plainly see my personnel folder lying open before him. I suppose he thought it was a way of softening me up before he got to the direct questions.

"Now, let us proceed to the night when you murdered your wife," he said it accusingly and then paused, waiting for an angry outburst. I sat stoically and stared at him.

"Do you have a response, Mister Ironcutter?"

"To what?" I countered.

"About the night you murdered your wife," he said with a smirk.

"I'm waiting for you to ask a specific question, Counselor. That's what we're here for, isn't it?"

"I'm asking you about murdering your wife."

"Oh, could you please repeat your question? I could have sworn all you did was make an asinine statement."

"So you do not deny you murdered your wife?"

"I deny murdering my wife," I replied. He didn't expect me to admit to anything, he was merely attempting to anger me. But, his little ploy didn't work. I wasn't some greenhorn, I'd seen this tactic many times. If he was smart, he would've known this.

"Alright, were you present on the night of February 1st, 2014, when your wife was murdered?"

"No," I replied. He looked confused for a moment.

"Are you trying to play games, Mister Ironcutter?" he asked scornfully.

"No."

He stretched his arms dramatically and smiled. "You're the person who called 911, is that correct?"

"Yes."

"So, you *were* present when she died."

"Is that a question?" I asked.

"Yes, it is."

"The answer to your question is no." I replied. Obviously, my simple answers were annoying him. He grabbed his glasses, pulled them off of his nose, and slapped them onto his legal pad. I wondered if he thought that would intimidate me. There was an old captain in OPA, back when it was still called Internal Affairs. He would often use the same tactic.

"Well, then, please explain the discrepancy of your previous statements to your current position in which you deny being present."

"I've never stated I was present at the time of my wife's death, counselor."

"But you're the one who called 911, correct?"

"Correct," I answered.

"So, you were present at the time of your wife's death," he declared. I could have let him go on and on, but decided to help him, but only to get things going.

"When I came home, I discovered my wife was dead, so I called 911." I leaned forward. "You see, Counselor, she was alive when I left and dead when I returned. Is that a satisfactory explanation?"

He appeared flustered at first, and then he smiled like he had me cornered.

"I'm glad you brought it up, Mister Ironcutter. Where did you go when you left your residence on the night of February 1st of 2014?"

"On the advice of my attorney, I am not going to answer that question."

"You don't have a choice," he replied forcefully, like he was speaking to a recalcitrant teenager. He couldn't contain his grin as he pulled some papers out of a folder and slid them across the table. William picked them up and examined them.

"The Motion to Compel order was a splendid idea, Counselor," James said to William. "So, after explaining to the judge your client's past refusal to answer this simple question, he agreed to the preemptive motion." James continued to grin smugly at his perceived victory as the three of us looked over his motion.

When he made his proclamation, I scribbled a note to Sherman; is it valid? Sherman gave a small nod. I sat silent for a long minute, looking at the table. James finally cleared his throat. I looked up to see him staring at me expectantly.

"You may now answer the question, Mister Ironcutter," he said pleasantly.

"Alright, Counselor, I'll answer your question, but I believe the answer will require some back story if you want a full understanding of what happened that night."

James looked at me curiously before nodding. "By all means."

"It started back in 1995 when a young secretary for the West Precinct came to work one morning wearing a large pair of sunglasses."

"This is irrelevant!" Raymond suddenly burst out. James scowled at him.

"Shut up, Perry, or leave."

"Oh, I insist he stay and hear everything," I responded and then fixed Perry with a stare. "But, heed the advice of your attorney and shut your mouth." Perry gave me a hateful stare, with his little lips pinched so tightly I thought he was trying to pass a kidney stone, but he kept his mouth shut.

"So, like I said before I was rudely interrupted, 1995. Michael Ironcutter was the day-shift lieutenant at that time. He realized something was wrong. He took her back to his office, spoke to her gently, and finally convinced her to remove her sunglasses. He discovered she had a black eye, given to her by her husband, a disgusting little man by the name of Raymond Walker Perry."

"That's a lie," Perry said. He sounded pitiful, like he was being demonized.

"Oh, it's the truth and you know it. You're a despicable, cowardly, woman beater," I said, stared at him a second, and then turned to James.

"Uncle Mike, well, he was having his own marital issues. The two of them found they had many things in common and formed a friendship. It soon lead to an affair that lasted for several years, until the night in question."

"What happened?" James asked.

I explained everything. I told of the phone call from Uncle Mike, how I met them at the hotel, how I cleaned everything up and got them home, and then after I returned home, discovering my dead wife. It took about thirty minutes, everyone listened raptly.

"Was a police report filed?" James finally asked.

"Not until the next day," I answered. "Uncle Mike reported he was waylaid by a couple of thugs who robbed him and took the car."

"Did either of them go to a hospital for treatment?"

"No. They didn't suffer any major physical injuries. Uncle Mike got a black eye and a knot or two on his head. Mrs. Perry's injuries were more – emotional." I paused a moment. "I tried to get her to go to the hospital, but she refused."

Assistant Chief of Police Raymond Perry stood suddenly. Too suddenly, he must have gotten dizzy. He steadied himself for a moment, eyed me like I'd committed a mortal sin, and then walked out without a word. There was a long minute of silence while James took notes and then reread them several times before looking up.

"Not to be insensitive, but since your uncle's death, it doesn't seem like this story can be substantiated," he said. I didn't respond. There was enough to substantiate it, if it was needed. There was the stolen vehicle report on file, and he could always depose Raymond's wife. I didn't bother pointing it out.

"You said the affair ended, correct?" James asked. I nodded.

"It's my understanding it ended that night. The last I heard, Mrs. Perry went to live with her sister in Arizona."

"Were those two men ever identified?"

I looked at James a long five seconds. "I wouldn't know."

He stared back at me, knowing that I was lying, but decided not to pursue it.

And so it went. I thought it'd be over quickly after my admission, but the questioning continued for over six hours. Often times, he'd ask the same question three or four times before Sherman would admonish him. He pointedly did not ask me about the arrest. I guess he thought if he ignored it, it wouldn't be brought up in the civil trial.

After a particularly long lull in which Counselor Hensley stared at his notes with a confused expression, Sherman spoke up.

"Counselor?" he asked. James looked up. "It's getting late, do you have any other questions for my client?"

James stared at his legal pad for a long minute, and then conceded defeat. "There will be no further questions at this time, but we reserved the right to depose Mister Ironcutter again at a later time if and when new evidence comes to light."

Sherman acknowledged him and dismissed Simone. She had her equipment packed away quickly, said goodbye, gave me a look, and hurried out of the door, muttering something about rush-hour traffic. I stood and stretched.

"Sherman, I appreciate all of the time you've spent on this," I said.

"Not at all," Sherman answered with a tired smile.

"Go home, old man," I said. He nodded and stood. William was about to follow him out, but I motioned for him to stay.

"Why don't you and I walk down Second Avenue and find a place to have a drink?" I asked him. He looked at me, started to decline, but then he must have sensed I needed to talk to him, which I did. We settled on Hooter's, which was located at the corner of Second and Union. We were seated by a girl with a big smile and even bigger breasts. We ordered a couple of beers.

"There's something important I need to tell you," I said.

"I figured," William replied as he watched another cute waitress walk by.

"I don't want to worry the old man, but there is a distinct possibility my life is in danger."

William's eyes widened when he realized I was serious. It took three beers for me to tell him everything and a couple more to fully answer all of his questions.

"So, there it is," I said. "He knows I'm onto him. He's playing a little bit of psychological warfare on me at the moment, but it's only a matter of time before he takes it a step further."

"We need to report this," William contended.

"I've left a couple of messages with Reuben Chandler. He's the Special Agent in Charge. So far, he hasn't called back."

"What about Metro?" William asked.

I shook my head. "I have nothing but conjecture at this point. The only solid evidence I have is his affair with Leona Spieth. Hell, unless the DNA shows a match, I don't even have any hard proof he was doing my wife."

"What can I do?" William finally asked.

"If I turn up missing or dead, contact Detective Percy Trotter and tell him everything. Right now, he's in California following up on a missing person's case. He should be back in a couple of days. All of the information I have is stored on one of Ronald's computers. I've no doubt it's all encrypted. And that's about it."

William nodded slowly. "I'm glad you told me. If something were to happen, at least I'll know how to respond." He paused a minute and looked at me. "I don't know what else to do."

"I don't either." I looked at my beer, knowing all of the information I had on Enrique was sparse, barely even reaching the level of reasonable suspicion.

"Alright, let's get out of here." I started to fish my wallet out, but William stopped me.

"I've got it," he said, fishing his own wallet out and pulling out an American Express Gold card. I nodded my thanks.

I watched the streets and the people as I walked back to my truck. Enrique was nowhere around. I got in my truck and went home.

Chapter 40

After the depositions were over, I had time to really think about Special Agent Enrique Hernandez, Marcia, Lester, Robard Trucking, my arrest, and all of the other nonsense. I was fairly certain the only way to get personal closure was to get closure on all of these other issues. The question was, how in the heck was I going to do it? It took an entire cigar and a pot of coffee before I figured out a plan. A brilliant plan. Or so I kept telling myself.

I picked up the phone and said a name.

"Hello?"

"Teresa?" I asked.

"Yes, who's calling?"

"Hi, it's Thomas."

There was a moment's pause before she answered. "Oh, hi, Thomas." I honestly couldn't tell if she was glad I called or apprehensive. I plowed ahead anyway.

"Hi. Listen, I'd like to meet with you, if you have time. I have something I'd like to talk to you about in person, maybe over a drink, if you're interested."

"Why, Thomas, are you asking me out?" she asked with a soft laugh.

After quite a bit of small talk, and maybe even a little bit of flirtation, Teresa agreed to meet with me.

I picked an out of the way bar on Harding Pike, sufficiently seedy enough and far enough away from the FBI office so we wouldn't run into any of her co-workers. The clientele had changed since the place had first opened, mostly Hispanic now, but nobody paid us any attention. I picked a booth in the back.

"What'll you have?" the waitress asked as we sat. She was a buxom blonde with a meaty backside, hinting of at least eight or nine kids back home.

"Vodka gimlet," Teresa said. "Please use some decent vodka." The waitress nodded indifferently.

"I'll have the same," I said. We made small talk until the waitress returned.

"The bartender used Kettle One, okay?" she asked with a touch of insolence.

"Perfect," I answered and gave her a pleasant smile. Her mouth formed a tight line before she walked off. Maybe it was a smile, maybe it was gas.

"Nice place," Teresa commented. Her sarcasm was evident.

"It used to be, years ago. I chose it because I didn't want anyone to see us together."

"Gee, you sure know how to make a girl feel good," she quipped.

"Oh, I didn't mean it like that, honest. What I meant to say is I have some stuff I want to discuss with you in confidence."

Teresa looked around. "You've certainly chosen the right spot then. Assuming no cholos come in and try to start trouble." She took a small sip, tasting it carefully. Apparently, she approved and took another, larger sip.

"Enrique's dirty," I said. She looked at me coolly.

"That's a pretty harsh accusation," she said. "Perhaps you should explain."

"He inserted himself into Robard Trucking and –"

She cut me off. "That's how it works, Thomas," she said dismissively. "We get word of a business engaging in organized crime and we investigate. Enrique went in undercover. It was all done by the book."

"May I ask where this incriminating information originally came from?" I asked.

She'd recovered now and looked at me steadily. "I'm not at liberty to say."

"That's a flippant answer," I said. She didn't respond. "Okay, I'll help you out. All of the evidence, all of the criminal activity, originated with Enrique. The Spieths weren't trafficking any drugs until Enrique came along. He appealed to their greed and convinced them they'd make a lot of money. It makes for a pretty good entrapment defense."

Teresa scoffed now. "Yeah, good luck with that one." She took a long drink. "We've seized over a million from the Detroit bank and there're several indictments in the works. With Enrique's help, we've made a good case." She looked at me pointedly. "There is no entrapment, Thomas."

"Yeah, about that, are you familiar with Tag First Distribution?"

"Of course," she said. "It was a shell corporation used by the Detroit bank to launder money."

"Who created Tag First?" I asked.

She shrugged. "One of the mob mopes."

"The Articles of Incorporation show Javier Garcia as the president and CEO. That's Enrique's nom de guerre, am I right?"

She rolled her eyes with an air of indifference.

"He set up the money laundering scheme through Tag First Distribution, his shell corporation."

"Easily explained," she replied.

"There's more," I said calmly.

This time, Teresa laughed as she signaled the waitress for another drink. "Oh, do tell, I'm all ears."

"He's been sleeping with Leona Spieth for a couple of years now." She was in the middle of swallowing when I dropped that one on her. She choked and started coughing.

"Sorry," I muttered, although I wasn't, and waited for her to recover.

She wiped her mouth daintily with a cocktail napkin and then fixed me with a hard stare. "What in the hell are you talking about?"

I told her about Herman Alsup and the video he'd taken. "When I confronted Leona about it, she told me everything."

"You've spoken to her?" she asked. I nodded. "And, there's a video?"

"Yep. Leona made me delete it, but I have a copy," I said and patted my iPhone. "Got it all right here, among other things. Would you like to watch it?" I asked. "Not to be crass, but Enrique really put it to her." She didn't answer. I sat there a moment and waited until she'd almost digested what I said and then dropped another one on her.

"He's committed murder too. More than one, in fact."

She gave pause now. The waitress set two fresh vodka gimlets down and walked off without comment. I hadn't ordered a second one, I'd barely touched my first one, but whatever.

"You are accusing a Federal agent of murder," she said it very slowly, as if I'd spit it out so quick she missed something.

"Maybe not as much an accusation, but I have enough evidence to warrant strong suspicion."

"And it's all in your iPhone, right?" she asked with an arched eyebrow.

"Some of it," I responded vaguely and took a sip of my first drink.

"Okay, I'll bite, whom has he murdered?" she asked. "Oh wait, let me guess, you think he murdered Lester."

"Yep."

She laughed again, but this time it was forced, contrived. She took a long sloppy swallow. "Why would he do something so absurd?"

"Remember back when you three served the search warrant?" I asked. She gave a slight nod. "You didn't get everything." Of course, it was a lie, and normally I detest lying, but this was the FBI I was dealing with. They had in fact taken everything, but she didn't know it. I pressed on.

"Lester knew all about Enrique, and knew he was dirty. He knew Enrique was sleeping with Leona and he knew Enrique killed my wife."

Leona stared at me hard. She was wondering if I was drunk, crazy, or a combination of both.

"Your wife, Thomas? Really?" Sarcasm now. "And why, pray tell, would an FBI agent want to murder your wife? Really, Thomas, you've lost your mind. You should seriously consider seeing a therapist."

I sipped my first drink quietly. She attempted to put a hard stare on me, probably in hopes I'd break down and apologize for my transgressions, or at least offer up a valid reason. I waited. She blinked first.

"Okay, why on earth do you think he killed your wife?"

"Because she was pregnant with his child."

Now, she dropped her glass, spilling its contents on the table. There was one of those metal napkin containers sitting on the table. She hastily pulled a few out and made a halfhearted attempt to clean up her mess before grabbing the drink meant for me and taking a healthy swallow.

"You're a liar, Thomas Ironcutter. I don't know why you're making these ridiculous accusations, but you need to back off."

"You seem to be taking this personally," I said. "Why?"

She glared at me. "Because you're besmirching the name of a highly respected co-worker."

"I have proof," I said plainly, maybe even with a hint of mystery, or so I hoped.

"If you have proof, you should turn it over," she said a little nervously.

"I intend to, but not yet."

"Why not?"

"I still have a couple of loose ends to tie up," I said.

"Like what?"

"Although I'm positive of the outcome, I need to submit Enrique's DNA for comparison testing."

"How did you get Enrique's DNA?" she asked suspiciously. "You didn't get a search warrant, I'd know if you did."

"Nope, no search warrant."

She tried to laugh again, but it sounded more like she was trying to clear some phlegm out of her throat. "So, you have no proof. Hell, Thomas, how do you even know the kid wasn't yours?"

"Oh, I've already covered that one." No, not really, the tests hadn't come back yet, but she didn't know that.

"One of my buddies with the homicide unit has already run a DNA comparison to see if the child was mine. It wasn't." Actually, I didn't know the answer yet. The tests probably wouldn't be complete for another couple of weeks, but she didn't need to know that.

"So, you think she was pregnant with Enrique's child." She scoffed now. "You have one hell of an imagination."

"Oh, the affair was real." I told her about the connection with Robard and the insurance company.

Teresa scoffed. "So, you've made this, this magical nexus between Enrique and your wife," she said as she held eye contact. "That's not enough probable cause for a search warrant."

"You are absolutely right. I thought I'd hit a dead end. No way to prove my theory that she was carrying his child. No probable cause for a search warrant, and we both know Enrique would never voluntarily submit to testing. And then I remembered, Enrique smoked a couple of cigarettes at my house, and I still had the butts sitting in my ashtray. Well, as you can imagine, when I remembered those butts, it became a simple matter of running another test. I haven't done it yet, but I will."

"Why not?" she asked.

I shrugged. "I've had a couple of delays, but I'm back on track now. All I need to do is send them off to the lab, unless the FBI would like to get involved with this."

She stared at me steadily.

"What do you think?" I asked.

"I think you're out of your ever-loving mind, accusing Agent Hernandez of murdering two people." She scoffed again, as if I'd just proclaimed Jesus was nothing more than a snake oil salesman.

"Actually, he's killed three people," I corrected. "He killed Rhoda Gwinnette too. Before you ask why he killed her, I don't know why, other than the fact he's a full-blown psychopath. Hell, for all I know, he's killed more than three." I stood. "I need to hit the head. Be right back."

I walked down a short hallway to where the restrooms were located, waited ten seconds, and then eased back and casually peeked around the corner. There was a plastic plant sitting on a table beside the hallway. It was covered in a thick layer of dust, which pretty much defined the state of this bar. I crouched down behind it to hide from Teresa, although I probably looked like a drunken idiot crouching down behind a plant. As I knew she would, she was texting furiously. I waited another minute, watched her slam down the drink intended for me and ordered another. I waited thirty seconds and returned to the booth.

I smiled pleasantly as I sat. "Where were we? Oh yeah, Enrique. Let me ask you something, are you sleeping with him?" I asked casually. Her eyes widened a moment before she recovered.

"Of course not," she said coolly. Her phone vibrated. She glanced at it quickly, but ignored it. "But even if I was, it'd be none of your business. Are you implying that I am?"

I shrugged innocently. "I'm wondering if he's done something else like this. What do you think?"

"I wouldn't know," she answered and picked up her drink. Seeing me watching her, she tried to make it casual as she took a swallow. "I've only recently transferred to Nashville."

"Oh? Where from?" I asked.

"Tulsa," she replied.

"I went through there once, Oral Roberts University is there, right?" I asked.

"Yeah, but I went to Oklahoma State."

"You guys need to investigate him, find out if he's done stuff like this before. How about I give your boss a call. What's his name? Chandler?"

"I'll speak to him," she responded quickly.

"Good," I said with mock excitation. "Set up a meeting. We'll nail the bastard."

Before Teresa could respond, her phone rang. It wasn't a text this time, but a real phone call. She looked at the caller I.D. and frowned. "I have to take this," she said, stood, and walked toward the restroom.

I'd done as much damage as I could and motioned to the waitress. "Do me a favor, beautiful," I said as I paid the tab and gave her a sweet tip. "Wait about five minutes or so and then tell my date I'm sorry but I had to leave."

"She won't be happy," she said as she eyed me like I was a lowly scoundrel.

I leaned forward a little. "Can you keep a secret?" I asked. Now she looked at me curiously.

I hooked a thumb toward the restrooms where Teresa was standing with her back toward us, talking on her phone, leaned in and lowered my voice.

"We've been talking about marriage, but I just found out she's been having an affair and is pregnant with another man's child. That's probably who she's chatting with right now."

"That bitch," she said contemptuously. "My ex did the same thing with me and left me and the two kids for her. Now I have to moonlight in this shithole to make ends meet." She looked toward the restrooms. "And that bitch is drinking while she's pregnant," she said, shaking her head. I shrugged, gave her another ten, and walked outside.

Chapter 41

I thought it'd be harder to follow Teresa. I mean, she was an FBI agent, trained in counter intelligence, surveillance detection techniques, all of that fancy horseshit. It only took a couple of minutes before she exited the front door in a hurry, obviously agitated. She threw a superficial glance around the parking lot, but totally missed me. Maybe because I was currently in Mick's car, a late model Buick. And, maybe, her thought processes were hampered due to all of the vodka gimlets I'd bought her. She hopped in her car and left in a hurry. I had no problem following her as she headed toward downtown.

She took the Shelby Avenue exit off of the interstate and parked in one of the parking lots near the Titan's football stadium. I kept driving and parked at a building which hid me in case she was watching. Said building was the Juvenile Justice Center. It's where kids went when the mean police arrested them. Getting out, I made my way around to the other side of the building and looked for a vantage point where I could spy on her unseen. I worked my way in between two parked cars, but before I even got hunkered down, I was spotted by a security guard who stormed up on me angrily.

"This is a secure area, what the hell are you doing here?" he demanded. When he got close and shone his flashlight in my face, he recognized me. I recognized him too.

"Ironcutter?" he asked.

"Hey, Bernie," I replied. Bernie Skaggs was a former Metro officer. A drunk driving conviction ended his career in law enforcement, but a local private security firm had hired him. He smiled broadly at me; I guess he thought we were friends since we'd both left the department in less than desirable circumstances.

"What are you doing?" he asked as he walked up and shook my hand.

"I'm working a case," I said, motioned him to squat down, and pointed over at Teresa's car. I hoped she hadn't seen me.

"A case?" he asked.

"Yeah, I'm doing PI work now," I said.

"Oh yeah? What kind of case?" He was curious now.

I pointed toward the big parking lot and Teresa's dark blue Ford, parked about a hundred yards from us. "One of those infidelity cases. A woman in that car out there is suspected of screwing around on her husband."

Bernie's eyes lit up. "No shit?"

"I shit you not," I replied. I could be a convincing liar when I had to be. As we watched, a black car drove up. Teresa got out of her car, stomped over, and got in the black car.

"Wow, looks like you caught her," Bernie said as he stared.

"Yeah."

"It's too bad those windows are tinted. You could've gotten pictures of them screwing each other," Bernie remarked and glanced at me. I guess he noticed I didn't have a camera. I made a show out of taking a couple of pictures with my iPhone.

"Yeah, but I think I've got enough." We watched the cars in silence. I could have gotten a tag number, but it wasn't necessary. I knew who was driving the Black Dodge Hemi with dark-tinted windows. It was my good pal Enrique. So, my suspicions were right on the money; Teresa was in cahoots with him. How far did their relationship go? Was she another dirty cop or was she simply stupidly in love. Hell, I was stupidly in love with Marcia, so I guess I could sympathize. I turned to Bernie.

"I'm going to head out and give the husband a call," I said. "Hey, I'd appreciate it if you'd keep this between us."

"You got it, partner," he replied. I didn't know we'd become partners so quick, but whatever made him feel relevant was fine with me. "Hey, are you needing any help?" he asked. "I've always had an inquisitive mind, I'd make a pretty good PI, if I do say so myself."

"Work is iffy," I replied. "This is the first case I've had in over a month."

Bernie looked dejected. "Oh."

I handed him a card. "But, we can keep in touch," I said.

Bernie nodded and gave me a friendly slap on the back.

"How did you know she was boinking Enrique?" Anna asked. She was sitting on the front porch with Henry and Tommy Boy when I'd arrived home. By the time I'd parked, she had a cold beer waiting on me.

"I had a hunch," I replied. "I'd seen them swap a few looks back and forth when they served the search warrant on me and I kind of figured it was more than simply a working relationship."

"That's all?"

"Yeah, sort of. When I asked to meet with her, I was testing the waters. I threw out a couple of statements and watched how she reacted. If she wasn't hooked up with him, she would have been eager to contact her boss and set up a meeting." I took a swig of beer. "Her behavior gave it away."

"What'll you think she'll do?" Anna asked.

"She's already done it. She's told Enrique everything I've accused him of." I told her of the phone texting and how I followed Teresa to her rendezvous by the Titan's stadium.

"I bet he's freaking out," she said.

I nodded, but was doubtful. I mean, if he took the time to think it all out, he'd realize all I could really confirm was he liked to sleep with as many women as he could. As far as instigating the heroin trafficking with Robard, well, good luck proving that one. And don't even get me started on the murders. I didn't have anything more than a few bits of circumstantial evidence and my gut instinct. I said as much to Anna.

"All I've done really was stir up the doo-doo," I concluded. "He'll either slip up or he won't. But, in the meantime, we've got to be careful. He might do something really crazy."

Tommy Boy had meandered up from wherever he'd been and jumped up on Anna's lap. "This is a sweet cat," she said as she stroked him.

I rolled my eyes.

"He's a sweet cat," she said again, then grinned at me. "Now we have two men in the house named Tommy."

I wasn't going to respond at first, but then couldn't help myself. "Back when I was a rookie in the academy, all of my friends called me Tommy Boy."

"Really?

"Yeah, we all had nicknames for each other. Let's see, you've met Dickie Do. Oh, and you met Sammy. We called him Saigon Sammy, even though he's Chinese. We had two Jacks, so one of them was Smilin' Jack and the other was Cactus Jack. We had a Barney, short for Barney Fife, Tex, Lefty, Rummy and Bulldog."

Anna laughed. "Weren't there any women in your academy class?" she asked.

"We started with four, but three quit. The only one left was redheaded, so we called her Red Robin."

I remembered Robin fondly. We'd hooked up after a party one night. The next morning, she informed me she was seeing someone else, and our interlude was nothing more than a one night stand. She stayed a cop all of eighteen months before entering law school, and was now a successful divorce attorney. Those were actually some good times.

"There were twenty-five of us in total, but only a few of us formed a tight bond."

"What was Percy's nickname?" she asked.

"You know, we never actually pinned a nickname on him. I always called him Big Percy. Dickie Do called him Big Pussy one day, but Percy set him straight real quick."

Anna laughed. "I bet he did." She carefully put Tommy Boy in my lap and stood.

"I'm going to take a shower and do some reading. Don't forget the vet appointment tomorrow," she reminded.

"Yeah, I know." During Henry's yearly appointment, the vet once again admonished me for not having Henry's balls cut out. Anna was present and sided with the vet. Feeling ganged up on, I reluctantly agreed. Henry and I swapped looks.

Chapter 42

My phone rang at about three, giving me reason to resume my practice of turning it off before going to bed. I was about to do so when I looked at the caller I.D.

It was Enrique.

"This ought to be good," I mumbled and answered. "Hello, killer," I said.

"Who the fuck do you think you are?" he growled in his distinct accent. His words were slurred, liked he'd been drinking. That meant I was getting to him. Good.

"Is that why you called?" I asked. "To make sure I know who I am? You must be estúpido."

There was a long pause and then I heard a quiet laugh.

"Oh, Thomas, Thomas, Thomas. Do you even know how thin the ice is that you're walking on?"

"I believe so. How about you?"

"You are a man of limited abilities, do you know that? Even your wife said so."

"You're probably correct, Enrique, but in the end, you'll be the one spending the rest of your life in prison, not me."

"Do not be so sure of that, my friend."

After Enrique hurled a few more expletives at me and hung up, I grabbed my gun and checked the house. I also visually checked each camera feed. I had several, some of them were out in the open, and some were camouflaged. Call me paranoid, but I never regretted spending the money on it. Not satisfied, I actually walked the entire perimeter of my property.

There was nothing going on. All was quiet. Even Tommy Boy, who had a habit of nocturnal wanderings, was curled up beside Henry. Even so, I had a hard time getting back to sleep.

I slept fitfully the rest of the night and awakened early. Anna joined me at the breakfast table.

"What time is the appointment?" she asked.

"Two," I said as I glanced down at Henry. He looked back suspiciously. "I think he knows."

Anna laughed. "It's for the best, Henry," she said and scratched him behind the ears.

"What're you doing today?" I asked.

Anna buttered a piece of toast. Tommy Boy jumped up in her lap and stuck his nose over the kitchen table. Anna tore off a small piece of the toast and gave it to him. "I'm meeting some friends for lunch. What about you?"

"I'm meeting Simone for lunch."

She grinned. "Good for you." She then leaned forward. "If you treat her right, maybe she'll give you dessert." She giggled then while I frowned.

I met Simone at a bistro in the hip area of east Nashville known as Five Points. It was never called by that name until the movie, The Gangs of New York, came out, but now everyone acted like it'd been called that since the beginning of time.

I'd already secured a booth by the time Simone arrived. She turned a few heads when she walked in. Her short summer dress showed off a pair of lean tanned legs. I waved to get her attention. She smiled and walked over. A few twenty-something hipsters eyed her backside as she walked by, and I met their stares. Yep, she's here to see me, eat your hearts out.

I stood as she approached and smiled. Simone smiled back and kissed me before sitting. A waitress approached quickly.

"A glass of your house wine, please," Simone said. I opted for a beer.

"I'm glad the slave driver allowed you a break for lunch," I said.

Simone laughed. "Sherman is probably the best employer I've ever had. He's a good man."

"Yes, he is," I agreed. "How did you two meet?"

"I got a job at his firm as a paralegal a few years ago. He approached me one day, said he needed a personal assistant and asked if I'd be interested."

"Nice, does he keep you busy?" I asked.

"The usual stuff. At this point in his career, he does a lot of delegating."

"Yeah, the old man doesn't need to work anymore."

"True, but you know Sherman, he'll never retire. Right now, there are a couple of legal cases involving intellectual property rights. Sherman has me busy helping him with *amicus curiae* legal briefs."

"Sounds interesting."

Simone nodded. "Very, but only if you can get past all of the boring legalese."

I chuckled. Our conversation was interrupted by my phone. I looked at the caller I.D. and frowned. "I need to take this one."

"We got luckier than a dog with two dicks!" Flaky exclaimed loudly.

"I hope that's a good thing," I said and caught Simone eyeing me.

"We were driving down I-24 and decided to check out a truck stop at one of the exits outside of Manchester. We found two Robard trucks sitting in the parking lot."

"That's great," I said. "Any issues?"

"None whatsoever," Flaky said proudly.

"A dog with two dicks?" Simone asked after I hung up.

"Well, you see, if a dog had two dicks, he'd be twice as lucky, get it?" I saw an older woman sitting at a table across from us look at me and frown in disgust. To my surprise, Simone laughed.

"Oh, I get it. I mean, I get the joke."

We enjoyed our lunch while we talked. I mentioned the two of us going on a date Saturday night when Simone stopped eating and stared at me.

"I have something to tell you," she said with a hesitant smile. "Madison is going to be gone all weekend. One of her friends is going to King's Mountain with her family and invited Madison to go with them."

Oh my, I think the door was being opened for me to spend the weekend getting to know Miss Simone Carson a little bit better. Or maybe she was simply engaging in casual conversation. No, stupid, she was being very clear. I cleared my throat.

"Why don't we go somewhere? How about a road trip to Gatlinburg or something?"

"How about you find a nice, secluded cabin and make a reservation?" she suggested. I immediately got on my iPhone.

Chapter 43

Henry was so dopey from the anesthetic I had to carry him to the truck. I put him down on the passenger seat and he hardly moved the entire trip home, even when I rolled the window down for him. I occasionally reached over and scratched him behind the ears, talking to him as I drove.

"I'm sorry we had to remove your family jewels."

He looked at me, as if to say, if I weren't so doped up I'd bite off *your* family jewels, asshole. I chuckled and scratched his head again.

On the way home, I took care of a few errands, finishing by stopping off at a convenience store to pick up some beer and milk. I bumped into a man as I walked back to my truck.

"Well, I'll be damned. It's Thomas Ironcutter." I looked around and it took me a few seconds to recognize him.

"Rabbit Cooper," I responded in surprise. Franklin "Rabbit" Cooper was stockier than the last time I saw him and had a shaved head. When I'd arrested him five years ago, he was a wiry twenty-one-year-old kid with a full head of dark hair. He'd gotten himself in a drunken barroom brawl, and unfortunately for Rabbit, the other drunk hit his head against the corner of the bar and died as a result. Now, he'd muscled up a bit and was sporting a funky-looking goatee. The happy-go-lucky grin was gone. Prison sure had a way of changing people.

"Out on parole," he replied as he shook my hand.

I nodded in understanding. "That's good. How's it been going for you?" I asked.

"Not too bad, it's taken some adjusting." He pointed up the road. "My mother lives in a house over yonder. I'm living with her until I get my feet on the ground."

"You working?"

"It's hit or miss. I get temp work at a labor staffing agency, but I can't seem to get anything regular. You know how it is."

I nodded in understanding.

"You still a cop?" he asked.

"No, I'm doing PI work now." We talked for several minutes before I set the plastic bags down and fished a business card out of my wallet.

"Listen, I've got to get back home, but shoot me a text tomorrow with your information. I'll make a few calls and see if any of my buddies who owe me favors has some kind of work."

"I appreciate it, Thomas. You know, even though you were the one who arrested me, I always thought you were a stand-up guy." We shook hands again and I hurriedly drove off, worried my beer was getting warm.

It was growing dark when I pulled into the drive and the first thing I noticed was the house was dark. As in, all of the lights were off. Even the outdoor security light mounted over my garage doors.

Instead of driving around to the back of the house, I stopped several feet down the driveway. Fishing my iPhone out, I attempted to access my surveillance cameras, but the system was not responding. I then tried to call Ronald, but my phone was indicating I had no service.

Odd.

My police instincts took over as I got out of the truck with my Springfield forty-five in hand. Not wanting to make any additional noise, I didn't shut my door and walked along the trees lining the drive. I heard a plaintive meow and looked up. Tommy Boy was up in one of the trees. Not very unusual, that damn cat liked to explore, but my intuition had the hair on the back of my neck standing upright. I worked my way around to the back of the house and listened. All was quiet. I wondered where Anna was. Standing to the side of the door, I turned the handle and pushed it in.

"Good evening, Thomas. Please come inside." The distinctive accent was unmistakable. It was Enrique. I maintained my position off to the side of the door and out of the line of gunfire.

I surprised myself at my calmness as I activated my iPhone. I may not have been able to get telephone service, but that didn't mean I couldn't use the record app.

"I think I'll decline, Agent Hernandez. Why don't you come outside?" My request was met with a clucking of his tongue. "I've already called the police," I added. He clucked his tongue again.

"Thomas, Thomas, Thomas. Do you think I am really so stupid? I have a cell phone jammer. That is why you could not access your surveillance cameras and why you are unable to call 911."

Damn. Well, that explained it. "What can I say, I bluffed," I said.

Enrique chuckled. "There is someone who would like to say hello to you," he said.

"Thomas?" It was Anna. It was frustrating that I couldn't see inside my darkened house, but it sounded like they were in the den. It made sense, he had a clear shot at whoever entered either the front or back door.

"Are you hurt?" I asked while trying to keep a level voice.

"I can assure you she is a picture of health," Enrique said. "For now. Whether she lives or dies is entirely dependent on you, my friend."

"Why are you holding Anna, Agent Hernandez?" I couldn't overdo it, otherwise he'd figure out I was recording him.

"You know why," he retorted.

My brain was spinning. I was trying to think of a peaceful resolution to this, but damned if I could figure one out.

"Thomas, are you there?" Enrique asked.

"I'm still here," I replied. "As for coming in there, I believe as soon as I come inside you're going to shoot me and then shoot Anna. You'll probably hold the gun against her head, just like you did to my wife, hoping the detectives will rule it a murder-suicide. Right?"

Enrique chuckled. "Oh, that is very astute of you, Thomas. That little whore you called your wife had the nerve to get pregnant with my child, even after insisting she was on birth control. She deserved to die. With a young vivacious woman like this girl living in your house, it won't be hard for those fat, doughnut eaters to believe you two were sleeping together and you had somehow scorned her." He ranted on and on, and I let him. When he paused to take a breath, I asked more questions.

"I'm curious, Enrique, why did you kill Lester? He had no idea about your involvement and couldn't have done anything to you that you couldn't talk your way out of."

Enrique laughed derisively. "Lester Gwinnette was an annoying fly that needed to be swatted, just like his wife."

"Yeah, about that. Why'd you kill her? She was a harmless, sad woman."

"Then I did her a favor," he replied in a tone suggesting he really thought he had done her a favor.

He chuckled again. "The woman didn't even put up a fight, Thomas. Even when I was tying the rope around her neck." He continued laughing, like the memory was a pleasant one. What a sick fuck.

"You don't have to do this," I said. "Why don't you just walk out the front door, take my truck, and disappear? The keys are still in the ignition."

He made that clucking sound he liked to make. "Thomas, you know why I'm here. You will give me everything you have regarding – my activities."

"I bet you've already searched my house."

"I have indeed," he replied.

"And you didn't find jack shit," I said with a laugh. "None of it's here. All of the evidence I have against you is locked up in my attorney's safe. As soon as I meet with Chandler, I'll turn it over to him. The best thing you can do is turn yourself in and hope for leniency. I'll be glad to speak on your behalf."

Enrique responded with a derisive laugh. "You are a funny man, Thomas. Come in here, now, or else you will force me to harm this beautiful woman."

"I don't think so, Enrique. You're going to kill her whether I walk through the door or not."

There was a sudden gunshot and the door frame splintered mere inches from my face. The stab of flame from his handgun gave me an indication where he was, but I dared not shoot. If I hit Anna by accident, I wouldn't be able to live with myself.

"Well then, since you have no desire to leave, why don't you let Anna walk out the front door and we can settle this man-to-man?" I invited.

He answered with another gunshot. "The next one is going into Anna," he growled. "Maybe I won't kill her outright, maybe I'll shoot her in the feet and work my way up. What do you think, Thomas?" To accentuate his threat, he did something that caused Anna to cry out in pain.

I gritted my teeth together so hard my jaw muscles ached. "I want you to know, if you hurt her, I'm going to kill you very, very slowly," I threatened.

Enrique had a good laugh at my threat. Yeah, it sounded lame, like something in one of those idiotic TV shows.

I was in a quandary. I knew he was going to kill the both of us and he was too smart to fall for any stalling tactics. Now, he was forcing the issue by hurting Anna, and as I was thinking this, Anna whimpered. I had to do something quick.

I was debating on how many bullets I could take before I got close enough to kill him without accidentally shooting Anna. Seeing no other alternative, I crouched and was preparing myself to charge in when I saw something amazing. Henry came out of the darkness like a bullet. He ran past me and through the doorway faster than I could say holy sheep shit.

Henry found his quarry in under a second and I heard a mixture of a mad dog attacking and Enrique screaming in pain. It was the break I was looking for. I ran in and sidestepped to the left of the doorway. A shot was fired, but I don't think it was toward me. I heard Henry emit a bark of pain, but he didn't stop his attack. I cautiously peered through the doorway and could see the outline of all three of them struggling in the darkness.

This was it. I charged in. My house was dark, but my eyes had adjusted and I could at least make out who was who. Henry was clamped down on one of Enrique's arm, twisting back and forth like a possessed demon while Anna was grabbing his other arm in an effort to keep him from shooting again.

They were moving around too much for a clean shot, so I charged low and took Enrique in the legs, knocking him to the floor. He actually growled at me as I punched him with my free hand and then stuck the barrel of my weapon under his chin.

Time stood still for a long moment. Even in the darkness I could see him staring at me with a look of pure hatred on his face.

He squeezed off a shot, which went through the ceiling, and tried desperately to wrestle his arm free so he could shoot me, but Anna was holding on tight, screaming at him the entire time. I shot once and he slumped lifeless. I squeezed the trigger again, but my handgun was pressed so hard under his chin it went out of battery. I pulled the slide back and put another round in him. Just to make sure. Blood and brain matter splattered my face.

My ears were ringing. Even so, I could hear the heavy breathing from both Anna and Henry. I stood and kicked Enrique's gun away. Using my lighter, I inspected him closely. The forty-five slugs, I mean, projectiles, did their job. I'd never admit it to anyone, but it was a satisfying feeling. I turned to Anna, who was still breathing heavily.

"Are you hurt?" I asked.

"He shot Henry," she wailed. Her voice was unsteady, she was trembling. Telltale signs of someone on the verge of shock.

I grabbed her by the shoulders and worked her away from Enrique's corpse. "It's okay. It's all over, right?" I repeated it a few times and waited until she nodded her head. "Alright, hang on, I'm going to get some lights on."

I worked my way to the utility room where the circuit panel was located and turned the main breaker back on. By the time I made it back to the den, Anna was sitting on the floor and had Henry cradled in her lap. Tears were flowing freely from her eyes.

"He's dead," she croaked out. I turned on additional lights and checked her carefully. She had a bloody lip, one of her eyes was swelling shut and I could see the imprint of fingers around her throat.

"Anywhere else?" I asked.

She pointed at one of her breasts. "I thought he was going to squeeze it off, the pervert." She ignored her injuries and continued stroking Henry's head. The sobs were coming out freely now.

I found the cellphone jammer sitting on my kitchen table. It was a simple-looking, box-shaped object with four stubby antennas sticking out of it. I located the switch and turned it off.

Reluctantly, I called 911. I didn't want to. I could have buried the SOB back in the woods and nobody would have been the wiser.

The call taker answered gruffly, like she was on the tail end of a double shift or something. "Where is the exact location of your emergency?" she asked in the tone of an order. I gave her my street address and started to tell her there was no number on the mailbox, but she cut me off.

"Are you currently at this address?" she asked with the same gruff, demanding tone. I started to reply with a smart-assed answer, but instead told her I was indeed at the address of the emergency. After a couple of additional stupid questions, she finally got around to asking me why in the heck I was calling 911.

I gave an articulated response. "An FBI agent broke into my house, took my roommate hostage, and tried to kill me. He's currently deceased due to lead poisoning."

Danged if she didn't ask me a million more questions. She even went as far to suggest I should perform CPR on the recently expired Special Agent Enrique Hernandez. She also insisted I stay on the line with her until the police arrived, but her attitude was irritating the shit out of me. I mean, I just told her we'd been the victims of a home invasion and I shot the intruder, and this lady, sitting in an air-conditioned office and guarded by armed security was acting like I owed her something.

I hung up, used my iPhone to reboot the security system and then called Ronald to ensure he was getting a live feed. Unfortunately, he didn't answer. I left a message, called William and ended up leaving a voice mail with him as well. I looked down at Anna, who was still sitting on the floor holding Henry.

I gave Enrique one last look. Two rounds in the head from a forty-five at close range sure could do some damage. I put my gun on the den table and reached out a hand to Anna.

"Come on," I said, and the two of us walked out to the front porch and waited.

Chapter 44

The first officer arrived rather quickly. He was a young man who looked like he was fresh out of high school. I quickly explained everything and then gently guided him in what actions he should take. He did really well. Unfortunately, other personnel began arriving, and soon it was a three-ring circus. There must have been twenty people on the scene within thirty minutes and every single one of them insisted Anna and I tell them everything that happened. I declined and told them the primary investigating detective was the only one we needed to give a statement to. This was not what some of them wanted to hear.

So, as you might expect, someone decided I needed to be handcuffed and stuffed into the back of a patrol car. I sat there looking at the scene. It was lit up in a luminous cacophony of flashing lights. Everyone was acting like typical cops; they were going in and out of my house like it was a peep show at a carnival. After they'd gotten a good look, they all stood around, talking about what they'd seen.

An older detective, one I recognized but for the life of me I didn't know her name, walked over to the patrol car I was sitting in and opened the back door.

"There's a dead DEA agent lying on your den floor. They said you killed him." Before I could answer, Detective Jay Sansing appeared.

"What's going on?" he asked. I looked over at Jay.

"Would you mind seeing to Anna?" I asked.

"She's fine," the older detective said. I peered at her closely, wondering what she had up her sleeve before looking at Jay again.

"Jay, please take care of Anna."

"You got it," he said and walked off looking for her.

The other detective continued staring at me as I watched Jay find Anna and escort her over to his car. I then looked over at the detective, wondering exactly what she was doing. Perhaps she'd been ordered to guard me, or perhaps she thought her mere presence was so intimidating I was going to break down and confess all my sins.

Jay rejoined us a minute later. "Alright, I've got her locked in my car. The bosses want the two of you brought downtown for questioning," he said. "I'm assuming you're going to refuse to give a statement."

"Detective Sansing, would you please record what we're about to talk about?"

Jay looked at me warily. He knew I was up to something, but he pulled out his cell phone and tapped on the screen.

"We're now being recorded." He rattled off the date and time, our current location, and everyone who was present. He said the name of the other detective, Kettleworth. I'd heard of her, but I'd never interacted with her. From the best of my recollection, she was a domestic violence detective. I wondered what she was doing here. I took a deep breath before speaking.

"Anna is the victim of a kidnapping, assault, and sexual battery, and yet, she is being treated as a suspect, would you two detectives agree or disagree?"

"The only suspect here is you," Detective Kettleworth declared. Jay looked at her sharply.

"Detective Kettleworth of the Metropolitan Nashville Police Department has just accused me of being a criminal suspect, I am therefore invoking my rights. As for Anna, when exactly is anyone going to provide her with medical assistance?"

Jay looked at me a moment before stopping the recording. "Good job, dumbass," he said to Kettleworth. She glared at him, but he ignored her and walked back over to Anna.

"I don't recall either of us ever working together," I said to her.

"We didn't," she replied gruffly.

"Well, I don't want you to take this the wrong way, but you might want to distance yourself from this and make an Irish exit."

"Why do you say that?" she asked.

"You've just called me a suspect," I replied. "And since I'm in handcuffs and sitting in the back of a patrol car, it's clear that's the prevailing mindset."

"Yeah, so?"

"Well, if you'll take the time to remember any of your training, you and your people are inside a crime scene without the consent of the homeowner, that would be me, and without the authority of a search warrant." Even in the strobe light effects, I could see her face suddenly harden.

"There's an emergency exception here, there's no need for a search warrant."

"What is the emergency, Detective?" I waited for her to answer, but none was forthcoming. "That only works on TV shows, not in real life."

Kettleworth didn't respond. After a moment, she shut the car door, walked over to the group of other officers and began a frantic, hushed conversation with them. They looked over at me several times during the conversation. In any other circumstance, I would've been highly amused.

So, there I was, handcuffed, my knees up against my chest in the undersized back seat. At least my ribs were sufficiently healed now. Eventually, I saw a black unmarked car drive up and Percy got out. He looked around and walked over to the group of officers, said a few words, and then he walked inside my house.

Within seconds, there were three other officers being shoved out of my front door. There was a lot of yelling, but Percy didn't back down. I could hear him through the closed car as he yelled at a patrol sergeant, and then the sergeant directed two officers to stand in front of my door, belatedly standing guard in order to prevent crime scene contamination.

"It's about time somebody showed some common sense," I muttered as Kettleworth pointed in my direction. Percy strode over, practically ripped the door open and pulled me out. He roughly took the cuffs off and put them in his back pocket.

"How was California?" I asked amicably.

"Shitty," he answered gruffly. "You're going to go sit in my car until I get this all straightened out."

"I appreciate it."

"Where's Anna?" he asked. I gestured toward Jay's car. Percy motioned for me to follow as he began walking.

“Get her to the hospital,” he ordered. Other officers and detectives had gathered around now and some of them began murmuring in disagreement.

“I’ve been told to transport her downtown,” Jay replied.

“Don’t screw this up, Sansing. Get her to the hospital, right now.”

“I’m alright,” Anna said.

Percy cut his eyes at her. “No you’re not!” he barked. “You’re injured and traumatized.” He pointed a finger at Jay. “Now, get her to the hospital.”

Anna looked over at me. I barely nodded, indicating I agreed with Percy.

“I’m traumatized,” she said to Jay. “I need to go to the hospital.”

Jay gave all three of us a look. “Are you going to take charge of the scene?” he asked Percy, who nodded. Jay nodded back and started the car. I watched him weave his way through all of the patrol cars as he exited the driveway.

During this cluster fuck, nobody thought to confiscate my phone. So, once I got seated in Percy’s car, I tried to call William again. He answered this time and gruffly informed me he was in the middle of dinner at a restaurant in Bellevue. When I told him what was going on, he didn’t hesitate.

“I’ll be right there,” he said. “In the meantime, don’t say shit to anybody.” Fifteen minutes later, I spotted him jogging down my driveway. I stepped out of Percy’s car and waved him over.

“I had to park on the side of the road,” he said. “I hope I don’t get towed. How are you?”

“I’m okay,” I said and brought him up to speed. It took about fifteen minutes. When I finished, he looked at me somberly.

“Do you want me to call my grandfather?”

I thought about it. I really wanted him here, but I saw how much the depositions fatigued him. The old man didn’t need this nonsense in his life anymore. “You know what you’re doing. We’ll call him in the morning when you get it all straightened out.”

William grinned at me. "I always wondered whether or not you thought I was any good. I guess this answers my question." He looked around. "I'll decimate these cops."

"Percy's on our side," I said and pointed. "He's the big one over there. Take my advice and don't piss him off."

"Duly noted," he said. "I'll go over there and introduce myself."

It lasted the rest of the night and well into the next morning. Before it was all over with, in addition to all of the Metro cops, personnel with the FBI, and even the Federal District Attorney's office were at the scene. The good thing is, Metro brought their mobile command post to the scene. It even had a compartmented room where people could be interviewed.

William made them get a search warrant and refused to allow them to obtain a statement from either Anna or myself until the processing of the scene was complete.

"It'll make them speed up the processing, otherwise, they'll hold the scene for days," William said. He then looked at me and grinned. "I learned that one from Gramps."

"Clever," I said. Unfortunately, they didn't complete all of their fancy processing until three o'clock the next afternoon. At some point during all of it, Jay had brought Anna back with a clean bill of health, more or less.

"A few bruises and her eye is going to be swollen shut for a couple of days," Jay whispered to me. "But no sexual assault. Well, let me clarify, he squeezed and twisted her left breast pretty hard, which technically is a sexual assault, but nothing else happened."

I nodded gratefully to him.

I was tired as hell, so was Anna, but on the advice of William, we agreed to submit to an interview. That lasted until almost six. I thought they'd be overjoyed when I told them I had recorded everything on my phone, including Enrique's admission to the three murders, but they responded with stony stares.

"We'll look into it," Special Agent in Charge Chandler said.

They probably would have gone on the rest of the night, but William finally stopped them, pointing out we'd been awake for over thirty hours.

"Unless, of course, you people would be willing to fix them dinner and clean up all of the blood." That earned William a few disdainful smirks, but at least one of them realized they were pushing the bounds of legalities.

They shooed us out of the mobile command post while they conferred amongst themselves. After approximately twenty minutes, they came out and told us they were going to allow us to get some rest. It took another thirty minutes or so before they all packed up and left.

William, Jay, and Percy were the only ones left.

"We've talked on the phone with the chief," Jay said. "There is a formal meeting scheduled for seven in the morning."

"What about the Feds?" William asked.

"They'll send a representative, but I'll wager they'll cut Metro out of the loop," Percy said.

"Alright," I said and gave them all a look. "You guys go home. Give me a shout tomorrow and let me know what's going on."

"I can help you get this mess cleaned up," Percy offered.

I shook my head. "It'll wait. I'm too damned tired to worry about it right now."

Chapter 45

Enrique had been hauled away in the M.E's van, but they left Henry lying on the den floor. After everyone left, Anna and I wrapped him in a couple of blankets and put him on a table in the garage. Back inside, Anna poured us both a glass of scotch while I surveyed the damage.

My flooring was terra cotta tile, so at least it wouldn't be hard to clean it. The rear door frame was damaged from Enrique's gunshots and there was an additional bullet hole in my ceiling. I hoped it wasn't going to rain anytime soon. My former co-workers had apparently ransacked the place looking for who knew what.

In short, my home was a wreck. We sat at the kitchen table, surveying the damage, drinking in silence.

"Well, I've gone and done it," I said.

"He deserved it," Anna said.

"That too, but more importantly, I've got you hooked on scotch." I thought it was funny, but Anna didn't laugh.

"What now?" she finally asked.

I let out a long yawn before responding. The accumulation of several hours of stress was now replaced by sheer exhaustion. My watch informed me it was only seven, but I was dead tired.

I stood stiffly. "I think I'm going to bed. All of this can wait until tomorrow."

Anna finished her scotch, stood, and followed me.

I awoke as the sun was coming up. Anna was curled up beside me. I guess she didn't want to be alone. Hell, neither did I. She was awake when I emerged from the bathroom, stretched, and followed me to the kitchen. We had to carefully walk around the mess. All of my kitchen cabinets were standing open and everything was askew.

"I've got a lot of housework ahead of me," I remarked disgustedly as I found the coffee pot.

"I'll help," Anna said tiredly. I nodded my appreciation. We watched the coffee brew in silence and then took our cups outside to the picnic table.

"Where do we start?" Anna asked.

The crime scene techs had taken the clothes we'd been wearing, but neither of us had bathed. I suppressed the urge to scratch myself and nodded toward the garage. "Let's bury Henry. We'll worry about the rest of the stuff later."

When we walked in the garage, we found Tommy Boy laid out on top of Henry. Anna stifled a sob.

"I don't think Henry liked Tommy Boy, he just put up with him for us," she said.

"Yeah, most likely," I replied. "Maybe the little bastard is like an angel of death or something." Anna looked at me. "Think about it. First there was Lester, then Rhoda, now Henry." Tommy Boy stared at me and offered a meow. "I bet he's the reincarnation of Thanatos."

"Who's Thanatos?" she asked.

"In Greek mythology, Thanatos was the demon personification of death."

Anna eyed me coolly. "Sometimes your sense of humor is inappropriate," she said. I shrugged. I mean, really, making a correlation between the little orange bastard and Greek mythology was true genius, but it was apparently lost on my perky-breasted partner. I made a mental note to force her to expand her cultural horizons.

We chose a spot under an oak tree in the back yard. I recited a rough version of the Lord's Prayer and threw in a couple of dog adjectives. Anna sobbed loudly and I put a comforting arm around her.

"I think he loved you the first time he laid eyes on you," I said to her. "When he heard you scream, he didn't hesitate to come to your rescue."

"He was a sweet dog."

"He was a hero. As soon as I get some money saved up, I'm going to get him a custom headstone," I said. "I was thinking about what to put on the engraving. How about, Henry the Magnificent? Or, Henry the Hero?"

Anna indicated her agreement by burying her head in my chest and crying some more. Our moment of bereavement was interrupted by the familiar sound of a car coming up the driveway. I grabbed my shovel.

"If that's anyone with the media, I'm going to bust their damn heads open," I growled.

"Yeah," Anna echoed as she grabbed hers. The two of us angrily trod to the front of the house. To our surprise, it was Ronald. I realized I hadn't called him after everything had settled down. He walked up tentatively, staring at the two of us. I imagined we looked quite the sight, red eyed, sweaty and brandishing shovels.

"Are you two okay?" he asked nervously.

"Yeah." I guided us to the front porch where Anna and I took turns telling him everything.

"I'm sorry guys," Ronald lamented. "I was gaming all night and didn't get the message until an hour ago. I tried calling, but your phone was turned off."

"It's okay, buddy," I said. We sat in silence for a couple of minutes before I stood.

"I'm going to fix another pot of coffee. Do either of you need anything?" They responded with head shakes.

I looked at the mess while I waited for the coffee to brew. The biggest issue was going to all of the dried blood. I was thinking it over when I heard another car coming up the driveway and stomped back outside. It was Duke. And another car was behind him. William and Sherman. And, Simone.

"You didn't answer your phone," Duke remarked as he shook my hand and hugged Anna.

"Yeah, they seized both of ours during the search warrant, along with my laptop."

"Sounds like typical cops," Duke growled.

"Yeah, and they took the clothes we were wearing as evidence," I said.

"They even took my panties," Anna added. "I told them I hadn't been raped, but they took them anyway."

"Typical cops," Duke repeated.

Sherman looked at William. "Let's see what we can do about getting their phones and computer back."

"I'm on it, Gramps," William said and jotted some notes on the legal pad he brought with him.

Duke walked back to his car, fumbled around and came out with several bags from Burger King. "I brought breakfast," he announced. It wasn't until I caught a whiff of the food that I realized how hungry I was.

"It'd be best if we ate outside," I said and motioned all of them to follow me to the picnic table in back. Henry's grave was visible nearby. We filled them in on what happened.

"So, that ugly ass dog came to the rescue?" Duke asked.

"Henry wasn't ugly," Anna quickly retorted and started tearing up. I frowned at Duke.

"Sorry," he said. "I didn't mean anything by it."

"Yeah, Henry saved the day," I said, and pointed at his grave. "He'll always be with us." I couldn't play the tough guy when talking about the mean old cur. I grabbed one of the napkins and wiped my eyes.

"Oh, before I forget," Ronald said and pulled a data stick out of his pocket.

"He disabled the system somehow, but before he did, I got some good footage of him coming here and breaking into your house." I nodded gratefully and handed it to William. There were several minutes of silence as everyone ate, which gave me enough time to compose myself.

Finishing my cup of coffee, I stood and stretched. "Well, who's going to help me scrub all of the blood and gore off of my floors?" I asked with a hint of sarcasm.

Ronald quickly stood. "I think I should go home." I could see he was getting a little anxious, perhaps thinking I was going to make him help. I motioned for him to follow me and I walked him to his car.

"I'm sorry, Thomas, I can't go inside and look at that stuff," he said. "I'll have a panic attack."

"That's okay, buddy, I was kidding anyway."

"You ought to hire one of those biohazard cleaning services," he suggested.

I shrugged. "I think I can handle it."

Ronald pointed back at the house. "I've been thinking about your other problem. I've got an idea for a backup system in case someone tries to disable the system again."

"I tell you what, when I get the house all cleaned up, you come back out and we'll look it over. Then we'll have some soup and crackers together." Ronald smiled now and tentatively held out his hand.

I grabbed him in a bro hug and held him tightly. "You're a good friend, Ronald."

"You are too," he said meekly as he strained to breathe.

I watched Ronald leave and turned to walk back to the house. Simone was standing a few feet away. I walked up and hugged her.

"I'm sorry for standing you up," I said.

"I'm glad you two are okay," she said. "Although I would've rather heard about it from you directly instead of watching it on the news."

"Yeah, I'm sorry. At one point, they took our phones and kept me pretty occupied. When they were finally finished, I crashed and slept all night." I didn't say anything about Anna crawling in bed with me. Although nothing had happened, I'm not sure she would have understood.

We continued hugging each other for a long minute.

"You're spending the night with me tonight," she murmured. "We'll put Anna up in Madison's room."

"That sounds wonderful," I said giddily.

Chapter 46

"I got some news about Doug yesterday," Anna said as we sat in the parking lot of the FBI headquarters on Elm Hill Pike.

"Oh, yeah?"

"Yeah, the liaison for Diff, you remember her? She called and said Doug had pled guilty to misdemeanor vandalism. The violation of the order of protection was dismissed upon payment of court costs."

I grunted. "Plea bargaining at its finest. Let me guess, he got probation."

"Yeah. He's supposed to pay restitution. She said to send a copy of the bill to the probation officer assigned to him."

"I'll make it out for an even five grand," I said with a laugh. "Jay told me he'd resigned, so at least he's not a cop anymore. The law enforcement community has enough problems without having hotheads like him."

I looked at my watch as William drove into the parking lot and parked beside us. "Late as usual," I muttered.

"Oh, by the way, William and I have a date tonight. I'd appreciate it if you didn't make any wise-ass remarks."

"Whatever time he told you he's picking you up, plan on waiting an extra hour," I said as we exited the car. William joined us with a big smile and a cup of Starbucks for the both of us. He gave Anna a kiss on the cheek, set his briefcase down, and shook my hand. I had to admit, the coffee tasted delicious, maybe he'd be good for Anna after all.

"Alright you two," I said. "Time for a little talk. When on FBI turf, always assume there is some means of a surreptitious recording going on, even in the lobby. So, be mindful of what you say."

"Gotcha," William replied. "I'm ready if you two are." We were as ready as we were going to be, so, the three of us walked inside. A uniformed security guard met us at the entryway, walked us through a metal detector, signed us in, and used a contraption that scanned our driver's license. It printed out an adhesive visitors badge with our names and pictures printed on it.

"Wear these at all times while you are in the facility or on the grounds," he ordered. I peeled off the backing to the adhesive and stuck it on my lapel, upside down. If he noticed, he didn't say anything about it, and instead pointed toward the lobby area. "Wait there."

After several minutes of impatient waiting, a stern-looking woman walked out of a side door and looked over the lobby. Whether she was an agent or an administrative assistant, I didn't know, but the ring on her finger kept me from staring too hard. She called out to us curtly, checked our identifications, frowned at me, and led us through the security doors, down a hallway with offices on both sides, and into a conference room. We passed cubicles along the way, not unlike any office in America. In fact, if not for the handguns holstered on everyone's hips, one could have easily confused this for some nameless corporate entity.

Special Agent in Charge Reuben Chandler was flanked by other agents carrying thick files as they entered the conference room. He sat at the head, of course, while the other agents hurriedly tried to get the closest seats to him, kind of like musical chairs. He nodded toward me before sitting, but didn't offer to shake my hand. He frowned at William as he booted up his tablet and then activated the video app, but said nothing, which was good. He knew that I knew they were surreptitiously recording us.

"Thomas, it's good to see you," he said.

"Likewise," I replied. "Will Special Agents Ridgeway and Jeffreys be joining us?"

"Ah, no." He didn't explain further and looked over at William.

"Is this your attorney?" he asked me. It seemed like a silly question. William was on the scene after the shooting and sat in during the formal interviews.

William spoke before I made a smart-assed retort. "Yes. My name is William Goldman. I am the attorney of record representing both Thomas Ironcutter and Anna Davies."

"Yes, very good. Let's begin." He started by introducing everyone in the room while William rotated the tablet, focusing the small camera on each person as they introduced themselves. Their names were unimportant, their titles are what caught my attention. There were several FBI agents, all of which had titles identifying them as their own version of OPA, and even a couple of Justice Department attorneys. Nobody present was from my old police department. Interesting, like Percy predicted, they'd been cut out of the loop. One of the agents laid out a bounded set of papers in front of Anna and me.

"These are transcripts of your statements. Initial each page and sign at the end," she directed. Anna started to reach for a pen, but William stopped her.

"My clients will respectfully decline," he said, and then directed his attention to the two Federal district attorneys.

"Let's begin this meeting the proper way. Do you intend to charge my clients with any crime?" William continued looking pointedly at them. They returned his stare before glancing at each other.

"At this time, it appears to be a case of self-defense. We do have follow-up questions, but unless and until new evidence is discovered, there will be no charges forthcoming."

"Do you intend to present this case to a Federal Grand Jury?" he asked. That one got him a few looks, but Reuben answered straightforwardly.

One of the DOJ attorneys spoke up. "It is standard protocol to present, but at this time, we don't see any issues."

"What about at the state level?" William pressed.

"No, not at this time," Reuben answered. "Have we made our position clear?"

William nodded in satisfaction. "And one further question, does the FBI intend to investigate the Metropolitan Nashville Police Department for any civil rights violations they may have committed against Thomas Ironcutter Junior?"

"Yes," Reuben answered curtly. "But I am not going to go into the particulars of the investigation at this time."

Inwardly, I took a deep sigh of relief. The only new evidence they were going to discover would be, I was certain, more evidence of Enrique's corruption in other cases. And, as far as the civil rights violations, I wasn't really particularly interested, but

William was smart enough to know this would help tremendously in procuring a favorable settlement in the lawsuit.

The meeting lasted a little over an hour. It consisted mostly of them asking questions and us answering them.

Reuben Chandler had remained mostly quiet during the entire question and answer session, but I noticed more than once he was watching me carefully.

"Does anyone else have any questions?" one of the DOJ attorneys asked.

"I believe I have one," Reuben said as he continued to stare at me. "Thomas, I'm curious about one thing. How do you think Special Agent Hernandez knew you were going to leave the house on the night he killed your wife?"

"It's my belief he intended to kill us both, and perhaps make it appear to be a murder-suicide. It was only by serendipitous fate I was called away."

The only other explanation is he somehow convinced the two thugs to waylay Uncle Mike and his lover. However, if I were to offer this up, it'd lead to how I helped Uncle Mike locate them, whereupon he killed them and threw them in a sinkhole in a rural part of Hickman County. This information was going to go with me to the grave.

Reuben looked at me solemnly for a long five seconds. "I thought so as well," he finally said.

After it was all over, we signed receipts for the return of our property, although one of the junior agents was tasked with escorting us to our vehicle before he handed over my handgun, unloaded, of course. We waited until he went back inside before speaking.

"That went well, all things considered," William said with a proud grin.

"Yep, it seemed to," I said.

"So, what's next?" Anna asked.

"Gramps and I have a phone conference scheduled with the mayor this afternoon. I'll inform them of the Fed's decision. I've no doubt it'll push them toward a more favorable settlement."

"You think so?" I asked.

William gave a confident nod. “I’m certain of it.”

Chapter 47

It took another three weeks of proposals and counter proposals before we got to this point, which was pretty quick in matters such as these. Sherman had chosen his conference room for us to meet. I was the last one to get there. The only person in attendance for the other side was James Hensley, the city's attorney. He looked uncomfortable. Simone came in and greeted me with a warm smile and a carafe of coffee.

"You are a wonderful woman," I said as she filled my cup. Her hand lingered on my shoulder a moment before she walked out. I held the carafe up for Sherman, who waved me off.

"I'm trying to cut down," he explained. I turned to Hensley and started to offer him some, but he was pointedly ignoring me, which was what he usually did. That was fine with me. I sat the carafe down and decided to needle him a little bit.

"Just think, Counselor. If that idiot Perry was run off back when he should have been, I'd still be poor and Metro would still have a few million in their coffers." He looked up sharply at Sherman.

"The terms of the settlement are to remain confidential, Counselor," Hensley declared. "Perhaps you should remind your client of that little fact."

Sherman chuckled. "Come now, James," he responded. "There is no need to be so sour."

Hensley ignored him, opened his briefcase and pulled out a stack of papers. "I have taken the time to put a sticky tab on each page that needs your signature," he said as he peered at me over his bifocals. I nodded as Sherman loaned me a pen.

"I'll need copies of all of this," I said as I began signing.

"Of course."

The process took about thirty minutes. Once it was completed, I poured myself a fresh cup and leaned back in my chair. Counselor Hensley closed his briefcase and stood. Sherman stood as well and offered his hand. Hensley shook, looked over at me, nodded and left. I sipped my coffee.

"I'm sure you'll take the time to read all of the terms of settlement, but I'm obligated to go over them, nonetheless."

"The settlement is confidential, I'm not to discuss it with anyone. I'm not even allowed to discuss my treatment leading up to the law suit. I'll receive my compensation in the form of structured payments in which your fee has already been deducted. Consider your obligations met." Sherman responded with a smile, reached into a desk drawer, and retrieved a bottle of scotch. I looked at the label. It was a forty-year-old single malt Balvenie. I happened to know that particular flavor retailed for a smidgen under five grand a bottle.

Sherman saw me looking. "I save it for special occasions," he said with a warm smile as he poured us two shots.

"It's too bad the only one we got out of there was Perry," I said. They agreed to put Perry out to pasture, but the only other action they took was to transfer Bartlett out of OPA. He was now the commander of the CID unit, which Percy let me know in no uncertain terms he was unhappy about it.

Chief Blair weathered the storm unscathed; his politics ran deep. Marson was transferred back to patrol. The little shit should have been fired, but no such luck.

"We've not discussed Robard lately," I said. William and Leona had been indicted on multiple charges last week. It was a big media event.

"Your biker colleagues have performed admirably," Sherman said. "They most certainly would not have been my choice, but they've recovered a total of six trucks and trailers. More than I could have hoped for. We also recovered over a million dollars in funds. A very successful effort. Judge Conway is most pleased."

"So, we're done with it?" I asked. Sherman nodded. We toasted again. The scotch went down smoothly. It had to be the best alcoholic beverage I'd ever tasted.

"Okay, I've got to ask, why did Judge Conway appoint you?"

"Let's just say, a few years ago Leona Spieth had a relationship with an unnamed person. She took him for a lot of money and spent all of it on various hedonistic pursuits."

"I think I have a light bulb going off in my head," I said.

Sherman nodded. "It was a very costly ordeal for this unnamed person, both financially and emotionally. There might have been a long, frank discussion between myself and someone, and we might have formulated our own plan of action."

Wow, those two old men were downright devious. I drank the rest of my scotch and withheld any thoughts I had on the matter.

"I have always trusted your discretion, Thomas, and I trust the details of this conversation will not leave this room."

"Goes without saying," I said.

Sherman nodded and smiled. "Let's play some golf this weekend," he suggested. "I'll get us a tee time for Saturday, how does that sound?"

"As long as we're done before four. I have a date Saturday evening with your lovely assistant."

We talked some more about inconsequential things before I left. Simone was nowhere to be found, so I meandered back down to the parking garage. As I approached my car, I stopped and stared. I'd finished the paint job a week ago, but this was the first day I'd driven my first love, also known as a 1967 Buick Wildcat.

She was beautiful.

Sitting, I fished out a cigar and lighter. I clenched it between my teeth and brought the lighter up, but stopped. Try as I might, I could not bring myself to lighting it. The blue flame of the butane burned in a quiet hiss as I held it, lost in thought. I had my car back. Hell, I had my life back. The lawsuit was a done deal, and the lingering suspicions about my wife's death had been put to rest.

It was almost surreal.

My phone emitted a strange chime right about the time I put my lighter back in my pocket. I looked at the screen, and after a moment realized what was going on. Anna had apparently downloaded the word of the day app onto my phone. I read the new word thoughtfully, and then took the battery out.

I needed to truly be by myself, at least, for a little while. I drove around town aimlessly and soon found myself driving by the Spieth's residence. There was a for-sale sign in the front yard and all of the curtains were drawn. I headed out into the Bellevue area and eventually found myself driving down my old street, Front Runner Road.

I drove slowly, recognizing familiar landmarks and spotting changes. The Porter family had put a new roof on their house, the Simpsons had finally cut down the persimmon tree in their backyard. My old house had a fresh coat of paint on the front door and I even saw a swing set in the backyard.

I tried to understand why my wife had an affair. Perhaps I worked too many hours, perhaps I didn't treat her properly, or maybe she simply found Enrique more charismatic than me. I didn't know. I'd never know. I circled the block once, stopped in front of the house for a few minutes and stared. I was lost in my thoughts and started to dab at my eyes with a handkerchief when a woman's voice startled me.

"Excuse me, can I help you with something?" A woman who had the aura of a soccer mom was standing beside my open window. A little girl was standing beside her, holding her mother's hand and staring at me the way little kids stare at grownups.

I cleared my throat. "Oh, no ma'am. I didn't mean to bother anyone." I gestured toward the house. "I used to live here." She stared at me curiously. "Are you familiar with the word hiraeth?" I asked.

Her expression turned to a frown. "I've never heard of it."

"I just learned of it myself. It's a Welsh word, it means a sad longing; a homesickness for something you can never return to."

She continued staring at me. Recognition dawned on her face. "I believe I know who you are."

"Yes," I answered quietly. "Is this your home now?"

"Yes it is."

"Good. It's a good home and deserves a good family." I started my car and left.

I made my way to Mick's place and parked. Looking through the plate-glass windows, I could see two different baseball games on the flat screens. Good, I needed something to distract me. Reluctantly, I reinserted my phone's battery before going inside.

"Well, Dago, are you a rich man now?" Mick asked as I lit my cigar.

I shook my head. "If I discuss even the smallest items of the settlement, I have to forfeit it. So, with that in mind, my answer to your question is none of your damned business."

Mick expressed his displeasure at my response by scratching his backside. "Well, answer me this, are you going to keep doing PI work?"

"That is a question I can answer. Yes, I believe I am."

"Good, you need a way to pay your tab, otherwise I'm going to have you scrubbing the toilets."

Leave it to Mick to bring me back down to reality.

Made in the USA
Monee, IL
01 May 2022